CIRKUS

PATTI
FRAZEE

NEW YORK

Published by Alyson Books,
P.O. Box 1253, Old Chelsea Station, New York, New York 10113-1251.
Distribution in the United Kingdom by Turnaround Publisher Services Ltd.,
Unit 3, Olympia Trading Estate, Coburg Road, Wood Green,
London N22 6TZ England.

First edition: May 2006

06 07 08 09 10 a 10 9 8 7 6 5 4 3 2 1

ISBN 1-55583-935-5
ISBN-13 978-1-55583-935-2

Library of Congress Cataloging-in-Publication Data has been applied for.

Book design by Victor Mingovits

To my parents,
Joan Frazee and the late Robert Frazee,
for their consciousness, love, and humor

Contents

Prologue

The Journey

The Atlantic Ocean
March 1900

hanghai lies sleeping on the top bunk, clutching a leather-bound diary to his chest. It is all he has left of Milada.

And he dreams of fire. The heated air rising around his arms, fire whooshing around his head, the burn crossing his forehead. He clutches the batons with his small fingers. Women gasp. The crowd applauds, and there, off to the side, Milada watches him. He performs for her.

The fire rises above him, around him, within him. He moves with the flame, throwing it here, pulling it there. The fire tugs at his short arms, rising and falling around his head, his torso. He dances with the fire, feeling the heat in the very core of his body. The flames drawing Milada closer, closer.

Thunder cracks and rumbles. He feels someone tugging on his diary; the journal that he wrote for Milada, about Milada. Milada. How he longs to dream of her now that she's gone.

The tugging continues. He wakes, his eyes puffy and sore. He tries to open his eyes but can't. The ship rises up and down as the sea continues to thrash. He feels the presence of the *jezibaba*. He hears her talking gibberish . . . that crazy Gypsy talk. *No,* he wants to say. *No, stop whatever you're doing.* But his mouth is too dry, his tongue stuck to the roof of his mouth. He wants to get away, but now he remembers that he is trapped here with her. Jakub put him here. *No* . . .

Sleep, she whispers, *sleep,* and a wave of peace falls over him like a blanket. And he feels Milada's soft lips on his, her breath entering his mouth and lungs, and he feels right again.

Sleep. Fingers brush the hair away from his forehead. His mother? Can it be after all these years? No. He opens his eyes and sees it is the Gypsy, Mariana. Words fall from her mouth. Her hot breath spills onto his face. But he's too tired now to be afraid of her. He pulls his face away from her grip. He only wants to sleep.

She takes something from his arms.

Sleep. He relaxes and lets her take it away. What is it?

He doesn't know. He glances her way and sees she is reading the book he was holding. Why was he holding a book?

He closes his eyes and once again dreams of the fire. The fire spinning around his head, his shoulders, his torso. Women gasp. The crowd applauds. And there is only the fire.

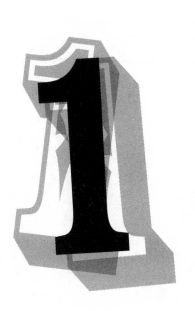

TO WATCH *Milada fly was like dreaming—the rhythmic swinging, the small squeak that came from the bar while hundreds watched in quiet amazement, her soft curves etched against the white top of the Big Tent. She curled and flipped twice in midair before catching the other bar. The audience gasped in fear, then roared in delight.*

It was then that I knew I wanted to be part of the show. As Jakub's Cirkus traveled the Bohemian countryside by wagon, stopping at villages and castles, playing for hundreds and hundreds of people, I fell in love with her.

I imagined my mother telling the story: "Once upon a time, there was a dwarf who threw fire. He ran off to join the circus and fell in love with a beautiful woman who soared through the sky." Mother's story would be simple, and the dwarf would always be happy.

I thought this would be simple. I thought love would be simple.

Sometimes when Milada runs her hands over the odd curves of my body, I wonder how she can love me. But she whispers "I love you" when I am about to throw fire; she speaks it when we are saying good night; she moans it when we are making love; she glances it when her fiancé is standing by her side.

Soon, Jakub's Cirkus will close down and we will go to America, and this will all be different.

Life will be simple. Love will be simple.

—Shanghai's diary, August 1899

New Arrival

Grand Island, Nebraska
May 2, 1900

ariana attempts to draw the crowd in with her hands as she sits on a wooden stool sewing on multicolored garments, the likes of which these midwestern women have never seen, of azure, crimson, fuchsia, and emerald green. A hand-painted sign with elaborate cursive writing sits in front of her small tent on the midway and boasts that she is the best fortune-teller in all of Europe: PALM READINGS, TAROT READINGS, AND FORTUNES TOLD is printed in smaller letters. She stops sewing to fan herself with a circus flyer and watches the men and women file past her without a glance. Their focus is on the banner of the Sideshow Tent that stands directly across from her. The women's long dresses kick up dust as they walk, and the hot, still air makes them perspire so heavily that sweat soaks into the fabric below their high necklines. Most of them carry parasols, clasped in white-gloved hands. The children are dressed in their Sunday best, and the men wear suits with neatly pressed collars that appear to make their heads immobile.

The formal attire makes Mariana think of Shanghai's diary, safely tucked away beneath a pile of neatly folded fabric in her tent. She has read it so many times that it is easy to recall the fine craftsmanship of the diary itself—the leather cover, the strong binding, the linen-paper pages. She is sure that the brothel madam bought this for Shanghai—perhaps as a sincere gift to his words, perhaps as a desperate attempt to keep him.

There is a distant roll of thunder far off to the west, beyond the red and blue flags of the Big Top, where a dark cloud threatens to swallow the horizon. Mariana looks up and sees that, for now, the sky above the circus grounds is deep blue and the sun stands strongly above the Nebraska plains, beating down on the sprouting corn of early summer. It has been only two weeks since Mariana left her homeland of Bohemia, and she already misses the rolling hills, the castles dotting the countryside, and the soft sounds that sift through her native tongue. She has learned English from Jakub over the past twenty-five years, ever since she joined Jakub's Cirkus outside of Český Krumlov.

Jakub has always vowed to come to America to seek his fortune. He spent two years here as a teenager working for his uncle Vladan's circus and has spoken dreamily of the miles and miles of sky and prairie in the "land of Barnum." "There are hundreds of circuses traveling throughout the country," he spoke like a true showman, "making more money than you have ever seen!" Mariana told him time and again that it would not be a good move, but when Jakub's Cirkus failed to make money last year, she had no choice but to concede to his whim. His uncle Vladan offered him the job as manager and part owner of the Borsefsky Brothers Circus, and Jakub gladly accepted, bringing with him his most faithful performers.

And despite the problems, Jakub brought Shanghai, too. It was on the ship to America that Mariana gained possession of his diary, during those two nights that they spent together in her cabin, she his caretaker, he distraught over lost love. She helped him forget the pain he held inside his heart. She took the diary away so that he couldn't ever remember again.

Now, her attention shifts to a gathering of people who stand in the distance watching her, discerning her. Business is slower for Mariana here than it ever was in Bohemia. She has been studying these American crowds over the past two weeks to learn their weaknesses. Although these God-fearing farmers and their wives will not approach her, they pause to watch her sew her long loose skirts with matching scarves, or one of the elaborate costumes for a performer. The crowd now thickens around Mariana, and they gaze silently as her fingers quickly pull the needle through the fabric; her movements are smooth and hypnotic, like a spider building a web. Even the men, standing patiently behind their wives, find her work spellbinding.

Once she begins to spin her web, they forget that she looks unlike anyone they've ever seen. Like all married Romani women, she wears a *diklo*, a scarf that covers her head. Her black hair with thin strands of gray hangs freely out the back and falls below her shoulders. Her deeply set eyes are magnetic and mysterious: the right one is brown, the left is green. Among the Gypsies, Mariana is considered beautiful; among strangers, she is considered exotic. Now, with the Nebraska sun browning her smooth, perfect skin, she is almost dangerous to the women surrounding her.

A man pushes his wife, a small, shy woman, to the front of the gathered crowd. "Go on, honey!" the man's voice is mocking. "Get on up there and get your fortune told!" He looks around at the crowd, and they laugh uncomfortably as his wife pushes her way back into the semicircle of onlookers.

Mariana notices two smaller children clinging to the woman's skirt and two older children standing behind her, their faces guarded. A man standing close to the couple says, "Why don't you get on in there, Joe? Maybe you'll find out how your crops'll do this year!" Joe straightens his upper body and tugs lightly on the bottom of his vest. "Maybe I will!" He walks toward Mariana, but she can see through the pride on his face.

"No!" his wife whispers as she tries to pull him back. "She's a Gypsy."

Joe dismisses his wife with a wave of his hand and walks past Mariana into her small tent. The wife's eyes are turned to the ground as Mariana studies the woman's stance. When she closes the flap of the tent, she sees the quiet defeat on the children's faces.

She sits at a small table opposite the man and slowly unfolds a silk scarf that holds, in the center, a deck of tarot cards. As Mariana lines the cards in the shape of a cross, she delights in watching tiny beads of sweat roll out of the man's thin, reddish hair. Her long, slender fingers flip the cards over so that each one smacks the table, making exclamation points through the silence. The tiny blue veins beneath Mariana's cinnamon-toned skin rise to the surface. Unlike the Romani women who raised her more than thirty years ago, Mariana has short nails and wears little jewelry. She has one ring on her right index finger—silver with a dark blue stone. On her left hand she wears a large silver ring, wrapped like a serpent all the way up her middle finger, a trinket she stole from the hand of a dead woman when she was twelve.

Through the tarot cards, Mariana tells Joe what he wants to hear. "You will have good fortune with your crops." Her Czech accent is thick. "Your children will grow up and have many children of their own . . . You will live a long, happy life." Mariana sees the man's shoulders relax.

Just as she uses her hands outside the tent to draw the people in, she uses them now to gain her patron's trust. This is how the Romani queen taught her to read palms, in a way that borders on the sensual. Her fingers knowingly trace the deep lines of the patron's open hand; she strokes the curves of his fingers and gains his trust as she tells him his fortune, looking deeply into his eyes, embracing his sweaty palms between her cool hands.

She strokes the veins in Joe's muscular forearm, follows the trail to his wrist, and feels his pulse nipping at her finger. She almost tells him the secret that he does not know, thinking he will be as joyful as she was carrying her own child. But then a picture takes hold of her inner vision and stops her from speaking. She closes her eyes and sees the man's face fill with fire as he kicks his wife repeatedly. She forces her eyes open and releases the man's hands quickly. "Thank you for coming."

"That's it?" the man says.

"Yes, that is all you need to know right now."

"You didn't tell me nothin' I didn't already know!"

She ignores his mocking tone. When he leaves the tent, Mariana watches him with his family until she cannot bear it. He grabs his wife's arm and pulls her away while the woman struggles to soften his grip by tugging on his strong fingers. The children wail dramatically, even the two older ones. Mariana feels herself inside their eyes, looking back at the dark woman hiding behind the curtained entrance of the small tent. She sees herself frozen, her grip on the curtain as strong as the man's grip on his wife. She closes her eyes, and her mind is filled with the vision of her mother lying on the ground, blood pouring from her womb, her father kicking and kicking until he is sure the baby is dead.

Mariana wipes her face with the bottom of her skirt and returns to her stool out front, trying to focus on the whirling motion of people walking across the midway, pushing her father out of her mind. She tries to thread a needle, but her fingers fumble and shake, so she rests her hands in her lap, closes her eyes, and breathes in, then exhales all emotion, until her body buzzes with numbness and blindness overcomes her inner vision.

A strong wind picks up from the west, and a blast of dirt stings Mariana's face. She hears the Sideshow canvas flap in the wind and imagines the larger-than-life painting of "Shanghai, the Fire-Breathing Dwarf." LIVE ONSTAGE! is printed at the bottom of the bright-yellow rectangle that has a caricature of him. His head is three times larger than the short, fat body drawn on the banner. It is not how she sees Shanghai at all; his body is muscular, his face strong. He pulls his nearly shoulder-length hair back in a ponytail, whereas in the drawing his hair is wild and stands out from his head in every direction. The clothes on the caricature are dumpy, but Mariana takes extra care to make clothes that flatter his three-foot, six-inch frame. She finds for him the softest material and makes him an array of different-colored, loose-fitting shirts with short sleeves and black trousers with suspenders. She finds peace as her mind's eye traces the huge word *Shanghai,* following the curves of each letter like the lines of a palm.

"Have you no customers?" a man asks, and when she opens her

eyes, a tall, slender image casts a shadow upon her. She shields her face from the sun with one hand until Jakub's head perfectly blocks out the glaring light.

"*Buď trpělivý,*" Mariana says. "You have to be patient; it is a reluctant crowd."

Jakub looks toward the towners, who are breaking up and moving on, then turns his attention back to Mariana, "Well, if anyone can bring them in, it is you." With Jakub in profile, Mariana sees how his dark hair is graying at the temples. His skin is darker than that of most Czech men, and even as dark as Mariana's by midsummer.

He lowers his voice and leans into her. "Good luck is on my side today, my dear." When he smiles, his dimples cause long creases in his cheeks and his hazel eyes light up.

"Yes?" Mariana turns her attention to threading the needle.

"Can you take yourself away for a moment? I need your advice." The crowd glances her way but moves toward the Sideshow. Shanghai's performance on the Bally-ho platform will start soon.

"I may have a few more customers," she says.

"They don't look very interested in you at the moment. The snake charmer will have their full attention soon enough."

Mariana reluctantly follows Jakub behind the Big Top into the backyard. They walk between the cookhouse and wardrobe tents, past the draft-horse stable, toward the railroad tracks to the north of the backyard. "I know that it is difficult for you to look at the human oddities, my dear," Jakub slows his pace.

"Another oddity?" Mariana stops in her tracks. "Don't you have enough?"

"I have only seven. Barnum had ten, and now everyone has ten."

Mariana's voice becomes sly, "Have you asked your uncle about this?" Although Jakub is in charge here, it is his uncle Vladan who has the final say in the circus operations. He does not travel with them but works at the winter quarters in Fairbury, Nebraska, making arrangements for future stops and overseeing the finances. Vladan receives a weekly summary from Jakub's logbook and a detailed list of receipts. He is aware of Jakub's financial difficulty with his cirkus back in the old country and watches closely to make sure that there is no mismanagement of the Borsefsky Brothers Circus.

After Mariana's comment, Jakub rolls his head around to stretch his neck, twisting it to the left, then the right. A smile crosses his face, and he looks Mariana dead in the eyes. "You will need to make a suitable costume, and I need to know if you can do that."

Mariana smiles at Jakub's avoidance. "Of course," she says simply. Jakub leads her to the sidetrack where his boxcar sits at the end of the train. The car is painted bright red, and characters from Czech fairy tales are carved into each corner and painted gold. On one edge, a tall, thin man holds a stone that catches light like a diamond; opposite him, a blindfolded man holds an acorn in his outstretched hand; carved into one corner, then spreading to the opposite corner, is a short, fat man holding a ring that appears to be made of solid gold. But it is the side of the boxcar that Mariana loves the most: the finely crafted mural of Charles Bridge and Staré mesto, Old Town, in Prague. The brick bridge sits in the foreground, and rising to the sky behind it is the domed building of Jesuit Klementinum, the twin-spired Týn Cathedral, and the tower of Old Town Hall. The painting is so vivid that Mariana can hear the streets filled with people at the weekend market, their tongues gently rolling in their mouths as they speak Czech, and, off in the distance, the clopping of horses' hooves on cobblestone streets.

She is lost in this vision until she steps onto the train and sees the anomaly that Jakub is so excited about. She gasps at the two-headed person sitting on the settee. Jakub speaks English, "Mariana, I am pleased to introduce Anna and Atasha." He opens his hand toward each twin as he introduces her. Mariana glances from one set of brown eyes to the other. They look to be about seventeen years old. Their bodies are joined just below the shoulder and down to their hip. Each one has one arm. Mariana casts her eyes downward along the seams of their finely made dress. The girl on the left turns in slightly toward the other girl. Mariana is shocked at the sight of their feet at the bottom of their skirts. There are only three.

"Girls!" a man behind Mariana bellows. "Where are your manners? Say hello to the woman!" Both heads speak at once, although the one on the left struggles to get the words out of her mouth.

"Is it a trick?" Mariana addresses Jakub in Czech.

"No, it's not a trick!" the man behind her barks. Mariana turns and sees that a woman is sitting in a chair next to the man. She is crying uncontrollably.

"The parents," Jakub nods in the couple's direction. "They are from the old country." Mariana looks back at the two-headed body and steps closer to Jakub, pulling herself away from the bad spirits that surround the twins. She has never been happy about this part of circus life, the oddities that border her existence. She believes in her heart that bad spirits certainly caused these freakish afflictions. If she were ever to look into their souls, one of the bad spirits might attach to her, leaving her to find nothing but misfortune the rest of her life. After all these years, Mariana still gets a bad feeling when she is close to the circus oddities; she stands near them only long enough to sew their costumes and make alterations.

Even with Shanghai, she knows that she can never see into his soul as she can with any other man. She will never know what Shanghai holds inside, and she has already come closer to him than she should have dared when she placed the spell on him. She must keep her attraction to him under control, not only for the appearance of her marriage but also for her own well-being. His diary—it lets her see his heart without breaking his skin.

And now as Mariana looks at the twins, she sees only their physical self. She does not allow herself behind their eyes, beneath their skins. "Mariana, may I see you outside?" Jakub holds onto her hand as she steps off the boxcar. "I'm going to offer to send the parents fifteen dollars per head each week for them," he whispers to her.

"Thirty dollars a week?! No. It is too much."

"Too much!" Jakub laughs. "My dear, you have always been unrealistic when it comes to the anomalies. No. No. This is too much to pass up. We will have people coming far and wide to see them. They will pull in hundreds of dollars a week."

"Did you see the mother?" Mariana says plainly.

"The mother? You were looking at the mother?!"

Mariana dismisses his sarcasm. "She is very ill. They did not bring the girls here to get a good price. They brought them here to unburden the mother."

Jakub looks toward the boxcar and rubs his chin, "Yes, but the Ringlings, even the Cole Brothers, would give them much, much more. If I don't offer them a fair price, they may go to one of the other circuses and we will lose."

"The parents are tired. The mother is weak. We are a Bohemian circus. They are Bohemian. We are family to them. The parents will not go to the Cole Brothers, or to the Ringlings. They want their daughters here, where they will get fed Czech food, where they will have finely made clothing, and where they will be with their heritage. Offer them seven dollars a head per week."

Jakub takes a handkerchief from his back pocket and wipes his forehead with it. "Are you sure?"

Mariana smiles. "Do you doubt me now, after all these years?"

"No, of course not. Seven dollars a head?"

Mariana nods. Jakub takes a deep breath, then rolls his hand out toward the steps for Mariana to enter the boxcar before him.

The twins are kneeling in front of their mother; her hands are nestled between theirs. Jakub waves the father over to the opposite corner of the room, and they speak in low voices. Mariana sees that the mother's eyes are surrounded by sickly pink skin and dark circles. A veil of fog seems to lie over the black of her pupils. Mariana closes her eyes and feels the mother's pain, low in her abdomen—a sharp, stabbing pain. She forces air out of her lungs and opens her eyes. *"Nes te'sorthene,"* she says to herself in Romani. *Bad spirits.*

13

✦   ✦   ✦   ✦   ✦

SHANGHAI STANDS at the end of the parade wagons as he prepares for his act in front of the Sideshow Tent. His torches, which were specially made just for him, are smaller to fit perfectly in his hands. He pours gasoline on each end, soaking them so that they will take the flame easily. Jarmil, the Human Torso, says hello as the Strong Man carries him toward the Sideshow. Shanghai looks up and tries to remember the first time he saw Jarmil, tries to remember how he reacted.

He has been plagued by some strange memory loss since he arrived in America. He remembers leaving Madam Zora and his home at the brothel, traveling with Jakub's Cirkus, and performing in the Sideshow. Last night, someone mentioned that he joined the circus because of Milada, the trapeze flyer, and he doesn't remember that at all. These are the spaces in his life that read in his memory as a dark hole, like dropping a coin into a well and looking down into it to see this one little glimmer, but then there is only blackness.

Ah, yes! He does remember meeting Jarmil. It was the day of his arrival—backstage at the Sideshow. They talked about juggling, but Shanghai was distracted. Now, a train rattles as it makes its way out of town and passes the sidetrack where Jakub's boxcar sits. The wheels spark on the rail, and it jars Shanghai's memory to a moment on the train platform in Prague. All of the performers were on the train, ready to go to America. He was waiting for Milada to get on the train, too, Shanghai remembers, and he wanted so badly for her to be next to him. But Zikmund, the Sideshow spieler, held his arm around Milada, keeping her close to him like a treasure. Zikmund looked directly at Shanghai as he made the announcement that he and Milada were going to Vienna. "We are getting married!" he announced in delight.

Jakub was shaking Zikmund's hand when Milada broke away from him and ran to the train. Shanghai reached down for her from the window, but his arms were too short to touch her, so she jumped up and held onto the window's edge like a true acrobat. She kissed him quickly and whispered to Shanghai that this was the right thing to do, then returned to the ground before Zikmund even noticed.

Now Shanghai wonders what she meant, that this was the right thing to do. And why did she kiss him? He tries to remember something, anything else, about this moment. He squeezes his eyes shut, but there is nothing but the dark, hollow well.

Shanghai opens his eyes just as the twins are stepping out of Jakub's car. He watches them step down with the ease of a one-headed, two-legged person. The far-left leg almost seems to dangle, just barely touching the ground, while the right and middle legs work as normal. He saw a picture once of Chang and Eng, the original Siamese twins, but he has never seen one in person.

He quickly picks up his torches when Jakub and Mariana appear from the boxcar. Shanghai ducks behind one of the idle parade wagons and leans against a wheel as he listens to one of the twins speak with a stutter, "Mama, can we g-g-go to the Big Top now?" The mother cries, and Shanghai watches the good-byes through the spokes of the wagon wheel.

"No. No, my sweets." Their mother pulls the twins close and places her head between their heads. "We are not going to the show after all."

"Mama . . . " the twin on the right says, but Shanghai cannot hear the rest of her sentence beneath the mother's cries.

"Watch them," the father warns Jakub. "They are budding young girls. Don't let them get into trouble here." Jakub shakes the father's hand. The father pulls his wife away from the twins' grips. "This is the best thing for all of us. Please, girls, don't make it any harder."

"No! Mama needs us!" the twin on the right yells over her sister, who is now wailing.

The entire scene is painful to Shanghai. He remembers that day almost sixteen years ago, when his mother left him at the age of five.

15

He thought she was coming back, so he didn't cry. He envies the twin that cries; maybe her parents *will* come back for her. He holds this hope for her as he watches Jakub motion to Mariana. She crosses to the mother of the twins and gently pulls her away. The mother transfers her anguish from the twins' shoulders to Mariana's, her lament becoming uncontrollable, and Mariana maneuvers her so that her back is turned to the twins. Jakub puts his arm around Atasha, the twin on the right. Like a top, Atasha spins their large double body out of his reach. He quickly grabs the arm of the other twin, Anna, and pulls the girls toward him before they get too close to their mother again.

Mariana whispers something into the mother's ear, and it immediately calms her. *Jezibaba,* Shanghai says to himself. *Witch.* It is what everyone in the circus calls Mariana. Everyone has stories to tell of her Gypsy ways. He shudders when he thinks of those days he spent locked away with her on the ship. She was as close to him then as she is to the twins' mother now. He watches the *jezibaba* calm the mother with words, and he's sure that she has cast some sort of spell on him. Ever since he was forced to spend those days in her cabin, his heart has been emptied. He knows that he must have been in love with Milada, who is now married to Zikmund, because otherwise why would he have joined the circus for her? Why would she have whispered in his ear and kissed him good-bye? Shanghai knows he must force himself to remember, no matter how painful, in order to rid Mariana's spell from his body.

Jakub leads the twins into the backyard; the one on the left struggles to free their bodies from Jakub's strength, but the one on the right stands tall, trying to get a final glimpse of her mother's eyes. The parents don't look back. They walk over the railroad tracks and cross to their wagon and horses; the father holds the mother's head tightly to his chest as she cries into the fabric of his suit coat.

Mariana straightens her skirt and wipes the tears from the shoulder of her blouse. She turns her eyes to the treetops and the horizon, as if trying to check the direction of the wind, then her eyes quickly dart toward Shanghai. He immediately turns and tucks his head down

16

toward his bent knees, trying to hide from the *jezibaba*. When he looks up, Mariana is standing next to him, staring down. She smiles, and the hair on Shanghai's arms rises.

"Excuse me," he says and picks up his torches. He can feel the Gypsy watch him as he scurries toward the midway.

✸ ✸ ✸ ✸ ✸

"STEP RIGHT up, folks!" Vincent stands on the Bally-ho platform, his high nasal voice rising over the crowd. His middle-American accent draws out every word and hums through his nose at the end of each proclamation. "Come and see the amazing anomalies of nature. We have the one and only world-renowned Gizela the Dog Woman! But don't get too close! She has been known to bite! And just to give you an idea of what you'll see inside, we have a spectacular performance from one of the most famous performers in all of Czechoslovakia . . . Shanghai, the fire-breathing dwarf!"

Mariana looks across the midway, over the heads of the patrons, as Shanghai takes his place on the platform. She's happy that the arrival of the twins did not make her miss his performance. She sees Shanghai only from the neck up as he raises two unlit torches into the air. The crowd is silent. Vincent takes a match to the torches, and the flames reach high up into the sky, then flame down. There is a collective shriek of delight from the crowd. The flames spin above Shanghai's head, twisting and rolling with the movement of his arms and hands. The flames whoosh through the air, and Shanghai throws them up, catches them low, rolls them under his arms; they fly up behind him, then spin effortlessly in his hands before they fly up again. The crowd shrieks, then applauds, then shrieks again.

Before the flames stop flying, Radovan approaches Mariana. He is Jakub's confidant and serves as the boss hostler, the man in charge of the horses. He had been part of Jakub's Cirkus even longer than Mariana. His gray hair is thick and slicked back behind his ears. His red, sunburned face sets off his white, untamed eyebrows. "Our little friend seems to be doing much better since we left the homeland," Radovan says, more as a question than a statement.

"Yes," Mariana agrees, "much better."

"Have you had any contact with Milada since our departure?"

All those years ago, when Milada was a little girl, she was sometimes like the child Mariana lost. When Milada grew older, she and Mariana became friends. She was the only friend Mariana has had in all these years with the circus.

Mariana smiles, knowing that anything she tells Radovan will go back to Jakub. "No, I have not. But I sense that she and Zikmund are very happily married."

"That's good. Very good." Radovan looks toward Shanghai on the platform as he is bending down out of sight, then his head quickly appears again. He swishes something around in his mouth, holds up a baton of flames, then spits the liquid out of his mouth so that flames shoot up even higher than before. The crowd breaks out in applause as the batons spin again above Shanghai's head. "Well," Radovan puts his hat on, "keep an eye on him, and let us know if he's up to any more mischief, will you?"

Mariana glares at Radovan. "Yes, yes, of course," she lies. "I will let you know." Radovan walks away as Shanghai puts the tip of the baton in his mouth and pulls it out with the flame extinguished. He does the same with the next one, then bows to the audience.

As the crowd disperses and lines up for the Sideshow, Shanghai looks at Mariana across the midway. Mariana wishes she could wipe the fear from his face every time he looks at her. She wishes she could replace that fear with love. Instead, she closes her eyes and thinks of his diary, keeping the words for herself. In the distance, thunder rolls across the prairie and lightning flashes in the sky.

✹ ✹ ✹ ✹ ✹

THE CIRCUS compound is quiet when a rumble of thunder shakes the passenger car that holds the women of the Sideshow, including Atasha and Anna. This rain canceled the evening show, and everyone returned to the sleeper cars early. Atasha listens to the pounding rain on top of the metal car as Anna tries to stop weeping. Their bunk is not nearly wide enough for both of them; Atasha lies on the edge, and Anna is uncomfortably propped against the wall, a long pillow from home tucked beneath her.

Across from them, Judita, the six hundred–pound woman, is splayed out in her bed like a melting giant, snoring loudly; the thick rolls of her skin look soft and pliable as they hang off the edge of her mattress. She wears a gown of dark blue fabric dotted with tiny white stars. The bunks above the twins and Judita are empty, at least for now.

Another roar of thunder shakes the train. Atasha closes her eyes and thinks of how thunder lulled her to sleep back at the farm in Holdrege, Nebraska, her only home since birth. And when she woke in the morning, the smell of wet prairie grass was sweet and pleasant. But now, this land, this sky, this place—all seem so foreign to her.

Anna drifts in and out of sleep. Her breath is slow and even, but it quickens when she wakes, and she twists her body slightly, trying to get comfortable. Atasha reaches over to readjust the pillow behind Anna; it is the one their mother made for her so that gravity doesn't pull Anna into an awkward, painful position. The pillow is stuffed with goose feathers and runs the full length of her body. It took their mother nearly two years to collect enough feathers for it. Atasha feels Anna's heart beat strongly enough to rock their bodies. Every now and then, Anna gulps in air, like a dying fish, her lungs burdened by hours of crying.

Judita's snoring drowns out the cries of a wild animal across the compound—an animal unlike any Atasha has ever heard before. Not a wolf or a cat in heat, not a dog or an owl—no, this animal is haunted, and its mourning fills the night air like a lonely train whistle off in the distance. Atasha closes her eyes, but opens them abruptly when a gruff voice asks, "Mluvíte Çeský?" "Do you speak Czech?" A person whose face is covered by coarse-looking hair stands over the twins; the only clue to her sex is that she is wearing a dress. The woman's appearance startles Atasha enough to wake Anna.

"What is it?" Anna asks.

"Ano," Atasha replies to the woman. "Yes."

"What's going on?" Anna asks Atasha.

"You're in my bunk," the woman says.

"Jakub gave us this bunk. He told us to sleep here."

"Well, it's mine. You're a First of May, a greenie. You don't get a bottom bunk."

"Gizela," Judita barks across the small aisle, "it's true. Jakub gave them your bunk."

Atasha remembers seeing a block on the banner for GIZELA THE DOG WOMAN, but she didn't expect to see someone quite like this. Hair covers the woman's hands; long nails protrude from her fingertips. She can't tell how old the woman is but guesses that she is in her twenties.

"But they're First of Mays!" Gizela protests.

"I told Jakub that you wouldn't like it, but look at them." Judita's voice is heavy and filled with gasps.

"I'm sorry," Atasha says. "We can't crawl up there. My sister is weak and doesn't balance herself well."

Gizela growls at the twins. Atasha looks for fangs when Gizela bears her teeth, but there are none. Her teeth are rotten, and a few are missing. Judita admonishes the Dog Woman, "Gizela, just go to sleep. Talk to Jakub tomorrow."

"Why don't you take the top bunk then?" Gizela snaps.

Judita laughs and her bunk squeaks beneath her weight.

Someone yells, "Lights out!" and the sleeper car becomes dark. Gizela mumbles under her breath and rustles around. She sticks her foot under Atasha's back as she climbs onto the top bunk. Once she is above them, she moves around as if she can't get comfortable. The twins lie still and quiet until Gizela's restlessness stops and silence fills the night air.

"I m-m-miss Mama," Anna whispers.

Atasha tries to breathe in the smell of their mother that lingers on their clothes and on Anna's pillow; it is the scent of talcum powder and fresh bread, and it's beginning to fade in the stale, hot air filled with the smell of sweat. "I do, too," says Atasha.

Anna cries softly at first, but then she can't stop. Atasha reaches her arm across her body to stroke the hair at Anna's temple. Anna's crying lessens. *"Shhhh,"* Atasha tries to comfort Anna the same way their mother would, *"shhhhhh."* She strokes Anna's hair until the crying has stopped and Anna slips into a dream.

ANNA'S EYES flutter as she sees herself and Atasha, high in the air, floating above a large tub of water. The skin between them is stretched so far that they can twist and turn independently of one another. They are peaceful at first, but then their bodies fall suddenly from the air, down, down, until they splash, belly first, in the water. A crowd of people laugh, and Anna sees that it is all of the circus performers and workers, a group of faces that she recognizes but does not know. There is the man that cuts up the meat for the lions, a group of black men that began working after the show was over, and the Sideshow freaks, including Judita and a growling Gizela. Their faces are huge, three times bigger than their bodies, and their laughter creates a wind that blows on the surface of the water and causes giant waves. Atasha leads Anna to the side of this large tub, where Jakub stands waiting for them. He pulls them out of the water and throws them once again into the air. They fall downward, landing with a painful splash, and all the people laugh. They swim to the side of the tub opposite Jakub, trying to get away from him, but he simply walks around the tub, grabs them once again, and throws the twins higher into the air. Anna feels that she cannot swim any longer, and as she falls down, down, down, she cries to her sister and Jakub that she is going to drown. They plop into the water, and Jakub once again pulls them out and throws them back into the air.

This time, as she is falling, Anna wakes from the dream with a start. Judita's snoring has become louder, and somewhere nearby, a lion roars over and over. Pain bites into Anna's spine and she tries to move, but Atasha is deep in sleep. She's trapped between her twin sister and the wall with her pillow now lying on top of her; her chest is tight, her arm stuck behind her. She raises her knee in the air because her leg is the only part she can move. Her arm is painfully asleep. She can't move her body enough to release it. She wants to scream, she wants to run. "Atasha!" she whispers. "Atasha!" But Atasha is a sound sleeper, and Anna cannot wake her. Instead, she closes her eyes and tries to ease herself into this new prison.

The First Day of the Sideshow

Grand Island, Nebraska
May 3, 1900

utside the passenger car, Atasha and Anna watch a dizzying array of activity move through the compound as the circus prepares to open the gates at midday. Atasha seeks out a morning view of the Nebraska plains. She craves to see the tidy lines of farmland reaching out to the horizon and the wide-open blue sky that seems to go on forever, even all the way to California, and blankets the earth with the heat of the day. But her vision is filled with clowns with painted faces treading through mud and caged lions as they are rolled across the grounds. She is caught in the momentum of the agitated lions desperately pacing in their cages until her eyes rest on the purple coneflowers that dot the high grasses surrounding the compound. Back home, she would pick the flowers, delicately pull the soft petals off, and press the most perfect ones between the pages of a book. But in this place, the flowers' appearance looks sad to her—like drooping purple sunflowers, their red-orange centers being scorched by the hot summer sun. *Everything looks different here,* Atasha thinks.

A giant gray mass fills her vision, and when it turns, the twins are looking into the black eyes of an elephant. The elephant reaches its trunk out and sucks on Anna's sleeve. Taken aback by the giant beast, she lets out a shriek. A man appears from behind the elephant and pokes it with a stick, yelling out commands. As the elephant's trunk retreats, the man removes his cap, bows to the girls, and greets them. "Nazdar." He then turns his attention to the elephant. "Bruno! BOW!" The elephant bends both front legs and rolls its trunk out to the girls, this time without touching them. "Welcome to the show," the man says in Czech. Soon the great mass is moving off into the distance, trampling the coneflowers and tall grass as the man's barking orders trail behind.

The girls watch in wonder as the giant creature joins other elephants in the line of parade wagons that spans the length of the circus yard. A small wagon, much like their father's, is at the front, and the other parade wagons are lined up behind it. Restless horses are hitched up to each wagon, kicking dust beneath their feet as men in colorful outfits keep them in place. Eight gray horses lead a large wagon with instruments carved on the side. It is trimmed in gold and carries several band members high off the ground. Following that is the equestrian group, saddled on their statuesque white horses. The poodle cages, lion cages, and tiger cages are followed by a blue bandwagon and two more lion cages, a red bandwagon, a caged buffalo, and black and white horses on which six men dressed as Russian soldiers try to maintain control. Another bandwagon, oxen, camels, ten elephants, and the calliope wagon, with various-size pipes rising from the center.

At the rear of the calliope, Atasha sees Shanghai sitting on an overturned bucket. She immediately notices the strong features of his face offset by the kindness in his eyes. He is a handsome man, she thinks, but his body is strangely condensed. His elbow is balanced on his knee, and he rests his chin on an open palm. His gaze is fixed on the girls. Atasha feels Anna twist slightly to adjust the fine petticoat their mother made for them; it is Anna's habit to dig her fingers into the waistband and pull it around until she finds comfort.

Shanghai steps toward the twins with his hands in his pockets. Atasha feels Anna's body retreat until their ribs are touching; each vertebra of Atasha's spine cracks with the movement. Shanghai stops several feet from them; his eyes look down the length of the twins' bodies, then slowly ascend back to their faces. He motions toward the inner compound with a movement of his head, beckoning the twins to follow as he turns and walks away.

Atasha steps forward, then tries to move the twins' shared leg, but Anna stands frozen. As Atasha tries to move their foot and Anna stands firm, their bodies rock with the momentum of their adverse wills. "Anna, move!" The force of Atasha's voice causes Shanghai to stop and wait for them. Anna straightens herself up and releases the grip on their leg.

Although Anna's left leg barely touches the ground, dangling like a rag doll between steps, Atasha knows all too well that the control belongs to both of them. When the girls were almost seven years old, Atasha wandered from their house. Anna began whining that she didn't want to go, but Atasha led them closer to the creek out beyond the field where the cows grazed. Atasha thought she had full control because Anna never led them anywhere; if Anna wanted to go in a particular direction, she told her sister. Atasha led them to their mother or to Anna's favorite doll with button eyes. But it was when Atasha neared the creek that she felt Anna's control over their shared leg; the muscles tensed, the knee locked, and Anna pulled her body backward, throwing Atasha off balance. Anna curled her body into a ball and sent them into a forward roll.

Now Atasha wonders if Anna will send them tumbling as Shanghai leads them to the Sideshow Tent, with its painted front and flags snapping in the dry Nebraska wind. Vincent, the pock-faced American with greasy blond hair, stands at the entrance as the girls approach. "Afternoon, ladies." His grin exposes his graying teeth and the sour odor of his breath. Atasha feels the hair rise on Anna's arm. "Nice day for a show, ain't it?" He laughs as the twins slip past him and into the tent.

Inside, one large stage sits at the opposite end of the tent, and several small stages line each side, the whole making a horseshoe. One stage has a series of barbells on it for the Strong Man, while another holds a crate full of snakes for the Snake Charmer; on the next stage, Jarmil, the

Man with No Legs, happily pulls himself around using a small piece of wood on wheels. He stops to look at the two heads staring up at him and mumbles something in Czech. Anna nudges Atasha to look toward the stage just left of center. Gizela is shutting herself into a rattling cage, wrapping her hairy fingers with long nails around the bars. While her dress last night was clean and fashionable, this one is ragged and dirty, and shows off the lower part of her legs, which are also covered in the same coarse hair. When she sees the twins, she violently shakes the cage and growls at them. Anna nudges Atasha, and they turn their attention to the small stage right of center, closest to the main stage, where Judita stands next to Ladislav, the Skeleton Man. Shadows appear all over Ladislav's body where his bones protrude through translucent skin and delicate blue veins.

"Ahoy," Judita says as the twins approach. She sucks in air through her mouth, and her large chest expands with each gasping breath.

"Have you seen the little man?" Atasha asks Judita.

Before she can answer, a voice comes from the main stage. "Girls, I have been waiting." Jakub is sitting on the steps at the side of the stage. "I sent Shanghai for you." He motions for the twins to come closer. "You will be the main act on this stage." He slaps the steps with an open palm. "Vincent will announce you when the time comes. Until then, you will stay behind the curtain. You cannot let any of the towners see you. Understand?" Atasha nods to Jakub. "I want you to go to Mariana for a costume. We cannot have you sit here in your church clothes."

Atasha and Anna approach him. "These are not our church clothes. These are the clothes our mother made for us, and they suit us just fine," Atasha says.

Jakub places his arm around Atasha's shoulder. His fingertips lightly touch the back of Anna's neck. "No, I'm sorry. We cannot have you looking so much like our patrons. They do not come here to see people who look so much like them; they come to see everything that they are not." He squeezes Anna's neck slightly. "Now, I want you to go see Mariana. She will fit you with a suitable costume." He pulls out his watch. "The circus parade starts soon. Then you must be ready. When you return, please use the back entrance."

"The back entrance?" Atasha asks.

Jakub leads the girls behind the stage and points to a low-cut slit in the tent. "The back entrance." He bends down and exits through the slit, holding it open for the girls to follow.

✶　✶　✶　✶　✶

MARIANA SORTS through two trunks of material and unwillingly imagines the conjoined bodies on the Sideshow platform. Just this morning, Jakub gave her the request: "They must have clothing that shows off their connection, but does not make the women faint." Mariana looks at the stretchy material she has for the high-wire performers but tosses it aside, deciding it is too tight. She keeps digging. At the bottom of the first trunk is the azure crushed velvet she used many years ago for the only child star this circus had ever seen.

Milada was only ten years old when she began to perform on the trapeze. She was strong and agile, and was the first performer with Jakub's Cirkus to fly without a net. She quickly gained top billing. The crowd was in awe of her. They held their breath when she released her grip from her father's arms and sailed to the top of the tent, her small body in a ball, then somersaulted back down and straightened her body just in time to grasp her father's arms once again. The crowd fell in love with her as she flew into a double twist and caught her brother's arms on the other side of the trapeze. The crowd jumped to their feet and cheered until Milada performed a backward twist and flew into the safety of her father's arms.

The moment Mariana found this fabric, she knew it was special. She spent many, many hours making Milada an outfit that, while she complained of the weight of it, made her look like a little princess.

And when Milada's legs lengthened and her body began to blossom, Mariana held onto the fabric, hoping that she could use it again one day for Milada's child.

But Milada has left her, left the circus, and Mariana now imagines how the light in the Sideshow Tent will make certain parts of the costume shimmer, how the fabric will lay against the twins' connection, rolling with their bodies like the tall grasses of the Nebraska plains. Still, she is reluctant to use this fabric for an anomaly.

"Mariana," Jakub sings as he pokes his head inside the tent, "you have company." When Jakub sees the fabric Mariana is holding, he enters the tent alone. "That is brilliant!" He strokes the fabric draped over Mariana's arm. "Yes! This is perfect for them!"

Mariana embraces the fabric, holding it tightly to her chest. "No. It is Milada's. It is too precious to use for Siamese twins."

Jakub becomes fatherly. "Milada is gone, Mariana. She has long outgrown this fabric. Use it for the twins now, before the moths eat it." Mariana strokes the fabric like a cat. "Milada is in Austria, Mariana. We are in America. Use the fabric." Mariana releases her tight grip on the velvet and nods her head. "Shall I show the girls in?"

"Yes." Mariana closes her eyes momentarily and inhales, trying to prepare herself for the sight of them. "Yes, show them in."

The twins are as shocking to her today as they were yesterday. The one just seems to dangle there, hanging off her upright sister. Her leg looks limp, with just her tiptoes touching the ground. Mariana wonders how the one sister can stand as upright as she does with all the weight of the other one pulling her off to the left. The angled sister's arm hangs loosely. Her head tilts slightly, and Mariana tips her head to address the tilting sister. She tries to speak with a softened voice. *"Jach se mas?"*

"We are fine," the upright sister says to Mariana.

Mariana straightens her head and snaps at Atasha in English, "Does your sister not speak for herself?"

Atasha looks down. "She is shy."

"Ah. Well, she will have to get over that, now, won't she? Tell me, what are your names again?"

Atasha's voice quivers. "I am Atasha; this is Anna." Mariana pulls a tape measure through her fingers like a magician contemplating the next trick. "Your English is very good, madam," Atasha says meekly.

"Yes. I had to learn to speak well to serve the patrons in America."

"We hear that you are a fortune-teller. Is that true?"

"I am."

"Mama says that only God can see what lies ahead," Atasha says cynically.

"Many people in America believe as your mother does, don't they?" Mariana asks in a way that prompts no answer. She motions for the twins to turn. Anna balances their bodies with her big toe on the ground, and Atasha shuffles them around so that their backs face Mariana, who now feels the heaviness of her breakfast churn in her stomach.

"Our m-m-mother made us this dress," Anna says quietly.

Mariana gulps in air as an attempt to settle her stomach. "And a beautiful dress it is." She focuses on the fabric to regain her composure, taking the skirt into her hands and rubbing the seam between her fingers. "Very nicely made."

Anna straightens up. "Our m-m-mother is the best seamstress in Phelps County. She won awards at the county fair."

"Anna," Atasha reprimands her sister. Anna looks at Atasha innocently.

"You will have to take the skirts off for me to measure you," Mariana says reluctantly, trying to prepare herself for the twins' disrobed body. She can't help watching the girls' arms work together, their elbows moving in time to each other, as they unbutton the front of their clothing. The dress first goes over Anna's head; then she hands the bunched-up fabric to Atasha to pull the rest over her head. Atasha holds the skirt out, waiting for Mariana to take it.

As she sees the twins' broad shared body in front of her, she chokes down bile and focuses on the oddly made camisole and three-legged

29

bloomers the twins wear. They are unlike anything Mariana has seen before. Half of each piece of clothing is held together by bits and pieces of more fabric.

"Can you sew a pocket for Anna's handkerchief on her side of the dress, please?" Atasha asks.

"A handkerchief?" Mariana asks. A handkerchief is unclean. Just the thought makes Mariana cringe, but the *gadjikane* way is not the way of the Romanies.

"She has problems with her nose running."

"Why is that?" Mariana immediately regrets asking, knowing that she doesn't want a response.

"The doctors said it's because she didn't grow right."

Mariana forces the answer out of her head and starts to measure the girls' chest, quickly realizing that she cannot spread her arms wide enough to grab the tape measure from the other side. She hands one end of the tape measure to Anna, then walks around to face the twins to get the measurement. She presses her fingers between Atasha's left breast and Anna's right. She is shocked to feel springy, boneless tissue there, beating to the rhythm of one or the other, or both, heartbeats. She walks around the twins and leans onto a sewing table to control the lightheadedness she is feeling.

"Are you all right, madam?" Atasha asks.

"Yes." Mariana stands upright and smoothes her skirt. She clears her throat. "How long ago did your parents come to America?"

"In 1879," Atasha says quickly.

"Yes, just a few years b-before we were born." Anna comes to life when speaking of her parents. "They had friends who moved here five years b-b-before them and heard reports of how good the farming was."

"Your father is a farmer?" Mariana directs her question to Anna as she steps behind them and looks at their wide back. There is a valley, a dent, where their bodies would have separated them. She measures the length of Atasha's shoulders, pushing her thumb into the small crevice; she is surprised at its inflexibility.

"Yes, and a good farmer, too. He has the b-b-best corn and gets a good p-p-price for it."

Mariana feels Atasha's body nudge into Anna's as she measures the girls' waists. She searches her mind quickly for a new question to ask the twins so she won't have to think about how their hip bones feel strangely aligned beneath her palms.

"Madam, can I ask a question?" Atasha asks.

"Yes," Mariana says firmly, trying to prepare herself for anything from the two-headed person.

"What is it that we're supposed to do?"

"Do?"

"Yes, on that platform, with all those people?"

"My dear, the people will come to you. They will look at you. They will go home."

"I don't want them to l-l-look at us," Anna whines.

Mariana sits on her knees to measure Atasha's inseam. "But that is what they are here for. That is what they pay for. That is what you are here for."

"I d-d-don't want to be here," Anna says firmly.

There is a moment of silence, then Mariana asks, "The illness your mother has . . . What is it exactly?"

"It is nothing," Atasha says abruptly, but simultaneously Anna says, "She had many months of complaints. Then they thought she was pregnant. The d-d-doctors."

"But she is not pregnant?"

"No, she is not," Atasha says. Anna bows her head.

Again, Mariana sees Atasha signal Anna with her body. Atasha's rib cage moves into the shared space between them; the bottom rib pokes out from her skin and meets with Anna's rib cage. Mariana quickly turns her head and walks toward her sewing table. "Well, we are all done here. Your costume will be ready before you take the stage this afternoon."

"But we have to be ready when the parade ends. That's what Jakub

31

told us," says Atasha to Mariana's back.

"Yes, I know. Just go to the costume tent behind the Big Top. Your outfit will be ready there."

"It took our mother days to m-m-make our clothes," says Anna in the same surprised tone as Atasha.

"Yes. Well," Mariana says. "I am not your mother."

✦   ✦   ✦   ✦   ✦

ANNA TOUCHES the fabric of their new dress. It's soft when she runs her hand toward her hip and strangely resistant when she runs it toward her breast. It hugs their waists and breasts, then falls off their hips like a waterfall. Anna's momentary peace is disturbed when a man yells, "Doors!" just outside the Sideshow Tent.

Vincent bursts through the tent, and his voice booms, "It's showtime!" Soon the crowd's voices fill the tent, and beyond the curtain that hides them, Anna hears Gizela shriek and growl. Her cage rattles so violently, Anna imagines that it is about to fall over. Her breath leaves her in a silent, uncontrollable puff. She quivers. She tries to stop herself, trying to will herself to be as strong as Atasha, but the harder she tries, the more she shakes.

Her nose runs and she reaches into the small pocket for her handkerchief, but she also finds a small piece of wood shaped like an *S*. Its edges are smooth, and tiny snails are painted on it. It is a piece of a puzzle made for them by their father. The Gypsy must have found it in the pocket of their dress and placed it in their new costume. Just a few days ago, Anna tucked it in her pocket to put into her keepsake box as a token from childhood. Their father burned the puzzle a day before their journey to the circus. Now Anna understands why.

Everything happened so fast, and she never had the chance to put it into her keepsake box as planned. Anna feels stupid for not recognizing how odd it was that her parents had everything packed for the impromptu journey to see the circus. How could the twins have overlooked all the clues? A two-day journey, well-packed suitcases, their mother's nearly constant tears.

The voices that fill the tent become stronger in number, and they slowly trickle to the other side of the curtain that separates the twins from everyone else. Vincent introduces Jarmil, who happily rolls across the stage, his wheels squealing as they jump over each board on the platform. "Look at that freak," the voice of a man says. "How sad," a woman says. The crowd becomes strangely silent.

Atasha whispers into Anna's ear, telling her sister that they have to show the crowd they are human. "Let me answer the questions. We cannot let them hear your stutter." Anna feels protected but ashamed. She twists her ribs around, trying to loosen the tightness in their new dress. "And don't fidget! We have to look like one person, Anna. We are not like the rest of them here."

Judita and Ladislav are introduced. A man yells out, "Are you married to each other?" Unable to understand English, the pair stand silently, looking back at the crowd with wide smiles on their faces. Some in the crowd begin to laugh, and Judita and Ladislav join in. "What a couple of idiots," a man says. Judita laughs from her belly; her breasts and chins bounce with the movement.

"Yes, folks, it's true, they are married," Vincent lies, and the crowd bursts into a cacophony of laughter, with Judita and Ladislav laughing along.

Anna feels Atasha's anger rise; she feels it in the pounding of Atasha's heart, the tightening of her stomach muscles, the rushing of blood between them. "See! They are being made fools of because they cannot understand English! I can't bear this anymore." Atasha moves their body from behind the curtain and steps onto the main stage. She yells out in Czech, "The man asked if you are married." Judita stops laughing for a moment and looks at Atasha, who repeats the question as she motions to the man who asked it. The man is now looking at

Atasha and Anna in shock. Judita turns to Ladislav and they lean into each other, faking little kisses on each other's cheeks, and then Judita breaks out in another belly-rolling laugh. But it is too late; the crowd's attention has shifted.

The crowd walks toward the main stage in shocked silence. Judita stops kissing Ladislav and yells back to Atasha, "Why did you have to get involved? I knew you would come in and take over the whole show!"

"I was only trying to help," Atasha yells over the heads of the crowd to Judita, as Anna pulls Atasha back behind the curtain. She is more aware of the crowd swelling in front of them than Atasha.

"Well, mind your own business next time!" Judita yells.

Vincent runs from the small stage, leaving Judita and Ladislav behind, and leaps up the steps to the main stage. Before he has a chance to introduce the twins, a man standing just below the platform addresses Atasha, "Does the other head talk?"

Others in the crowd echo him, "Yes, does she talk?" and soon even the women are begging for Anna to speak. Anna covers her face with her hand and bows her head. Atasha faces the crowd, but Anna feels her body tremble, too. Anna's knees begin to shake. "Don't say anything, Anna," Atasha whispers in Czech. "Think of good times, like Mama told us to do. 'When you get scared, think of good times.'"

With her eyes closed, Anna inhales. For a moment she thinks she can smell the wildflowers that filled the air around the family farm. She tries to focus on the whinnying of horses outside the tent, but nothing can drown out the sounds of the crowd, begging for her to speak. Anna opens her eyes to see that the crowd is growing. People are jammed around the stage, and the heat from the group is making Anna's armpits burn. Sweat dribbles down her arm. She thinks of the small trips her family made to Holdrege, Nebraska. People stared when the girls walked down the street, but they all knew of the twins and celebrated them as a miracle. Even the richest family in town invited the twins into their home to share a meal.

Vincent grabs Atasha's arm and pulls the twins to the center of the stage. "That's right, folks, two people, joined from shoulder to hip! Two heads, two arms, three legs!" He turns his back to the crowd for an instant and whispers to the twins, "Spin around, girls. Let them see you from front to back." Anna looks into Vincent's black eyes, then glances at Atasha, who is staring at him, her body firmly in place. Vincent sighs in exasperation, then turns back to the crowd. "But don't stare too long; legend has it that these girls were born after their mother visited a sideshow in Berlin and saw two people just like this. Next thing you know," he puts his finger into his cheek and pulls it out, making a popping noise, "out popped the Borsefsky Brothers Circus Siamese Twins!"

Women in the crowd gasp. The men gently put their hands on the small of their wives' backs and nudge them along. Vincent smiles in delight and winks at Anna as he turns to leave. Anna closes her eyes and remembers the real story of their birth.

When they were five years old, their mother told them the story of how her womb opened up and there was a great flood of water. The twins were caught in the pounding rush, their bodies tossed into the walls of the birth canal like a log in a raging river. Their mother pushed and pushed until the twins broke free, and the midwife caught them in midair.

The midwife marveled at their entanglement. These bodies connected from shoulder to hip; one body with two heads, two arms, and three legs. She was sure that they shared organs as well as skin, muscle, nerves, and ligaments.

The midwife told their mother that the twins could not possibly live. But their mother held the twins in her arms and said, "How lucky you girls are to have each other—to always have each other. Life will be good to you." The twins heard this from their mother throughout their lives, even yesterday on their way to see the circus.

Now the crowd moves along, but a new set of faces come in to take their place. Atasha stands strong and stares down the crowd. Anna leans into Atasha until her spine aches. For every move they make, a collective gasp is released from the ever-changing crowd. A scratch, a readjustment, a whisper makes the staring faces plead for more. The twins sit; a woman faints. Anna closes her eyes. Backstage, Judita laughs; Gizela growls.

Anna remembers when they were little girls and their mother held them on her lap; Atasha straddled their mother's right leg, and Anna straddled the left. Their mother tucked her head between the girls' heads. This is how she told them stories. Stories of fair maidens and dragons, of great dances and princes from far-away lands.

Anna's favorite story was of a two-headed maiden with silky hair. She was often sent into battle to fight women jealous of her beauty and men fearful of her intellect. Sometimes she fought dragons that breathed words of fire and hatred. The two-headed fair maiden soon became a hero throughout the land. A prince from a neighboring town heard of her bravery and beauty. The prince rode a long distance on a white horse to meet the two-headed maiden and instantly fell in love with her. There was a grand wedding, attended by royalty and people of great wealth. The two-headed fair maiden went to live in a beautiful castle and became a princess.

"My girls," their mother would say, putting her arms around the girls and squeezing tightly. "How lucky you are to always have each other. You will go through your lives never feeling lonely, and maybe someday you will be blessed with a handsome prince who will take you away to his castle high up on a hill."

Anna tries to think of all the stories their mother had told them over the years. Of wood maidens and *jezibabas,* of the flaming horse and Prince Bayaya, of magicians and Long Beard the dwarf. Her head fills with images that once seemed so strange to her but now seem oddly real. Finally, after hours of daydreaming, the crowd in the Sideshow Tent goes away.

Just an hour later, an eerie silence falls inside the tent. Judita's laughter and Gizela's cage rattling have stopped. The air is thick with the smell of sweat. Anna hears loud applause from the Big Top. She is startled by Vincent's voice. "Jakub would like a word with you girls after the big show." He seems delighted with his statement. "Go to the end of the train; you'll find Jakub's boxcar. Be there at ten. And don't be late."

RAIN TAPS on the metal roof of Jakub's car, a soft, steady rain, not nearly as violent as last night's storm. Atasha reaches across her body and pats the leg between herself and Anna. She wiggles her fingers, begging for Anna's hand. When Anna reaches over, Atasha locks fingertips with her sister as they sit on the same settee they did yesterday in this boxcar. Atasha takes in her surroundings. Rich cherrywood everywhere and, placed against the wall opposite the entrance, a bed for two. It is neatly made, covered with a handcrafted bedspread. The colors are bright and look like all of the costumes of the circus. A locked liquor cabinet lines the wall between the bed and a small but heavy-looking desk. The settee on which Atasha and Anna sit faces a soft chair with a low back, and, directly above that, there is a small window. Atasha sees Jakub approach. He uses his suit coat to guard his head from the rain; his face glows in the light of the lantern he carries.

He steps into the car and crosses to his desk without a word. Atasha clears her throat in an attempt to gain Jakub's attention. He ignores her as he drapes his wet jacket over the back of his desk chair and slowly unbuttons his collar. Atasha feels Anna's grip on her hand tighten. Jakub takes a cigar from his desk, bites off the end, and spits it into a basket. He then turns his attention to the twins. His voice is soft but firm: "Vincent tells me that you girls refuse to perform for the people."

"We are not performers," says Atasha.

Jakub smiles. "You *were* not performers, my dear." He waves his

37

cigar through the air as if he were conducting an orchestra. "You are now part of the circus—and in the circus we are all performers."

Atasha looks down at her lap. Anna moves their shared leg, tapping its foot on the floor. Atasha feels how her sister makes the calf muscles tighten and relax.

"I'll tell you what," Jakub scratches a match on the top of his desk, and the flame lights up his face as he puffs on the cigar. He shakes the match and blows smoke as he speaks. "I will have Shanghai show you around, have him stay by your side for a few days—teach you about our ways. You know Shanghai, don't you?" Jakub motions Shanghai's height with his hand. Atasha shakes her head yes. "Anna?" Jakub blows out smoke. "Anna!" He rises from his chair, puts his cigar in an ashtray, and approaches the twins. Atasha feels threatened by his tall figure towering over them, but he squats in front of the silent twin and gently cups her chin in his hand, raising her eyes to meet his. "Do you know Shanghai, Anna?"

Atasha watches Anna close her eyes tightly and then nod her head as it rests in Jakub's hand.

"I know you are frightened," he whispers to her. "You miss your family, don't you?" Anna opens her eyes and nods. "Yes, I suppose you would." He draws the back of his hand down her face. Atasha tenses, and her grip tightens on Anna's hand. "You will find a home here soon enough." Jakub wipes a tear off Anna's face with his thumb. "You will feel at home here one day soon." Anna nods.

Jakub pats the twins' clenched hands and returns to his desk. He becomes businesslike once again. "We leave at midnight. Curfew for the women is at eleven. You must be in your bunk by then."

"G-G-Gizela," Anna says meekly. "She is angry that we took her bunk."

"Don't worry about Gizela. I will take care of Gizela." Jakub dips his pen in ink and makes a note.

"We don't want trouble," Atasha says quickly.

Jakub stops writing and smiles at Atasha. "My dear, Gizela will not give you trouble. She will know her place soon enough." He returns to writing, then says dismissively, "Is there anything else, girls?"

Atasha looks at Anna, then asks, "Where are we going?"

Jakub shuffles some papers on his desk. "Tomorrow, we will be in North Platte. Ogallala the next day. Then we go to Colorado."

"Colorado?" Atasha asks. "But that's so far away from home."

"In a few days," Jakub smiles, "that is home."

MILADA TELLS *fantastic stories of the Gypsy woman of Jakub's Cirkus—the very same woman she sent to find me that day in Prague.*

When Milada was a little girl and learning the trapeze for the first time, she felt so afraid—afraid of falling, afraid of disappointing her father, afraid of hurting her brother as she flew to his arms. She wished in her heart of hearts that Mariana were there, for she had a way of easing everyone's restlessness, of calming their spirits. Milada simply thought, "I wish Mariana were here," as she climbed the pole to stand on the platform that very first time.

When all was quiet and her toes were clutching the edge of the platform, Milada heard Mariana's voice inside her head: "You can do it, my little girl. You can fly. Hold the bar firmly but gently and let yourself go. Trust your body—it is the body of a flyer. It is in your blood." Milada felt gentle hands on her elbows, pushing her wrists toward the bar. She opened her eyes, and with her small hands wrapped around the bar, she stepped off the platform for the first time. She felt like a bird sailing above the circus grounds. She felt free and peaceful as her body arched with each direction change.

The Gypsy is Milada's friend. I must accept that. But I fear that Mariana will get too close to me. I fear that she will see beyond my stunted growth and find the truth.

I tell Milada this over and over again, but Milada says that Mariana cannot see inside the soul of anyone like me. It seems that when the Gypsy was herself a little girl, she traveled to a nearby village with her mother. A man—a one-armed, one-legged man whose face carried all of life's hardships— sat on the street. Mariana watched the man; she was mesmerized by his affliction. The man smiled at her and beckoned her to come near. When she did, he grabbed her arm forcefully and spit upon her, then yelled words of hatred about the Gypsies and how they cursed his life. Mariana, only five years old, screamed and tried to pull herself away from the man. Her mother wrenched Mariana away from him and pulled her to safety.

That day, Mariana's mother bent down to her little girl and held her shoulders firmly. "Did you see into his soul, Mariana?" she asked. "Answer me!" Mariana said no. Her mother told her that day that a seer can never go into the heart of those afflicted in body or mind. "You will get lost in there, Mariana. You will get lost." Mariana knew then that she must never cross the boundary of skin of the anomalies.

That is the story that Mariana told Milada, and Milada assures me that the Gypsy sees me as one of the afflicted.

One of the afflicted. I wonder what my mother would say to that.

The Gypsy worries me.

No matter what Milada says, I must keep my distance. I must keep away from the woman with the serpent ring twisting around her finger.

—Shanghai's diary, May 1899

Mariana's Walk

Grand Island, Nebraska
May 3, 1900

he rain has stopped, and the darkness that surrounds the circus compound is that of the night sky. Mariana stands at the edge of the circus grounds without shoes and feels the thick mud seep between her toes. The earth is cool and inviting. She feels as if she could grow roots from her toes and dig down deep into darkness. She holds her loose-hanging skirt up above her knees and begins to dance like the Gypsy women who raised her. She arches her right arm above her head as her left arm curves along her stomach, her hand clutching the black skirt. When she lifts her feet in dance, she kicks mud high up into the air. She lets out a laugh. If the troupers were to hear her, they would say she cackled like a *jezibaba,* a witch from the old Czech fairy tales.

This is how she begins her nightly walks, exactly the same way she began them long before she joined the circus. When she was a girl, her mother sent her out to wander the Romani caravan to ease her restlessness. As she moved through the darkness, she listened at the backs of tents, pausing to the shapes of people's lives. She learned of passion and love, deceit and sorrow. She knew her Romani family secrets, even though she was too young to understand them.

Now she knows the secrets held within the circus. She knows which men are here escaping the law—having set a fire, stolen a horse, or even murdered someone. It is an addiction for her. She sees through the disguises, breaks through the stone of their faces, and touches the pulses of their souls. As she recalls the pages of that diary that she knows so well, she thinks of Shanghai's words about her. What makes him so afraid? But what Milada told Shanghai was right: she does not allow herself to see into the souls of the anomalies, the freaks of the sideshow. She does not enter their bodies because of the evil spirits that surround them. She fears that she will suffocate if she digs through the layers of fat in Judita. She imagines herself becoming twisted in the coarse hair that covers Gizela's body. She has nightmares that she falls into Jarmil's body and is trapped inside the stumps of his legs with no way out.

None of the troupers will come near her. When Mariana read Shanghai's diary tonight, she realized how they all fear that she will see into their souls to learn their secrets. And she does. She must see what's going on and how people behave, or misbehave. But even as intrigued as she is by Shanghai's talk of a secret, she cannot allow herself into his soul. She can only watch him from the outside.

Mariana stops dancing and again sinks her feet deep into the mud, letting it rise up to her ankles as she walks toward the men and horses tearing down the show. She finds her way by the pale moonlight, which tonight is muted by thin clouds. The trees whisper in the night breeze, their leaves restless. The leaves shimmer in the light, and drops of cool water fall on Mariana's head, sinking into her *diklo*. On the other side of the compound, a lion growls, and when Mariana closes her eyes, she can see it, beneath the canvas cover, behind the bars, pacing back and forth in a space no bigger than her fortune-telling tent. Her heart races as if trapped in her body, pounding against her rib cage. The lion's anguish rises in her chest.

She walks to the edge of the compound where the thick scent of manure lies heavy in the air; the smell of urine burns inside her nose. The horse tent is gone, having been loaded on the first train, which will soon leave. Some of the horses stand here, waiting for their work loading up the next train. Beyond the horses, four of the elephants are lined up like tombstones. Big clumps of dung, mixed with sawdust and hay, are smashed down into the mud by their enormous feet.

It is here, by the restless animals, that Mariana makes herself invisible night after night. She removes her *diklo* and pulls back her long hair, tying it with a purple ribbon she stole many years ago from a merchant in Prague. She closes her eyes and draws in a deep breath, filling her lungs with the spirit of the night. The spirit dances inside her chest; her breath swirls like a tornado in her lungs. She knows that someone is filled with intense grief and longing. Her chest aches, and she slowly releases her breath like a dying woman.

Mariana first made herself invisible long ago when she was still in the family. One night before her father began drinking, she let him hold her in his arms. His breath smelled of garlic and sausage. She grabbed onto his beard, her small hand encircling the long, rough hair; she combed his graying beard with her small fingers, running them through the tiny curls. He told her the story of the Romanies, the Gypsies. Long ago, they walked a great distance from India, a land far, far away. They crossed the sea and found their way into Bohemia, their feet blistered, their spirits tired. A whole tribe crossed over together. "Yes, dear heart," he said, his voice rough from so many years of whiskey, "we traveled as family even back then. Family is our history." Mariana pulled out a few loose hairs from his beard. "Never, never betray your family."

She traced the lines under his eyes with her finger. Even at the age of five, she was trying to read his face. "You are my little moneymaker, aren't you?" he said, pulling Mariana up above his head, her arms and legs dangling like a rag doll. "My little moneymaker!" He pulled her close to his chest where the scent of cigars filled Mariana's nostrils. She knew what this meant. The women were the ones who begged, borrowed, and stole. The better they were at it, the higher price they were sold into marriage for. Mariana knew this, and it made her tremble in her father's arms.

He lifted her once again, high above his head, "You'll stay pure for your papa, won't you, my dear heart?" Mariana squirmed like a cat. "Stay pure so that your papa will get more money for you when you marry." She didn't understand what he meant by pure, but it was the same word her uncle used to reassure her after he made her put his . . . çrak into her mouth. As she looked down at her father, Mariana felt the fear rise in her throat from deep in her belly. She tried to hold it in, but the fear was too much. An explosion flew from her mouth, an explosion of chewed-up sausage and chunks of potatoes mixed with a stinking liquid that ran down her father's face onto his dusty dark suit.

Her father growled from his chest, his eyes wild. He turned her over on his knee and pounded on her, his voice rising over her head like a wave. When she felt her father's cigar burning the back of her neck, she drifted away. When she woke, her mother was holding a cold cloth on her forehead. "Mariana," she whispered, "it is time for you to learn the secret of the Romani women in our tribe. Sit up, sit up." Her mother pulled on Mariana's arms and steadied her as she stood for the first time since she passed out. "It is time for you to learn how to make yourself invisible."

Her mother taught her how to breathe in and out rapidly for several minutes. "This is fire-breathing," her mother said. "You must learn how to use your breath; it is the key to making yourself drift away into the landscape." Mariana did this fire-breathing until she felt she would pass out once again. "Good, good," her mother said. "Now breathe in." Mariana mocked the way her mother held her hands out like a ballerina, then pulled them toward her face as if helping the air go into her mouth and nostrils. "Now let it out . . . slowly . . . slowly . . . good. Now you will put yourself into the place where you are finely tuned into the world." Mariana closed her eyes. "When you are in tune, you will draw in that breath and hold it until your chest burns. Then you will slowly, more slowly than you ever have before, let your breath out, let it out. As you do this, you will feel yourself fade away. You will slowly breathe in one more time, and you will stay invisible as long as you can hold the last of that breath inside yourself."

By the time she was seven years old, Mariana was able to expand her lungs well enough, and let out the breath slowly enough, to walk beyond the boundaries of the compound. The first time she wandered away, her mother sent several men to look for her, fearing that she had been stolen by *gadjes,* for slavery. When they told her mother that they found Mariana one-half mile from the caravan, her mother became very unhappy. She took Mariana by the hand and dragged her to the edge of the compound.

"You must never use this power to betray your family. This is our secret, Mariana; the men do not know we can do this." Her mother poured a line of salts onto the earth. "This is the line you must never cross when you are a shadow." Her mother spit onto the salt. "If you cross this line as a shadow, your breath will be held inside your chest, trapped like a man in prison. It will not cross your lips no matter how you force it. You will blow up like a dead man and turn blue. Watch where I put this salt, Mariana. It will blow away, but the line will remain, drawn in the psyche of the earth." Mariana understood that a curse had been put on her. She never again crossed outside that Romani compound when she was invisible until she married and left the family.

Now, Mariana feels her body fade into the moonlight. She backs away from the elephants when she sees some of the working men approach. Once she has seeped into the pores of the night, she follows the men pulling the elephants toward the Big Top. The first train left moments ago, just after the ticket wagons were loaded, and headed for North Platte. After the evening show started, the men, draft horses, and elephants loaded up the cookhouse, the parade wagons, and the draft-horse top. One passenger car with the menagerie and layout crew went with that train.

While the second train is being loaded, Mariana walks among the men as they roll up the large canvas and heave it onto the canvas wagon. The black men sing as they work; the white men look at them with scorn. "Can't they just keep quiet and get the job done?" one man mumbles. But their songs rise in the air, and Mariana hears the mournfulness in their voices. It is the same sadness they carry within their bodies, the same grief shown on the skin of their backs. But she knows that there is hope in their spiritual lament. She feels that hope as a small spark deep inside their bellies.

An elephant suddenly cries out, and she turns her attention to one of the crewmen slapping it with a stick. Before he can hit it again, Mariana throws her hand between the elephant and the stick and snaps it in half. Her hand stings from the force. The man looks surprised and throws the stick to the ground. As he searches for something else to strike the giant animal, Mariana gently guides the elephant to the center pole of the Big Top. It is here where all of the elephants help pull out the center poles and haul them onto the sides of the wagon. When the man returns, he finds that the elephant is in place, his trunk curled around the bottom of a pole.

Radovan hitches the horses onto the front of both the canvas and the pole wagons so that the horses can take them to the tracks. Mariana makes her way to the train, where the engine is followed by several stock cars and then the flatcars. Jakub stands on the end flatcar at the top of the ramp where the wagons are loaded. He barks out directions in English to the American workmen, directing the order in which the wagons will be loaded onto the flatcars. "Pole wagon! Canvas wagon! Seats wagon! Rigging!" The horses bring each wagon to the ramp. The men hitch them up, pull them onto the cars, and navigate them toward the flatcar closest to the engine. Pieces of wood serve as a bridge between the cars so that the wagons can be loaded toward the engine in the order they are needed the next morning. "Ring stock wagon!" Jakub yells, and Radovan and his horses bring to him the wagon carrying trunks filled with costumes, saddles, and plumes. "Generator! Lights!"

Mariana moves to the sidetrack, where the sleeper cars and the pie car wait to be attached behind the flatcars and taken to the next city. Inside each sleeper car is an entire community. There is one for the female Sideshow performers and another for the male Sideshow performers and staff, one for the female Big Top troupers, and one for the male troupers and staff. The workmen have their own sleeper car. She feels how some sections of cars are darker than others. The space inside those dwellings is cavernous, and the darkness twists and turns into hidden places. The workmen's car is the worst of these; the flea-filled bunks line the walls, and many men have to sleep two to a bunk. The air is heavy with sweat and other forms of body odor, and the stink is so bad that Mariana will not venture inside it. But there is another air that hangs heavy in this car; it is an air of deceit and hiding. Many of the men are transient and will drift out of circus life when they feel the law getting too close.

Mariana is most entertained these days by the Americans, and she approaches Vincent, one of the troupers who remains from Uncle Vladan's circus before Jakub took over. He leans against the Sideshow car smoking a cigarette. She steps through the mud to stand face-to-face with him. Vincent's eyes wander off to a tree, where the soft coo of an owl echoes over the treetops. He snorts in, swirls the liquid around in his mouth, then spits off to his left. Mariana steps back, disgusted, then moves forward and studies his face again. The lines on his pocked face are filled with dirt; he has a scar above his right eyebrow and a long, deep scar running down the left side of his face. His eyes are black, empty, lifeless. Mariana has seen eyes like this before. A chill runs through her veins.

She steps away from him, pulls a packet of fine white dust from her cleavage, and empties it into her palm. *"Bùh s tebou,"* she whispers. "God be with you," and blows the fine powder toward the man. He looks around as if he has heard something, but then returns to his cigarette when he sees no one lurking in the darkness.

She steps toward the pie car, where several of the troupers are eating bowls piled with ice cream. She is looking for Shanghai. He is the one Mariana consistently searches out on these walks. She has been unusually drawn to him since that first time she saw him with Milada, and now that she reads his diary, she is even more intrigued. She wonders if the "secret" is that he was once Madam Zora's lover. Or is it that his mother left him when he was just a young boy? Shanghai sits with some of the other Czech troupers: the Lion Tamer, several male aerialists, and Simon, the circus's best clown.

Shanghai is telling Simon and the others a story, one that Mariana has heard over the past decade. Every time it is repeated, it shoots darts into Mariana's heart. It's a story about her. But this is the first time she has heard Shanghai tell it, and the story suddenly seems romantic. It is the way he speaks of the sensual that changes the story from being dirty to being mysterious and enchanting. "The *jezibaba* took a patron into her tent—he was a man of great wealth." Shanghai's body seems to grow every time he tells a story. His chest puffs out, and his arms reach high into the air as if he were twirling his torches of fire. "He wore a fine suit and walked with a cane. Everyone who saw him that day said that he was filled with sorrow. They didn't have to tell fortunes to see how much weight he carried on his shoulders.

"Many say that the *jezibaba* offered herself to him that day. Milada says that one of the children saw her. They peeked below her tent and saw the *jezibaba* bent over the man as he sat in the chair. She was rubbing his feet, her fingers moving over his crooked toes as if she were playing a piano. Her hands moved up under his pant leg, and the man groaned. The man's eyes were closed as the *jezibaba* stood and began speaking in the language of the Gypsies. She spoke in whispers, and then she leaned down and gave the man a long, soft kiss. Milada's friend counted the seconds, and the kiss lasted more than the child could count! When the man opened his eyes, his face looked ten years younger. He emerged from the *jezibaba*'s tent happy and fully satisfied."

She delights in his story, the same way she did when she saw herself in the pages of his diary. He thinks about her; he wonders about her.

Vincent makes a grand entrance to the pie car and yells, "Let's get this show on the road!" in his best spieler voice. He joins the English-speaking ticket sellers, who sit with the Strong Man. Shanghai stops momentarily when Vincent arrives but then continues his story about the rich man and how he showed up the next day, bringing Mariana gifts of fine silk. The Americans glare suspiciously at the Czech group. "What do you think they're talking about?" asks one of the ticket sellers.

"They're talking about the mitt catcher, the Gypsy," Vincent says plainly. Mariana is surprised. Jakub told her that Vincent had ties to the homeland, but neither of them knew that Vincent could speak the native tongue. She wonders why Uncle Vladan didn't mention this either.

Jakub walks in, looking tired but satisfied. He pauses at the Americans' table to say hello, and when he joins his Czech comrades, their conversation abruptly changes.

Jakub hasn't begun drinking yet, and Mariana admires the clarity of his eyes. It reminds her of the man she was attracted to all those years ago. Jakub was twenty-four years old when she met him, and he had handsome, dark features like a Romani. She was enamored of him immediately. But now she knows too much about him to have any romantic feelings. She sees the dark, hollow space he holds in his chest; she sees how his desire lives in that space. She saw it the first time she gave him a reading all those years ago but chose to ignore it because she had devised the plan to gain her freedom.

She was fast approaching fourteen, then the oldest age of marriage. Her parents were beginning to talk about the day they would find her a husband. She had been nervous about the prospect for some time, sure that her fate was to spend the rest of her days unhappy with a man not unlike her father.

The day after the *abiav*, the wedding of a member of the family, Mariana and her friend Rupa decided to sneak away. The family had been celebrating for one day and one night with roasted pig and drink upon drink. As the celebration continued, the adults were so drunk that they preferred the children make themselves scarce rather than be underfoot. It was the perfect time for the girls to sneak away from the compound.

Rupa told Mariana that she had seen a circus flyer the day before when she went into town with her parents. JAKUB'S CIRKUS was printed boldly in large red letters, and there was a picture of a young woman standing on a beautiful white horse. Mariana didn't need the slightest encouragement to seek out the magic of the circus with her best friend.

The girls held hands as they walked through the countryside. Spring flowers were beginning to burst out of the ground. They passed by the ticket sellers on the midway, who made rude comments or whistled when Mariana walked by, her beauty beginning to blossom. They sneaked past the man taking tickets for the show to the Big Top, and squeezed their way onto a bench in the front row to watch the circus unfold.

That day—as Mariana watched the clowns, ponies, dogs, flipping acrobats, jugglers, unicyclist, equestrians, and flying woman in a shiny suit—she longed to be part of it. Jakub stood to the side, giving orders, directing the next act on the timing of their entrance. When she saw his dark hair, dark skin, and handsome features, Mariana thought, *Oh, yes, he could easily pass for a Rom.*

She knew she couldn't tell Rupa of her plans, so she only told Rupa to go back to the caravan alone. "I will be along soon. Don't say anything to anyone." Rupa protested at first; she didn't want to walk back alone, or leave Mariana there alone. "They might steal you," she said. Mariana knew her father would track her down if she left with the circus right then. He would want to get the *darro*, the dowry, for sure. And Mariana would spend the rest of her life watching out for him, or anyone else in the family. And then there was her mother's curse. She imagined herself blowing up and turning blue. No, she must do this the right way.

"You go back without me. Go on," she said. "I'll just be a few steps behind you." Rupa protested once again, but finally gave in.

Mariana made her way through the departing crowd to the area behind the Big Top and asked around for the dark, handsome man until one of the troupers finally led her to where he was washing his face and arms in a basin. Up close, he was even more striking.

Mariana, standing only to the height of Jakub's elbows, looked up at him and asked him to please take a seat on an overturned water bucket so that she could talk to him face-to-face. He obliged mockingly.

"The circus needs me," she said, her voice thin and high. Even though she could not tell her own future, she knew this to be true.

"Needs you?" Jakub laughed, wiping his arms with a clean white towel. "How could we possibly need a little girl like you?"

"I read fortunes. I can give you a reading now if you'd like." Mariana grabbed another bucket and carried it over to the smiling man. His well-defined arms were crossed over the white undershirt that hid his muscular chest.

"Please, please, be my guest." His voice quivered with laughter.

Mariana inhaled deeply, licked her lips, and put her hands out, motioning with her fingers for Jakub's hands to come to hers. He obliged by placing his hands in her tiny palms, and she gripped them tightly. His hands were large and brown, his fingers long and thin, his palms smooth like a girl's. She turned his hands so that his palms faced the sky, and she traced the lines. He was the son of a wealthy family, she said; he had inherited the circus; he yearned to prove his worth to his father by running a successful show.

Yes, it was all true, Jakub said, as he looked from his hands back to Mariana. Then she pulled a sewing needle from the hem of her skirt. "Do you trust me, sir?" she asked, twirling the needle between her index finger and thumb, the light catching so that Jakub's eyes were fixed on it.

"Yes," he choked out, shaking his head convincingly.

Mariana placed the fingertips of her left hand onto the wrist of his right hand; her palm rested in his. She slowly pulled her fingertips down Jakub's hand, stroking his index finger, making small circles on the tip. She poked the needle into his fingertip, squeezing a bright red bead above the skin. Just as her uncle taught her, she took his finger into her mouth and let the red bead roll onto her tongue, tasting the salty warmth as it spread to the back of her throat. She sucked lightly on his fingertip and slowly pulled his finger out of her mouth, leaving her tongue on the tip, making circles around the small puncture.

When she felt his excitement rise, just like her uncle's, she softly kissed his fingertip and whispered, "Success will follow you now, for I have breathed blessing into your blood."

Jakub cleared his throat. Yes, Mariana must be part of his circus.

In the pie car, the voices of the Czech troupers rise, and Mariana watches as Jakub pours the contents of his flask over the ice cream in his bowl. The brown liquid sinks into the creamy white ice cream, then pools at the bottom. Radovan steps into the car, and Jakub raises his flask. "Ah! Radovan, my friend, you are just in time!" The Americans glare as Radovan joins Jakub's table. Radovan turns the chair and straddles it, just as he did when Mariana first met him. She recognizes it as a power play now, but in that first meeting, she fell for it. She immediately thought that Radovan was Jakub's boss, and in that first conversation, she tried to win him over as well.

He leaned his chest into the back of the chair and asked, "Why doesn't she just leave with us—like all the other outlaws and runaways?"

Jakub pulled Radovan aside and explained to him Mariana's situation. How her mother had a curse, how her father would search her down, how Rupa would surely break her silence, being unsure of her friend's safety.

"And this will cost money?" Radovan's voice rose loudly enough for Mariana to hear it. "What is so special about this girl anyway?"

Before Jakub answered, Mariana piped in, "It is only temporary, sir, the cost of money." She looked from Radovan to Jakub and back, "While it's true, you will have to pay a *darro*, a dowry . . . "

"Yes, and how much will this dowry be?"

"My father will consider how much money he has spent in my upbringing, and he will decide how much money I will make in the future. That will be the dowry."

"No, Jakub!" Radovan turned to the handsome young man. "It is too much. We cannot possibly pay her those fees in advance."

"But sir," Mariana says, "at the end of the *abiav*, we will receive gifts of money that will nearly match the amount you will have to pay."

"I will have to pay, Radovan—me," Jakub stressed. "It is my money, it is my circus."

Radovan's face softened, "This *abiav* . . . What is that?"

"It's the wedding," Jakub said plainly. "Mariana has been telling me about the Gypsy ways."

"It sounds like trouble to me," Radovan said.

Mariana tried not to plead, "I will make more money for you than you can imagine, sir."

Jakub stopped her. "There is no need to beg, dear girl. I am in charge of this circus, and I say you shall join us."

Mariana looks at Jakub now as he sits at the end of the table and wonders how anything could have been different for her. She wonders if there was any other way to leave her Romani family behind. But her fate was to be married, and in a marriage to any other Rom, she would have had no control. Here in the circus, her role has been adviser and confidante. The circus is her life, and in the circus she has power. She took fate into her own hands.

Jakub tells stories of tonight's teardown like a true showman. He embellishes the truth at every turn. Everything went either serendipitously well or horribly wrong. The elephants nearly trampled Radovan to death. Two crewmen got into a fight and had to be pulled off one another. But always, the loading of the wagons onto the train worked like magic. Jakub, with his clipboard, yelled out, and everyone took his orders. A wagon went on; Jakub crawled to the top. He called out for the next wagon and jumped onto it like one of the dancing pony riders. He called for the next one and the next one, and leaped from wagon to wagon barking his orders to the men down below. Jakub was a puppet master, an acrobat, a dancer when he worked to load the wagons.

Shanghai cocks his head to the side as he listens to Jakub. Mariana admires Shanghai's strong brow and high cheekbones. She is mesmerized by his deep brown eyes and nearly allows herself to drift inside them. She feels his pulse in her temples, and when he stands up, she is quickly reminded of his mutation. She closes her eyes to pull herself away from his spirit. When she feels in control of herself again, she watches Shanghai cross back to his chair, his small body swaying back and forth, as he carries another bowl of ice cream, grasped in his stubby hands.

Jakub continues his story, getting louder as the alcohol fills his veins. His eyes droop. Mariana longs to hear Shanghai tell a story instead, but Jakub drones on. Her heart feels lifeless toward him. She thinks back, all those years ago, to a time when she did have feelings for him. A day after they met, Jakub came to the Romani camp with Radovan. They were both dressed in fine suits. Jakub's face was clean shaven. When he saw Mariana, a smile filled his face, and, for the first time in her life, she felt giddiness in her heart.

Radovan's demeanor had changed, and he looked ready to conduct business. Jakub relinquished control and stood back. Radovan took charge, playing like he was Jakub's father. *"Sastimos,"* Radovan approached Mariana's father who was still hung over from the previous wedding celebration. Radovan put his hand on Jakub's shoulder. "My son is ready to marry,"

"Yes, of course." When Mariana's father took in Jakub's appearance, his brow furrowed. "How, uh, how old is your son?"

"My good sir, I'm afraid that the death of his mother last year has made him appear older than his eighteen years. He is much more advanced in manners than his counterparts. I assure you he will make an excellent husband."

"I'm sorry for the death of your wife, sir. What tribe did you say you were from?"

"I did not say. I apologize." Radovan extended his hand to the father, "We are from the Machavaya tribe in Austria. We have come a great distance."

Mariana's father lit a cigar. "So you have. Were not the tribes closer to you able to provide a wife?"

"We went to many tribes, yes, but I am afraid none of the women was quite right for my son. He needs an extraordinary woman, for he is an extraordinary man. We have heard through the years how the

Kalderash tribe, such as yours, has exquisite women of great intellect. We have no Kalderash tribes close to us at the moment, so we made the extra effort to find you here."

"Well, welcome to our camp." Mariana's father turned to his wife. "Marika! Bring the girls ready for marriage here to us. Please, come and have a seat. The girls will be here momentarily."

While the women were rounding up their young daughters and making them presentable, Jakub and Radovan spoke quietly with Mariana's father and shared a drink of whiskey.

Ten girls lined up before Mariana's father, Jakub, and Radovan; the girls' parents stood behind them. Like all good Romani men looking for wives, Jakub and Radovan spent a good amount of time asking questions of the parents. How were the girls at housework? How was their health? Their attitude? They looked at the women's teeth, looked through the parts in their hair for lice, felt their hands for strength. Jakub's eyes lit up as he stood before Mariana. She had dressed in a red skirt and spent an hour that very morning braiding her long hair just for him. Finally, Radovan said to Mariana's father, "Sir, excuse me for a moment so that I may speak with my son."

"Certainly, take your time, please."

Jakub and Radovan walked to a nearby tree and acted like they were talking about the girls, making sure that they looked back toward the small gathering, as if sizing up the girls once again.

Finally, they approached Mariana's father, "Sir, at last I believe my son and I can celebrate. We are prepared to invite one of your girls into our family."

"Yes?" Mariana's father began stroking his beard. "And which girl have you chosen?"

"The girl with one brown eye and one green eye," he pointed to Mariana, "there."

"Ah, an excellent choice, sir! You see, you have chosen my very own daughter."

"Is that so?"

"Yes." He winked at Mariana. "Shall we go to my tent and discuss the *darro?*"

"Indeed. Son," Radovan pulled on Jakub's sleeve and signaled for him to follow.

"No, no, no," Mariana's father put his body between Jakub and the tent. "This is between parents only."

"I'm afraid, sir, that since my wife died, my son has been helping me with money matters. Please indulge us."

Mariana's father thought for a moment, "Well, then, I suppose we will make an exception this one time."

"You are very kind."

Mariana waited outside nervously. Her mother and some of the other women were already beginning to celebrate. "Such a handsome young man," some of the women said.

"He certainly is," said Mariana's mother, "and so well mannered."

"It's a shame about his mother," one of the women clucked her tongue.

Mariana eyed Rupa, who was one of the ten girls being considered for marriage, wondering if she might have recognized Jakub from the circus. "What do you think of him?" Mariana asked.

"He is pale," Rupa said, "but handsome, I suppose."

"Yes, I think he is handsome."

"The elders say you are joining the Machavaya tribe."

Mariana searched Rupa's face for any hint of a disguise, for any hint of a lie, but she appeared to not recognize Jakub at all. "Yes, in Austria."

"I will miss you, Mariana."

"Yes." Mariana saw her father's brother standing beyond Rupa, signaling her to come to him. "Yes, I'll miss you too." Mariana begrudgingly obliged her uncle's call. She knew it was the last time she would ever have to do what he asked of her.

And it was. When Mariana thinks of her uncle now, she is filled with fire and hatred. As Jakub raises his bowl into the air and the Elephant

Trainer rises to fill it with more ice cream, Mariana feels herself lose control of her breath. She quickly slips out of the pie car and into the darkness. She braces herself on the side of the train, her breath leaves her, and her body becomes fully visible once again. She tries to forget this part of the story every time, but it floods back into her brain. She choked on the semen running down her throat, and now she gasps for air. As she walks back to her own car, she pushes her memory forward to the moment when her father lifted a glass of wine and drank it—a symbol of his acceptance of Mariana's new husband-to-be. "Mariana is a very talented girl. She will provide years of service to you."

"Indeed," said Jakub, winking at Mariana. She giggled, but stopped when her father glared at her.

The celebration began immediately. That evening, there was a large feast, and a Romani band played their fiddles, guitars, and accordion. Jakub pulled Mariana into the middle of a circle of people and danced like a natural-born Romani: he arched his hands in the air and made small steps around Mariana in time with the music. At that moment, Mariana witnessed his great showmanship and fell madly in love. Jakub observed, then performed without hesitation, the dancing and mannerisms of the Rom.

Mariana felt like she was flying as she danced with Jakub that night. Her heart soared; her feet barely touched the ground. She was so close to escape. They danced until her feet ached and she had to sit down. Her father waved Jakub over to join them in drink. Mariana sat between her mother and Rupa the rest of the evening, watching Jakub raise drink upon drink until he passed out by the campfire. Still, his face was soft and peaceful.

Now, Mariana returns to the boxcar she shares with Jakub. In the daytime, it serves as his office. At night, it is her sleeping quarters, her home. She pulls the ribbon from her hair and wipes the mud off her now visible feet. She climbs into the double bed and rests at the very middle of it. She knows that Jakub won't be coming home tonight, just as he didn't come home the night before and just as he won't come home tomorrow night. He uses the boxcar now for circus business only. She laughs at herself, thinking back on how she tricked herself into believing that Jakub would be different from her father. She remembers how Jakub looked the day after the celebration. His eyes were swollen, and he squinted in the bright afternoon sun. How strange the tribe must have found his attire at the *abiav.* He wore a black suit with tails and a black top hat. Mariana wore a simple white dress with long sleeves and a high neckline.

They stood in the middle of a circle of people. Kvido, an elder of the tribe, stood before them. Mariana grabbed Jakub's hand and felt the blood warm her chest when he began to stroke the back of her hand with his thumb. They promised to stay true to one another; Mariana promised to be faithful; they promised to spend their lives together. Kvido gave them each a piece of bread and handed Mariana a needle; she took Jakub's finger and again poked it. She handed the needle to Jakub, and he stuck it quickly into Mariana's finger. They each placed a drop of their blood on the pieces of bread, then exchanged the bread and ate it. Jakub didn't let his gaze stray from Mariana as they slowly chewed. A cheer rose from the crowd.

Before the celebration began, Mariana left with her mother and grandmother. They cried as they took the ribbons from Mariana's hair, untwisted the braids, and combed out the tangles with their fingers. Her grandmother tied the *diklo* on Mariana's head. "You are a wife now," her mother whispered. "You must never be seen in public without the *diklo.*"

"Yes, Mama." Her mother hugged her so tightly that Mariana's heart ached. "I'll be all right, Mama. I'll be fine." The music began to play, and Mariana pushed her mother away. "It's time to go to the celebration."

Her mother wiped her eyes and blew her nose. "Yes, go join Jakub now. He is your new family."

That evening's celebration was even larger than that of the night before; there was wine, bourbon, whiskey, roasted pig and chicken, and more dancing. Mariana's father urged Jakub and Radovan to drink more and more, but finally Jakub told him they must leave. Mariana rode off in a wagon with her new husband and Radovan. Her mother waved a handkerchief and cried. Her father held up a bottle of whiskey. Mariana waved good-bye, then turned to her future.

She lies alone now in the bed she is supposed to share with Jakub. She imagines him raising his glass to the group gathered in the pie car, "To our successful season in America!" he yells. She used to care about sleeping alone night after night, but now she is content to have the car and bed all to herself. She hasn't trusted Jakub for many years now, ever since *bibaxt,* bad luck, visited them.

She snuffs out the lamp and pulls Jakub's pillow to her chest. The train begins to move. She closes her eyes. Her sleep takes her into a story that Shanghai tells in a dream only to her. His hands flutter around his head like birds. Mariana can hear his voice, but she is not listening. Instead, she watches his mouth form the vowels; she watches the shape of his lips as his tongue executes the soft *sh*'s of the Czech language. She begins to take in his story. "Long ago, when King Charles IV began work on Karlův most, the Charles Bridge, he made a proclamation to get everyone in Bohemia involved. He asked that all villages bring eggs to the construction of the stone bridge. People came from as far away as Slavonice, bringing with them wagons full of eggs. The workers mixed these eggs into the cement that now holds the stone bridge together." Shanghai's voice is animated and mellifluous, as if he were telling a bedtime story. "But there was one village that thought the eggs would rot before they ever made the journey to Prague. The villagers found a giant pot and boiled the eggs so they would survive the long trip." His eyes are clear with little gold flakes that dance in the hazel irises. "Can you imagine those workers? Breaking open the eggs only to find a hard center!" *How soft his face is,* she thinks, and as he's talking, Mariana reaches out and rubs the back of her hand across his cheek. As he finishes his story, he takes her hand and holds it in his palm. When his story is done, he leans down to place a kiss in her open palm. She feels like his story is a gift just for her. She opens her mouth to thank him, but no words will come out. Shanghai leans in and places a kiss on her parted lips.

The train begins to move, and it gently pulls Mariana out of the dream. Half-asleep, she happily recalls the kiss. Her chest is flooded with warmth, and, for a moment, she imagines returning the kiss, having Shanghai's full bottom lip between her lips, her tongue grazing the ridge. She softly falls back into the dream. Shanghai's lips are soft and warm. Shanghai pulls away, and his hands suddenly become rigid and cool to the touch. When she looks down at his hands, she sees that she is now holding the branches of a tree. There, standing before her, is a small, thick trunk with short, stubby branches coming from its center. Something violently tugs at the back of her head. Her *diklo* is ripped off, pulling some of her hair out with it. Mariana spins around, but no one is there. She touches her head and feels her scalp where chunks of hair have been pulled out. Mariana hears a wind. No, wait, it is something shaking, like the dry Nebraska grasses. She turns to the small tree that used to be Shanghai and sees her mother carrying the *diklo* with long strands of hair dragging on the ground, pouring salts around the trunk of the tree.

The train jerks to a stop, and Mariana's eyes snap open. Her heart is pounding wildly as she realizes how far the dream took her. She gets out of bed and pours water into the basin. She wipes her arms and face, and holds the towel over her eyes, trying to cleanse herself of Shanghai's magic. She must stop thinking about him—always thinking about him. Now that he has entered her dreams, she is beginning to lose control. *Where did this all begin?* she wonders. She thinks back to the time when she learned of his affair with Milada. Perhaps that was his secret? She watched them—stealing glances and touches, meeting secretly for a passionate moment or hour—and it made her yearn for that kind of love. He was devoted to Milada, and Mariana didn't have to cross the boundary of his skin to see the affection in his eyes. He is an oddity, yet Mariana doesn't feel an aversion to him. *After all, dwarves bring good luck to the circus.* She has been faithful to Jakub over the past twenty-four years, but she can't keep her thoughts from turning to someone else. *Jakub has broken his vows,* she reasons. But this is different. A normal man would be bad enough, but Shanghai . . . *It's not right, it's not natural. It is taboo.*

The Great Feast

Ogallala, Nebraska
May 6, 1900

fter less than a week, Atasha accepts the new routine of waking up late, putting on a costume, and sitting on the stage in the Sideshow Tent until late in the evening. On this day, Judita stops them on their way to the costume tent. "Today is dark," she says plainly. Anna looks to the sky. "No," Judita says, "what I mean is, there is no show today."

"No show?" Atasha says. "What do we do then?"

Judita laughs. "Whatever you wish. But this evening we have the Great Feast, and Jakub will expect you to be there."

The trains rest on a sidetrack by the grain mill at the edge of town. "We can walk," Atasha points to the prairie beyond the silos that rise to the sky, "even down to the lake we saw from the train window?"

"Yes. You can walk wherever you please as long as you don't let the towners see you for free. The feast is at six o'clock. If you are not back by then, Jakub will send some men out looking for you."

Atasha excitedly leads Anna through the tall grasses and toward a row of cottonwood trees. "Slow d-d-down!" Anna protests as she huffs in air while Atasha pulls her along.

"Come on!" Atasha yells. "I want to touch the water!"

"I can't go so . . . ," Anna takes a few labored breaths, "fast."

Atasha stops to let Anna catch her breath and bends over with her sister. "Look around," Atasha says excitedly. "See the columbine over there? Just as beautiful as the columbine that grew along the fence of the pasture."

Anna breathes heavily. "I feel light-headed."

Atasha sighs, "Let's sit down but only for a minute." Atasha leans her arm back to help them ease into the grass. The weight of Anna's body pulls them backward so they are lying on the ground, cushioned by the tall grasses. Atasha feels her blood rushing through her with anticipation, and she tries to calm herself by taking in the sounds of larks and sparrows, breathing in the scent of pink bee-bush and gaillardia, and watching the brilliant blue sky with white clouds whose shapes change as the wind moves them southward.

The tall grass encircles them like a cocoon. "Remember the day that Mama lay down in the grass with us and put her head right here," Atasha puts her hand between the twins' heads, "and watched the clouds with us?"

"We must have looked like a p-p-pinwheel," Anna giggles.

"If the clouds could have watched us, we must have moved like a pinwheel!"

"Do you think Mama and P-P-Papa miss us?"

"I think Mama does. Papa? I don't know."

Anna is quiet for a moment. "Do you think he's right?"

"About what?"

"That we are the reason Mama is so sick?"

Atasha closes her eyes, but the sky's brightness won't allow her to slip into darkness, even behind her eyelids. She thinks back on the night, just one month ago, when their father came in from the fields in his increasingly common bad mood. He found them next to their mother as she lay in bed. Atasha was pressing a cold cloth on her forehead as Anna held their mother's hands where they were clenched over her abdomen.

"Seems like one of you could have got dinner on the table," he barked.

Atasha snapped, "Mama's having one of her spells."

"Seems like she's always having one of those spells. Seems like since you two been born she has not been quite right." He stepped to the bed and looked over the three of them. "Anna, Atasha, get over there and make some dinner. Your mama will be fine here by herself. Hain't nothing you can do for her." The girls hesitated to move. *"Prominté!"* their father yelled.

He stood over their mother, who was curled up in a ball, her bright-red face streaked with tears and sweat. He stroked her gray and black hair and said quietly, "We'll call the doctor tomorrow."

At the dinner table that night, Atasha and Anna sat with their father in silence. Halfway through his dinner, he began to cry. Anna looked toward Atasha, who stopped eating and searched for Anna's hand under the table. "What did you girls do to us?" His voice was shaky. "We were fine before you came along. You messed her up inside. You messed her up." He pushed his plate off the table and stormed out the door.

A sudden wind blows the grasses, and Atasha imagines the sounds of the sea. Their mother often told the story of the long voyage to America. Of how she and their father slept at the bottom of the ship, sharing a long, narrow room with hundreds of others. The couple slept closely in a tiny bunk, and sometimes in the middle of the night, their mother felt rats crawl over her body, or mice nibbling crumbs down by her feet. But always, their mother loved the sound of the sea: the waves licking the bottom of the ship, rocking her, shush-ing her to sleep night after night. Atasha opens her eyes and, for a moment, thinks that she sees their mother's face in the shapes of the clouds, but the clouds break up and she sees nothing. Her heart becomes heavy. "Maybe father was right," Atasha says softly.

"I'm ready to walk," Anna says, and together they hoist up their body. Anna digs her foot into the ground and leans into Atasha, who braces them with their middle leg and pushes them up with her leg and arm. They continue over the small hill, picking up their feet to get through the grass. Atasha has slowed her pace for Anna. The seeds from the cottonwoods dance around them like bits of clouds fallen from the sky. Some of the little puffs stick in Anna's hair, and Atasha reaches over to pull them out, then feels in her own hair for the fuzzy seeds.

Just over the hill, the trees line the water's edge. Atasha sees a path, and leads Anna to it. She drags Anna through the damp, overgrown ground and toward the sound of trickling water. The mossy smell of the underbrush fills Atasha's nose, and she breathes it in so deeply that she can smell the wet dirt beneath it. "Perhaps we'll find m-m-mushrooms in here," says Anna. As she searches the ground, Atasha turns them sideways and pulls them down the narrow path.

"Anna, lean into me," Atasha moans.

"It hurts, Atasha! Can't we turn and walk forward?"

"There's too much brush. Watch out for poison ivy, will you?"

As they near the water, Atasha hears splashing and stops abruptly. Anna tries to regain her balance, and Atasha unconsciously helps. "What's wrong?" Anna cries.

"*Shhh!* There's someone here, I think." Atasha pushes Anna back toward the trees.

"We're going to get in trouble," Anna whines. "I just know it."

"*Shhh!*"

"Do you see anyone?"

"No."

Anna excitedly takes in a gulp of air and points to the middle of the river. "Over there!" Atasha follows Anna's finger to a person's head bobbing on top of the water. "It's the d-d-dwarf!"

Shanghai dives headfirst into the water, and Atasha catches a brief glimpse of his toes as they sink under the surface. She pulls Anna toward the edge of the river. When Shanghai's head reappears, Atasha yells out his name.

Shanghai is startled and quickly rubs the water from his eyes, then sinks down so that the water is just below his mouth. "Hello," he says shyly. He moves toward shore, but keeps his body below the surface of the water. "Could you turn around, please? I would like to get out, and my clothes are over there." He motions his head toward the small shirt and pants draped over a rock.

Atasha's face burns red. "Yes, of course." She and Anna slowly maneuver a 180-degree turn. The twins face the trees as Shanghai dresses behind them. "You had the same idea we did," says Atasha.

"You can swim?" asks Shanghai.

"We tried to swim once, but now we just like to stand with the water up to our knees."

"Atasha l-l-likes to. I don't."

"Anna's afraid of water. That's why we couldn't swim."

"I'm not afraid. I just d-d-don't like it."

"Can we turn around yet?" Atasha moans.

"NO!" Shanghai answers quickly.

Atasha feels uncomfortable and finds words to fill the space between them. "How long have you been with the circus, Shanghai?"

"Not too long before we came to America," Shanghai says. "I guess it has been a year now."

"What did you do before you joined the circus?"

Shanghai is silent, and Atasha hears the rustle of clothing. After a long pause, he answers, "I, uh, that is a long story, and you would find it tedious."

"No, we wouldn't," says Anna.

"How did you end up here, then?" asks Atasha.

Larks fill the gap in conversation until Shanghai finally says, "Milada—she was a flyer, a trapeze artist, with Jakub's Cirkus."

"I don't remember meeting her, do you, Anna?" Anna shakes her head no. "Is she still here?"

Shanghai appears in front of the girls, fully dressed. "Jakub told me that we need to work on an act for you."

Atasha is startled by Shanghai. This is the first time she's been so close to him and didn't realize that he stood only to her breast. "Yes, that's what he told us. But we don't have any talent."

Shanghai meets Atasha's eyes and smiles. "You are from a farm?"

Atasha blushes. "How did you know that?"

"Everyone knows," Shanghai shrugs.

"But that's not fair!" Atasha whines. "We know nothing about everyone else."

"Soon enough you will know more than you ever wanted." Shanghai winks at Atasha, who turns her eyes to the ground. He steps close to her and puts himself into Atasha's sight, looking up into her face. She raises her eyes to his once again. "What did you do on the farm?"

"We cooked," Anna's voice is meek, "we cleaned the house, we, we, fed the chickens and gathered eggs."

Shanghai raises one eyebrow and stops Anna. "Eggs?"

Anna looks embarrassed, so Atasha says yes.

Shanghai's eyes light up. "Have you ever juggled?"

"J-j-juggled?" Anna says.

"Oh, yes," Atasha says sarcastically, "we were juggling all the time."

Shanghai laughs shyly. "You could juggle eggs. Have you seen one of the postcards that Judita has?"

"Yes, she sells them after Vincent introduces her."

"You could do that same thing." Shanghai speaks quickly. "We could write a little story about how you began juggling eggs when you were three years old. You were so good at it that people came from far and wide to see you gather and juggle eggs, then they would buy them from you faster than the hens could lay them. I think it would work."

"You tell a very good story, Shanghai, but we do not juggle," says Atasha.

"N-n-no, we do not juggle eggs at all," says Anna.

"You will learn. I can teach you," Shanghai searches the ground for equal-shaped rocks. "This should work. Here," he hands one rock to Atasha and the other to Anna, "here."

"We cannot juggle," says Atasha.

Shanghai pulls the rocks from their hands. "Watch." He throws them into an arch over his head. They spin so fast from one hand to another that Atasha can't see anything but a blur. He slows them down, then speeds them up. "Can you see what I'm doing?"

"Yes, you are throwing rocks in the air," Atasha says dryly.

"Watch." Shanghai throws as slowly as possible. "This rock goes into the air over my head, this one goes into the other hand; as I catch this one, I throw the other one. See, it is easy." He stops and puts a rock in Anna's hand and the other in Atasha's, then steps back. "Go ahead, try it."

Atasha throws her rock in the air, and it hits Anna on the head. Anna shrieks. "See! We cannot juggle!" Atasha yells and reaches over to rub her sister's head.

"Perhaps we should start with something softer." Shanghai scratches his head. "Are you okay, Anna?"

"I think so." Anna rubs her head. "There's a bump there. Feel it, Atasha?"

"Yes. That is a stupid idea, Shanghai. We cannot juggle."

Shanghai scans the ground for something softer. "You can. You will get the hang of it."

"But, Shanghai," Atasha is frustrated, "you forget that each of us controls one arm. We'll never have the same kind of coordination you do."

"How do you walk?"

"What do you mean?"

"You each have a leg, and that one in the middle. How do you coordinate walking?"

"I don't know; we just do it."

"Can you feel each other's legs?"

"We can feel the leg between us."

"I can f-f-feel your leg, Atasha."

"Can you feel her arm?" asks Shanghai excitedly.

Anna thinks for a moment. "I can feel her clench it sometimes. I can feel her make a fist."

"See? You can juggle. I just know it. We will work on it, starting tomorrow." Shanghai looks skyward. "You should spend your time here by the lake well. It looks like just a few more hours before the feast."

"What is this feast? Judita was talking about it earlier."

"Ah! You will have to come and see for yourself!" Atasha smiles at the way Shanghai's face lights up as he speaks. "There will be more food than you have ever seen on your farm."

"Shanghai, I still don't think we can juggle," says Atasha.

"Yes, you can," Shanghai reassures her. "I will help you, every day if I have to. Besides, this is the circus, and in the circus anything is possible."

"Shanghai?" Atasha asks. "What happens in the winter here?"

"What do you mean?"

"I mean, do we travel? Even in winter?"

"No," Shanghai laughs, "we do not travel in the winter. People do different things. Some go back to Europe; the Americans will go to wherever they live during the off-season. Some stay at the winter quarters."

"You mean, we could go h-h-home?" Anna asks. "Back to the farm?"

Shanghai's voice softens. "You can go wherever you wish." He looks at Atasha and gives her a soft, knowing smile. She feels a wave of embarrassment rush through her and quickly looks away so that he can't see her blush.

A horn sounds in the distance, and Shanghai says, "I will see you at the feast then?"

Atasha looks up quickly. "Oh, yes! We'll be there." She feels her heart race as Shanghai disappears into the woods.

AS THE twins near the circus grounds, Atasha sees a trail of smoke rise into the air, and she smells fat drippings from the fire. Off to the left, men are juggling knives. To the right a woman is carrying a snake.

Farther ahead, poodles are walking on hind legs begging berries from a man feeding a chimp. They pass a group of men playing horseshoes, while off to the left, a pig is roasting on a spit, the flames licking its pink underbelly. The cookhouse is lined with tables; most are set simply, but the one at the front of the cookhouse is draped with a red cloth, and fresh-cut wildflowers sit in empty bottles arranged down the middle.

Jakub startles Atasha when he puts his arm around Anna. "Girls!" His voice is booming. "You're just in time!" Jakub leads them past some tables set outside the tent where the workmen sit. The gritty body odor from these men permeates the air. Their eyes follow the twins with amazement, and jealousy. The tables inside the cookhouse are filled with the Americans, some of whom are performers, but most deal with the business of the circus. Jakub navigates the twins to the head table. "The cook is about to serve the blood soup. Come, you will be guests at my table."

"But we don't like blood soup," Anna says meekly, directing her statement at Atasha.

"Nonsense! All Czechs like blood soup. Here," Jakub directs them to a bench placed toward the head of the elaborate-looking table, "we had a seat brought here especially for you and you."

"But we really don't want any blood soup, sir," Atasha says.

"Shanghai!" Atasha follows Jakub's call and sees the dwarf approaching the table. He is dressed in pants and a white shirt that look too big for him. His hair is slicked back with a few long strands hanging down in his eyes. His stride causes him to sway back and forth as he walks. He crawls up on the chair opposite Anna. Atasha looks down when he makes eye contact with her. "How is your head, Anna?" he asks.

Before she answers, Jakub yells across the tables and waves Radovan over. He greets every person as if he or she were his special guest for the evening. Radovan, Shanghai, the Lion Tamer, Jarmil, and Simon the clown, without his makeup, sit along one side of the table. Vincent sits next to Atasha, and on the other side of him sit the parents of the trapeze family. Judita sits at the end opposite Jakub. Her skin creates thick rolls from her chin to her arms, and her breasts disappear in the thickness of her torso. Her body spreads out to fill the entire width of the table.

The cook begins to ladle the dark red soup. Jarmil squeals with delight and claps his hands like a child. The cook sloppily drops soup into Atasha's bowl, and she watches the crimson liquid spread as it soaks into the tablecloth. "Eat, girls," Jakub says like a concerned father. "It's full of nutrients for you—surely a two-headed body needs plenty of that." Jakub slurps in a few spoonfuls.

Atasha shakes her head no. Anna picks up a spoon and manages to take a few sips. Atasha's stomach turns. Before Anna takes another spoonful, Atasha stops her. "We really do not like blood soup, sir," she says strongly to Jakub.

Jakub doesn't hear her because he is engaged in a conversation with Radovan. Shanghai clears his throat, and, as Atasha turns her attention toward him, he picks up his bowl of soup and turns it over, dumping the contents onto the ground. He smiles at Atasha, and she feels a sudden warmth rush through her body. She smiles back, glances at Jakub, then dumps her bowl of soup on the ground. "But Atasha," Anna whispers.

"Just do it, Anna." Anna puts down her spoon, but doesn't make a move with the bowl. Shanghai's eyes move to Anna, so Atasha looks at her sister. "Anna!" she scolds as she grabs the bowl and dumps the soup.

"I d-d-don't want to be in trouble."

"Jakub didn't even notice."

"I don't like blood soup either." Vincent leans over and flashes his toothless smile at Anna.

Atasha looks back toward Shanghai, who is now engaged in a conversation with Jakub and Radovan. She scans the rest of the table and notices that Mariana is missing.

"Anna," Atasha whispers, "the Gypsy isn't here." Anna looks down along each side of the table, then shrugs her shoulders.

"Who are you looking for, miss?" asks Vincent.

Atasha looks carefully at Jakub, then back to Vincent. "The Gyp . . . Mariana."

Vincent laughs and leans into the girls, whispering as if he were telling a ghost story, "I've heard that the witch doesn't eat animals."

Atasha tries to move away from Vincent. "She doesn't?"

"No. Radovan says that she can feel their souls. He says that when she was a little girl, she was visited by the spirit of one of the animals that she ate for dinner. It crept up on her in the middle of the night and bit into her flesh." Vincent makes a biting gesture at Atasha's neck and laughs wickedly. Atasha jumps in response to his gesture and moves closer into Anna.

The cook brings a steaming platter of pork ribs to the table and sets it in front of Jakub, who stands with a glass of wine in his hand. "To the family gathered here! May we all become rich beyond our wildest dreams!" Atasha follows Shanghai's lead and raises her wineglass in the air during Jakub's toast. "And we welcome to our table tonight some Americans, Atasha and Anna, who are bringing us much success. And Vincent! What a surprise it is to find out we have another American in our midst who can speak Czech! *Na zdraví!*" The entire cookhouse echoes him, *"Na zdraví!"*

Vincent leans over the twins to Jakub and says, "How did you know that?"

"A little bird told me." Jakub's eyes light up. Vincent looks around the table suspiciously, his eyes studying Shanghai more than anyone else.

Jakub piles the plates up with food and passes them down each side of the table. "Judita!" he yells across the table to the gigantic woman. "This is yours!" He scoops a huge mound of potatoes onto the center of this plate, which is larger than everyone else's, then pours thick gravy to cover every inch. Next, he stacks as many ribs on top of the potatoes as the plate will hold. He hands the plate over Anna to Atasha, and gravy drips off the side as she passes it to Vincent. She watches it travel down the row to Judita; a few of the ribs fall off before it gets to her. "Eat well tonight, Judita! Just fifty more pounds and we can claim that you are the fattest woman in all of America!"

"Yes!" Radovan adds, "Only those Ringling bastards have one fatter than you!" The whole table laughs.

Jakub fills another plate to pass down the row. "Here," Vincent says as he puts his left arm around Atasha and reaches across to take a plate of food from Jakub, "let me help you with that." Atasha turns her head toward Anna because Vincent's hair smells as if he has been rolling his head in a pigpen. The sweat and dirt make his hair stick to his forehead in thick strands.

After the food has been passed around the table, Vincent removes his arm from Atasha's shoulder and places his hand on her thigh. "I've been meaning to tell you," Vincent whispers in her ear, "you're much prettier than your sister." He squeezes her thigh. She grabs his hand and pushes it away. Vincent's laughter comes from deep inside his belly, and Atasha smells how his breath rots from there. She feels embarrassed and looks at Shanghai; his eyes have narrowed, and he scowls at Vincent.

Vincent leans over his plate and begins devouring the ribs and pork chop. He licks his fingers clean of pig grease and gravy, smacking his lips on each finger like he is cleaning the meat off a bone. Shanghai glances back and forth between Vincent and Atasha. Atasha gives Shanghai a slight smile.

"You know," Vincent leans into Atasha as he points a pork rib in Shanghai's direction, "our little friend over there used to work in a whorehouse."

"A what?" Atasha sounds agitated. Shanghai cocks his head as if he's trying to hear what Vincent is saying.

"I heard Jakub talking about it last night."

"I don't know what you're talking about," says Atasha.

"Watch this." Vincent raises his voice and speaks in Czech, "Shanghai, tell me, how did you come to breathe fire?"

Many conversations around the table stop. "Why do you ask?" says Shanghai.

"Well, it's just not something you'd learn in your everyday life, so I was just wondering."

"It is a lengthy story," Shanghai says.

"No, please, indulge us. I'm sure we're all interested in hearing it. Right, Atasha?" Atasha meekly nods her head.

Everyone's attention is focused on Shanghai. He gazes at Atasha, then Jakub. "It's up to you," says Jakub.

Shanghai raises his eyebrows, as if a spark ignited in his brain. "Well, Vincent, I did not learn it at all. It is part of my heritage. You see, long ago, when my father's father's father was just a boy, he lived in a village in the far southwest corner of Bohemia. At the edge of the village there was a giant ground lizard, as long as this table, who breathed fire. The ground lizard crossed the countryside on its belly, setting bushes and grasses on fire. It is told that my father's father's father once found a tree stump burned to a crisp; close by, a tree lay on the ground nearly intact, the bottom of it singed. My father's father's father estimated that twenty feet of the tree between the trunk and the top had been turned to ash. The ground lizard was not really hurting anyone but was causing the town much grief over the bush fires they had to put out day after day."

Judita smacks her lips as she eats, and Jakub shushes her, delighting in Shanghai's story. Judita puts down the half-eaten rib, drinks her whole glass of water, then stops to listen.

"Something had to be done. The ground lizard was consuming the countryside with fire, and the villagers were becoming very tired. They tried catching him but he was too fast, and every time they got close, he started another fire.

"You have heard the expression 'Fight fire with fire'? Well, it was at a dinner table, much like this one, that my father's father's father sneezed violently. When he did, a flame shot out of his nose and burned the carcass of a chicken down to nothing. The family sat silently around the table staring in amazement and fear at the charred remnants of the boy's sneeze. His mother scolded him and asked him if he'd been playing with the ground lizard. 'No, Mama,' he said in shame. It was then that the boy's father, my father's father's father's father, came up with the idea.

"The next day, they set off for the charred countryside with a bottle of fresh pepper. They walked quietly through the last field of wildflowers, and sure enough, the ground lizard was happily basking in the sun. The boy was amazed at the lizard's enormity and its emerald-green skin.

"When they got about ten horse lengths away from the ground lizard, the boy's father dumped a mound of pepper into his hand and held it out to the boy. The boy took a deep breath, and when he sneezed, a great flame shot from his nose and burned the ground lizard to a crisp.

"So that's how . . . ," Shanghai begins to twitch his right eye and wrinkle his nose. He looks toward the sky. *"ah . . . ahh . . . "* Vincent pushes his seat back from the table. "AH-CHOO!" Shanghai lets out a sneeze that blows out the candle in front of him. "Now where was I? Oh, yes, so that's how my family came to breathe fire." Shanghai looks directly at Vincent.

Jakub begins laughing, as does everyone else at the table. Vincent scowls at Shanghai. "You're quite the storyteller, little one. Perhaps you should not breathe fire at all. Perhaps we should set you up in a corner of the Freak Tent and have you tell stories to the little children. They would be so happy with someone their own size."

"Vincent," Jakub pours himself another drink, "I'm sure many of us would like to know . . . how is it that you came to the circus?" Vincent's smile immediately disappears. "That's what I thought." Jakub takes a sip, savors it, then swallows. "We have a code here. We do not ask someone about his past unless he willingly offers the information. It is best, I think, for you in particular, to live by our code."

Atasha finds herself staring at Shanghai, who suddenly seems magical to her. In her heart, she now believes that he can actually teach them to juggle. As darkness falls, she notices how Shanghai's face seems extra bright in the glow of the candles. She sees how, in Shanghai's eyes, there are little gold flecks that dance and spin like the falling leaves of autumn.

Her thoughts and feelings are completely her own. Anna's thoughts and feelings soon become a backdrop, a voice among other voices, drifting slowly into the background as Atasha becomes mesmerized by Shanghai's dancing eyes.

✷   ✷   ✷   ✷   ✷

AS SHANGHAI tells his story, Anna watches Jakub's animated face, reacting at every turn. Her knee is pressed against his beneath the table, and the thrill of this contact courses through her veins. This euphoria began the other night when Jakub talked to the girls after the show. The way he drew his finger down the side of her face and held her chin in his hand not only surprised her but also made her feel special, even separate from Atasha.

His face is dark and rugged. His blue eyes shine as he laughs at Shanghai's story; his dimples bring softness to his face. She feels as if she can trust him. His gaze pauses on hers, and he smiles. Anna looks down, embarrassed to be caught looking at him in this manner. Below the table, Jakub pats Anna's knee, and when she looks at him he winks like a father would. She has to catch her breath and smiles back at him. Anna wonders if her sister has the same romantic notions about Jakub. The same ideas that he is, perhaps, their prince. She imagines his hand back on her knee, rubbing her leg, holding his palm on her thigh as if he never wanted it to be anywhere else. She delights in this fantasy until someone mentions Mariana in a conversation.

She looks at his face again. How strong he is, how kind. And she wonders how a fine man like Jakub could possibly be married to a *jezibaba*.

IN ALL *my life, I have only ever seen the cheating side of marriage. Those married men who came into the brothel carried their shame like a heavy cloak, removing it only long enough to indulge in pleasures with one of the ladies. And when the men stepped outside the front door, the change was visible on their faces—as if they had just put that dreaded weight back over their shoulders as they began their long walk home.*

Now, I am wearing that cloak as I am on the other side of cheating. Milada tousles my hair and tells me that I am innocent in all of this—that she is the one doing the cheating, but still, I wear that heavy cloak of shame, of guilt.

I see so many here wearing that cloak. Jakub's cloak weighs his shoulders down so much that he must drink himself light again. I saw him, just last night, with another woman, a woman other than his wife. I saw the woman at the evening performance and knew immediately that she was looking to make extra money. Jakub didn't have the decency to take her somewhere away from his wife. I saw them, right beneath Mariana's wagon, on the ground, making noises that could wake the horses. His wife surely heard those sounds.

This morning, Jakub's eyes were still clouded from alcohol, but the weight was visible on his shoulders. And when the Gypsy looked at him, he avoided her eyes. I thought an argument would ensue, but all they discussed was business. All they ever discuss is business. And in the end, it seems that Jakub removes that cloak of shame and guilt and gives it over to his wife. I can almost see the transference: his spirit becomes lighter, and hers becomes heavier.

I do not want to wear that cloak, Milada. You must find a way to free yourself from Zikmund so that we can live without guilt, without shame—without a weight so heavy on our shoulders that we can never speak from our hearts again.

—Shanghai's diary, July 1899

Dětátko

Ogallala, Nebraska
May 6, 1900

ariana sits at the base of a tree at a clearing by the river. She moves far away from the circus grounds on days of the Great Feast. She enters the woods, where she can't smell the cooking flesh or hear the dripping grease popping in the fire, which sounds to her like cracking bones.

She closes Shanghai's diary. Each time she has read this passage, it has made her feel heavy all over again. She closes her eyes and leans her head back on the trunk of a tree, trying to erase the words written about her marriage. She wishes she could shut down a few chosen senses and walk among the troupers as they chew on animal flesh. Instead, she heightens her sense of hearing. Soon, Shanghai's words float above her head and replace the words that he wrote. She loves to hear him tell a story. *The ground lizard, is it?* She can see his face in her mind as he speaks. His eyebrows raise, first one, then the other, then both. He moves his hands through the air as if his words were clay that he can form and mold until he constructs this giant sculpture of words. And those words form a picture that Mariana carries in her mind all the time. When she brings the image back, it is Shanghai's voice she hears in her head over and over again.

It takes her away from the memories she fights today. It was exactly sixteen years ago when Mariana dreamed of a flood. In her dream, the water rose up and wiped away her Romani family: Papa, Mama, and her sister Nona. Nona was a baby, and she rode high on a wave, her little body tossed about like timber. She would cry, then her cry would disappear into the water, then she would scream, then her scream would become a gurgle beneath the surface, then her scream was clear again, then a gurgle. Mariana called out for Nona. Called out for her mama or papa to help, but they were long gone, washed away to the sea.

Mariana woke from this dream with Jakub beside her, sleeping soundly. The bed was soaking wet; sweat poured from her face. She knew it was a bad dream and that her Romani family was not in danger, but she also knew that something was terribly wrong. She was doubled over in pain, and when she felt between her legs, she felt the sticky texture of fresh blood. "Oh, no! Oh, no!" she cried, and Jakub shot up from his sleep.

"What is it? What?"

"*Dětátko! The baby!*"

Jakub jumped out of bed and ran to the lanterns to bring light into the wagon. "What? Are you sure? It's too small. It can't be the baby."

"I know. I know," Mariana cried into the night. "It is too early. Get someone! Get someone!" Jakub ran to get help, leaving her in the dim lamplight to watch the bright red blood sink into their bed. She knew that it was already too late.

Days of silence passed between them. One evening, as they were lying in bed, Mariana said plainly, "It was the freaks. They brought *bibaxt* with them."

"You think they have brought us bad luck?" Jakub spoke softly and rubbed her back, but she pulled away. "No, my dear, it wasn't the freaks. They had nothing to do with this."

"They joined us two months ago, just after *Dětátko* was conceived. And now he is dead. Do you think that is a coincidence? They are surrounded by bad spirits, and now those bad spirits have surrounded us."

"Mariana," Jakub whispered to her, "this would have happened whether the freaks were here or not. The doctor said it was from your rigorous work schedule. He said you should have been resting these past few months." It was in these days that Jakub's Cirkus traveled by wagon, and the doctor thought the constant movement and daily work had been too much for Mariana's baby.

"No," Mariana began to cry, "no, I don't believe that. Mama carried me, and Nona, while the caravan traveled town to town more rigorously than we do now. Mama washed clothes, told fortunes at the side of the road, helped steal chickens . . . She only miscarried when Papa beat the baby out of her. The freaks, they have cursed us."

"Please stop saying that. They have brought us the money we've needed lately to get by. They are just human beings like us. They need a home. Just like us."

Mariana stopped talking then. She didn't talk to Jakub for a week, two weeks, three; she lost count. Jakub told her that she didn't need to return to work so quickly. She said nothing, and the next day, she was in front of her tent, sewing garments and telling fortunes. At night, she sat in a chair and wept. Jakub tried to comfort her. He threw out the stained mattress and brought in a new one. Mariana still said nothing to him. She had no words to say.

After the third week of silence, Jakub and Radovan were sitting next to a bonfire when Mariana stood on the top step of their wagon and released a moan so loud that the two elephants cried with her. Jakub and Radovan dropped their bottles and covered their ears for several minutes until the awful wailing stopped. Mariana stepped down the stairs, dragging a blanket behind her, and disappeared into the woods. She sat beneath a tree, holding the bundled-up blanket in her arms. She held herself, rocking and humming a Gypsy tune.

Jakub cast a lamp on her, and she shut her eyes to keep the brightness out. He tried to pull the blanket from her, but her grip was too tight. "Mariana, let go. It's over." She hummed louder and began to shake. A vision of her father flooded her brain.

"Did you do this to me?" she whispered, her eyes fierce and wild.

"What? No!"

She lifted her blouse and showed Jakub her abdomen. "There are bruises, see?"

Jakub knelt down and looked at her dark skin. It was smooth and pure. There was not a mark on it but Mariana felt it, felt the pain deep inside her body. "Mariana, look, there are no bruises. You're just having a bad dream, *hmmm?* Come back to the trailer with me. You need more rest."

She ignored him and continued humming while she rocked her baby's blanket. Jakub's voice quivered with fear. "You are coming with me right now!" He stood up and motioned for her to take his hand. "Come!"

She glared at him. He grabbed hold of her arms and tried to pull her up, but she was too heavy, as if gravity were holding her as tightly as she held the blanket. "This is ridiculous. Come on, now. Stand up!" Jakub demanded, but Mariana didn't move. He yelled out for Radovan, keeping his lantern cast on Mariana's small, curled-up body. When Radovan made his way through the brush, Jakub demanded that Radovan pick her up and carry her back to the wagon.

Radovan refused. "She's a Gypsy. She may put a curse on me."

"Nonsense!" Jakub handed Radovan the lantern and lifted her like a baby. She began to wail, her cries again setting off the elephants.

"Jakub!" Radovan chastised. "Leave her be!"

"No! I am tired of this!" Jakub yelled over her cries. "She needs to return to the world of the living." He carried her to the wagon with Radovan following. He put Mariana back into the wagon and commanded Radovan to find a sturdy lock. Mariana's wild cries turned into weeping, and they shut the door to the wagon. They wrapped a chain around the door and locked Mariana in. "You will stay there until you learn to be human again, Mariana!" Jakub yelled. Two days passed. On the third evening, with the caravan ready to leave for the next town, Jakub opened the door to check on her, but Mariana was gone. "Radovan!" he yelled, and his hands were flying around as he gestured wildly. "Where is she?! Where did she go? What have you done with her?"

"Who?" Radovan backed up, fearing that Jakub would strike him.

"Mariana. She's not in the wagon!"

"What? She has to be . . . ," Radovan headed for the wagon to search for Mariana. When he came out he said, "Something's not right, Jakub. Let's just pack up and leave her here." Jakub pushed Radovan into the side of the wagon and held him by the collar—they stood eye to eye—but then Jakub released him. Radovan backed away from Jakub, but said, "I told you in the beginning that having a Gypsy along with us was trouble. How did she break out of the wagon? That's what I'd like to know." Radovan's voice trailed off, and he motioned for Jakub to look toward the trees.

Mariana was standing at the edge of the woods, holding tightly to a piece of the blanket, watching the whole scene play out. She walked toward the wagon and sat on the steps. Clutching the ripped piece of fabric to her chest, she began to cry.

The mumblings of Mariana's escape into the woods that day ran through the circus grounds, and everyone began to fear her. She knew that they watched her suspiciously and reported any odd behavior to Jakub. They reported watching her dance in the darkness, appearing beside them from thin air, and crying in the middle of the night from beyond the tree line. By the end of that season, even Jakub was convinced that she was a *jezibaba*.

After several months, she came out of the spell she was in and begged Jakub to try to conceive another baby with her. He refused. She tried to seduce him, but Radovan told him to stay away from her completely. She'd lost her baby and her husband.

Soon enough, Jakub was sleeping with town girls and whores. Mariana looked the other way, but more and more she was beginning to see the change in his face, the resemblance to her father. And now, reading Shanghai's diary, she sees her marriage from the outside. She remembers the night that Shanghai describes, when Jakub had sex with a woman on the ground, right beneath Mariana's bed, grunting like wild animals.

He disappoints her in so many ways. But the most unforgivable is that he has forgotten their child. He doesn't mark this day anymore—the day of their child's birth and death. *If only he didn't try so hard to forget, maybe he wouldn't behave in such a way.*

Sometimes Mariana thinks she can still feel that little life moving inside her, but she knows her baby is dead. She buried the blanket that day in the woods outside of *Český ráj* so she could remember his death. And she held onto one corner of the blanket, just one little piece. Every year, when Jakub's Cirkus returned to that spot, she clutched that piece of blanket to her chest as she placed flowers on her baby's grave. This is the first year that she will not visit that place. This is the first year that her baby will experience the same loneliness that she feels every day of her life.

But even today, there are times when she feels the same kind of light-headedness, the same kind of nausea as that of a pregnant woman. She steps down to the water's edge, cups the cool liquid in her hands, and lifts it to her face. From the circus grounds, Jakub's laughter wafts above everyone else's and drifts over her head. She turns her eyes to the sky and screams out once again. Birds flap wildly from the treetops and fly away on the air of her scream. Then it is silent.

She stays by the river until it turns dark, then she returns to the compound. As she steps into her train car, she can hear the voices rise and fall, and laughter circles the grounds. She searches through her trunk for that little worn piece of fabric. She holds onto it and imagines returning to the woods of *Český ráj* to stand over the place she marked as a grave for her baby. Her flesh and blood. She cries for the sorrow that fills her heart and for the sickness she feels being so far from home. Throughout the night she dreams of her baby all alone in those woods, lying on the ground, crying out for her. Each time she wakes, she uses that little piece of cloth to catch her tears.

EVERY NIGHT *in every village, hundreds of people come to Jakub's Cirkus. They sit in the Big Top, waiting for the most magical night of their lives. They have never seen anything like this before: instead of horses that work the fields, they witness dancing ponies; instead of two musicians standing on the street corner, they hear a full band playing throughout the show; instead of a beautiful woman walking down the street, they watch her flying across the length of the tent; and they have never seen anything like the contortionist clowns, performing elephants, parading camels, and roaring lions.*

As the show goes on, the crowd shrieks, gasps, laughs, and breaks into thunderous applause. It is unlike anything I have ever seen. I will be in the Big Top someday soon. Milada is sure of it. She sometimes laughs at Jakub's ignorance. "If he only saw the truth, Shanghai, he would know that you are the best performer of them all!"

I do see myself in the Big Top, throwing fire as high as Milada's bar and catching it in perfect rhythm. Or perhaps I can learn to roll on a barrel while juggling fire; then the crowd will gasp throughout my entire performance, worried that I too will catch on fire as I roll around the ring. Milada and I even talk about how I could learn to fly the trapeze, to be the man on the other side of her act. I could catch her as her father catches her, and no one would even be able to tell that I was a dwarf. I would simply be a man, swinging from a bar. The audience would never know any different.

When I meet Milada in the Big Tent, after the night's performance, we talk about all of the possibilities.

It seems that everywhere I look now, all I see are the possibilities.

—Shanghai's diary, May 1899

Shanghai Flies

Ogallala, Nebraska
May 6, 1900

hanghai sits around the campfire with the usual group of men—Jakub, Radovan, Vincent, the Czech troupers—and tonight he listens for the slurring of their voices as the empty bottles of alcohol fall to the ground with a clink. The women's curfew has long passed, and even the workmen have settled into their bunks for the evening. When Jakub's eyelids begin to droop, Shanghai makes his move and sneaks away, unnoticed.

Lately, he has been drawn to the Big Top. He now remembers meeting Milada there, night after night. They put on a show together, pretending they were the whole circus. Then they climbed the ladder . . . and his memory stops there. But every time he steps into the big tent, more comes back to him. Somehow, being in the large, open space of the Big Top, he is able to recall certain details about her. He picks up his lantern and makes his way along the side of the train, his feet crunching on the small rocks that surround the railroad ties. His lamplight is so low to the ground that if one of the troupers were to look outside a car, he or she would see only a dim glow pass the window. They may even see it as a ghost—a spirit of the plains—and they would quickly go back to sleep before it haunted them.

He hurries past the *jezibaba*'s car, noticing that her light is still on. He hears soft whimpers from inside, but they stop as his feet shuffle by. His heartbeat quickens. He leaves the trail that follows the sidetrack and makes his way to the Big Top.

✹   ✹   ✹   ✹   ✹

MARIANA RESTS her hand on Shanghai's diary, holding on to the word *possibility*. She lies quietly on her bed, listening to the nocturnal sounds of this new place, comparing them to the sounds of home. Only the men's voices, rising into the air like the campfire embers, sound remotely like Czechoslovakia. How well she knows the words that Shanghai has written. She puts the diary back into her trunk, exactly where it belongs, hoping to put these foolish thoughts away with it. Then she hears familiar footsteps pass by, the person's gait uneven and rapid. Her heart jumps. She steps out into the steamy night air and watches Shanghai's lamplight disappear into the Big Top. *No*, she whispers, *no, I will not.* But then she thinks again of the possibilities. She cautiously slips past Jakub who is sitting close to the fire. His state of drunkenness makes her feel less guilty. She finds her way to the elephants and draws her index finger along the rough skin of Bruno. He twitches at her touch and the wrinkled skin tenses, but when the giant beast looks into Mariana's eyes, he relaxes once again. She breathes in and out, in and out. The smells from a nearby pig farm bite the air. She focuses on the expansion of her chest, on the movement of air through her nostrils, and allows herself to fade.

She steps into the big tent, where Shanghai stands in the middle of one of the two rings. She takes her place in the empty stands, sits in a chair, and watches his performance. Every time she sees Shanghai this way, her heart feels light. Shanghai turns, as if gathering a round of applause from a full house, then raises his hands in the air and falls into a series of handstands—one, two, three, four—until it appears that he will flip right out of the ring. He stops and curls his body, reverses direction, and does a series of forward rolls. When he stands, he again throws his arms in the air and addresses all four sides of the empty stands as if he has done something never achieved by man. Mariana sits on her hands to stop herself from applauding. She delights in watching Shanghai's show.

He rolls a large wooden spool into the ring, and, balancing himself on it, he tries to navigate it around the ring. He falls off and gets back on; he rolls it into the sides of the ring, backs up, and keeps nudging forward until he makes one full circle. Since their arrival in America, he hasn't mentioned his desire to be a Big Top trouper, but it's obvious to Mariana that his dream is still alive.

As he climbs the pole toward the fly system, Mariana feels like stepping out of the shadows to make herself known. Instead, she remains in the darkness and watches Shanghai ascend the rope, which sways recklessly as he climbs higher. When he gets to the top platform, he reaches for the trapeze, but it is tied a foot above his grasp. As he jumps for it and misses it, a tingling fear runs throughout Mariana's body. He sits at the edge with his feet dangling over the side of the platform. He sways his body, reaching his arms out in pantomime of the trapeze performance. For one minute, Mariana can see his body leap from the edge and sail through the air, over one ring, then the other, his body thrown smoothly back and forth like a pendulum, his legs arching one way, then the other.

. . . all I see are the possibilities, Mariana thinks to herself.

SHANGHAI CLOSES his eyes and thinks of Milada. He doesn't know if he is imagining or remembering, but regardless, he sits with this picture of her in his head, and the picture makes his heart feel warm again. Her body is long, her movements smooth, as she glides through the air. He watches her not from a distance like an audience member but from beside her. He focuses on her hands first—how they grip the bar. The small thin bones of each finger in the back of her hand protrude as if they are tiny muscles; the curve of her knuckles is white with her grip; her thumb curls up beneath the bar like a baby. Her forearms are smooth and solid. Shanghai follows the definition of a muscle from her wrist, watches it curve around her elbow and form a deep groove as it disappears under her costume. For that moment, she is so clear to him that he feels as if he could paint a portrait of her. Her breasts form soft curves above her rib cage, and he longs to run his fingertips over the groove below them, above them, around them. He imagines running his finger over her nipples, then following the curve down to her ribs and over each bone to her abdomen. It is tight and solid as she swings.

He makes his way up to her neck, where her veins form tiny blue trails that disappear into the soft waves of the dark hair at the back of her neck. Her ears, her eyes, her lips . . . her hair . . . her eyes, her lips. Shanghai has lost the image. He pulls himself back to the platform and puts his hands over his eyes, hoping the darkness will bring her back. She is swinging. She is swinging. She is swinging, but he cannot she her face anymore. He sees only a long, slender body, flying through the air, toward him, away from him—faceless, nameless, fearless.

★ ★ ★ ★ ★

MARIANA STEPS off the bleacher and onto the dirt floor. When she looks up, Shanghai has stopped rocking and pulls his nearly shoulder-length hair back into a ponytail. His eyes are shadowed by his heavy brow line, but Mariana can still see his strong features: his high cheekbones and square jaw, his flat, round nose. She knows how badly he wants to fly; Milada pleaded his case when he joined Jakub's Cirkus. But Jakub would have none of it. "No, no, no," he said. "Look at him . . . he will never get from one bar to another; his arms are too short." Milada put her arm around Shanghai, pulling him close so that his head was just below her right breast.

"He could do it," Milada protested. "He has the body of an athlete."

"Is that what you see?" Jakub laughed. "Well, my dear Milada, you can see whatever you'd like, but I can tell you that he has the body of a Sideshow act." Jakub sat at his desk where he had piles of drawings and notes. "No, if he wants to stay with us, he will be in the Sideshow; he is a fire thrower. I saw it myself this afternoon." Jakub's face lit up when he thought of his new acquisition—as if Shanghai had fallen from the sky.

Shanghai stands on the platform, and his shadow spreads from the bottom of the big canvas to the top. By the look on his face, it almost seems that he can remember his lover, but it's not possible; the spell Mariana put on him was too powerful. Mariana steps into the ring below him. She can almost feel Milada's presence here, as if Shanghai had conjured her up. She can almost hear the young woman's voice.

She remembers the night that Milada first told her about Shanghai. It was in Lidice, a village just outside of Prague. Mariana was lying in bed, listening to the creak of branches and the rustle of a small animal in the underbrush as she drifted off to sleep. Before she entered into darkness completely, Milada's soft voice came to her, "Mariana, Mariana . . . " It compelled her to step out of her own dream to follow the pull of Milada's will.

She entered Milada's dream through a maze of flying rings of fire. Her feet sank into scorching white sand, so she released her attachment to the earth and drifted above the ashen land. She passed a group of little girls, holding hands and giggling as they spun their circle around. She floated above a bed of shining knives where Milada's father lay sleeping. She entered a dark tunnel that hummed like a thousand bees, a sound Mariana found comforting and disturbing all at once. On the other side of the tunnel was a dark green meadow full of bright yellow wildflowers surrounded by trees. Milada performed floating acrobatics above the treetops, her lean athletic body gracefully twirling, her long, dark hair tumbling behind her. Mariana willed Milada's body to the ground.

"I'm so glad you came!" Milada said.

"Could this not wait until morning?" Mariana watched bubbles of light dance behind Milada's head.

"You must take Jakub to Václavské náměstí, Wenceslas Square, in Prague tomorrow. When you get to Karlova Street, go west. At two in the afternoon you will find there a man who will bring tears of joy to Jakub's eyes. He is my friend, and I want him here."

Mariana caught sight of a juggling chimpanzee dressed in a tiny vest swinging from branch to branch in the trees off to the left. "How will I know this friend of yours?"

"He is a little person. He stands only to my ribs."

"What is your friend's name?"

"Shanghai."

"And why should he be here?"

Milada twirled around as if she could not help herself. "He is truly enchanting, madam. You must see for yourself."

"How did you meet this fellow?" A crowded street in Prague appeared behind Milada; horse-drawn carriages kicked up dust, and the sound of a crowd rose over Milada's head.

"Yesterday, when Zikmund and I went into town. Zikmund went into a bar for a drink, and I wandered the streets. When I turned the corner, there was Shanghai with a crowd of people gathered around."

"And did Zikmund meet Shanghai as well?"

"No, of course not. Shanghai and I talked while Zikmund was in the bar. Shanghai wanted to come see me perform last night, and I didn't want to tell him no. I find him intoxicating. His talents are being wasted out there on the street." Milada's emerald eyes glistened like jewels.

"And Shanghai, he wants to join us?"

"Oh, yes, he wants to be here more than anything."

"So why does he not go directly to Jakub and talk to him?"

"There is a complication."

"A complication, how?"

A dark cloud rose from the ground and swallowed the street. "Zikmund is coming, madam, I must go. But please . . . I beg you . . . Shanghai will die in that place if we do not save him."

"I will consult the cards on it, Milada. If the cards bode well for us, I will talk to Jakub." Milada was sucked into the dark cloud. The pull was strong enough that Mariana had to fight to step away from it. She walked back through the buzzing tunnel, out the other side, and saw that Milada's father was no longer sleeping on the bed of knives. She thought that he was, no doubt, part of the dark cloud that had pulled Milada away.

As Mariana walked through the dancing rings of fire, she forced her eyes open. She thought she saw a miniature shadow standing next to her bed, watching her sleep. The pear-shaped head looked like Shanghai, but when Mariana's eyes finally focused into the state of waking, the shadow had disappeared.

Mariana imagined how Zikmund would react to finding his fiancée with Shanghai. How Milada's overbearing father would react. *Yes, this could be fun,* she thought. "Yes, Milada," Mariana whispered into the darkness, "I will take Jakub to Wenceslas Square tomorrow afternoon. I will tell him that I need some fabric for costumes. We will see just how enchanting your little friend can be."

Indeed, Mariana did find him enchanting. Even now, she is more enchanted with him than ever before. When he spins fire, he mesmerizes. When he tells a story, everyone is captivated. As she reads his diary, she finds herself wanting to seek him out more and more. He is a guilty indulgence, and she yearns to be close to him.

SHANGHAI HEARS a whisper of hay move below him. He looks down on the two rings; each one frames a mixture of sawdust and hay. He sees no one, but again he imagines a tent full of people, looking up at the height of him. He becomes a giant, filling the platform, reaching the top of the tent, and the crowd looks at him as if he can do anything. As he gazes across the open space to the opposite platform, Milada's image again flashes in his head. He tries to force the image of her into flight, but Milada disappears as quickly as she entered his mind's eye.

Shanghai grabs onto the rope ladder and glides down without putting his feet on the rungs. When he reaches the bottom, he wipes his hands together with small claps. He blows on his burning palms as he enters the ring directly below the free-hanging trapeze bar. He looks up and feels as if he has been here before, feels that he should know something about standing just below the bar, but he can't remember. His neck is stretched out, his head relaxed back, so that he looks skyward, and he can't seem to remove his eyes from the wires and ropes and bars of the trapeze.

✴ ✴ ✴ ✴ ✴

MARIANA WATCHES as Shanghai stares at the empty trapeze. Sadness has taken over his face. No doubt his attempts to recall Milada have failed. Mariana longs to see him happy and almost feels compelled to remove her spell so that he can remember once again. No, that would simply bring him a new form of sadness. *Has Milada's longing for Shanghai perhaps filled my own heart?* Mariana wonders. *Are these perhaps not my longings at all?*

She remembers the anticipation she felt at meeting Shanghai face-to-face on that one-hour journey to Prague. As Jakub led the horses across the Charles Bridge, Mariana suggested that they tie them near the Týn Cathedral and walk to Old Town. She knew it was the only way they would "happen upon" Shanghai.

"But my dear, the time, the time." Jakub pulled out his pocket watch.

"There is no show today. What is your hurry?"

Jakub put his watch away, grabbed Mariana's hand, and kissed it. "All right, my dear, whatever you wish." Whenever Mariana went out in public, Jakub felt that men's eyes lingered too long on her mysterious beauty. Even though he no longer slept with his wife, he did want the greater world to know that she belonged with him. So they walked arm in arm through the streets of Prague. Jakub wore his top hat and tails, and Mariana wore a purple and blue skirt with a white blouse and a purple diklo. They walked proudly, fully aware of how people stared at them. Mariana heard the whispers as they passed. "Gypsies," one woman muttered, but her friend corrected her. "The circus is in town." The women nodded approvingly.

Ignoring the whispers, the couple made their way to Wenceslas Square where people walked along the street broad enough for the horse-drawn tram and carriages going either way. Mariana led Jakub toward the general store but made sure that they walked past Karlova Street, where Shanghai was to perform. "Let's see what is going on here." She tugged on Jakub's arm, and he followed her toward a small crowd that was gathered. She pushed her way to the front, pulling Jakub with her.

In the center of the crowd, Shanghai was throwing sticks of fire into the air, flipping the flames under his arms and back up toward the sky. As they spun down into his hands, his eyes never left the flaming sticks. Mariana looked at Jakub and saw the smile stretch slowly across his face.

Shanghai held a stick up to his mouth and blew a great flame into the air. Jakub laughed in delight and applauded wildly. Shanghai juggled the flames high. His grip was firm; his arms moved so quickly that they appeared to be of normal length. He stopped juggling and put one stick in his mouth to extinguish the flame, then did the same with the other stick. The crowd threw coins at Shanghai's feet. Jakub pulled Mariana aside and said excitedly, "We must ask him to be part of our show."

"Him?" Mariana tried to remain calm, knowing that Jakub had to think that this was his discovery.

"Yes, yes, he is brilliant."

"He is good, yes."

"Well, that's that. I must have him. Our Sideshow would do well with him in it." Shanghai was picking coins off the street as Jakub and Mariana approached. "Pardon me, young man, but may I have a word with you?"

"Of course." When Shanghai straightened up, Jakub seemed surprised that he stood only waist high.

"You are a little person?"

"Yes, sir. I am a dwarf." Mariana watched the gold flakes in Shanghai's brown eyes dance like falling snow.

Jakub looked to Mariana with shock. "Did you see that he was a little person?"

"He does look bigger when he is throwing fire."

Even now, Mariana has to remind herself of Shanghai's stature. His shadow is tall and slender as he looks toward the top of the tent, his arms spread wide. He gazes out into the big empty space between poles where one trapeze bar hangs, lonely and still. Mariana smiles as she remembers Shanghai's look of discernment as he sized up Jakub on that first meeting.

"My good fellow, I am the owner of Jakub's Cirkus. I don't know how much money you are making out here doing this, but I guarantee you that you will be making much, much more money if you join us. And, of course, you will travel all over Bohemia and see places you've never imagined."

Shanghai appeared to be thinking this proposition through as he ran his fingers through the coins in his hat. Mariana noticed the strength and agility in his hands. "It is a very tempting offer, but you see, I do not belong to myself. I am the employee of a brothel just up the street."

Jakub looked at Mariana, then leaned down to Shanghai, whispering, "A brothel?"

"Yes, sir. My mother, she . . . ," Shanghai looked at Mariana, then continued, "she lived there when I was born and, before I learned how to count, sold me to the madam, buying her own freedom."

Jakub straightened up and tugged on the bottom of his jacket. "Well, that's easy enough. Madams have a price for everything. Please, lead us to this brothel. I will have a talk with your madam."

"I wish it were that easy. You see, Madam Zora, she has a certain attachment to me."

Jakub bent down to Shanghai and slowly enunciated each word, "Every madam has her price." He stood upright again. "Now, take us to this brothel."

Shanghai shoved the coins in his pockets and picked up the torch paraphernalia. Jakub and Mariana followed him down the narrow cobblestone street, shadowed by rows of two-story buildings on either side. He led them into a row house, through a dark, narrow hallway, and into a small room where perfume filled the air like the swirling smoke from a cigar. Shanghai exited into another room. Lacy curtains partially obstructed Mariana's view of women lounging on pillows and large chairs.

"Wait here, my dear." Jakub followed Shanghai through the curtains.

Mariana grabbed his arm and pulled him back. "I'm going with you." It was one thing to have Jakub take up with these women when she was not around, but it was a betrayal if he took up with them when she was standing in the next room.

Jakub whispered, "Mariana, do you understand what this is?"

She peered over Jakub's shoulder into the room with curtains. She had to admit, too, that she felt a certain curiosity for what went on inside this house. And she wanted to ensure that Shanghai would be coming with them that very day. "Of course I understand, but this is business. I am involved in this transaction as much as you are."

Jakub thought for a moment, then rolled his hand out, signaling for Mariana to walk ahead of him. Shanghai was nowhere in sight. The ladies stared in shock at Mariana as she looked around the room. The women looked similar to the women of the circus: bright clothing and bright makeup piled on nearly as thick as the clowns'. These women wore more revealing clothing and black stockings; otherwise, they could be part of the circus. A woman with long, thin legs and a scarlet petticoat approached Jakub and drew her finger across his chest. She then walked to Mariana and cupped her chin in her hand. Mariana's heart quickened as the woman's finger grazed her lips. The prostitute spoke to Jakub. "Such a beautiful woman. I could teach her a few things if you'd like."

Jakub laughed. "I think you would be surprised at what you would learn from her! My wife has powers of perception that are far beyond any follies of the flesh."

The woman looked at Mariana with craving eyes. "Is that so?"

"Yes," Mariana fearlessly met the woman's eyes, enjoying the game they were playing, "that is so."

Mariana suddenly wonders if the desires she feels for Shanghai are merely part of a game—a game that started with Milada. Mariana imagines, briefly, how Shanghai would react to seeing her shadow next to his on the wall. A look of shock would cross his face, or perhaps a look of shame. Or maybe he would dance with her shadow, convinced that Milada had returned for him. Or maybe, just maybe, he would move toward her and kiss her hand, his soft lips touching her flesh. Mariana walks the perimeter of the ring. Shanghai is now staring at his giant shadow on the canvas wall. He raises his arms up so that the shadow elongates his limbs; he bends his knees, experimenting with the shadow, making it shorter, then taller, wider, then longer. As she circles the ring, Mariana almost hopes that the lamp will cast her image onto the wall with his. I am old enough to be his mother, she quickly thinks. But Madam Zora is her age. And how shocking it was to see her for the first time as she followed Shanghai into the perfume-filled room. She wore a heavy purple velvet dress. Her large breasts were pushed up so that they spilled above the tight fabric.

"Ah!" Jakub said. "Are you Madam Zora, the lady in charge?"

"I am. Shanghai tells me you wanted a word with me."

Jakub removed his hat. "Yes, madam. I am Jakub, the owner of Jakub's Cirkus. I would like to purchase this young fellow from you."

"You would like Shanghai?"

"Yes, I would." Jakub nudged Mariana. She reached into her blouse and pulled out a wad of cash, handing it to Jakub. "I am prepared to offer you 100 corona for him."

The madam's eyes widened as she watched Jakub count out the money. A few of the women gasped. "My good sir," the madam swallowed hard, "I'm afraid that Shanghai is not for sale."

"Not for sale? Why madam, everyone has a price—name yours."

"I really don't think that Shanghai wants to leave. You see, we have a special relationship."

"Ah, indeed. Well, perhaps we should ask Shanghai." Jakub looked down to where Shanghai was surrounded by the black-stockinged legs of the ladies. "Sir! Would you prefer to stay here or to travel with the circus?" He leaned into Shanghai. "Believe me, I would not blame you if you chose to stay." The ladies giggled.

Shanghai looked up at the madam. "You have been good to me over these past fifteen years, but to be honest, I want to travel with the circus."

"You see? He wants to go with us. So, I am prepared to offer you 150 corona to let him go."

Madam Zora bent down to Shanghai and, placing her finger under Shanghai's chin, looked deeply into his eyes. "This is what you want then, my little one? You know they may not be as understanding to your ways as I."

"Yes," Shanghai pulled the madam's hand from under his chin and squeezed it between both of his hands, "this is exactly what I want."

"Well then," the madam straightened up, a tone of anger in her voice, "give me 250 corona and he is yours." The madam released her hand from Shanghai's grip. "Shanghai, gather your things and get out of my sight. Perhaps the two of you will join me in a drink to seal the deal? Or, sir, maybe you would like to enjoy the delights of one of my many offerings—on the house, of course."

"No, no," Jakub waved off the madam's offer, as he looked nervously at his wife, "a drink will suffice."

"Yes," Mariana toyed with the woman with hungry eyes, "a drink will suffice."

The madam led Mariana and Jakub to another smaller room where rows of bottles were lined up behind the bar. Her tone was one of suspicion, "And Shanghai will be in your Sideshow?"

"Yes," Jakub said, signaling for a refill, "yes, he will draw quite a crowd."

"And where will he live?"

"Madam Zora, I assure you that he will lead a very comfortable life with us."

"Well, good. I . . . ," her words are forced, "I want Shanghai to be happy. I do not keep anyone here against their will." Mariana saw through the madam's deceitful tone. This seemed far too easy.

Jakub raised his glass. "That is quite admirable, madam."

Shanghai appeared from the stairway carrying a well-worn brown leather bag with handles. Jakub stood to greet him. "Are we ready then?"

"Oh, how about one more drink? Just one more for old times' sake, Shanghai?"

"No." Shanghai let Jakub take the bag from him. "I think it's best if we leave now."

Jakub placed his hand on Shanghai's shoulder and led him back into the parlor and toward the door. Mariana followed the pair, and, as Jakub opened the door, she felt a rush of air pass by her. She watched as the madam fell to her knees, throwing her arms around Shanghai's chest so tightly that her knuckles turned white.

"Please don't leave! Haven't I been good to you? Haven't I treated you well all these years?" Her cries spilled into the street and echoed off a neighboring building. Jakub handed the bag to Mariana and pried

Shanghai from the robust woman's grip; he quickly lifted Shanghai off the ground and tucked him under his arm like a doll. The madam latched onto Shanghai's feet, and Mariana watched as the madam was dragged out into the cobblestone street.

Mariana walked behind this spectacle as if it were nothing unusual, but bystanders watched the wailing madam being dragged down the street. Shanghai was laid out, facing the sky, with Jakub pulling from under his armpits and Madam Zora pulling on his feet. As Jakub dragged her, her skirt got twisted and torn by the friction from the cobblestones. "Madam, have some dignity!" Jakub yelled.

"Shanghai, don't leave me. I'll give you anything. I'll give you money, more than you'll ever know what to do with. I'll stop whoring . . . anything! Please! Please!" Shanghai's right shoe came off, and Madam Zora could no longer keep her grip on him with just one hand. She finally let go, her knees and feet bloody and torn. Mariana stepped over the woman, splayed out on the street with her skirt twisted up around her torso. She moaned and rolled from side to side. As the trio walked through Wenceslas Square, the painful cries of the madam still filled the air. Jakub let Shanghai down, and he wobbled all the way to the carriage with only one shoe. Mariana imagined that the other was still clutched in the madam's hand.

Mariana wonders what kind of spell Shanghai has to make people behave in such an abnormal manner. And how has she herself fallen victim to it? Shanghai begins to dance with his own shadow, swaying back and forth, stretching his arms up to an invisible lover. Mariana yearns to make herself visible. But it is not right, she thinks; these feelings are not right. For now, Mariana decides to remain in the darkness and watch Shanghai dance alone.

SHANGHAI SEES Milada as a shadow, spread across the Big Top wall, flying high above his shadow. He can see her when he doesn't have to imagine her face. Yes, he remembers! His heart beats wildly as the image sneaks into his brain. It was here, in the Big Top, where they would meet. He would stand on the ground and watch her shadow swing. Yes! It was the first night he ever stepped foot into the big tent. He watched her perform—he was just one in the crowd, gasping for her, clapping for her, pleading for more. He remembers the exhilaration he felt watching her soar from one pole to the other, her legs clutching one bar, releasing, then catching the next bar with her strong hands. He remembers her being so far outside himself and his life that it didn't seem possible to ever be close enough to touch her.

Shanghai kneels down in the ring, drops to his hands, and tries to focus. Focus. Yes! After the show, he waited for her, just as she asked. He waited inside the tent by the empty cages where the lions performed. She walked toward him, her hair falling down her shoulders. He remembers! She walked toward him and whispered something in his ear, something sexy and soft; then she grabbed his hand at the very moment the generator was turned off, and it became blackness inside the Big Top. He felt her lips on his and he leaned into the kiss, but she pulled away. He heard a flame flare up, then saw the glowing lantern in her hand. Soft light spread up from her arm, encircled her chest, and surrounded her face so that he couldn't see through the light. She pulled him toward the center ring and left him next to the lantern as she climbed to the top, her shadow spreading across the wall. She grabbed the bar and began to swing. Her hair fell off her head like rain when she flipped upside down and outstretched her arms toward him on the ground. Shanghai watched her shadow. He reached his arms up, and their shadows touched, briefly, quickly, then released as if in a dream.

And then . . . and then . . . and then is what Shanghai can't recall. It is only the shadow. Only the times that were like a dream.

★　　★　　★　　★　　★

MARIANA RECOGNIZES the yearning on Shanghai's face. It is that same look he had the first night she saw him—it was even before she stepped into Milada's dream. She watched them in the Big Top. Milada swung slowly back and forth, hanging off the trapeze bar with her arms outstretched beneath her. Shanghai's shadow reached up to hers, and their arms met, then released, met, released. After several passes, Milada let go, and her lean body flipped through the air until she landed in the net below. Shanghai climbed into the net. Milada pulled him on top of her, her thighs clutching his feet, then rolled him over so that she was on top and kissed him full on the lips. She pulled away and giggled as Shanghai lifted his head, trying to prolong the kiss. Milada braced herself by holding his arms down on the net and kissed him quickly again. They looked like they were encased in the net; Shanghai's muscles bulged through the ropes. He laughed as Milada repeated the kiss but then rolled her and placed his right hand at the nape of her neck as his left hand clutched the net. He ran his tongue along her top lip, then took her bottom lip into his mouth.

Mariana felt the passion rise in Milada's heart and turned to leave the lovers as they tumbled through the net and fell out, rolling onto the freshly laid sawdust. Milada pulled herself from Shanghai and ran to the platform where the unicyclist performed. Shanghai held her satiny dress in his hands and walked slowly toward her. He dropped his suspenders and began to unbutton his shirt. Mariana was at the entrance of the tent when Milada's passionate whispers fluttered over her head. "Will you join the circus?" Milada asked Shanghai.

"Yes," he said.

Now Milada is long gone, and Shanghai orchestrates his dance alone. Mariana stands at the edge of the bleachers, her hand on one cold red chair as she thinks, *How I wish to be on the other side of his dance.*

She once again fights the urge to step into the lamplight with

Shanghai; she has her vows, and she remains true to Jakub. This is how it was destined to be. She was supposed to grow up, marry, and bear many children. But that, even that, she cannot do right. Her marriage is all for show. Romanies say that a marriage isn't even a marriage until the first child is born. And her baby—her baby was a dream. There is no grave for her baby. No proof that he ever existed. But there is the spot where Mariana buried that blanket under a tree in the woods outside of Český ráj. When she stepped onto the ship bound for America, she felt like she was abandoning her baby once again. When would she next be able to spread flowers on the ground in the place she lost him? When would she be able to commemorate that short little life? The one little being she so desired and so loved?

That longing on Shanghai's face, yes, she understands it because she has that longing too. That longing turns into sorrow and regret for ever leaving the homeland.

Now Shanghai bends over and drops to all fours. Mariana is shocked by this image. He is rocking back and forth, as if some memory has taken hold. And all she can see is herself—her uncle holding her down into his lap. She knows how it feels to be on all fours like that. She wants to yell to Shanghai, *Stop, stop now! She doesn't know what he's doing. Why he's doing it. It's some awful memory that has sneaked into his heart. Into her heart. That's a good girl, her uncle said as he pushed her into his lap. Slowly now, slowly, he said, that's good. And when he had pleased himself, he said, Don't tell anyone—do you want your parents to know that you're a whore?*

The baby, it was the one way she could redeem herself. The baby was her chance to be a mother, to be a woman, not a whore. The anguish builds inside throat and she tries to run, but she can't carry herself outside the Big Top fast enough. She lurches forward and vomits on the sawdust floor behind the bleachers.

"Hello?" Shanghai yells from the ring.

Mariana collapses to her knees, wiping her mouth with the back of her hand. Shanghai approaches her cautiously and whispers her name for the first time, "Mariana? Would you like me to get Jakub?"

"No!" she yells. She coughs and spits, then laughs at how pitiful she must look. She hides her face in her hands. Shanghai grasps her arm and gently helps her up. He offers her his handkerchief. "No," she gasps, "no, I am all right. I am . . . I am fine." She waves Shanghai away, but he doesn't leave. He puts her arm around his shoulders; they are surprisingly strong, solid. Mariana melts into him. He stands only to her waist, but he is able to help her through the circus grounds and past the glowing fire. She hopes no one sees her like this. The spectacle of her. She knows that stories would pass all over the circus grounds tonight of how weak the Gypsy is, of how sick she looks.

She knows she could walk onto the boxcar herself, but she lets Shanghai help her. She feels the strength in his grip around her waist. Milada was right—he does have the body of an athlete. Mariana breathes the scent of his fresh sweat. She holds onto him as if she'll never let go. He leads her to the bed and helps her stand as he pulls the covers back. He eases her down on the bed, where her head rests perfectly on the pillow. She wants to grab him and pull him close to her. He takes her slippers off and pulls the blanket over her. She wants to beg him to stay with her on this night. She wants to say, *We're both feeling lonely, sad, desperate. We should share the night. We should lean on each other.*

Instead, she clutches his handkerchief in her fist and lets him go without a word.

A Letter Home

Ogallala, Nebraska
May 6, 1900

hanghai runs from Mariana's car until he feels a safe distance from it. He leans over to catch his breath as he makes his way back to the Big Top to get his lantern. He closes his eyes to the thought of the *jezibaba* clutching his shoulder, digging her slender fingers into his muscle. He felt nauseous himself helping her back to her boxcar, but he knew he couldn't just leave her on her own.

A small voice calls his name from somewhere in the darkness. He looks around and fears that the *jezibaba* is following him. "Over here," the voice calls. Shanghai moves his eyes to the entrance of the Big Top, where the two-headed figure stands.

"What are you doing here?" asks Shanghai. "It's past curfew." He looks around to see if Jakub or Radovan might be nearby. The twins would be heavily fined if they were found to be wandering about after curfew.

"We wanted to take a walk," says Atasha. "We saw this light inside the Big Top and wanted to see who was there, but there was no one."

"You should be back in the train sleeping." Shanghai rushes over to them and takes the lantern. "Jakub cannot find you out here." Jakub told him a few days ago that not only would he teach the girls to juggle but he would also be caretaker for the twins. The responsibility weighs on his shoulders.

"Anna couldn't sleep. Her back is hurting."

"Is there something wrong?"

"It's the bed on the train," Atasha says. "It is too narrow for both of us and Anna's pillow, so she has to do without."

Shanghai imagines the twins lying down, and the awkwardness of Anna's body. He sees, from the angle of her body, how Anna would be pulled away from her sister by gravity. "Can't you lean against the wall?"

"I can, but then it hurts here." Anna rubs the back of her neck.

Shanghai understands this kind of pain. He wakes every day with pain in his knees, his hips, and his swayed back. "I will talk to Jakub about it tomorrow. We cannot have you living with such pain, especially if you are to juggle. Besides, Jakub will do anything to keep his best draw content."

"Best draw?" Atasha asks.

"He and his uncle are making many profits from the two of you. Surely they are paying you well."

"We get fifteen dollars a week. Our parents get the rest."

"That's all right with you?"

"Our mother," Anna says meekly, "sh-she is sick."

"Yes, I saw her that day you came here. She didn't look well." Shanghai sees both of their chests expand and deflate as they take a deep breath. He begins to turn away and repeats to the twins that they should try to rest up for the busy day tomorrow. "You will have another juggling lesson in the morning, before the afternoon show."

Atasha blurts out, "Will you help us write a letter to our mother?"

"A letter?" Shanghai turns back toward the twins. "Why don't you write it yourself?"

"We can speak Czech, but we cannot write the language," Atasha says, "and our parents can speak English but read very little of it. Please? It would mean so much to us."

"You want to do this tonight?"

"Yes!" Anna says excitedly, then pleads in a high pitch, "Please?"

Shanghai looks past the twins into the dark cavern of the Big Top. He tries to recall the image of his ghost lover. He closes his eyes to picture the color of her hair and the curves of her face, but he can barely see the shape of Milada's head. Since his attempts are futile, he tells the twins to meet him in a half hour at the Snake Charmer's parade wagon, parked at the edge of the compound. "It has glass sides and snakes carved into the wood," he tells them. "And bring a pencil and paper."

While the twins find their way to their passenger car by the light of the glowing campfire, Shanghai considers what he can do to help alleviate Anna's pain. He takes the steps he uses to get into the car he shares with the Sideshow men and places them below the flatcar that carries the wagon. He then goes to the cookhouse and checks each chair until he finds the sturdiest one. He pulls the chair outside, and, even though it causes pain in his lower back, he drags the chair across the grounds. The legs of the chair leave a thin double trail in the sawdust and dirt all the way to the parade wagon. He pulls the chair up the steps and feels a strain in his neck as he maneuvers it through the door. He places the cookhouse chair next to the snake charmer's chair. "Shanghai?" Atasha calls his name from outside the wagon. He finds the twins standing at the bottom of the stairs. Anna holds the paper and Atasha holds the pencil.

He helps them onto the wagon. "I brought a chair for you from the cookhouse." Shanghai holds the back of the chair as if pulling it out from a table for Anna to sit. The twins turn and relax back into the chairs, but they are at an uneven height. Anna moans in pain.

"I can't s-s-sit here, Atasha." Shanghai runs to Anna's side and helps her stand as if she were a pregnant woman.

"Shanghai, what about the bench from the cookhouse?" Atasha asks.

Shanghai looks down in shame. "I couldn't carry it."

"We'll just sit on the floor," Atasha says quickly. Shanghai holds Anna's hand as they ease themselves onto the wooden floor, covered loosely with hay. They lean against a nonglassed wall. Shanghai silently doubts that he's the best caretaker for the twins and apologizes to them.

"Please, Shanghai, we are fine," says Atasha.

He feels as if he has failed them in some way. "I just wish I could help more."

"No, no," Atasha reassures him, "writing the letter for us means so much. You have gone out of your way to make us feel like a part of this circus family. Not to mention that you are teaching us to juggle."

Shanghai drags a bucket from the corner of the wagon, turns it upside down, and sits across from the twins. "Dear M-M-Mama and Papa," Anna anxiously begins. Shanghai hesitates, then looks down and scratches pencil on paper.

"No!" Atasha says quickly, and Shanghai stops writing. "We are only writing a letter to Mama. Papa doesn't even care that we are here."

"Atasha," Anna whines, "he's still our papa."

"Anna, I do not want to write a letter to him. I have nothing to say. Besides, we need to ask Mama if we can come home for the winter." Shanghai's eyes follow from one twin to the next as he waits for a decision to be made. He watches how their body moves together, one nudging the other, and how neither one can fully see the other's face when they speak. He considers the best way to teach them to juggle.

"Don't you love Papa anymore?"

"Yes," Atasha says unconvincingly, trying to comfort Anna, "but I can tell Mama to send our love. I don't want Papa to read this letter."

"He will read it, though. He might even have to read it for her."

"Then he can wonder why it is not addressed to him."

The twins both look at Shanghai, who sits with his elbow on his knee, his chin resting in the palm of his hand. "Well?" Shanghai asks.

Atasha looks at Anna, then back at Shanghai, "Dear Mama."

"Yes," Anna concedes, "Dear Mama." Shanghai crumples up one piece of paper and begins a new page. As the twins update their mother on their new lives with the circus, Shanghai writes furiously. Even though he listens, he thinks about all the letters he's written to his mother since he was four years old. Madam Zora wrote them for him at first, but he wrote them himself as he got older. He never got a response, but then, in his heart, he knew that Madam Zora never sent them anyway.

Atasha says, "We are eating well, and we are being treated well, except for our sleeping arrangements. We work less than we ever did on the farm and sometimes ask the horse trainer if we can help wash down some of the horses. He seems not to mind it, but he worries that Jakub will catch us."

"Why does Jakub not want us washing horses?" Anna asks Shanghai, who is at first oblivious to her question. "Shanghai?"

Shanghai looks up abruptly. "Well, there are rules. You are Sideshow performers; he is an equestrian. You have your job, he has his. Jakub does not want you washing horses, getting tired, and not performing your job in the afternoon and evening."

"But we enjoy it," Anna whines.

"Once you start juggling, you will find soon enough that you will get too tired to perform in the Sideshow and wash horses. You will need to rest after all of the towns we visit on this trip."

Atasha nods her head for Shanghai to continue. "Mama, sometimes I think the show is why Anna cannot sleep at night. But we are faring well. We grow weary of having people stare at us day after day. Some of them are not very kind. One night a man asked us if we both had brains."

"And a woman asked me if my b-b-brain was smaller." Anna looks down in shame.

Atasha pinches and rubs a piece of fabric from her skirt between her thumb and index finger. "We are learning to juggle for the show. Shanghai, our new friend, is teaching us how." She flashes a smile at him, and his pulse quickens from her attention. For the first time, he sees how attractive she is: her hair falls below her shoulders; she doesn't pull it back like most women do. Her eyes are warm and kind. Her skin is smooth like porcelain. He realizes that he is staring and quickly averts his eyes toward the side of the wagon. The lamplight casts his and the twins' reflections on the glass, and he sees that Atasha is still smiling at him. He feels awkward and returns his eyes to the page.

109

He clears his throat. "Go on."

Atasha giggles, then continues, "We are learning of all the places we will travel this summer. We have been to Kearney, North Platte, and Ogallala."

Anna says, "And tomorrow, we go to Colorado."

Atasha adds, "They tell us that we will travel along the mountains and go across to Utah and Idaho."

"They say there is snow on the m-m-mountains, right in the middle of summer!"

"Slow down! Slow down!" Shanghai says, stopping momentarily to rub his right hand. He has never seen any mountains either, but his mother used to tell him of a range she saw in Austria when she was a little girl. She talked about them so much, he thought that maybe she would go back to those mountains that day she left the brothel. Either that or she would travel to Shanghai, the city he was named for. She heard about it from one of her regulars. "They have people there with dark skin like tea. And their whole world is filled with color. The women wear long silk robes and slippers all the time. And the women's hair is like that, too—long, black silk." Shanghai comforts himself with thoughts that his mother has settled in this magical land. That she has become one of the dark-skinned women who wear silk robes and soft slippers all day.

He recalls the strong smell of her perfume when she knelt down to hug him good-bye. He doesn't remember tears or sadness, only her voice whispering in his ear, "You be good for Mother." He can't distinguish her face from any of the other women at the brothel, can't pick her out of his memory. He can only see black-stockinged legs and bustiers. He does remember her hair, piled high on her head when she was working. He remembers that, and when she prepared for sleep, she let it fall down to the small of her back and combed it out. "Count with me," she said as she brushed through it. The bristles sounded harsh but left her black hair shiny and smooth. "One, two, three," they said it slowly together, but Shanghai lost his way when she got above twelve. So he spoke with her the higher numbers, and was always a beat behind: "fifty-nine, sixty, sixty-one, . . . " and she let him run his fingers through the silky ends, twisting strands around his fingertips, "eighty, eighty-one, eighty-two, . . . " He remembers her face and the smile that crossed it when she wasn't working, a dreamy look reflected in the mirror, " . . . ninety-nine, one hundred!" she said gleefully, then turned to pick up Shanghai's small, light body.

He remembers her hugs because she squeezed so tight that he could barely breathe. But that last time he saw her, she barely squeezed at all. She merely rubbed his head, kissed his cheek, and said, "Now don't cry, okay?" She raised her index finger in front of his face as he nodded, and all he remembers was that he felt no need to cry because he thought that she would return. She would come back from the mountains, or from Shanghai, and maybe even bring him a little surprise that she had picked up. She opened the door, and the bright sun made her a shadow in the doorway. She stopped and stood there for a long time with her back to him. Madam Zora took Shanghai's hand and stood next to him. His mother was holding a suitcase, but he thought nothing of it. She stepped out onto the street and turned to close the door. That familiar smile crossed her face when she looked at Shanghai, and then she was gone.

"Are you ready, Shanghai?" Atasha asks. He nods himself out of the daydream, and she continues, "And one of the Americans told us that, in Colorado, the sky turns pink at sunrise and the mountains reflect the rising sun in the East so that gold trims the mountaintops.

"We get to sleep on the t-t-train, and sometimes at night, we tell each other your stories to help one another fall asleep. And we think about how you used to hold us on your lap when we were little girls."

Shanghai is writing so furiously that he doesn't notice that the twins have stopped talking until he runs out of words to write. He looks up and sees the sisters holding hands. Atasha is rocking Anna as their heads lean into each other with their temples touching. He looks down at the page. "Would you like me to read to you what we have so far?"

"No," says Atasha sadly. "Just finish it with, 'We miss you and think of you often. We hope to come home in the winter when the circus is not traveling. Shanghai says that we can go anywhere we want, and we want to be with you. Please consider this, Mama. Love, Anna and Atasha.'"

"Atasha," Anna whispers, "what if . . . ?"

"We won't think about that now, Anna. We'll just wait for Mama to reply."

Shanghai feels sadness well up inside for the twins' misery. He scribbles down the final words, folds the paper, and softly says, "I will have Radovan take it to town to mail. It will go out tomorrow." He begins to feel restless. "It is long past midnight and past your curfew. We need to get you to your car. You should get your rest." His eyes keep falling on Atasha, even against his will.

Anna stretches her arm behind her and cringes in pain. Atasha twists with the movement. "We will talk to Jakub about your sleeping arrangements." Shanghai smiles at her. "I know we can come up with something that will work better for you."

"That would be nice. Thank you," Atasha says as the twins turn their backs to Shanghai and step out of the wagon.

"Here! Let me help you. I don't want you falling off the platform. Jakub would be very unhappy with me if you were to hurt yourselves." Shanghai laughs nervously as he brushes past the twins. He holds onto Atasha's hand as she steps off the train, and when he does, a familiar electricity runs through his veins. He looks into Atasha's eyes and sees her clearly without her attached sister. His heart races. "You are quite lovely, you know," he says without thinking. Atasha's face reddens, but it is Anna who says, "Please, you embarrass us."

THE NEXT morning, Shanghai walks alongside the parade wagons with the twins' letter. When he finds Radovan hitching horses to the bandwagon, Shanghai gives him the letter to take into town. "Their mother," Radovan says, "she is quite sick."

"Yes, they told me." Shanghai tries to keep his conversation with Radovan brief, knowing that anything spoken will be twisted from the truth. "Have you seen Jakub?"

"He is inspecting the elephants." Radovan points to the end of the wagons lined up for the parade.

Shanghai walks past the bandwagon, where five of the band members pull their instruments to the top; five other band members stand on the ground and pass up more instruments. The equestrians are lined up, and Shanghai tips his hat to the man who lets Atasha and Anna wash the horses. He walks alongside the brightly painted and decorated show wagons, which hold no purpose except to dazzle the audience with their fine craftsmanship. Each one is carved or painted with images from fairy tales. The Snake Charmer sits inside her glass-walled wagon and lets two large snakes wrap themselves around her throughout the parade. He passes the lions, the mirrored wagon, the camels and elephants. "Neviděl jste Jakuba?" Shanghai tries to use pantomime to communicate with the American camel handler, asking if he has seen Jakub. Then Shanghai simply repeats his name, "Jakub. Jakub." The annoyed camel handler shoos Shanghai away. He continues on, looking for Jakub's form beneath the legs of the elephants. He passes the calliope wagon and finds Jakub talking to the Elephant Trainer. He pulls on Jakub's pant leg. Jakub is in a jovial mood, but dark circles hang like shadows under his eyes. "I want a word with you. About the twins," says Shanghai.

"All right, after the parade." He tightens a bridle on one of the horses.

"We won't have time then. Our schedules don't match—you know that."

He gives his attention to Shanghai. "Can you be brief?"

"Yes." Shanghai pulls him aside and speaks quickly. "You asked me to watch over the twins and, well, . . . "

"Yes, yes," Jakub tries to hurry him up.

"The smaller one—she cannot sleep at night because of the bed."

"They have ample room, I assure you. Their bunk is as big as Judita's!" Jakub laughs.

"Yes, I know, but it's not good enough. Anna, she says that her back hurts and her neck, too. It's the angle she is at. She needs the pillow her mother made her, and the bunk is not wide enough for both of them and the pillow."

Jakub sucks on his front tooth as he thinks. "Let me think about it. Tell the twins to come to my car tonight before curfew. I will talk to them."

"Thank you," Shanghai yells over the sound of the bandwagon beginning the parade. "We will be there later."

"Not you, just them. They can talk to me on their own." Jakub steps up on a carriage with Radovan holding the reins.

Before Shanghai can protest, the horses circle around him; he moves out of the way and watches Jakub's head bounce into the distance with each movement of the carriage. At first, Shanghai found the twins to be a burden—a project to take away his happy solitude. But now, he wants to make sure they are well cared for. He even looks forward to seeing them again. As the wagons roll past him and out onto the main street of town, Shanghai scurries off to the midway. His heart pounds as he approaches the Sideshow Tent for their next juggling lesson. He stands at the back, watching Atasha and Anna on the main stage, practicing as they wait for him. He feels nervous and takes a deep breath. Atasha tosses an egg that arcs over her head and into Anna's open palm. Anna looks straight ahead, as if she were on a high wire, then carefully hands the egg across to Atasha. Atasha is much more relaxed, and she takes the egg from her sister, then confidently throws it back into the air. It once again lands in Anna's open palm.

Shanghai wonders what it's like, having another person attached to one's body. He thinks of how strong Atasha is, and how weak Anna seems to be. Atasha is a whole person, he thinks, and Anna is almost a parasite. Atasha has to carry her around, has to adjust for the pains her sister holds.

Shanghai smiles at Atasha's confidence, not only for the fact that she's beginning to make the juggling work but also because her confidence reminds him of Milada. He wipes the sweat from his palms and approaches the stage.

THAT NIGHT, the show is ready to move on, and the workmen tear down the Big Top. The elephants pull the poles from the ground, allowing the large canvas to fall slowly to the earth on a puff of air. The men's voices rise over the circus compound as they roll the canvas and load it onto the pole wagon.

Shanghai steps onto the dessert car and sits with Ladislav and the Strong Man. Their bodies are a shocking contrast to each other. The Strong Man is burly, wide, and gruff; he could easily break Ladislav, the Human Skeleton, in half. Yet they sit drinking coffee, laughing like a couple of soldiers returned from battle. The Strong Man's hands are wrapped around his coffee cup so that it looks as if he is drinking from his palms. "When I traveled with the circus from Pardubice," he says, his voice gravelly, "I had to help set up the tent. We all had to help."

"Yes." Ladislav shakes his long skull in agreement; his jaw tenses and releases. "My circus asked me to set up the outhouses once." They laugh together like old comrades.

Jakub walks in, and all the men yell a greeting to him. He sits across from Shanghai and pulls a bottle of whiskey from beneath his suit coat. "Fellows! We're on our way to Colorado. The train leaves soon." He pours whiskey into each glass around the table, then takes a swig from the bottle.

Shanghai yells over the men's voices to him, "Have you talked with the twins?"

"Yes, yes," he waves off Shanghai's question, "they're all taken care of. Vincent is showing them where to sleep right now."

"Vincent?" Shanghai is startled. "You let Vincent take care of them?"

"Drink, little one. Everything is under control."

Shanghai pounds his fist on the table. "I thought I was to be their caretaker. Wasn't that what you asked of me?"

"Vincent is capable. They'll be fine."

Shanghai rushes past the Strong Man, who is already refilling his glass. The Strong Man picks Shanghai up and raises him over his head like a barbell. The room breaks out in laughter. Shanghai doesn't struggle. Instead, he crosses his arms and firmly says, "Put me down."

"Jonathan, let him go," Jakub scolds, and the Strong Man returns Shanghai to the floor. Jakub yells toward Shanghai as he bounds out the door. "The train leaves in fifteen minutes!" Shanghai runs to the passenger car where the twins sleep. He surprises Gizela, who is standing half-clothed beside the twins' bed. She pulls a sheet up to hide her hair-covered body.

"Where are the twins?"

Gizela shrugs and says, "I have my bed back, that's all I know."

Judita says, "Vincent took them to the flatcars."

Outside, men are yelling, horses whinnying, elephants crying. Shanghai runs toward the front of the train where the wagons are loaded. He looks under cars for three-legged bodies and for Vincent's too-high pants. He looks on top of cars for any sign of the twins. Then he sees it—at the very front of the train, just behind the engine—one lone parade wagon. The rest have all gone on the first train, and this one looks terribly out of place sitting next to the pole wagons and simple carriages. He stops abruptly as Vincent leads the twins onto the Snake Charmer's wagon. Shanghai peers through the glassed side and watches

Vincent stroke Anna's hair. She pushes him away. Atasha says something with a frown on her face. Vincent laughs lightly, then holds Anna's chin in his hand. Shanghai tries to formulate a plan. Vincent leans in to kiss Anna, and when Atasha pushes him away, he grabs the back of her head and kisses her violently. Before Shanghai can react, a voice comes from the entrance of the wagon. "Vincent! Isn't Jakub waiting for you in the dessert car?" The voice is firm and angry. Shanghai squints his eyes, and Mariana appears from the darkness. Her stance is strong, her face stern. She appears large and powerful, and, for the first time, Shanghai is grateful for her presence. He ducks under the train car as Vincent steps off the wagon; his skinny legs carry him back to the pie car.

"Thank you, madam," Atasha says. "Thank you so much."

Mariana's voice is controlled and firm: "You may keep my lantern here with you. Rest well, girls. We have a long ride tonight."

There is silence in the car except for a few whispers between the twins. Shanghai waits to see Mariana's legs step down from the train and walk off into darkness. When the train whistle blows, signaling that they will be leaving in minutes, Shanghai carefully crawls onto the train platform and looks through the side of the wagon. The twins are alone.

"Atasha? Anna? It's Shanghai." His voice is low.

"Yes?" Atasha whispers back. He drags himself up onto the wagon hitch and opens the door of the wagon. Anna has already fallen asleep. "Are you all right?" he asks Atasha. She nods her head.

The train begins to move. Shanghai knows that he should quickly jump off and run down to the dessert car to join Jakub and the others, but he wants to be here, with Atasha. He cautiously approaches her, then lies down on his stomach several feet from her. "Is she hurt?" he whispers.

"No," Atasha reaches over and strokes her sister's hair, "she's worn out."

"I'm sorry that happened to you. Vincent is a bastard. I knew it the moment I saw him. Jakub should never have let him take care of you.

That is my job." Shanghai's anger bites the air.

"You saw that?" Atasha is embarrassed.

"Through the glass. I'm sorry . . . I didn't know what to do."

"The Gypsy . . . she . . . "

"I know. I saw her." The train gains speed. Shanghai rolls over to his back. "It appears that I'm stuck here for the night. I'll stay over here, I assure you." He extinguishes the lantern, but he still looks in her direction, trying to see her through the darkness, letting his eyes rest on her face when she can't catch him staring.

"Do you think he'll come back . . . some other night?"

"Vincent? I don't think so. He's as afraid of Mariana as everyone else is."

"Can I promise Anna that he'll leave us alone?"

"Yes. Mariana will go to Jakub if she has to, but I think she alone was enough to scare him off. I'm glad she was here, but . . . " The train slows down and takes a curve; it jostles enough so that Anna moans.

Atasha says, "She scares me."

Shanghai shudders at the memory of spending several nights with Mariana on the ship to America. He closes his eyes and begins to fall asleep when Atasha asks him about living in a brothel.

"Why do you want to know?" he asks.

"You know so much about us, and I know nothing about you. Except that you tell a good story. Tell me a true story," she whispers. "Please?"

"Well," Shanghai sighs, "do you know what a brothel is?"

"No."

"Uh, it is a place," Shanghai chooses his words carefully, hoping that Atasha will not think ill of him, "where women give themselves over to men who are willing to pay money." Shanghai gulps. "Do you understand what I mean by saying they 'give themselves over'?" Atasha is silent long enough for Shanghai to worry. "Atasha?"

"No."

Shanghai tries to be delicate. "They have sexual relations with the men."

"With just any man?"

"Yes. Any man who is willing to pay."

"And . . . you grew up there?"

"Yes," Shanghai says softly, almost inaudibly. "My mother worked there."

"How? Why were you there?"

"I was born there, Atasha."

"Who was your father?"

"My father . . . he . . . he was a circus performer." Shanghai makes up a story on the spot. His mother never knew who his father was—she had it narrowed down to one week of her clientele, but she never told any of them of the possibility. "He was a juggler and a fire-eater himself. He was a lonely man, a little person, just like me. He sought the love of a woman, but he couldn't find it because of his stature. He fell in love many times, but his love was never returned. My mother, she loved him, but she had her work. Whenever he was in town, he came to see her. He paid her for a full night so that he could lay in her arms and sleep. It was during those nights that he felt truly loved."

"How often did you see your father?"

"He died." Shanghai thinks for a moment. "He suffered many burns one night when his hair caught fire. He never did get to see me. I was only one month old when he died."

"That's so sad, Shanghai." Shanghai feels guilty at the sincerity of Atasha's sympathy, "And your mother, is she still there?"

"My mother? No, she left when I was very young. She was able to buy her freedom, and she thought it best that I stay with Madam Zora until she got settled. But she never came back."

"Oh, Shanghai." Atasha sounds close to weeping.

He continues on quickly and begins to tell the truth. "When I turned thirteen, Madam Zora asked me to take on new responsibilities. I ran money here and there, escorted gentlemen from the train station to the brothel, got food and supplies for the house, and did whatever she asked. When I was fourteen," he says, "some of the girls took more of an interest in me. I didn't mind that so much, but then some of the customers started asking around about me." He pauses for Atasha's reaction to this, but there is only silence. He constructs his sentences in his head carefully before he speaks. "I knew I had to do something. You see, before my mother left, she devised a plan so that I would not fall into the trap of prostitution. Being a dwarf, she feared that I would become a party favor for the gentlemen who were looking for something different. Here I was, so many years later without my mother to watch over me, and I began to take things in my own hands. I began to edge my way closer to Madam Zora. I rubbed her feet at the end of a long day, I drew her bath, I brought her flowers from the town square. Soon enough, she began to take a particular liking toward me and," Shanghai thinks of a delicate way to describe his affair with the madam, "I spent every night with her."

"What plan did your mother come up with to save you from prostitution?"

Shanghai ponders this, then says, "I will have to tell you that another time. It's . . . complicated."

Atasha looks disappointed. "Was Madam Zora in love with you?"

"I never thought that she would fall in love with me, but she did. I became the man of the house. Before I knew it, all of the women in the house wanted to be with me. They tried to seduce me. It was a game for them. They not only wanted to see who could get me into bed first, but they also wanted to see how much they could get past Madam Zora. That's why I began to spend more time outside the house."

Words suddenly fall from his mouth without thought. "It was a circus performer, a friend of my father, who visited the brothel when he was in town, who showed me how to throw fire. I took to it quickly, and it soon became my escape. I began to leave the house more and more, and I came back with so much money that Madam Zora didn't object."

"Were you in love with her?"

"She was all I knew. She was my boss, never my mother, or sister, or family—she had been my boss since I was four years old. I didn't know there was anything else until I met Milada." Shanghai wonders if he has said too much.

The train bounces on the track. "You tell stories like my mother," says Atasha. "She used to tell stories all the time until she got so weak."

"My mother used to tell stories, too," says Shanghai.

"Milada was the flyer, wasn't she?"

"You've heard about her?"

"Yes, Gizela and Judita talk about her sometimes."

Even though he can't see through the darkness, Shanghai turns over and faces Atasha. "What do they say?"

"Different things. That she was amazing on the trapeze, one of the best in Europe. And that you and she were," Atasha pauses, "involved."

Shanghai moves closer to Atasha and asks excitedly, "Did they tell you anything in particular about us?"

"No, just that she stayed in Prague and married another performer."

"Nothing else? Nothing about me?"

"No. Why do you ask?"

"The Gypsy, . . . " he leans into Atasha as if someone else might hear, " . . . she put some sort of spell on me, and I can't remember anything about Milada. Well, sometimes I remember bits and pieces. I get a flash of a memory, and then it's gone. I try to bring it back, but I only see fragments. Then, I make up the rest of the story. Now it gets so I don't know what is real and what I've made up."

"Perhaps it's best not to remember. Gizela and Judita say she broke your heart."

"Will you . . . ?" Shanghai thinks about how much he wants to know. "Will you listen for me? Tell me if you hear anything about our relationship?"

"Are you sure you want to know?"

"I think so. I remember things so well, so vividly. I just can't remember her."

"Maybe the Gypsy did you a favor."

"I don't know . . . I have this emptiness inside, like a hollow well. I used to hold something there, but now it's all dried up and there's just this echo. And everyone around me knows something. They have all of the memories that should be mine. I want those memories back."

"I haven't heard anything. Really. Judita and Gizela barely talk to us."

He squeezes his eyes shut and takes a deep breath. "It's late," he says. "We should get some sleep now." He is so close to Atasha that he can hear her breathe.

The train rattles on the track, and the sound begins to lull him to sleep. Atasha reaches out and lightly touches Shanghai's hand. "I'll listen for you." Her voice is as soft as a kiss.

THERE WAS *a chill in the air when we walked across the bridge. Sunset. It had been only three hours since we met. I sat on the stone wall with Milada next to me. The River Vltava tumbled below us as we looked over the edge, her body pressed against mine. I wanted to ask her "Can you feel it?" Can you feel how the world seems so small right now and there is no one but you and me? There is no Zikmund, no Madam Zora, no lost mother, no angry father. There is only us.*

And we talked about water and the power of water, and I held on to the edge begging the powers not to let me fall. And as I drifted on her vowels, I knew for sure that I was falling and that somehow I would be swallowed whole by the churning waters.

As we balanced ourselves on the wall of the Charles Bridge, I dared myself. I motioned to her to lean in to me. She opened her mouth to ask me why, and I caught her words on my tongue. Her bottom lip welcomed me, and the words, her words, tumbled into my mouth, wrapped themselves on my tongue, clattered on my teeth. Her tongue grazed mine, and the words spun back into her mouth and rested on the roof—reveling in the space they had inside her.

"Come to the circus," she whispered, and she ran her tongue inside my ear, and then her teeth nibbled on the lobe.

She turned and moved back toward the city. Back toward Zikmund, and all I could do was whisper one word. Milada. I whispered it so that I could feel each movement of her name in my mouth. I felt the way the m *vibrated between my lips, how the* l *lightly touched my tongue on the back of my teeth, how the* d *dug into the roof of my mouth and then fell away on the curve of the* a. *Milada.*

And as I watched her disappear into the crowd at the mouth of the bridge, with the sun setting low in the sky, I knew there was only one thing left to do.

I knew that I must go to the circus.

—*Shanghai's diary, May 1899*

Secrets

Fort Collins, Colorado
May 10, 1900

he mountains rise up behind the circus grounds, daunting and untouchable. They are trimmed in pink as the sun sets in the West. Mariana imagines herself on the Charles Bridge with Shanghai. She wonders how her name feels in his mouth. "Mariana?" Jakub calls her name, and she takes one last look at the sunset before stepping into her boxcar to give her receipts to Jakub. He sets up office here from ten a.m. until ten p.m. every day, except Sunday, when there are no shows. She puts the money down on his desk. "Only fifty cents, Mariana? You had only ten customers?"

She wonders how it feels to be in love like Shanghai was in love with Milada. She looks at Jakub's weathered face and sees the twenty-four years of marriage. "I know, I know," Jakub says, looking back down at his books, "everything will be better in the next town." Mariana is silent. She is tired of making excuses for these American crowds and their apprehension toward fortune-telling.

She walks to her trunk and searches for some suitable fabric to mend a costume. She holds up each piece of fabric to the ripped satiny shirt of the Lion Tamer. "One of the lions get out of control?" Jakub asks.

Mariana thinks for a moment how Shanghai would make up a story—something much more spectacular than the fact that the Lion Tamer's shirt got caught on a nail from one of the wagons. She smiles to herself. "No," she answers. Jakub looks at her blankly for a moment, then continues counting money.

They share this car for an hour each day, from nine to ten p.m. Mariana uses this time together to mention some of the things that she sees going on, to make sure Jakub maintains control. That was one of the problems with his circus back in the old country: he mismanaged his people and mismanaged his money. Vladan is keeping an eye on the books; Mariana is watching everyone else. "Vincent is up to no good," Mariana says plainly. "You need to keep close watch on him."

Jakub sits back in his chair. "Vincent again, Mariana?" It was just a few weeks ago that she hinted at Vincent's connection to Vladan. She thought it interesting that he came from Vladan's circus and spoke Czech. His ears seemed much too big when he sat close to Czech-speaking performers. "Do you have something against him?" asks Jakub, a hint of sarcasm in his voice.

Mariana bites off the end of her thread. "He has intentions with some of the ladies that are not so honorable. You need to teach him our code," she says simply, without giving Jakub the details of the encounter with Vincent on the parade wagon.

Jakub does not reply.

"You are having the Snake Charmer's wagon travel on our train from now on?" Mariana asks. It is an extraordinary exception that Jakub has made. All of the parade wagons usually go on the first train. To have one alone travel to the next town on the second train is unheard of.

"Yes." Jakub seems annoyed. "It's all under control, my dear. There's no need to worry." He removes a flask from his desk drawer, takes a swig, then places it close at hand as he works in his logbook. There is a knock on the door. "Enter!" Jakub yells.

Shanghai rushes past Mariana and lays his receipts from postcard sales on Jakub's desk. Mariana tries to hide her feelings and maintains control by looking him directly in the eyes. He glances at her, then quickly looks away. She often toys with the idea of getting inside him to find out his true feelings toward her. She imagines his inner life is magical and full of spinning torches of light. But when he steps up on a chair to talk with Jakub, she is reminded of his physical deviation. "It appears that you'll need new trousers soon," Mariana blurts out to get his attention. Shanghai looks at the seat of his pants where there are some tears and burn marks. "I'll put that on my list."

"Thank you," says Shanghai, then he turns to finish his business with Jakub. He seemed pleasingly surprised that Mariana offered, and, for a moment, it appeared that he looked at her in wonder instead of fear.

After he leaves, Jakub tells Mariana that it will be noted in the books that she made a dollar-fifty in receipts today. "We will take the extra dollar out of Shanghai's postcard sales. It will be our little secret, *hmm?*" Mariana knows that Uncle Vladan has been concerned over her lack of sales. She feels a slight pang of guilt for taking from Shanghai, but she knows that her receipts must look better.

"Oh!" Jakub opens his desk drawer. "I forgot . . . we received another letter for Shanghai." Jakub crosses to Mariana and hands her the envelope. "Take care of it for me, will you?"

"Yes." Mariana folds the envelope and puts it aside. Ever since the letters first began to arrive, Jakub has asked Mariana to burn them. She hasn't burned one yet. She doesn't know why she feels the need to hold on to them. After Jakub leaves, Mariana unfolds the letter. She doesn't have to open it to know that it begins the same way every letter has begun, "My beloved Shanghai . . . " Mariana puts this letter on top of the bundle she has been collecting. She neatly ties the ribbon around the stack and runs her fingertip over the curves in Milada's handwriting before she locks the letters away.

IT IS nearly midnight when Atasha and Anna take an evening walk that helps ease Anna's pain. The stars fill the night sky in numbers never before seen by the twins. Atasha hears Shanghai's name mentioned from the campfire near Mariana's boxcar. She nudges Anna closer to the glowing light. Jakub, Radovan, the Lion Tamer, Vincent, Ladislav, and the Strong Man sit on overturned buckets passing a bottle of whiskey around the circle. As Atasha nears the fire, Anna chastises, "They'll see us! We'll get in trouble. It's past curfew."

"Don't you want to see Jakub?" Atasha has had an inkling of Anna's fondness for him lately. She feels how Anna's heart quickens every time he is around. Anna doesn't respond to Atasha's question, but gives in to the pull of her body closer to the fire.

Jakub's face glows in the light as he sways his arms in the air, with a bottle in his left hand. He is telling a story to Vincent, but he's so animated that everyone gathered there listens. "We were parked in Poděbrady, about fifty miles outside Prague." Jakub bites the end off his cigar. "The show started as usual. I was standing at the performers' entrance, looking around the crowd to get an idea of our attendance. Then I saw them." Jakub points into the darkness, directly at Atasha and Anna. Anna gasps, but Atasha knows they are too far away for Jakub to see them. "They were in the first, second, and third rows—best seats in the house—wearing clothing that matched our most ornate. And she was sitting in the middle of them all, there in the front row. Her eyes were a fiery blue."

"Atasha, let's go. Jakub's going to catch us."

Jakub continues, "I told Radovan to pull Shanghai from the Sideshow and bring him over to the Big Top. I thought she was there for him and that I would feed her hunger. You know, see what would come of it."

When Atasha hears Shanghai's name, she shushes Anna and whispers, "I want to hear this."

"But it wasn't Shanghai that Madam Zora was there for." Jakub drinks from the bottle and passes it on. "She was there for Milada."

"Milada?" Vincent asks, his teeth rotting bones in the campfire light. "Who? ..."

"Ah, Milada," Radovan pipes in. "She was the most beautiful aerialist this circus has ever seen."

"She was like a daughter to many of us," Jakub says. "Myself, Radovan, Mariana."

"Why was the madam there for her?"

Jakub laughs. "Because Madam Zora knew something I did not. She knew that Milada was involved in a relationship with Shanghai."

Vincent spits out the tip of a new cigar. "That freaky dwarf?"

Before Atasha's anger has a chance to rise, Jakub is on Vincent, quicker than being shot out of a cannon. Vincent didn't see him coming, and now Jakub has him on the ground, his knee across the American's chest, a knife at his throat. "My good man," Jakub talks through clenched teeth, "do not ever address anyone in this circus in that manner. Shanghai, Judita, Jarmil, Atasha, and Anna—they are all human beings and will be treated as such. Do you understand?"

Vincent gasps in air and nods his head. Jakub releases him and takes his seat on the other side of the fire. "Atasha, did you see that?" asks Anna. "He really does care about us." Atasha doesn't respond.

"Now, where was I?" says Jakub.

Vincent looks down at his shoes and says, "Milada and Shanghai, they were . . . ?"

"Ah, yes. Madam Zora. She was there for Milada. It seems that she had a spy traveling with us. Someone was sending her letters, informing her of the tryst between the two lovers."

"Who was sending the letters?" Vincent asks.

"To this very day, I do not know." Jakub picks up an empty glass and motions to Radovan to pour him a shot from the whiskey bottle. "But it was someone very clever. Shanghai said that he and Milada were very careful, because of Zikmund, and they were never aware of a spy."

"Who's Zikmund?"

"Zikmund was Milada's fiancé." The men laugh, as if they've never heard the story before.

"Oh, yes," Jakub points to Vincent, "Zikmund had your job back in the old country. He and Milada had been engaged for a year when Shanghai joined us."

"Atasha, let's go," Anna whines.

"Anna, be quiet. I'm trying to hear the story."

"I'm tired. Let's go to bed."

Atasha stands firm against Anna's pull. "Anna! Just a few more minutes, then we'll leave. Please?" She begs and Anna relinquishes her will to her sister.

Vincent looks at Radovan. "So what happened next? When you went to tell Shanghai?"

Radovan begins to answer, but Jakub talks over him. "Shanghai showed up in the Big Top. I didn't see him at first, not until the crowd began to laugh." Jakub points up to the stars. "He climbed the rope ladder, all the way to the top, and stopped Milada's act."

"Ah!" Radovan interjects. "But the other drama played out in the Sideshow Tent." Jakub glares at Radovan briefly, then puffs on his cigar and blows smoke rings above his head. "One of Madam Zora's whores was telling Zikmund of the affair between Shanghai and his fiancée. When he heard the news, his face turned as red as this fire, and his shoulders hunched up to his ears so that it looked like they would swallow his neck. I followed him down the midway, toward the Big Top. When we got there, Shanghai was just coming down from the platform."

"And that's when chaos ensued." Jakub puts his hand on Radovan's shoulder and raises his voice to take back the story. "Zikmund's jealousy made him oblivious to the audience, who was still laughing at the sight of a dwarf descending the rope ladder. When Shanghai got within reach, Zikmund pulled him off the ladder and held him up over his head."

"And like true showmen," Radovan says, "Milada and her father continued swinging up above. It almost seemed that the conflict were propelling them like the pendulum of a clock."

Jakub continues, "Shanghai squirmed in Zikmund's hands. With all his might, he wrangled himself to the ground. Zikmund picked Shanghai up by the collar and held him so that they were face-to-face. Shanghai began kicking and managed to hit Zikmund in a very sensitive place."

Radovan jumps in: "And when Zikmund bent over to hold himself, Shanghai grabbed him around the knees and knocked him to the ground. Shanghai sat on him and began throwing wild punches. By this time, Zikmund's hands were covering his face." The men look from Jakub to Radovan to Jakub as the story unfolds.

Atasha nudges her way closer to the fire, but Anna's footing is firm. Atasha relinquishes and steps back. Anna says, "Atasha, we should go; it's long past curfew."

"Anna! I told you that I wanted to hear this story. Aren't you interested at all?"

"It's not our business."

Atasha thinks of telling her sister that she told Shanghai that she would listen for him, but it is a secret. A secret she shares with Shanghai, and she wants it to be between them only. "Just a few minutes more, I promise. Just until Jakub finishes his story."

Anna sighs in resignation, her body releasing into Atasha's.

Jakub's voice fills with delight. "That's when Madam Zora and her entourage showed up in the ring, looking just like they were a part of the show!"

"The crowd didn't know any different," says Radovan.

"You mean, all this time, the audience thought that this was all an act?" Vincent laughs.

"Of course they did. A dwarf running wildly into the ring, climbing the ladder, a tall, wiry man running after him, lifting him above his head. Why, it was the best clown show they had ever seen! And to top it off, here comes a robust woman in colorful clothes and ornate jewelry to pull the punching dwarf off the wiry, tall man."

"Madam Zora?" asks Vincent.

"That's right. Madam Zora stepped in and plucked Shanghai off Zikmund. Shanghai's arms and legs were flailing about as the woman held him tightly around the waist. But Shanghai threw his elbow back and caught Madam Zora in the breast, an easy target, if you know what I mean." The men laugh. "Madam Zora dropped Shanghai, and before he knew what hit him, Zikmund had tackled him."

Radovan yells over the laughter, "Zikmund had a strong choke hold on Shanghai. His large hands were curled around Shanghai's neck."

Jakub says, "Madam Zora released the hold on her breast and stepped back into the fight to pull Zikmund off Shanghai. Several of her whores joined the battle. The crowd was laughing hysterically, and all the while Milada and her father swung above, watching the fight below. By this time, they weren't performing, they were merely swinging."

Radovan says, "Oh, yes. And Milada looked terrified as she watched this unfold, and her father . . . his face was as red as Zikmund's as he glared at his daughter."

Atasha feels a hand on her shoulder; the grip is firm and digs into her collarbone. She jumps and startles Anna. Anna screams.

"Who's there?" Jakub yells into the darkness.

"It's only me, Jakub." Mariana releases her grip on Atasha's shoulder and walks in front of the twins.

Jakub squints, trying to make out Mariana's form. "Are you all right, my dear?"

Mariana yells toward him, "Yes, I just tripped. I'm fine."

Jakub's voice becomes softer as he takes a seat with the circle of men and continues his story in a low murmur.

"It is past curfew, girls," Mariana chastises like a mother. "What are you doing out here?"

Anna begins to cry, her body shaking. Atasha says, "We were just walking, madam."

"You best go to your car and mind your own business. I don't think Jakub wants you hearing such stories."

"Yes, ma'am," Atasha says, and she quickly pulls Anna away from the *jezibaba*.

When they get back to the Snake Charmer's wagon, Atasha asks Anna not to tell Shanghai what they heard tonight. "Why not?" Anna asks. "He was there, wasn't he?"

"I know, but he might be embarrassed about it," Atasha lies to her sister. She wants to tell Shanghai in her own time. She wants to collect all the pieces of the puzzle of his missing memory and give them to him as a gift. A gift from her and her only.

Vision

Silverton, Colorado
May 23, 1900

nna squints her eyes when the flash goes off. She blinks to focus on the man who looks into a box on a stand with his head under a black cloth. Bright white spots blanket her sight. Jakub stands behind the man, looking like a proud father as he instructs the twins to take another pose.

Anna feels something simmering inside of her as she watches Jakub's arms fly through the air. She loves to watch him work because his whole body fills a room when he takes charge. His eyes spark, his jaw strengthens, his shoulders square up with his slender frame, and he seems to become more animated, more expressive.

"Raise the eggs above your heads," Jakub instructs, and he holds his arms up. His face is soft. He is a teacher, a father, a man with passion. "No, no, Anna, not so high. Keep your elbow bent. That's a good girl."

Anna is momentarily distracted by the collar of the new dress that Mariana made them—its lacy neckline scratches her skin. This is the fourth new dress that Mariana has made for them. "You shall have one new dress a week!" That's what Jakub told them. Anna has almost forgotten what their old clothes look like; she has become so accustomed to these new luxurious costumes that Jakub is dressing them in.

"Atasha, stay still for a moment," Jakub says as she also tugs at the collar of the dress. She holds the egg above her head and looks behind the photographer, behind Jakub, toward the door. Jakub told Shanghai to wait outside, fearing that he would disrupt the proceedings. Even

133

though he had the idea for these photos, Jakub has found the best photographer and is in charge of the entire project. The twins had to relinquish one week's salary to pay for the sitting and for the first five hundred cards to sell to their admirers, but Shanghai reassured them that they would get the money back twofold.

"Atasha, look here, at the photographer," Jakub's voice sings, but Atasha's mind drifts off to Shanghai. She loves being close to him; she's become accustomed to being in his presence. The twins have spent every morning with him for the past two weeks; sometimes he tells them fantastic stories about the old country, but mostly he teaches them how to juggle. She smiles when she thinks of how he works with them, how he cups her hand and squeezes her fingers to show her the proper catch and release. He told them that juggling would be simple if they just let their minds believe they could do it. And he was right. Atasha delights in how easy it is for her and Anna to juggle. She can feel Anna's arm fly through the air; she senses each grip and release. On the first night they performed their act, Jakub immediately wired his uncle Vladan and told him about how well his new acquisition was working out. Even though Jakub took the credit, Shanghai looked proud.

"Atasha! Hold still!" Jakub yells. "Keep your face somber, like this." He mimics a stone-faced look that makes Atasha want to burst out laughing. "And keep your arm up! Now, focus!"

Anna giggles at her sister, and Atasha giggles back. Jakub yells at both of them, then calms down when the photographer steps in to readjust the collars on their dress. The twins have flourished in their new life. People come from miles away to see them. There was even a story in the *Denver Post* about the juggling twins. Anna clipped the article and keeps it in a locked box in her trunk. She is saving all the mementos to give to her parents when the season is over and she and her sister return to the farm for the winter.

Atasha nudges Anna to look over Jakub's shoulder where Shanghai stands in the doorway. Atasha suddenly feels ridiculous holding this egg at ear height. Anna whines, "My arm is hurting. How much longer?"

Shanghai disappears from the doorway and steps out into the bright sun.

"Hold still, please," the man under the black cloth demands.

Anna's head begins to ache, and she knows she needs water. Altitude sickness has affected her ever since the circus got higher into the Rocky Mountains. She was sick for the entire day they spent in Durango, and threw up two or three times before Shanghai told her to drink water, and more water, and more water until she felt like she would float away.

Atasha feels her sister's pain and says, "Anna needs water."

"Hold still!" Jakub barks.

Another flash. Anna drops her arm. "Anna needs water," Atasha demands. Shanghai appears from nowhere, holding a canteen of fresh mountain springwater in front of Anna.

"Shanghai!" Jakub yells. "Didn't I tell you to wait outside?"

"Can you not see how pale she's getting? She needed this."

"Please, Shanghai. You are only distracting them."

Anna's eyes are focused on Jakub. How strong he is, she thinks. Atasha's eyes are set on Shanghai. How sweet he is, she thinks.

The man behind the cloth snaps his fingers. "Look here! Look here!"

Another flash goes off. The girls' eyes immediately return to the men standing off to each side of the photographer.

SHANGHAI LEAVES the canteen on the floor and steps outside, letting the twins finish their session. He wanders toward the edge of town, looking at the mountains that rise up in front of him, beside him. He wonders if, somewhere, his mother is taking in a view just as beautiful. He stops at the edge of town, in front of the saloon, and his eyes scale each peak. A voice calls out to him, and he looks up toward the sun, where a silhouette stands at the edge of the balcony, her arms spread out as if she has wings. He can hear her—Milada's voice floods his brain, and an ache rises in his chest. The ache comes from his spleen and attaches to his ribs like a creeping vine. Crawling across each rib, it starts low, then moves upward, and he can't seem to catch his breath. The vine begins to choke his heart, and pain fills the walls of his chest. Shanghai tries to catch his breath, but the pain is taking over and all he sees is Milada, all he hears is Milada.

"The first time I took flight," Milada's voice is clear, "she helped me. She spoke to me and said, 'You can do it, my little girl, you can fly. It is in your blood.' She can see right into my soul, Shanghai. She can see right into the heart of me."

Milada towers over him and then she drops. Shanghai gasps and holds his arms out to catch her, but her body doesn't fall. He looks up and suddenly sees the woman on the balcony. She says something to him in English. He puts down his arms as the woman leans over the rail; her breasts are heaved up and bulging from her dress. She fixes her eyes on his and doesn't speak another word—she doesn't have to—Shanghai knows what she is offering. He turns away and gazes toward the mountaintops, the faint memory of Milada still fresh in his mind.

He remembers now—the connection she had with the Gypsy. He closes his eyes and tries to hear Milada's voice once again, but all he hears is his own voice, arguing with Milada about the *jezibaba*. "If she can see into a person's soul, then she will discover the truth, Milada." The way that Mariana looks at him lately makes him shudder. Her gaze rests on his body too long; her eyes seek to discover his soul. He thinks of finding her, just a few weeks ago, throwing up in the Big Top, and he wonders what she was doing there. How long had she been there, watching him? And he thinks of the night that she caught Vincent trying to molest the girls. Where did she come from? His knees shake, and he grabs onto the horse hitch to steady himself.

He knows that Mariana could never be trusted with the truth about him. He knows that he must somehow gain her trust, just as he gained Madam Zora's trust those many years ago.

A carriage stops in front of Shanghai, and Jakub sticks his head from the covered window. "Are you coming with us, my friend?" Shanghai says nothing as he crawls into the carriage. Jakub rented it so that the townspeople could not get a free showing of his most prized act. The horses pull them through the small town, past the bank, another saloon, and the doctor's office. Once they are outside the city limits, they are allowed to open the curtains and look out at the peaks. Aspen trees surround them, their trunks tall and lean. Shanghai silently watches the scenery pass.

"Are you all right, Shanghai?" Atasha asks.

"He is fine, my dear girl." Jakub sits next to Shanghai. He jostles Shanghai's shoulder as he reassures Atasha.

"Yes," Shanghai clears his throat, "fine." He rubs the fabric that sits on the knee of his pants. Wondering, planning, worrying—thinking of Mariana.

Anna points to the sharp rise of the mountain over the creek on her side of the carriage. "Look!" Two mountain goats are sparring on the cliff above the water. The animals pound their heads together with a hollow thwack, their antlers scraping together.

"Can we stop and watch them, Jakub?" Anna asks.

He pats her hand and softly says, "No, Anna, my dear, we have an afternoon show."

Shanghai watches the goats back up, kick dirt, rise, then lock horns again. He feels too close to everyone right now but so incredibly lonely. He's spent more and more nights with Atasha, lying beside her as her sister sleeps, talking softly into the night. His feelings toward her are growing, and he wants to tell her everything, but it's not time yet. He knows that.

He doesn't remember feeling so vulnerable in the old country. Did Milada perhaps protect him? He doesn't remember how he came to know the methods to keep himself safe. The ways to keep his secret safe, especially from the *jezibaba*.

Soon, the flags of the Big Top come into view, and as they pull onto the grounds, Atasha points to a man on a ladder in front of the Sideshow Banner. He is painting on a huge square of the canvas, on the space formerly occupied by a Czech performer who did not travel to America with Jakub. The man is painting on a bright yellow background.

"It's us!" Anna squeals as they get out of the carriage.

"Yes, that's right," Jakub says. Shanghai is relieved that the twins' moods have lifted in recent days. They no longer cry at night. They don't struggle at their performances. They seem to feel at home. Atasha seems to feel comfortable with him.

Shanghai looks up at the black outline of the twins, their hair pulled back, eggs flying over their heads. "It's so big," Atasha says.

"Yes, well, you are a big deal around here." Jakub puts his arm around Anna.

"I have to prepare for the show," Shanghai says and nods at Atasha. He knows he will see her later, but now he must attend to Mariana. He tries to gain his courage as he walks into the backyard, toward the butcher block by the lion cages. He picks up one of the knives used for cutting the lions' meat, grasping its bloody handle. He pulls the trousers away from his knee and sticks the tip of the knife in, making a small cut. He tugs on the fabric and makes a bigger rip.

He shudders as he approaches Mariana in the costume tent, but he knows he must go through with this; it's only a matter of time. Mariana is working on a costume; pins stick out of her mouth like whiskers on a dog. He almost turns and walks away, but Mariana catches him in her sight.

She calls him over, and he stammers as he tries to get the words out. "It's my trousers, ma'am." She pulls the pins out of her mouth and sticks them into the dress. Shanghai can't look her in the eye. "A few weeks ago, you commented that I needed new ones and," he gulps, "I was wondering if you could make some soon." He shows her the rip in the knee of his pants. "These are getting more worn every day."

Mariana nods. "Yes, of course. Come and see me on Saturday. I'll be able to work on them then." Her eyes linger on his face so that he can see her longing, but her voice is so cool that Shanghai begins to wonder if she even has a heart inside of her body. As he makes his way outside, Mariana calls him back. "I need to mend those before you go onstage. You can sit up here, on the table, and I'll mend them quickly for you."

She clears the table for Shanghai and motions for him to use a stool to climb up. He studies her face as she concentrates on the fabric. She is so close; it would be easy to lean over and place a kiss on her lips. And in that kiss, she would lean into him, he knows she would. And in the intimacy that comes with being close to her, he could gain her trust and blind her vision. Every woman who has slept with him has held the secret close to her heart. But what kind of a man would he be then? The same kind of man who visits a brothel and uses women for his own amusement? The same kind of man as Jakub? The same kind of man as Vincent?

As she sews the tear in his knee, he flinches every time the needle pierces the fabric. Mariana tells him to relax. The way she says it makes him remember his time with her on the ship. She said that same word to him then, "Relax, relax," and he fell asleep. Was that part of her spell? He almost asks her outright, but fears that she will put another spell on him. He yells out a lie that he forgot to prepare his torches. "I need to go." He becomes frantic. Mariana quickly ties off the thread and lets him go without another word. He feels her eyes watching him leave the tent.

He scurries through the compound, oblivious to the twins as he passes them. They call his name, but he cannot hear them. He is only wondering how he can bring Mariana that close to his life.

IT WAS *many years ago that Medard taught me to throw fire. He came to the brothel with the batons tucked under his arms and let me play with them as he had his usual consultation with Nina. When his time with Nina was done, he came outside to the cobblestone street and showed me how to use the batons properly.*

I twirled them first without the advantage of fire. The batons were light and much too big for my arms. Still, I managed to twist them under my arms, over my head, between my legs. After weeks of practice, Medard brought me batons specially made, just for my height. "A gift," he said, "for the gifted." It was on that day that he finally allowed me to light the tips.

He held the lighted baton over his head and said, "Do you know that nature rejuvenates itself through fire? It burns off all of the old to make room for new growth." He spun the fire around his head, and I watched it burn. "Do not fear it, my boy."

I took the baton in my hand and was surprised at how heavy it was. I began to spin that one baton in front of me, just as Medard taught me, and it whooshed, whooshed, whooshed. Soon the fire had its own life; it was like dancing with a woman of great inner strength. The fire created a rhythm in my hands; it moved with my body and against my body. I had to guide its energy this way and that. Medard gave me the second baton, and the fire danced all around me. When I got the batons going fast enough, there was a ring of fire around my head, spinning faster and faster until I felt that I would be consumed by it.

I threw the batons, spun them, caught them. My size didn't hold me back. I was lost in the fire spinning around my head. I felt like a man of great presence; I felt like I was everything I wanted to be. I was not me. I was not the wrong person anymore. The flames nipped at my ears, danced between my arms, blazed at my face.

Medard stood with his mouth hanging open. A crowd of onlookers had gathered. I imagined my mother standing at the back of the crowd, seeing for herself that her son could embrace the fire.

—Shanghai's diary, June 1899

Something Special
for Shanghai

Telluride, Colorado
May 26, 1900

ariana puts Shanghai's diary away and steps out of the boxcar into a thick fog that blankets the ground like steam from the locomotive. The air is silent except for one magpie who knows instinctively that, despite the fog, day is breaking. No one else appears to be awake. Mariana hates mornings like this; she feels as if everyone around her is dead, unable to wake, and she wants to run to the animals caged and tied at the edge of the compound and let them loose. She imagines them running wild through the backyard, trampling tents and ticket stands, waking the tired performers suddenly, causing them to run, frightened, into the mountains. Give the animals power, she thinks, just this once.

She steps back into her car and picks up the small trousers she sews especially for Shanghai. She has already made one pair for him but has decided to give him another. She pulls the thread through the coarse fabric as she makes little pockets for his thick hands. Mariana knows that Shanghai will wear these trousers day to day, so each pair will have pockets. What a surprise for Shanghai; pockets are hard to come by in circus costumes. But this isn't the first time she has surprised him.

Almost two years ago, she wrote the letter to Madam Zora, telling her the circus was about to leave for America and that her beloved Shanghai had made the transition easily into circus life. "Shanghai is doing well," Mariana wrote, "and we are about to depart for America. Just a few more stops in Bohemia, and then we travel to Amsterdam and leave by ship. Shanghai and his new lover, Milada, will be traveling with us. Perhaps Shanghai has not written to you of Milada? She is a beautiful young girl and flies the trapeze. They are very happy together indeed. Do try to see us before we leave, won't you?"

She didn't expect a reply from Madam Zora and did not get one. She simply waited. And on that day, when Madam Zora and a troupe of her whores walked through the midway, Mariana knew that it was not only Shanghai who would be surprised. Madam Zora passed by the fortune-telling tent, gave a slight nod to Mariana, and walked on. The redheaded prostitute who flirted with Mariana at the brothel came over for a reading. "Pavlina, please, we do not have time for that nonsense," Madam Zora said. Mariana grabbed the redhead's hand and squeezed it tightly, rubbing a knuckle with her thumb. The redhead pulled away, her tough demeanor broken for one minute.

They walked toward the Big Top, pausing briefly at the Sideshow Tent to stare at Shanghai's likeness painted on the canvas. "It looks nothing like him," the madam protested.

After the show started, Mariana stepped into the big tent and watched backstage as Jakub called the order of Pradha's Prancing Ponies, the juggling Hatsa Brothers, and the clowns. She delighted in the shock on Jakub's face as Shanghai began climbing the rope to the trapeze platform. He didn't actually see Shanghai at first because he was looking skyward where Milada stood on one platform while her father stood on the one opposite her, preparing for flight. Only when the audience began to laugh did Jakub furl his brow and look around the tent for a show-off clown or perhaps a wayward parading poodle walking into the side ring on hind legs.

Mariana watched Jakub's reactions as Shanghai climbed the rope; the motion of his small body made it swing dramatically back and forth, much like his own gait. When he reached the top, he grabbed onto Milada's ankle. She leaned down to him, frantic, her face turning a shade of red.

He said something to her, and her eyes moved through the audience until they focused on Madam Zora who sat in the front row, stone-faced. Her girls sat around her, fanning themselves with circus flyers. They leaned into each other and giggled. Milada's father looked concerned and followed his daughter's gaze into the audience. Milada motioned for Shanghai to go away, and he began his descent on the rope.

When the fight broke out between Zikmund and Shanghai, Milada was flying from her father's arms, flipping, catching, then flying again. Mariana smiled at how the scene must have looked swinging upside down like that.

Madam Zora looked pleased as she watched the fight, but Mariana knew that she could not remain a spectator for long. Indeed, she and her whores left their seats and joined in the excitement.

Jakub had to regain control quickly, before his reputation was further damaged. He stepped in, holding Shanghai by the collar and pushing Zikmund back with a hand on his chest. "Stop it! Stop it, you two," Jakub yelled. "This is not the place for this! You!" Jakub nodded his head toward Zikmund. "Go back to the Bally-ho platform! And you," Jakub looked down to Shanghai, "go to the cookhouse. We will deal with this after the show!" Both Zikmund and Shanghai were sweating and panting. Neither one made a move in any direction. "Now go!" The crowd broke out in wild applause as Shanghai exited through to the backyard and Zikmund left through the audience entrance.

Jakub pulled his jacket down into place. "Madam Zora." He nodded to her.

"Sir," she nodded back. She looked at Mariana and smiled, "Madam."

Mariana returned her greeting and looked up at Milada as she fell into the net. Her father, who would normally jump onto the platform at the top of the pole, fell into the net below as well. He put his hand on Milada's shoulder and escorted her outside the tent.

Mariana hoped that Jakub would discover his own weakness for management and decide that he was not ready to manage a circus in

America. But Jakub is too arrogant for that. But Mariana also discovered that there was a small part of her that hoped that the love affair between Milada and Shanghai would end. It was selfish, she knows, but now that she reads Shanghai's diary, she realizes that Milada needed to be forced into a decision. I have done them a great service, she justifies. I have helped Shanghai. And besides, she didn't get what she really wanted in the end—she didn't get to stay in the old country.

As Mariana sews another pocket into Shanghai's trousers, she hears Shanghai's voice call from the entrance of her car. Her pulse quickens. "May I come in?"

"Please." Mariana stands halfway out of her chair, then tries to relax.

"My trousers. Are they done?" Shanghai's hair is pulled back into a ponytail; the lines beneath his eyes are deep, and Mariana feels drawn in by those lines, like following the seam on a dress.

"Yes. I am just finishing them up. Won't you take a seat while I make the final stitches?" Mariana bites off the end of some thread and effortlessly threads another needle. She doesn't need to look at the eye as her fingers pull the thread through on the first try. Shanghai crawls up on the settee and glances nervously around the boxcar. "How is this season going for you?" she asks.

"Good," Shanghai says abruptly.

"Ah," Mariana nods, "and you are teaching the twins new tricks?"

"Yes. They are learning quickly." Shanghai's tone is even, and Mariana can't get a read on him. He is as cool as the Rocky Mountain air. She smiles, but Shanghai looks away. His eyes wander from the desk to the wall to the ceiling to the window.

He looks back at Mariana, his eyes unable to focus on hers. He fidgets. "I can come back later."

"No, no." Mariana wraps the thread around her index and middle fingers so tightly that the blood looks like it will burst from her fingertips. She breaks off the thread. "I am done. I sewed some pockets for you."

Shanghai climbs out of the chair and crosses to Mariana. It seems that he wants to say something, and his hand rests on hers for a moment. Mariana looks him square in the eyes, trying to discern his intent. He quickly pulls the trousers from her grip, thanks her beneath his breath, and scurries out the door.

Mariana pushes the needle into the pin cushion and sits quietly for a moment. This isn't the first time Shanghai has been so cold toward her. She thought of all the unspoken worry she felt when he stood at the stern of the ship, staring out to the sea as if he could still see the homeland, still see Milada; as if he were watching her wedding unfold before his eyes. The strong cold winds pounded waves into the ship; ice formed on Shanghai's face, freezing his tears into permanence.

And the spoken grief when Jakub came to get her. "Shanghai is going to jump!" he said. The urgency of his voice made Mariana understand that Jakub was seriously concerned. When Mariana got on deck, she looked up to see Shanghai hanging on to the rail of the crow's nest. He spoke no words; he just stepped to the outside of the rail, his hands gripping the iron as he leaned forward and swayed precariously in the wind.

"Shanghai!" Mariana yelled as she struggled to bundle her sweater up around her neck. "I can talk to Milada for you if you just come down!" Shanghai acted as if he didn't hear at all.

"It's true, Shanghai, she can talk to Milada!" Jakub yelled up, his voice carried on the wind. "Come on down, now! We can help you!"

Shanghai looked down at Mariana and Jakub, but didn't make a move. "Mariana, tell him something through his mind," Jakub urged.

"I can't," Mariana said plainly, feeling that if she went into his mind, his heart, she would be forever lost.

"Of course you can. You do so with me, and you've done so with Milada. Now go on."

"No. I cannot."

"Oh, come now. That again? You know there are no evil spirits around him."

"I can't." Mariana was stern.

Jakub became resigned. "Shanghai! Come on down now. You can ask Mariana a question, and she will answer it for you. Ask her something that only Milada would know."

Shanghai considered this. "You can talk to Milada from here?" Shanghai's small voice reached the deck.

"Yes!" Mariana yelled back. "Come on down, and I will talk to her for you."

Shanghai crawled down the ladder, and the circus performers on deck cheered affirmations to him. "Yes. Yes," Jakub said to the gathering, "everyone go back to your beds now." He put his hand on Shanghai's shoulder and instructed him to go with Mariana. He pulled Mariana aside. "Take care of him, will you? I don't want you to let him out of your sight. He can sleep in your cabin tonight."

Mariana thought that Shanghai would fight this, but he was defeated in so many other ways that he lowered his head and followed her to the private sleeping cabin. Her cabin was small, but comfortable and much nicer than the large room of sleeping bunks all of the performers were sharing with mice during these many months at sea. She motioned for him to sit on the bunk as she sat in the only chair in the room. They looked at each other in silence. Shanghai began to cry. He covered his face with his hands, and his body shook with the force of his sobs. She wanted to reach out for him; she wanted to pull him close to her chest and hold him until the pain went away. Instead, she pushed back into her chair. She grew increasingly uncomfortable with Shanghai's emotional display and contemplated leaving the cabin. She reached for a scrap of fabric in a nearby bag and handed it to Shanghai. He wiped his face with it and twisted the piece of fabric between his fingers in silence. Mariana eyed the door and struggled to keep her body in the cabin with Shanghai. Her chest was tight, as if she were tied to the chair. Finally, she cleared her throat and said, "What is it that you want to ask Milada?"

"You can contact her for me?"

"Yes."

"I want to ask her if she is happy."

146

Mariana was taken aback once again. She had no intention of actually contacting Milada, even though she could, and it almost seemed wrong to lie to Shanghai. She was determined though; this was her game. "What?" Mariana asked, feeling distracted.

Shanghai spoke quickly, "I want to know if she is happy with Zikmund. I want to know if she misses me, if she thinks about me, if she wants me back."

She relaxed and closed her eyes. She knew that Shanghai thought she was contacting Milada, but her mind was running through all of the possible answers and the scenarios that would result.

Finally, Mariana said, "She will not answer as to whether she is happy with Zikmund." She reached over and held Shanghai's stubby hands; they were hot and moistened with tears. She rubbed them between her slender fingers, feeling their thickness, taking time to run her fingertips over the large knuckles. "She does miss you and thinks about you often." Shanghai nodded and smiled through his tears. "But she does not want you back." Mariana hated to see how Shanghai's face suddenly aged ten years with that one sentence. He abruptly pulled his hands away from her.

"I want to be alone right now," he said, his voice angry.

Suddenly, Mariana felt a strong desire to stay. "I cannot do that," she said softly. Shanghai's eyes became ice as he stared her down. Mariana's voice was stern, almost angry, as she emphasized each word, "I cannot do that."

Shanghai spat in her face. "You are a *jezibaba!* A witch! I have always felt that, and I feel that still." He stood up. "I don't believe you! I don't believe that you have talked to Milada at all!"

Mariana calmly wiped the spit off her face and leaned back into her chair. Her hands clutched the arms. "If that makes you feel better."

"Let me out of here," Shanghai said firmly.

"No. You are not well right now. You should rest."

"I'm not tired. Let me out!"

Mariana glared at Shanghai with ice-cold eyes. He bit his bottom lip and looked away from her, then climbed to the top bunk and pulled the covers over his head. Mariana stayed in the chair and watched him as she contemplated helping him forget. He tossed and turned, and she whispered, "Relax, relax." She needed for him to fall asleep so that she could have this power over him. Her spell was like poetry. She constructed the words carefully throughout the night. She had to be concise; she didn't want him to forget everything in his life, only the hurt that Milada brought on. She didn't want him to forget the time he spent in her cabin or the moment that they first met.

When the night was as black as the churning seas, Mariana had the spell ready. She steadied herself next to Shanghai's bunk. He was deep in sleep when she put her lips over his and softly spoke the spell into his mouth. The incantation rolled from her tongue and vibrated between his teeth. His breath smelled sweet and swirled warmth in her ear when she turned her head to steady her hand above his heart. She lifted the burning feeling right out of his chest. The ship moaned. She turned to his lips and spoke a blessing. *I wish only good for you, little one,* she said into his parted lips. Before she could stop herself, she touched her lips to his, pressing flesh on flesh. It was a soft, dry kiss that lasted only a moment before Mariana pulled herself away.

She sat in the chair and watched him sleep the rest of the night. In the morning he woke and asked why he was in her cabin. That's when she knew for sure that her spell had worked.

Yes, Mariana thinks now, *I have done him a great service.*

AS SHANGHAI steps away from Mariana's boxcar with his trousers in hand, his eyes focus on the ground. He chastises himself for being unable to do something, anything, even hold a conversation with her. *Coward,* he mutters. He stops and turns back to look up at her car. The mural of the Charles Bridge looms before him. He closes his eyes and wishes he were back in Prague, doing something else. And maybe, Atasha would even go with him. Maybe she would keep his secret safe. He never considered the energy it would take to hide such a thing, but then he'd never imagined meeting anyone like Mariana. He takes a deep breath and steps cautiously up to the *jezibaba*'s door. A step creaks, and he clutches the wooden rail. A splinter bites his middle finger, and he jerks his hand away from the rail. One more step and he's at the *jezibaba*'s door. Before he has a chance to knock, the door flings open. Mariana stands above him.

"Yes?" she sounds surprised but stands back, letting him in once again.

Shanghai focuses on the splinter in his hand, picking at it; blood beads to the surface.

"A splinter?" Mariana asks and Shanghai nods. "Come, sit down." Shanghai tries to steady his hand. His mind goes blank, and he instinctively pulls the wound to his mouth, holding his finger across his lips, sucking lightly.

She sits down next to him, a needle in her hand. She takes his finger in her hand and gently works the splinter out of his skin. His mouth is dry and he tries to swallow, but his throat is too tight. His foot, which sits just over the edge of the settee, is tapping the air. "I . . . ," he searches for something to say, "I . . . just came back to thank you again." He feels that he should do something. This could be his last chance to be so close to her. There must be some way.

"Got it," Mariana holds a small splinter in front of him.

He quickly jumps off the settee, his nervousness taking control. His heart beats up into his throat as his eyes lock with the *jezibaba*'s. And then he thinks of it: if he knows her secret, then perhaps his own secret will be safe if ever revealed to her. He gasps to catch his breath, to gain his courage. "What was it, madam, if I may ask," his knees begin to shake, "that upset you so much a few weeks ago?" His palms begin to sweat as Mariana looks at him with discernment. "In the Big Top.

When I saw you and helped you back here."

Mariana stands and walks slowly toward him. He backs up to the wall. She towers over him as she traps him, her body only inches away from his. "Why do you ask?" she says, anger rising in her voice.

Shanghai swallows the lump in his throat. His neck cramps from looking straight up at her. "I was, I am concerned." He speaks quickly. "I wasn't sure whether I should tell Jakub about it or not. I thought, perhaps, you are fighting an illness."

She steps away from him and returns to her chair. "No, I am not ill. I thank you for your concern, though."

Shanghai steps toward her. "If there's anything I can do. If you need to talk, I . . . I . . . " He can't bring himself to say the words. Air rises up from his stomach, and he catches it in his throat, then swallows it back down. "Well," he continues, "you know where to find me."

Mariana nods her head as Shanghai takes his leave. He crosses in front of the Sideshow Banner. He nervously picks at the stinging in his finger until the tiny scab comes off and another bead of blood rises to the surface.

★　　★　　★　　★　　★

SHANGHAI FOCUSES on the torches at his feet. The crowd buzzes around him, and Vincent's booming voice drowns into the background. When he learned to throw fire, he learned that he must put himself into a vacuum, where all else fades into the distance. His focus is always on the fire—always on the flames.

Vincent takes a match to one of the torches, then jumps off the stage so that Shanghai is alone. A flame bursts toward the sky. Shanghai puts the other torch to the flame. He moves his arms rhythmically as the flames spin past his ears, *whoosh, whoosh;* he feels the movement in his upper back, his shoulders—like the rhythm of the train going over the track, the pounding of the timpani in the Big Top. It's a low rhythm in his body, energy transferring from the deep orange flame into his arm, into his biceps, triceps, quads—*whoosh, whoosh.* He's in a trance until the act is over and he puts the flames into his mouth, swallowing the fire into his soul.

Mariana is at the back of the crowd, watching him from her tent. Tiny bumps rise across his arms when he sees her. He steps toward her, and her eyes light up. The hair on the back of his neck rises. As the crowd clears the midway, moving into the Sideshow Tent, Shanghai approaches her. His mind is blank; he's unsure what to say, how to talk with her.

"Madam," he says politely.

"Yes?" she looks eye to eye with him when she is sitting down.

He quickly searches his mind, then suddenly grabs the sides of his pants, clutching the fabric in his hands. "The pants . . . they fit perfectly."

A smile spreads across Mariana's face. Shanghai has never noticed before how white her teeth are; the top ones are perfectly straight, the bottom ones slightly, but unnoticeably, crooked. *She's really quite beautiful,* he thinks, and as he stares at her mouth he suddenly feels as if he's under her spell. He backs away from Mariana, and her face turns to a frown. "Thank you," he says quickly just as the music in the Big Top rises to a crescendo.

Later that night, as Shanghai sits in the pie car with the other Czech troupers, he tries to push Mariana out of his mind, but he seems to be consumed. *If she finds out,* he thinks, *what will happen?* He creates a story in his head, then creates a new one, and a new one, and a new one. He tries to look at it from all angles, but always, in the end, it is never good for him. He looks out the window of the pie car and sees that the workmen are deflating the Big Top; the huge canvas drops to the ground and kicks up sawdust. He cannot be alone in this anymore, and he knows that he must tell the one person he can trust. Atasha—she would understand. While he waits for just the right moment to leave the troupers and sneak off to Atasha's wagon, he thinks of the way to tell her. He tries it one way and then another. Outside, the workmen are loading up the last of the wagons. Shanghai keeps an eye out for Mariana, scanning the periphery of the compound for her figure, watching for her, waiting for her to appear from nowhere. When Jakub joins their group, he knows that the train will be leaving in about an hour. He keeps track of the time as he laughs and jokes with the men, just like he used to back in the home country. He used to enjoy being part of this circle, but lately, he has felt disconnected.

Every time Milada, her father, or Zikmund are brought up in conversation, the men's voices quiet, they glance his way, then someone changes the subject. He has gathered from the conversations tonight that Milada's father stayed in the old country to give his daughter away at the altar. The men don't seem to know that the *jezibaba* put a spell on him and that he can remember only fragments of his time with Milada. They don't know that his cavernous memory fills him with more grief than the moments he can remember.

It was their behavior on the ship to America that tipped him off that something was missing: the sideways glances, the concern they showed after he spent a few days with Mariana, the hushed conversations. They told him how dramatic it was to see him hanging from the crow's nest and how Jakub and the *jezibaba* talked him down. When he asked them why he even considered throwing himself out into the sea, they replied in shock, "Well, Milada, of course." He played along, pretending to know who Milada was and why she was so important to him. When he sat in silence during those long days at sea, squinted his eyes, and concentrated, his memory came back in fragments.

But lately, he hasn't wanted to sit alone to try to remember her at all. Even now, his mind is preoccupied with dismissing himself from this circle before the train begins to move. He wants to see Atasha. He needs to tell her everything. When Radovan joins them in the pie car, Shanghai excuses himself.

"Shanghai, my friend, where are you going?" Jakub's voice fills the pie car.

Shanghai arches backward, his hand on the base of his spine. "My back is hurting. I need to lie down."

"Your back has been hurting a lot lately," Jakub says with concern. "Would you like to see a doctor in the next town?"

Shanghai thanks Jakub but declines the offer. He doesn't take a lantern when he goes outside for fear that Mariana will follow him. He keeps his hand on the train so that he can follow it down the track. The metal is cool and smooth beneath his fingers. He scrutinizes the night air for anyone who might be watching him, and when he comes to the flatcars, he cautiously looks around for the *jezibaba,* then climbs up to join Atasha and Anna in the Snake Charmer's wagon.

Anna is asleep, but Atasha lies awake, just as he had hoped. He sits across from her, his knees pulled to his chest. "Is something wrong?" she asks.

He sighs and thinks of the emptiness that consumes him. "I . . . ," his voice shakes, "I have something to tell you." *If someone else knows,* he tries to reassure himself, *I won't feel so alone.*

"I have something to tell you, too. About Milada," her voice is soft and full of compassion. It seems much easier to listen to her than to speak any more words. "I heard Jakub telling the story one night— about you and Milada and Zikmund." He tunes into Atasha's voice dancing over the words. In this darkness, his vision is filled with her as one whole person. He forgets that her sister lies next to her. He sees only Atasha, her body long and lean. He sees the curve of her hip and breast. He watches her lips move over the words, how they bounce together and kiss each syllable. Her hair falls around her shoulders like silk. Her eyes are full of life, and all he can think in that moment is of how he yearns to be close to her. How he longs to touch her. How he aches for her to hold him. When she finishes her story, she looks his way, her neck straining against the pull of her sister.

"Can I . . . ," Shanghai rubs his hands together, " . . . can I lie next to you?"

Atasha smiles and shyly says yes.

153

He crawls over to her and lies down; she willingly wraps her arm around his small body. He drapes his arm across her abdomen, reaching out to rest his hand on her waist. His fingers are stopped by the spongy tissue that connects Atasha to her sister. He pulls his hand back and rests it on Atasha's belly.

"What do you think of my story?" she whispers. Shanghai shrugs. "You wanted me to listen for you, remember?"

"Yes, I remember." He feels her stomach move up and down with each breath she takes. When Anna takes a deep breath, he can't feel it in Atasha's body, but when she makes a slight movement, Atasha's body adjusts, too. He wonders what she feels right now, as her hand wanders over his shoulder, his back, his ribs. What does she notice in his body?

"Are you okay?" asks Atasha.

Shanghai whispers back yes but feels lost. He has no connection to the story about Milada and Zikmund, nor any connection to the men he used to call his friends, and he hasn't felt a connection to family for years. He has no fresh memories of his mother. Now, lying next to Atasha, he is so aware of her connection. He moves his hand back to the space of skin that joins her and her sister. It is there that he feels two heartbeats. The skin pounds like a drum beneath his palm. One heart beats beneath his thumb, the other beneath his pinkie. They form a rhythm, first one, then the other: Atasha's, then Anna's, Atasha's, Anna's. He runs his fingers over the stretched skin, and Atasha giggles. "Careful," she says, "you'll wake Anna."

Shanghai tucks his arms into the space between himself and Atasha, pulling his arms to his chest. Trying to hold his secret so close that she won't discover it, at least not tonight. Then, before he even thinks about it, he places a kiss on Atasha's neck, just below her earlobe. When he realizes what he's doing, he stops himself and whispers, "I'm sorry." He pulls away from her and crawls to the other side of the wagon. "You don't have to listen for me anymore," he says.

"Shanghai? I thought you would be happy. . . . Are you?" Atasha hesitates. "Are you mad at me?"

"No, I'm just tired," Shanghai says softly. "Thank you for listening, but I don't think I want to know anymore. I just want . . . " The train starts to move and the whistle sounds. He approaches Atasha once again. He wants to say it all, to tell her that he doesn't want to know anymore about his ghost lover and that all he wants is to be with her. He wants her to love him back. He leans over and places a kiss on her forehead. "It's time to go to sleep." Before he can pull away, she grabs the back of his head and guides him down to her lips. They are soft and moist, and the kiss lasts for only a moment before Atasha says good night.

AS DAYLIGHT breaks, the train shakes, then lurches forward. The jolt wakes Shanghai from his dream of Atasha on the high wire. She has a body of her own and balances herself on a coil strung from one of the fly poles to the next. She puts one foot in front of the other, her toes curl around the wire, and her arms are spread out at her sides. In those moments as he comes out of sleep, he smiles at her beauty.

A few voices rise out of the sleeper cars, and Shanghai knows that the men will begin to unload the train soon. He crawls over to the twins and places his hand on Anna's head, stroking her hair, then he leans over and kisses Atasha lightly on the forehead. He sneaks out of the wagon and returns to his own bunk before any of the workmen see him.

MARIANA WAKES when the train jerks to an abrupt stop. Her fingers and knees ache, like each one has been hit with a tiny mallet throughout the night. Every morning in a new town, she gets out of bed and looks out her little window. It gives her bearing on her surroundings. Today, another fog blankets the ground. Her senses feel dulled, but they awaken quickly when she catches a glimpse of Shanghai. He hurries past, his small body disappearing into the fog, which breaks up suddenly and lifts like smoke from a cigar. Mariana gets a feeling, something deep and daunting. "Mi`zak," she says. "Wicked." Her bones tell her that there is trouble ahead.

ONCE UPON *a time there was a beautiful girl who held something mysterious in her heart. She lived her life in two ways, one as a woman in love with a man who spoke smooth and angled words, the other as a woman in love with someone who built a wall of words around his short stature. The love for the man who spoke smooth and angled words was part of the show, proof to her parents that she was a normal girl with an extraordinary gift of flight. The love with the person who built a wall of words was pure, real, and forbidden. She hid these feelings away because her father, a man with a long neck and wings to fly, had a heavy hand. She feared that if her father found out about the other love, he would take away her wings and tell her never to return.*

One day, the beautiful girl cried and cried until the earth could no longer absorb her tears. The water puddled on the surface, then carved a gully into the land; the gully turned into a gorge, the gorge turned into a lake, and the lake turned into a river that pushed its way out to the sea. She told the man of short stature that her father, the man with a long neck and wings to fly, had promised her hand to the man who spoke smooth and angled words. The man with short stature told her that they could escape, give up everything and escape.

But the beautiful girl stepped off her perch and sailed into the arms of her father. She could not give up the extraordinary gift of flight. The man with the stunted stature watched her fly, night after night, and when she was bound to the earth once again, he tried to help her catch her tears. He told her that he had been constructing a ship of words and that they could sail away on the river of tears, going out to sea, far, far away from the man with smooth and angled words and the man with a long neck and wings to fly.

The beautiful girl became so paralyzed that all she could do was stay in the place that she already knew. And every day, she took flight, and every night, her tears dropped to the earth and floated out to sea.

—*Shanghai's diary, August 1899*

159

The Stranger

ariana watches the muddy river churn past, thinking of Shanghai's diary. *The river of tears.* She imagines it crystal clear and salty. Not anything like the Mississippi that rolls past her tent now. Earlier in the day, before the first show, she tossed a stick into the muddy water and watched it churn past the Big Top, the Menagerie Tent, and the Sideshow Tent until it was swallowed completely by the river as it passed beneath the dock. The river is like thick soup boiling over an open flame—constantly moving, bubbling, rolling.

This morning before the parade, Jakub lectured everyone about getting too close to the water. "People are swallowed alive by the river, never to be seen again." Mariana wonders if Shanghai is tempted to write his own story, perhaps about a dwarf who jumped in to save a beautiful girl. As she twirls her dark hair between her fingers, she wonders if—in her younger days—Shanghai would have found her to be beautiful.

A paddleboat full of people makes its way to the dock; the large wheel spins in the water, and steam pours from the top of the shaft. People are pressed against the railing of the boat, pointing toward the large tents and the banner of the Sideshow. Children jump up and down and shriek with delight. Adult voices buzz between each other, as laughter swells up over the water. Beyond the paddleboat, there is the tree-lined bank across the wide expanse of the river—Illinois. *One step closer to New York. One step closer to home.*

She is seated at the end of the dock, where the paddleboat has stopped, and people are carefully stepping down off the boat and onto the wooden planks. Jakub thought this placement might help her receipts, but as usual, the audience barely pauses to watch her sew. She swats a large buzzing water bug away from her ear. A man dressed in a black suit makes his way down the platform and removes his hat as he approaches. "Excuse me, please," he says. Mariana is startled by his Czech accent. As he continues, she watches his large Adam's apple bounce on top of his high white collar. "Do you know Atasha and Anna?"

"The twins?" she replies, squinting her eyes against the sun.

"Yes," the man says. She guesses that he is in his late thirties, the same age as she. "Yes, the twins. Do you know where they may be?"

"Of course, they are in the Sideshow." She points across to the crowd gathered in front of the Sideshow Banner. "See their likeness up there?" The man looks toward the drawing of the twins on the canvas.

"The Borsefsky Brothers Siamese Twins?" the man reads from the banner.

"Yes," Mariana answers, "the *Siamese* Twins." She emphasizes *Siamese*, not understanding that he questions the "Borsefsky Brothers" statement. The man walks away as if in a trance, and Mariana calls out to him, "Sir, what business do you have with the twins?"

"I have some news from home," he yells as he makes his way through the crowd. He spins his hat in his hand, rubbing the brim between his fingers.

She watches the man pay for his ticket and get in line. He is noticeably nervous. Vincent's spieling is so loud that the man must plug his ears. "Come one, come all, see the amazing wonders of the world! This is not for the faint-hearted!" The man looks up again at the twins' likeness on the banner, then follows the crowd into the Sideshow Tent with Vincent in the lead.

Mariana puts down her sewing, then starts along the midway to watch the man from backstage. Before she gets fifteen feet from her tent, a voice barks at her from behind, "Where are you going?" She notices the tall, thin shadow on the ground next to her shadow.

She tries not to show her surprise. "Vladan?" Mariana turns to face Jakub's uncle. "What are you doing here?"

"I was in Chicago for some business and thought I would stop here on my way home to see how my nephew is doing." Vladan glances out over the water. He looks nothing like Jakub. His skin is pale; his face is thin and bony. "Another boat will be along soon. Jakub tells me your receipts have not been good lately. Is that true?" Mariana narrows her eyes at Vladan. She knows that he fears her Gypsy ways just as Radovan does. She sensed it the first time she met him years ago when he visited the old country. His hands shook, his knees quaked, and Mariana delighted in the power of it. Now, he avoids eye contact with her and fidgets with his clothing. He glances at her as he waits out the silence and sees her dark eyes burning into his psyche. He backs away from her and says, "Yes, well, do whatever you like, but I believe that young man is looking for a reading." The young, awkward-looking man standing behind Mariana holds out a nickel, and, from just a quick glance, she can see that he is a bachelor hoping to be told that he will find a bride in the near future. She reluctantly takes the money from his hand and leads him to her tent. As he steps in, she gazes across the midway and watches the man in the black suit disappear into the Sideshow Tent.

VINCENT WALKS around the twins and gives his usual spiel, "That's right, folks, two heads, two arms, three legs, one body. These girls nearly killed their mother at birth ..." he continues as Atasha anchors her left leg, the twins' shared leg, and begins to spin the twins around slowly. They stop at each turn so that the audience can see them from front to side to back to front. Anna keeps them balanced as Atasha turns them. Vincent brings a sturdy wooden crate onto the stage and places it just behind Atasha. The crate is made of thick oak wood and is vibrant indigo with heavy metal corners painted gold. The blacksmith made large handles for the side and a gilded plaque with the inscription "The Borsefsky Brothers Siamese Twins" on the front. Vincent opens the crate and pulls out two eggs, holding them up for the audience to see. He throws one egg to Atasha, and she catches it in her right hand. He walks in front of the twins and hands the other egg to Anna. "Now prepare yourselves for the Borsefsky Brothers Siamese Twins!"

Atasha sets the first egg in motion, and Anna catches it. One egg bounces from Anna's hand to Atasha's, into the air, over their heads, before Anna catches it again and throws it to Atasha. It is nothing spectacular, but the crowd is mesmerized. The simple juggling continues until the crowd becomes accustomed to the spectacle. That's when Shanghai makes his entrance, stands on the crate, and juggles two eggs in the air. The crowd laughs at the juggling dwarf but is silenced when Shanghai throws one of the eggs over Atasha's head and into her hand. When they have mastered a rhythm with throwing three eggs between them, Shanghai sends the fourth into the loop.

Soon, the eggs are flying so fast that they are a blur. Atasha throws, Anna throws, Atasha catches, Anna catches; their timing is perfect. They can feel each other's movements. Shanghai jumps off the crate and pulls out two more eggs. He walks to the side of the twins, and they slowly turn toward him as they juggle. He tosses the two eggs toward the twins, and they throw theirs to him. Suddenly the two are working as three. Atasha throws Shanghai an egg as he launches another in the air; six eggs are flying between Shanghai and Atasha, Shanghai and Anna, Anna and Atasha, Shanghai and the twins. At the end of the act, Shanghai grabs a burlap sack from Vincent and lets each egg fall into it until all are gathered and the twins' arms are still.

The crowd erupts into wild applause. Atasha can feel the buzzing in her arms as if the movement has become a part of her heartbeat. She looks at Shanghai, who is holding the sack of eggs high above his head. Anna leads them in a bow.

Shanghai takes his leave without notice, and Vincent steps up to the front of the stage, just to the right of the twins. "Aren't they amazing, folks?! These girls came to us from a farm in Nebraska! We found them out in a chicken coop, juggling eggs just like this! Don't you worry. You can take home a postcard picturing these beautiful, bizarre young girls for just five cents. That's right, send it to your relatives or just keep it for yourself as a souvenir of the amazing Borsefsky Brothers Siamese Twins!"

The audience applauds and cheers, and when they quiet, Vincent asks them for questions. The twins answer the same questions they did on their very first day in the show: "Can both heads speak? Do both heads eat? If one gets a cold, does the other also?"

Atasha answers the questions politely; Anna speaks only when necessary to prove Atasha right. "Do both heads speak?"

"Yes," Atasha says, "we are two separate people, with two fully functioning brains."

"Yes," Anna manages to say, her voice quivering. She tries to control her stutter but usually fails. "We are simply joined to-to-together. Here," she runs her hand along their joined skin from shoulder to hip. The crowd gasps, then talks quietly until someone brings up another question. It is rare that the twins get an unexpected inquiry from one town to the other.

When the questions have stopped, Vincent steps to the front of the platform. "Thank you for your time, folks. In a few minutes, we'll be selling tickets for an added dimension of the show. No women or children, please; this is not for the faint-hearted. Gentlemen, in this special show you will see Gizela once again, only this time, you will see her in her full natural splendor. There is a gen-u-ine boy, born with the head of an alligator. And, something you won't believe until you see Patricka, a he/she with both male and female body parts. Just three cents gets you into this added show. Tickets will be sold right over there in ten minutes. Until then, step right up to the twins to purchase special postcards for five cents! That's right, only five cents for a souvenir that will last a lifetime!"

The twins step to the end of the platform, selling their postcards and smiling politely at the now timid audience. As Anna hands them out, Atasha collects the money. They rarely get questions as they sell postcards; the crowd becomes tongue-tied when they stand face-to-face with the conjoined bodies.

As the crowd thins, Atasha hears a man call her name. She scans the remaining faces. "Anna, Atasha!" the man says as he wildly waves his hands. Anna is happily handing out postcards and doesn't notice the man. "Anna," Atasha whispers, "look."

Atasha points into the audience as the man approaches their platform. "Atasha. Anna." The man becomes more somber as he nudges his way through the small gathering.

"Yes?" says Atasha, somewhat annoyed. "Would you like a postcard?"

"Girls," he says, "don't you recognize me?"

Anna's ribs push into Atasha's. The man speaks to the girls in Czech: "I have news . . . about your mother." He pulls a wrinkled and well-traveled piece of paper from his breast pocket. Atasha stares at the man with distrust in her eyes. Anna doesn't look at the man at all. "I'm your mother's cousin Viktor. We met when you were just this high. It was many years ago, just after I came to America. Remember?" Atasha frowns as she studies the man's face.

The crowd around the man silently looks from the man to the twins, anxiously waiting for the twins to speak. "Girls, I have bad news," his voice turns somber as he looks down at his shoes, then back up at the twins. "I found out the other day that your mother has died. Your father wrote me a letter, see?" Anna gasps for air, but Atasha furls her brow as the man holds up the worn page with fine cursive writing on it. "Your father wrote that he was going to wait until the end of the season to tell you, but I thought your mother would want you to know." Anna begins to weep, but Atasha squints at the letter, trying to authenticate her father's writing. "I saw that this circus was here and hoped that it was yours. I did the right thing . . . telling you," the man reassures himself.

"Okay, sir." Vincent steps in whenever someone lingers with an act for too long. "Let's move along now. The twins have other admirers." Indeed, Atasha recognized her father's swirling *s*'s and the way the hook above his *c* flared at the end. She is so stunned that she doesn't stop Vincent as he pushes the man toward the entrance.

"I'm sorry, girls." The man unwillingly moves forward, looking back at the twins until he is out of sight.

"D-d-does he t-tell the truth?" Anna whispers, her stutter more pronounced in her anguish.

The man's face is becoming clearer in Atasha's memory. She wants to run after the man and read the letter; she wants to see for herself how their papa wrote down his grief. "I think yes," she says, and Anna shakes uncontrollably.

ANNA FEELS the clouds choke out the last small spot of the exposed moon, and the wagon grows pitch-black. Her body is twisted, pulled one way by the weight of Atasha's body, pulled the other by gravity. It takes her by surprise—how uncomfortable she feels—and she closes her eyes to the increasing pain in the back of her neck and the small of her back.

Atasha breathes deeply, and Anna feels the stretching of skin between them. Her back strains with every one of Atasha's breaths. Anna tries to follow the breathing, but her lungs are smaller and weaker, so she can barely keep up. When it is silent and still, she can hear Atasha's heartbeat—especially when it beats opposite her own. Usually the rhythm can lull her to sleep but not tonight. Anna wonders if all the pain she feels is because her mother is dead. But inside her body, it isn't an ache she holds; it's a kind of numbness. She pulls her pillow to her face and breathes in, hoping to pull any trace of her mother into her lungs.

"What are you doing?" whispers Atasha.

"Trying to remember the way Mama smelled," says Anna. Her chest awakens from the numbness, and she cries softly. She reaches her hand over and rests it on Atasha's abdomen. Atasha locks her fingers between Anna's. The softness and warmth of their intermingled hands lift the weight from Anna's heart.

"Remember Grandfather Knowitall?" Atasha asks.

Anna smiles as warmth rises in her chest. "Yes, the fairy tale."

"There once was a land that was dreary and dark like a grave." Atasha strokes the back of Anna's hand just as their mother used to do. Despite her discomfort, Anna pushes her body as far into Atasha as possible. "In this land, Grandfather Knowitall had not been seen for many, many days, for he had been under the *jezibaba*'s spell. You see, Jezibaba called out to her friend . . . "

Anna interrupts, "You forgot that the *jezibaba* lived in a castle at the edge of the dark, dreary land."

"Did I?" asks Atasha and Anna nods. "Jezibaba lived in a castle at the edge of this dark and dreary land. You see, Jezibaba called out to her friend the Darkness, and the Darkness sent out the clouds to cover up Grandfather Knowitall's beautiful light. But what Jezibaba didn't know was that in this land there was a beautiful two-headed maiden. One of the heads answered to Lenka, the other to Ludmila."

"Who would be who?" Anna says, remembering how her mother would pose that question to the two of them.

"I would be Ludmila; you would be Lenka."

"Did you decide that or did I?"

"I can't remember anymore."

"Go on."

"You see, Lenka and Ludmila had a mother and father, both of whom had loved the sun, Grandfather Knowitall, their whole lives. Every night at supper time, their parents would cry . . . "

Her voice sad, Anna quietly says, "When, oh, when will Grandfather Knowitall ever return?"

"It was after the sixty-seventh evening of sorrow that Lenka and Ludmila decided that they must do something. They set out from their home, kissing their parents good-bye, and headed for Jezibaba's castle, just beyond the forest."

Anna's thoughts shift from the story and back into the heaviness of her heart. She interrupts Atasha, "Why do you think Papa didn't tell us?"

"You heard Viktor," Atasha says softly. "He wanted to wait until the season was over."

"Why?"

Atasha doesn't answer right away, then says unconvincingly, "Maybe he's too sad."

"Maybe, you're right." Anna begins to cry. "He d-d-doesn't love us." Anna thinks of how their father couldn't look at them when they were saying good-bye. Couldn't look at them when they were in Jakub's boxcar. Couldn't even look at them when they were in the wagon on the way to the circus. How he just let her and Atasha go on and on about all the things they were going to see at the circus. And how was it that they thought they were going to see the circus, not be a part of it? Anna tries to recall, but her head is pounding. She closes her eyes tight and tries to remember. Oh, yes, it was his words, not their mother's: "How would you girls like to see a circus?" His voice was excited like a little child's. It was the first time Anna had ever heard their father speak so joyfully and playfully. And on the way to Grand Island, Anna and Atasha asked things like "Will there be elephants? Will there be camels? Will there be clowns?" Their father played along for the first part of the trip. "Yes!" he said excitedly. "There will be all of those things and more that you cannot imagine!" Anna remembers how excited she was to see

169

her father that way: young and vibrant, ready to show them a whole new world. But after a few hours of their questions, their father turned silent once again. "If you girls keep talking about the circus, it won't be as exciting when you get there. Now quiet down!" he yelled. Anna recalls how quiet their mother was on that trip. How she sometimes sat in front with their father and sometimes lay in back with the twins, but she was always silent.

"Go to sleep now, Anna," Atasha says with the same tone of voice their mother once used, soft and caring. Anna releases the hold on her sister's hand and leans back onto the long pillow their mother made for her. She closes her eyes and listens once again to the *ba-boom, ba-boom, ba-boom* of Atasha's heart.

* * * * *

THE VOICE comes to Atasha in the darkness and whispers her name. The deep sound travels inside her ears and rolls in her head like a dream. "Atasha," it sounds again, and she opens her eyes. She feels the heaviness that she went to sleep with, that void inside her chest that is weighted by grief. "Shanghai . . . ," she begins to speak, but the air comes out of her lungs in bursts, the ache in her throat turning into a cry. She hears a rustle of hay, and then Shanghai is next to her, holding her hand.

"I heard," he whispers. His voice is strong and soothing, his hand soft and warm.

Atasha squeezes Shanghai's hand. "A man, Mother's cousin Viktor, he just appeared tonight. Did you see him? Vincent pushed him away before either one of us had a chance to say anything, to ask questions." Shanghai lies down next to her and cradles her arm close to his body. Atasha gives into the warmth of this closeness. She begins to cry, allows herself to cry, allows herself to be the weak one, just this once. She loses control, and her sobbing shakes her whole body. Shanghai readjusts so that Atasha's arm is behind his neck. He strokes her hair and wipes the tears from her face with his thumb.

When her sobbing softens, Shanghai tells her the story of how he once thought he saw his mother on the Charles Bridge in Prague. The woman was looking down into the River Vltava, as if watching her reflection shift in the gentle waters. "She was standing over the spot where Saint Nepomucký was drowned. Legend has it that the king, Václav IV, cut out the saint's tongue after he refused to tell the secrets of the queen from the confessional. Nepomucký was lowered into the water in a cage and drowned. But when they pulled him out of the water and looked into his mouth, his tongue had been restored. It was then that he became both a martyr and a saint.

"In my heart I hoped so badly that the woman standing in that spot was my mother. It had never occurred to me until that very moment, that quite possibly, she was no longer a whore. If she were out there, on that bridge, then she had escaped her life of prostitution. I was fourteen years old, and I still yearned to see my mother. As I got closer to her, I saw the woman's tears drop into the water below, breaking her reflection. I touched her arm and she jumped. When I saw her face, I knew it wasn't my mother. The woman looked shocked. 'It was a miracle,' she said. She turned back to the water and prayed. It was on that day that I stopped hoping to see my mother living in the world. I stopped hoping that I would see her with just one man and maybe a child or two. Living happily in a normal life—praying for saints who drowned in the River Vltava. I came to accept that my mother was a prostitute and that I would never see her again."

Atasha asks, "How long did it take you to stop feeling the hurt?"

Shanghai drapes his arm beneath Atasha's breasts, being careful not to touch Anna. "I still feel the hurt sometimes, but . . . ," he strokes her hair again, "it gets better. I used to look in the mirror, just to see something that would remind me of her. I have her eyes. It comforts me to see them looking back at me every now and then."

171

Atasha turns to face Shanghai but can see only his forehead. "I wish I could see your eyes right now," she whispers. Shanghai pulls himself up and leans over Atasha. He holds his face just inches from hers.

"I saw your mother only from a distance," he draws his finger down the bridge of her nose, "but I believe you have her nose. And her cheekbones." He softly kisses each cheek, then whispers to Atasha to go to sleep.

"Will you stay here tonight?" she asks.

"I'll be right over there," he whispers.

"No, please, stay here, next to me?" She can't make out his facial expression through the darkness, and it seems an eternity before he whispers his yes and eases his body close to her side. She feels comforted to have her sister's warmth on her left side and the warmth from Shanghai on the right. The train starts to travel northward, and Atasha slips into a dream of her mother, lying stiff, cold, and still on the table back home. Women from the church prepare her body—washing it, caring for it. Her father is outside, all alone, a shovel in his hand. He throws clumps of earth behind him and growls at the task. It is the same dream over and over. She drifts from inside the house to her mother's dead body to outside, where her father digs and digs and digs. As the train slows to a stop in the middle of the night, Atasha wakes to feel Shanghai next to her, his breath warming her neck. She shifts her arm, and he moves slightly, kisses her neck softly, then they both drift into sleep again.

Anna wakes in the middle of the night, calling Atasha's name. "Yes?" She feels Shanghai tucked in close to her. He moves slightly, but she doesn't know if he is asleep or awake.

"Atasha, I want . . . Mama. I want to see her . . . "

"I know, Anna. I know."

"It's not fair. Why couldn't . . . ?" Anna doesn't say anything else, but Atasha knows what she wants to say. She knows that Anna is too kind, too loving to say it. She knows that Anna wishes their papa had died instead.

172

"We have two shows tomorrow. You should rest." Atasha wonders how Anna will get through this. *She's so delicate, so vulnerable.* When they were little girls, the midwife told their mother that Anna had a weak heart—that she would be the reason that the twins might not survive. "Your heart is strong, Atasha," that's what their mother said. "It is strong enough for both of you." Atasha knew her responsibility. If the twins fell down and scraped their knees, Anna cried, but Atasha helped her mother comfort her. When their father yelled at the girls for some trivial reason, Anna cried, but Atasha remained steadfast and showed no emotion.

Now she has to carry her sister through this. "Anna?" she whispers, but Anna has fallen back to sleep. Grief weighs down on Atasha's chest. "Shanghai?"

"Yes?" he whispers to her, and his breath touches her ear.

"I don't know if I'm strong enough."

"You are, Atasha. You are strong enough."

"But Anna, she . . . How will she get through this? And what will we do at the end of the season? Papa won't want us. He was the one that brought us here. It was Mama who would have wanted us back. Now we have nowhere to go and . . . "

Shanghai hushes her and whispers, "I'll help you, Atasha. We will work it out together." His fingers move slowly over her cheek, and she relaxes into his hand. She closes her eyes and feels his fingers trace her brow, her hairline, her ear. And all she wants to do is sleep. Sleep with Shanghai by her side, and with Anna by her side—safe and comfortable. And soon, someday soon, the pain will go away and Anna will survive and they both will survive.

"How did we get here?" Atasha cries. She cries so hard that she doesn't know if she'll ever be able to stop herself.

"*Shhhh . . . shhhh.*" Shanghai kisses her neck. "I am so glad you're here. I have been so lonely, and you, you make me laugh and you make me want to care. To care about you."

Atasha laughs through her tears, then cries again. She hears the workmen outside, yelling, putting up tents, moving wagons. She cries and cries and cries, and Shanghai wipes her tears away until there are no more left. "Shanghai?" she says. "Please tell me a story."

Shanghai thinks for a moment then whispers, "Once upon a time there was a court fool who was a dwarf . . . ," and as he tells the story, Atasha feels herself let go. Her heart stops pounding wildly in her chest, and Anna's heart slowly beats with hers. She feels her body relax into the bed of hay that she lies on, and she feels Anna melt further into slumber. And as the workmen put up the Big Top and as Shanghai's words float around her head, Atasha's eyelids close over the ache in her eyes and she falls into a deep sleep.

Mariana's Plight

Davenport, Iowa
July 13, 1900

ariana sits on the settee in her boxcar examining the hem of her skirt. Just before the circus parade ended, Radovan sought her out and said that Jakub had business to discuss with the two of them. They stare quietly at each other as they wait for Jakub to join them. Radovan leans on the wall near the door, takes a cigar from his coat pocket, and strikes a flame.

"If you please," Mariana says, "you know I don't like smoking in here."

He glares at Mariana, then shakes out the flame on the matchstick.

"Thank you," she says as Jakub comes in. He is noticeably uncomfortable.

"Would you excuse us, Radovan?" he says.

Radovan stands up straight. "But your uncle said . . . "

"Forget what my uncle said," Jakub cuts him off in agitation. "I am in charge right now. Please leave me alone with my wife."

Mariana looks from Jakub to Radovan and back to Jakub. She hasn't heard him refer to her as "wife" in quite some time. "What is this about?" she asks. Jakub opens the door for Radovan and motions for him to leave. "What is going on here?" she demands.

Jakub kneels next to her and holds her hand. She pulls it away and sees the fear in his eyes. He sits back on his heels and puts his hands up as if surrendering to her. She says nothing. He pulls a chair close to her and leans in, his elbows resting on his knees, his hands clasped together.

He looks like he is about to beg, as if weakness has taken control of him. His voice is low and feeble. "Mariana, Uncle Vladan had a talk with me, and Radovan, before he left yesterday."

"Why was Radovan included in this talk and not I?"

"He . . . he just happened to be there. We were sitting around talking, and . . . he was just there."

"Go on." Mariana feels her face turn to stone; her eyebrows will not raise, her lips will not turn into a frown, the lines in her face will not deepen.

"I did not agree with what my uncle said, and I tried to tell him that we could do things differently; we could change the posters, we could get Vincent involved. Well, there are many things we could do, but," Jakub looks into Mariana's eyes briefly, then quickly looks away, "I just couldn't convince him differently. I know you will not be happy about this.

"Mariana," Jakub squirms, "Uncle Vladan wants you to move into the Sideshow Tent."

Mariana's eyes turn to ice as they fix on Jakub's fearful face. She speaks with controlled anger. "And Radovan knows about this?"

"Yes," Jakub rubs the palms of his hands together, "but that is not really the issue here. I tried to talk Uncle Vladan out of it, but he says, and I have to agree, that the Americans are not ready for a fortune-teller. They cannot possibly walk right up to you and sit in your tent for all of their neighbors and minister to see. Your revenues have been less than good, you must admit . . . " Mariana does not say a word. "The only way the towners will approach you is if we have you in the Sideshow Tent where Vincent can sell your talents. You will have to perform some simple telepathic trick first, and then you can tell fortunes in a corner of the tent. We will hang curtains for you, so you will be off to the side on your own."

As Jakub speaks, Mariana recognizes all of his nervous ticks: rubbing his face, cracking his knuckles, bouncing his knee, readjusting his vest. He talks to her as if she were one of the troupers. She may not be able to read her own future, but it is clear that Vladan has taken away her place in this circus, and Jakub has allowed it to happen.

"We are just not seen as a reputable circus having you out front. I know it is difficult to understand. But it is not done here, to have a fortune-teller out front. The Ringlings don't do it, the Cole Brothers don't do it, not even the Campbell Brothers. You will make more money in the Sideshow Tent. It is a plain and simple fact. I'm sorry. I'm shutting you down today." Jakub looks into her face for some reaction but gets none. Mariana watches the beads of sweat roll over his temples and break when they reach his sideburns. He backs to the door, turns quickly, and leaves.

Her blood burns beneath her skin. She closes her eyes, and, without effort, her body breaks into tiny pieces as it disappears into the background. She bites the inside of her lip until blood trickles down the side of her tongue and into her throat. She steps outside, and as she does a wind kicks up from the south, blowing dust over the circus grounds. Her body rises like a bubble, and she floats to the treetops. She has never experienced this sensation of flying before. She looks down at the circus grounds, out toward her little tent, now abandoned, and beyond the Sideshow Banner. On the Bally-ho platform, Shanghai's flames are licking the air; Vincent's voice rises above the masts of the tent and drifts off into the sky like a cloud. The flags of the Big Top snap violently, and Mariana spins like one of Shanghai's torches. How she wishes the fire could consume her. She imagines herself there, twirling between his fingers. She sees herself under his care day after day, being held in his hands, then dipped into a cool solution until it is time to erupt and spin from his hands into the sky but then to fall right back down to rest in his palms once again. She spins until she is so dizzy that she falls back to earth with a thud, the air forced out of her lungs violently, and she comes back into being.

She lies on the ground watching the clouds linger above her. She thinks back to the day in Czechoslovakia, in some unnamed town like all the other towns, when Jakub told her about America. He was unsure that closing down his circus and leaving Bohemia was the right thing to do. He asked her, begged her, to do a reading for him. "No, Jakub," she said, "you know that I cannot tell my own future."

"But Mariana, this is my future, not yours," he whispered. "Please?" he asked as he held out his hand.

"No, Jakub. Your future is my future. I cannot predict accurately. You know that I cannot. I could not see that our baby would die. I could not see that we would lose money in this circus. I cannot predict our future."

But Jakub would not give up. He got down on one knee and held her hands, begging her, as his wife, to please look at his future. "Please, Mariana, please," and once again he turned up his palm and placed it in her hand. Offering it to her as a gift. Almost as an impulse, she traced the lines with her finger. It wasn't the lines that she read. It was the vibrations that rose out of his palm and into her fingertips, and those vibrations put her into a trance. The vibrations are what she feels when she does a reading. They travel like a bee in a hive, buzzing into different alcoves of her body, through her veins, into her kidneys, her lungs, her spleen, each chamber of her heart. The vibrations from Jakub went so deeply that she could feel his heartbeat in her own chest. That is when he spilled out the questions: "Will I be successful in America?" "Is this the right time to go back?" "Will I be prosperous?" "Will I be healthy?" "Will I be happy?"

When he asked these questions, Mariana felt his heart quicken with excitement, and she told him, without a doubt, "Yes, yes, yes. You will be prosperous, you will be healthy, you will be happy." She told him this because she could feel his desire and knew that the desire was so strong, he could not help but be happy and healthy and prosperous.

When he left her after that reading, the residue of his visit made her heart heavy. She still held inside traces of the excitement that he felt, but like opium coursing through her veins, it soon left her. All that remained were her own feelings about going to America. Darkness enveloped her heart and consumed her chest. She knew this day would come. She tried to prepare for it. He had talked about America since their marriage began, but she always hoped that he would let go of his dream. When she was younger, the idea of leaving the home country didn't worry her. But as she grew older, she became settled on the land. To go to America meant that she would have to leave the earth that connected her to her baby. She tried to stop it with the letter to Madam Zora, but that failed and, as the day of departure neared, she knew that she had no choice but to get on the ship. Her husband was going, and she would have to go with him. What else could she do?

And now this has happened: she has been stripped of her power as Jakub's wife. She wants to run, but her body has melted into the ground like a rock. She cannot move her calves, her thighs, her arms, her head. Her mind begins to spin. She needs to go back to the home country, even if she has to go alone. "I control my fate," she mumbles over and over as a mantra.

Her mind doesn't stop moving. She builds a scenario, then lets it go; she builds another, then releases it; she builds another. She writes the story in her head. The story of the Borsefsky Brothers Circus. How vulnerable they are: riding the rail, surrounded by wild animals, vicious animals that would rather escape than go through another show. She thinks of the elements: flood, tornado, fire. Shanghai's torches turning in the air, so close to a tent that would easily catch fire, trapping the anomalies inside. Or perhaps the troupers could all turn on each other. The family torn apart. All the rules, spoken and unspoken, broken. "Yes," she says out loud, her lips able to form the words as she gets stronger, "how enjoyable that would be."

Her body feels light again, and she is able to pull herself up. She has left an imprint in the dirt like an angel in the winter snow. She thinks of returning to Czechoslovakia, the ground that she calls home. And no matter how the story plays out, she knows in her heart that Jakub must return with her. It makes her angry that she must depend on him, but she is a woman, a Gypsy, and she needs him, possibly more than he needs her. They will travel the country as two. He can publicize her, and she can have control of their fate for once.

She looks down at the ring that winds its way up her middle finger and recalls how it came into her possession. When she was twelve years old, she became friends with the Romani king and queen of her tribe. The woman was named Lyuba and the man Nanosh. They had been married for fifty years, and they still showed signs of happiness with each other. Nanosh brought Lyuba small tokens every day like a flower or a ribbon, or he played a song for her on his violin. Lyuba spoke of Nanosh in a way that Mariana never heard her mother speak of her father. Her voice was soft and loving, and her eyes gazed at him like she was newly married.

Lyuba taught Mariana how to walk lucidly in dreams. She visited Mariana there, on that plane, and taught her how to cross from her own dreams and into another's. But Lyuba was ill. Every day she was growing weaker. One day, when Lyuba was lying in her bed, she told Mariana that Nanosh was out in the field gathering a mixture of poisonous foliage, enough for both of them to take. She said that she and Nanosh had lived their lives together and would end their lives together. Mariana cried. Lyuba lifted her hand and put it on top of Mariana's head. *"Shh, shh, shh,"* she tried to quiet Mariana's tears. "We will be táttipáni soon." As táttipáni, spirits, Lyuba and Nanosh could travel anywhere, having been freed from the earth. Mariana held Lyuba's hand and traced the line of the serpent ring as it circled up past the knuckle on Lyuba's middle finger. When Nanosh came back, Mariana left. She waited until after supper to return to their wagon. She found the couple barely breathing and still warm. She pulled the serpent ring off Lyuba's finger, kissed her hand, and left the couple there to enter méripen, death, peacefully.

The next morning, Lyuba and Nanosh, the Romani king and queen of the Kalderash tribe, were found dead. The queen's ring, which was to be passed on to her successor, had been stolen. There was an outpouring of grief in the tribe. Mariana overheard her mother talk about the ring and the powers that it held. "No one knows," her mother said, "how potent that ring is. Whoever took it will be múladi." Mariana worried about being haunted, as her mother predicted, until one night when Lyuba visited her in her dreams. She told Mariana to keep the ring. "Its powers will be revealed to you throughout your life," she said. It wasn't until Mariana left the tribe that she began to wear the ring that once belonged to the Romani queen.

Another strong wind blows up from the south, and a blast of dirt covers Mariana's imprint in the rich Iowa soil. She twists the serpent ring around her finger and feels the strength of the Romani queen course through her veins.

THE NEXT day, Mariana steps onto the stage inside the Sideshow Tent in Cedar Rapids, Iowa. An impatient crowd waits for her to do something spectacular as Vincent whispers, "This is how it's gonna go . . . " She half listens to him, and her mind drifts away to the homeland. Their circus was smaller and traveled village to village by wagon. But Jakub was in control then, and Mariana was in control of Jakub. She closes her eyes and thinks of the Czech countryside: the smell of dirt and flowers and smooth, silky grasses. She's sure it smells the same way here in America, but she can't seem to find the fragrance; she smells roasted nuts and popcorn, sweaty bodies, and camel shit. At night, she smells the coal that fuels the train and the vodka on Jakub's breath.

"Are you ready?" Vincent is talking to Mariana but looking at the audience as if sizing them up. Mariana nods hesitantly, for at that moment she sees the anomalies standing off in the wings, behind a curtain, peering out at her as if saying "We told you that you were no better than us." And in front of them all stands Shanghai, his arms hanging loosely at his sides, his gaze somewhere between encouraging and mocking. For the first time, Mariana is to put on a show for Shanghai. Her knees begin to quiver, and her pulse quickens.

"Ladies and gentlemen!" she flinches at the thundering of Vincent's voice so close to her head. She steps away from him and puts her finger in her right ear to keep the sound from hurting her eardrums. She gulps down the lump in her throat. *This can't be real,* she thinks to herself, but before she has time to acclimate to being center stage, Vincent pulls the fabric across Mariana's eyes. As he passes his hands in front of her face, she smells the sweat and dirt of his palms and the musty odor of his wrinkled suit. The room becomes blackness, and it feels as if her eyeballs are being pushed into her brain. An image comes into her mind, and she tries to push it out before it takes control. She sees herself as a little girl, bending before her uncle, and he forces her head between his legs and she takes him into her mouth, shutting her eyes so tightly that they ache.

"You, sir! Come up here." Vincent's voice brings her back to the present moment as he beckons someone from the crowd to join them on stage. She struggles to pull in a deep breath, then tries to gain control of her racing heart. The more she tries, the more labored her breathing becomes. She fears she will vanish before everyone's eyes. But when she thinks of Shanghai on the sidelines, it somehow comforts her. She is able to take one deep, slow breath and maintain control once again.

"I am going to have this gentleman put down a number between one and fifty on this slate board. Any number between one and fifty, and Mariana, the most famous fortune-teller in all of Czechoslovakia, will tell us all what number he writes down. Okay then, go ahead and write down any number between one and fifty." Vincent emphasizes each word, his voice creating a rhythm, and it hangs on the vowels. "Ooooooneee and fiiiifteeee! Now show it to the folks, but don't say a word."

Mariana knows that Vincent will try to give her some code to tell her what number is written on the slate. He described this system to her before she was blindfolded, but she didn't listen. Vincent, and all the anomalies, too, doubt that Mariana can actually read minds and tell fortunes. She knows that they sit somewhere between distrust and disbelief when it comes to her powers. They want to believe that she can do it, so they can actually hate her, but they don't quite believe so that they can distrust her.

Mariana doesn't break Vincent's code as he speaks, but she doesn't have to; she can see the number written on the slate board in her mind's eye: thirty-eight. "Mariana can't see through the blindfold, can you, Mariana?" She shakes her head no, but she can see everything clearly by her other senses. She knows that Vincent is waving his hand in front of her face because she feels the heat and smells that dirty sweat once again. She hears the audience laugh at this spectacle, and her blood boils.

"Now Mariana is going to tell us all what number this gentleman has written on the tablet. Mariana?"

She imagines herself standing here, in the Sideshow Tent, a shadow of the woman who was given the Romani queen's ring, as if she were some kind of half-wit, some kind of anomaly, some kind of freak of nature. She knows what she must do. "Twenty-one!" Mariana announces firmly, resolutely. The audience becomes silent.

Vincent laughs nervously. "Now, Mariana, think hard. There is a different number written on the slate board. Think, think of what the number might be." Mariana almost wished she knew what the code was, so that she could delight in how Vincent was struggling to tell her the number.

"Oh, yes, I see it clearly now." Mariana's accent is thick but clear. "The number is four!"

People start mumbling, and Vincent quickly moves on. "Today only, Mariana's fortune-telling booth will be open to you for just five cents! Five cents gets you a personal, PRIVATE session with the best fortune-teller in all of Czechoslovakia!" Vincent removes Mariana's blindfold and says, "What's wrong with you, old lady?" Mariana smiles and steps off the stage as Vincent introduces Judita.

Jakub is waiting for her at the bottom step. "Is there a problem, my dear?" his voice drips with sweetness, but Mariana doesn't melt for him anymore. She looks him dead in the eyes, then retreats behind the curtained area that has been set up in the corner. Jakub follows her.

"May I?" he removes his hat and motions to the chair opposite her. She does not respond, but he sits anyway. "Mariana, I know you are upset with this new arrangement, but . . . " He removes his hat and runs his fingers through his thick black hair. ". . . this is the way it has to be for now. Please, I need your cooperation."

"You know that I do not belong here. I do not."

"Yes, of course, you are right. You don't belong here. But I can't do anything about it this time. Bear with me, just for the rest of this season. We have three months left, and I know you are resilient enough to stick it out. If you show good profits, then I can convince Uncle Vladan that you are worthy of pulling in the crowds outside of the Sideshow Tent. Next season, things will be different. You'll see."

"No, they will not be different. I can feel it. This is the way it is going to be for me as long as we stay in America, with your uncle running the show."

"Don't you remember what you said to me? 'We will be prosperous here. We will have success.' Mariana, my dear," Jakub takes her hand, "you have never been wrong."

"I said that you will be prosperous. I never looked into my own heart that day." Mariana snaps her hand back from him.

"Well," he stands and puts his hat back on, his voice stern, "I see we are not getting anywhere. You are here, in the Sideshow Tent, and that is how it has to be right now. The anomalies fear you, so you don't have to worry about them coming near you. Please, try to do your best so that we get good receipts. If you don't, I can't guarantee anything to you."

Mariana glares at Jakub and stands to meet his eyes. "What, exactly, are you saying to me?"

Jakub's voice softens. "Mariana, please, I am trying to make a good life for us. Someday we will return to Czechoslovakia and make our own circus again. You know how I feel about you. I want you by my side." He leans into her, grabbing her hand and kissing her cheek. "Just bear with me," he whispers in her ear. But she hears the quiver in his voice. She feels his hand shake with fear. And for the first time, everything becomes clear to her. He speaks with love and tenderness, but the only emotion that drives him to be next to her is fear.

Her mind is set. She will give him something real to fear.

Inner Turmoil

tasha dreams that she is suspended above a large tub of water that is as pure blue as the ocean that Shanghai once described in a story. She has a body separate from Anna, complete—with two arms, two legs, two feet, one heartbeat. Anna drifts in the pool below on her back, her own body bobbing on top of the water as she looks up at her sister in delight. Atasha floats downward, slowly, slowly, twisting like a feather until she plops into the water. A gathering of people cheers its approval. A man pulls her out of the tub and throws her again into the air, where she is held like magic for several moments, and then she slowly drops once again. She takes a long ribbon out of her pocket, and it streams behind her like a rainbow-colored banner until the warm water envelops her completely. She breaks the surface and swims to the side where Shanghai greets her. He pulls her from the pool, and as both of her arms are wrapped fully around his shoulders, she feels the air pass from his mouth and move over her earlobe.

When Atasha wakes, the train is moving, and she hears Shanghai's breath in her ear, in and out. She closes her eyes and feels that Anna is in a deep sleep. She rubs Shanghai's back, feeling how his shoulder blade sticks out, and runs her fingertip over the flat muscle that is stretched like the skin between her and her sister. Shanghai shifts and sleepily pulls himself closer to her ear. His hand moves slowly down her body and over her abdomen where the skin is smooth and taut. Atasha told him how her sister had the lifeline to their mother and carries the scar from it. Atasha has no bellybutton, no wound from their birth, but it doesn't stop Shanghai from circling her abdomen with his soft hand. He draws his fingertips up her body and circles her right nipple with the back of his fingernail. She breathes in, and Shanghai puts his mouth over hers, catching her breath on the exhale.

He snuggles his face into the curve of her neck and leaves a trail of tiny kisses. His mouth wanders until he finds the pulse in her neck where he wraps his lips and feels the vibration of blood pounding through the artery. He sucks lightly, then releases his lips from her neck. He pulls himself on top of her and smiles as he looks into Atasha's eyes. Anna stirs. Shanghai freezes, poised to dart into the darkness if necessary. "She is dreaming," Atasha reassures him. These past few nights, Shanghai has been touching her like this, but only this. And she wants him to keep touching, to keep kissing, to make her feel whole.

"Come to Prague with me," he whispers.

"What?"

"At the end of the season."

"You want me, us, to go to the old country with you?" He doesn't say anything; he just nods and smiles at her like a little boy. His grin is toothless and crooked. Atasha conjures up a life, there in the old country, with Shanghai and her sister. She sees herself walking hand in hand with Shanghai as they wander the streets of Prague, wearing their finest clothes. She would be a woman there. Not someone's little girl, not someone's charge. She would be grown up, living a life of her own, making her own decisions. And it would be a great adventure, to travel throughout the country. She imagines the cobblestone streets that her mother used to talk about and the village where her mother grew up— with castles on hills and vendors in the streets. "Tell me more," Atasha giggles as she whispers.

Shanghai slowly kisses his way down her neck, pauses, then looks at Anna. He breathes his words into her ear, "Jsi překrásná," "You are beautiful," and makes his way to her breasts, where he pulls her nipple into his mouth through the fabric of her nightgown.

★   ★   ★   ★   ★

ANNA'S LONG eyelashes flutter as she and Atasha fly through the air. They are like a feather falling out of the sky, drifting down, down, gently twirling from side to side. They plop into a pool of warm blue water. Jakub lifts them out, a smile crossing his face as he looks into Anna's eyes. He gently tosses the twins back toward the sky. A crowd of people cheers. Anna and Atasha ride a pocket of air as they begin to descend once again. Anna pulls a long, silky scarf out of their pocket, and it trails behind them like a flag. A spotlight lands on the twins, its warmth illuminating the fine silk costume they wear on their body.

Jakub pulls them out of the pool again, and the scene becomes a great wedding. She and Atasha are dressed in a silky white gown with a train so long that the clowns and midgets must walk behind them to keep it off the ground. Anna looks at the guests through her veil of lace. Her mother is sitting in the front row, surrounded by circus people. Anna is holding on to her father's arm. He is dressed in his finest suit, the one her mother made just for this occasion. Atasha is carrying a bouquet of flowers, much smaller than the bouquet that she herself is carrying.

They step up two tiny steps and onto a stage, where Jakub is waiting for them. He is dressed in a black tux with tails. He takes Anna's hand and kisses it. *"Jsi překrásná,"* he says. They turn to face the minister.

Anna hears a drum beating in the distance. Its thumping becomes louder and louder until she can feel it in her chest. She turns to face the audience and sees Shanghai standing to the side of her mother. He is holding a small drum, and he thumps it with a mallet. Anna turns back to face Jakub at the altar. The pounding drum soothes Anna at first, but then its beating becomes faster and she begins to feel dizzy. She and Jakub turn to the minister until the pounding becomes so consuming that Anna emerges from this dream.

As she wakens, the thumping continues. She first thinks that the drumming is the train rolling over the tracks, but she slowly realizes that the sound is Atasha's heartbeat. Anna wills her heavy eyelids open and feels Atasha squirming as her heart pounds rapidly. Anna almost calls out to her sister, who releases a soft moan from somewhere deep inside her chest, but Anna stops herself when she turns her head to see two small feet on either side of Atasha's neck.

Anna tries to comprehend the sensation she feels on the leg she shares with Atasha—soft hair grazing, tickling their inner thigh. She feels her pulse quicken with Atasha's, and a tingling rush rises up from her toes, into her calves, knees, thighs.

Anna squeezes her eyes shut as her own nipples harden. Atasha gasps. Anna lies still. Shanghai moans. Anna covers her left ear with her hand. Atasha sighs, "Yes." Anna knows what is going on. She heard these same sounds when they were little girls, before their mother became so ill. She and Atasha giggled about it then, when they were young. But now she feels the blood rushing through her sister's veins, pounding in her own ears. She tries to escape back in time to a place before she knew about such things. *Something happy, think of something happy.* Their mother teaching them how to cook a pie: *Roll out the dough, Atasha don't eat the dough. . . . Anna cut up the apples like this. . . . Be careful not to cut yourself . . . Won't Papa be happy to see how productive you are? Papa coming home from the fields, how she wanted him to pull them up above his head and throw them in the air like a proud papa, like she'd seen some of the fathers do with their children at church. How she wanted to be lovable, huggable, unbreakable. And when their papa mumbled something about "Why didn't you show them how to feed the chickens?" Anna began to cry, and Atasha said, "Don't cry, we have each other, for always and ever and ever."*

Atasha arches her back as her body shudders. Anna feels pain in her own gut, her stomach churning that evening's dinner. Atasha's heartbeat slows; her breathing evens out. Shanghai whispers something to Atasha as he moves off her body and curls up next to her. His fingertips graze Anna's shoulder, and she tries to lie perfectly still. Atasha giggles and says, *"Shhhh,* you'll wake her."

Atasha's childhood words dance in Anna's mind: " . . . we have each other for always and ever and ever, we have each other . . . "

Atasha was a liar.

Atasha is a liar.

★　　★　　★　　★　　★

IN THE morning, after the train has stopped at the edge of Des Moines, Anna wakes to Shanghai's touching once again. He caresses her sister's stomach and whispers into Atasha's ear. Anna can't hear what he's saying; she doesn't want to hear what he's saying.

In every fairy tale, in every story their mother told them, the two-headed fair maiden always found a prince—one man—who loved the two-headed maiden. One man who loved both. It was never like this— their mother never told a story of how one man would take the love of one twin away from the other. One man would come into their lives and change everything.

Anna keeps her eyes closed as Shanghai kisses Atasha. "The sun is coming up. I have to go." Atasha quietly begs him to stay, but Anna feels relieved as she hears him pick up his clothes and say, "No, no, no. I must go before everyone wakes." The lovers giggle through one last kiss. Anna feels Shanghai's hand on the top of her head briefly. Anna's muscles tighten.

This is not the prince they were supposed to have. Their mother never described a man with a swayed back, stunted arms and legs, stubby fists. She described a man who was tall and lean, charming and mysterious. Handsome with dark eyes, dark features. Someone more like Jakub.

Jakub could love both of them—Anna just knows that his heart is big enough for that. He wouldn't dream of coming between Anna and her sister. Anna closes her eyes and tries to imagine a real love with

Jakub. She imagines him touching her like Shanghai touched Atasha last night. She imagines caresses with soft hands. She imagines small kisses on her neck and shoulder, then she pictures Jakub kissing his way up Atasha's neck, placing a kiss on *her* lips. She imagines it so real that she sees herself sitting next to her sister as Jakub touches her hair, her body. She sees herself an outsider once again.

She opens her eyes and looks at the top of the wagon. Bolts hold sheets of metal together; her eyes follow the melded lines that the blacksmith created. She now realizes that she and Atasha could never share one lover. Their hearts could not hold the jealousy that would rise between them. There could never be one handsome prince between the two of them. It would surely be their death. Their mother was wrong.

"Anna, stop squirming." Atasha's voice is groggy and ragged.

Anna feels a flash of anger. *Stop squirming.* The words run through her head like an echo. *Stop squirming.* Is that what she should have said to Atasha last night as she carried on with Shanghai? Stop squirming, stop squirming, stop squirming. Doesn't her sister understand how their lives are changing? She twists against Atasha's skin even more.

"Anna!" Atasha comes further out of her sleep. "What's wrong with you?"

Anna can't think of how to answer her sister. She dreads the day. A day with no shows, a day they will spend with Shanghai—*she* will spend with Atasha and Shanghai. *She* will be the outsider. "I don't feel well," she snaps back. Atasha should know this. She should know exactly what Anna is thinking. She should know it as well as she knows herself.

"It's early. Go back to sleep."

Anna feels emptiness in her stomach, as if it is filled with only air and is expanding painfully. "I need to get up, Atasha." She wants to run away from here. She wants to get away from Shanghai and go back to something simpler. She wants to walk all the way back to the farm and sleep in the bed their father made for them. She wants to eat the food that her mother taught them to cook. She feels so far away from her sister now that she wants to bring Atasha back home.

Atasha whines, "Anna, it's early and I'm tired. Go to sleep now."

"Why are you tired?" Anna's words bite the air.

"What?"

"Nothing." Anna squirms some more. "My back hurts. I need to get up."

Atasha moans. Anna looks at the ceiling again—several sheets of metal, melted together, pounded by the blacksmith's hammer, molded, manipulated, bolted—and it seems as if it's closing down on her like the lid of a coffin. She tries to move, but the weight of her sister holds her down. Birds sing outside as the sun comes up. Anna tries to breathe in the scent of the tall grasses of the plains, but it's the hay on the floor of this wagon, and the metal of the roof, that she inhales.

"All right, all right." Atasha's voice is still groggy, "I'm getting up."

As Atasha pulls herself upright, Anna feels the tugging at her spine, and a pain crosses over her hip and goes all the way down into her thigh, her knee, and into her toes.

THAT AFTERNOON, in a field just outside the circus grounds, Anna looks at a single flower. It is just beyond Shanghai's left ear. *What is it?* Joe-pye weed? Rose mallow? Gaillardia? Atasha would know. She always knows the names of wildflowers. Anna looks at Atasha, but her eyes are locked on Shanghai. *What is it they're talking about?* Czechoslovakia? Bohemia? Home. Shanghai is talking about home. His home.

Anna looks back toward the flower. It seems so awkward, out in this field with no other flowers. Stranded. Its deep velvety red color screams out to be seen. A large bee hovers over the top of the flower; it circles, dips, comes up again, circles, dips, lands. The flower quivers from the weight of the bee.

"Wouldn't that be a good idea, Anna?" Atasha says.

Anna looks at Shanghai's face, then sees her sister out of the corner of her eye. They are looking at each other. They are including her only because she is there.

"What?" Anna snaps. She was content to watch the flower.

"Don't you think Shanghai's idea sounds good?"

"What idea?"

"Anna, haven't you been listening?" Atasha seems giddy. Anna's head aches. "He has the most amazing plan for us after this season is over."

"But," Anna feels an urgency to intervene, "we're going b-b-back to the farm after the season is over. To help Papa."

Atasha laughs. "Where did you get that idea?" Atasha speaks to Anna, but she is still looking at Shanghai. Shanghai shares a smile with Atasha. Anna thinks that he looks like an older man when he smiles; deep lines crease around his eyes. "No, Anna. Papa doesn't want us. Has he sent one word of Mother's death? Has he sent word that we are to return to Holdrege? We have to make other plans for our future."

"But what about Jakub?" Anna wishes she had been listening to the two of them come up with this idea they call a plan. She wishes she had been protesting this all along.

"Jakub?" Atasha giggles as she looks at Shanghai.

Anna looks back at the blood-red flower. Another bee is circling and dipping, circling and dipping. Anna speaks in English so that Shanghai cannot understand her. "Atasha, t-t-tell me what this plan is right now." Her voice is stern.

Shanghai looks from one twin to the other. Atasha begins speaking in Czech, but Anna stops her. "In English, Atasha!"

"What's wrong with you?" Atasha asks.

"You are making plans without me. That's what's wrong."

"But Anna, you've been here the whole time. You've been sitting right here while we've been discussing our future."

"Atasha, I don't want to be here with you and Shanghai!" Anna struggles to get the words to cross her lips. "I w-w-want to be with only you. I w-w-want to be home with you and P-P-Papa and M-M-Mama. I w-w-want everything to be like it used to be."

Shanghai stands and politely says, "I'm going to take a walk."

Atasha watches him walk toward the tree line, then turns to her sister. "Anna, things can never be like they used to. Mama's dead."

"What plans have you been m-m-making, Atasha?"

"They include you, Anna. Shanghai was talking about the wonderful circuses that travel throughout Czechoslovakia and Bohemia. Circuses much like this one. We would get to go to the old country, Anna. We would get to see the village that Mother grew up in. You'd like that, wouldn't you?"

"But maybe P-P-Papa has changed his mind now that M-M-Mother is gone. Maybe he's decided he needs us after all."

"Anna, Father has never wanted us. Not since the day he first laid eyes on us and found us joined like this. He can barely stand to look at us."

"That's not true!"

"Anna, Papa is the one who sent us here. Not Mama. Father wanted us out of his way."

Anna looks out at the little red flower and sees Shanghai bending down to it. "I don't want to go to the home country with Shanghai. I want to stay here. In my home. I want to see if Papa needs us. I want to write him a letter."

"And what if he says no, Anna? He will say no. How many times do you need to feel this way? To feel unwanted and unloved?"

Anna holds back her words. She wants to cry out, scream out, *I feel unwanted and unloved right now, Atasha. I feel so far away from you that we might as well be separated. We might as well live two different lives. I wish we were living two different lives. I wish you weren't my sister.* She holds back the words because she can't speak them without stumbling over each consonant, each syllable. She holds back the words because she has always been the one to keep the peace. Because her mother always called her my little angel. When Atasha threw tantrums, Anna remained calm. When Atasha talked back to their father, Anna said, "I love you, Papa." *My little angel,* her mother whispered at bedtime as if it were a secret between her and her mother. A secret she had without Atasha.

"What about Jakub?" Anna manages to say.

"Why do you keep bringing up Jakub?! What about him?"

Anna wants to say, *I love him,* but Atasha would find that silly. "Jakub takes care of us now. Don't we owe him something?"

"Anna, he doesn't own us. We work for him, but he doesn't own us. Shanghai told me so. We owe him nothing."

Anna squeezes her eyes shut. She doesn't want to talk anymore. She doesn't want to talk about going to Czechoslovakia, she doesn't want to argue about whether their father loves them, she doesn't want her sister to speak Shanghai's name again, she doesn't want Atasha to take Jakub away from her.

"We will ask Shanghai to write a letter to Papa for us tonight. You can ask him if he would like for us to come back to the farm. Okay?"

Anna opens her eyes and sees Shanghai pinching the stem of the red flower. It seems to droop in his hand; Anna can almost see the color bleeding out of it. He carries it in front of him, clasped in his stubby fist. He walks toward Atasha with a smile.

Anna tries to imagine life on the farm without their mother. She tries to imagine her father, coming in from the fields, sitting at the table with them, talking about his day. She tries to imagine going into town with him, shopping for supplies, going to church. She tries, but no matter what she does, she cannot imagine it, any of it.

For a moment, it all seems hopeless. She will have go to the old country with Shanghai and Atasha. She will have to do whatever they want, go wherever they want to go. But then she thinks of Jakub. He even said that they are his best act. Jakub. He wouldn't want to lose them, and she wants to stay with him. Anna knows that she must stop being the little angel. *There must be some way, just this once, for me to get what I want.*

Shanghai stands in front of the twins, holding that little red flower—

Anna's flower—and now, up close, she sees the little yellow trim around the edge of each petal. She watches as Shanghai gently tucks the stem behind Atasha's ear.

★　★　★　★　★

ANNA FEELS nervous as she and Atasha sit across from Shanghai at the Great Feast. She hates speaking aloud in a large gathering like this, but she knows she must do it. She looks at Jakub. His face is so strong. She enjoys the way his brown eyes scan the table from under his dark lashes. When his eyes fall on her, she looks down at her lap.

"Anna, what's wrong with you today?" Jakub asks as he passes potatoes in front of the twins.

She looks at Jakub and feels momentarily comforted by his smile. She shrugs and says, "Nothing."

"You're not eating enough. Here," he scoops a mound of mashed potatoes on her plate, "eat up. It will put a glow back on your pretty face."

Anna feels herself blush at Jakub's attention. She thanks him and forces herself to eat a few bites. She knows she must speak loudly. She must try to get those few words out without stumbling. She puts down her fork and dabs her mouth with the napkin.

"Shanghai," she almost yells out his name. Voices quiet around the table. Her voice starts to quiver. "Will you come over to write a letter to Father tonight?"

Atasha looks at Shanghai, then glares at her sister, a shocked look on her face.

"What's this about?" Jakub asks like a father. "You are writing a letter for the girls? After curfew?"

"Yes, I," Shanghai hesitates, "they want to write to their father about their mother's death."

Jakub looks suspiciously from Shanghai back to the twins. "Curfew is curfew, Shanghai."

"Yessir. You're right." Shanghai shrugs at Atasha.

As the conversations around the table pick up once again, Anna feels disappointed. Shanghai will still find a way to sneak over to their wagon. Anna tries to escape the thought of them, but it keeps coming back into her head. She feels Atasha's bliss: she feels it in the lightness of her body, in the rushing of her blood, in the tingling in her thighs.

Anna looks down at the napkin that she's twisting in her hand. Jakub puts his finger under her chin and raises her head to meet his eyes. "You haven't heard from your father since your mother's death, have you?" Anna shakes her head.

"No, Jakub," Atasha intercedes. "We haven't, and it seems very important to Anna for us to write this letter. Tonight seems to be our best opportunity. The sooner it is done the better."

Atasha, you're such a liar, Anna thinks.

"Yes, you're right, Atasha." Jakub takes a bite of food while he ponders the situation. "I'll tell you what. After dinner, we will go to my boxcar and write a letter to your father. As your custodian, it's only right that I should help you do this."

Anna's heart quickens.

"But Jakub, you're so busy," Atasha says, "we couldn't possibly take your time. Shanghai has helped us write letters before."

"Yes, all before curfew," Shanghai says quickly.

"No, no, no. I insist. This is very important to Anna."

Anna imagines telling Jakub of what happened last night between Atasha and Shanghai. She imagines the look of shock on his face, his disgust at the situation. But then she sees herself lying there, next to her moaning sister, Shanghai's hand unknowingly tangled in her own hair, being part of what happened. Jakub would feel disgust for her, too. *No, there's a better way to do this,* Anna thinks as she swirls the potatoes with her fork. She looks at Atasha and sees the anger in her eyes. Anna lifts a small amount of the lukewarm mush into her mouth.

✦　✦　✦　✦　✦

ANNA SITS on the settee, watching Jakub at his desk. He wears bifocals—she's never seen him wear bifocals before. It makes him look distinguished. All nervousness leaves her as she watches him take out paper from a stationery box. He dips the tip of his pen into ink and taps it lightly on the side. He looks over the rim of his glasses at her and smiles. He doesn't look at Atasha, and in this moment, Anna isn't even aware of Atasha's presence.

"Dear Papa," Anna pauses as Jakub swipes his hand over the clean page, as if dust is on the surface, then puts his hand to the page and begins to write. Anna imagines the fine cursive penmanship that Jakub must have: there must be curls and swirls twisting around each letter he puts on the page. Jakub looks up. Anna dictates to him, just like Atasha has done with Shanghai over these past months. She tells their father that they heard about their mother's death. She tells him that she misses home. She tells him that she is worried about what they will do during the winter months, when the circus does not travel.

She hopes for some response from Jakub, but he is focused on putting the words on the page. It is only when Anna stops talking that Jakub looks up. "What about you, Atasha? Do you have any words for your father?"

"No." Atasha's anger bites the air.

"No? Nothing at all to say?"

Atasha is quiet.

"I understand that you are in a predicament, girls." Jakub takes off his bifocals. He sits next to Anna on the settee. She likes the way he smells—like oranges and cigars. His knee touches hers, and he picks her hand up from her lap. She feels like a lady, the way her fingers rest delicately on his warm palm. "You don't know where you will go when the season is over. I'm not sure your father will want you back on the farm." He strokes Anna's hand and speaks softly. "I know that is hard to hear, Anna, but I believe it to be true. Your father, he . . . I've seen his kind before. He's a good man, yes? But he is a man incapable of taking care of such unique daughters. Listen to me, both of you. I want you to come to Fairbury this winter to stay with me."

Anna's heart pounds inside her chest. This is exactly what she wanted. She's so wrapped up in Jakub's eyes that she can't even look at her sister. She doesn't care what her sister feels at this very moment.

"Really?" Anna says.

"Yes, yes." Jakub laughs softly. "Of course. I wouldn't strand you."

As Jakub speaks, he looks directly into Anna's eyes. His focus on Atasha is brief and powerless. Anna is overcome by his sensitivity, his compassion. His words are so kind, so gentle. Anna feels how much he cares for them, for her. She leans forward, pulling Atasha with her, and places a kiss on Jakub's lips. She smells his sweet breath and feels the tiny stubble around his mouth. His lips don't welcome her at first, but then she feels them open up, and she leans into her first kiss even more. His tongue slips into her mouth, and runs along her teeth, along the roof of her mouth.

She doesn't know what Atasha is doing or thinking, and she doesn't care. She just wants to kiss Jakub. She just wants to feel him close to her. His hand rests on her thigh. Her tongue enters his mouth, touches his teeth, and she feels herself opening to his hand.

But his hand doesn't move any farther up her leg. His lips abandon hers. When she opens her eyes, Jakub is looking at Atasha. "I'm sorry," he says quickly to Atasha. "This is not right. I'm sorry." He looks at Anna. "Anna, no, I . . . I cannot do this. You two are like daughters to me. I . . . I was wrong. I'm sorry."

Anna grabs Jakub's hand as he stands, but he pulls his hand away from her. "Anna," he clears his throat, "Anna, this can never happen again."

"But Jakub . . . "

"No, Anna, this cannot happen again. I . . . I . . . " He struggles for words then blurts out, "I am a married man."

Anna knows that Jakub belongs to Mariana, but she's heard stories that he's cheated on her before. She knows that she could change him so that he would want to be true only to her because his heart would fill with love.

"Girls, despite what has happened today—which I trust will be just between us?—despite this, I do have a place for you in Fairbury. You will be well taken care of, and, of course, Mariana will be there with us. Understand, Anna?"

Anna looks down at her hands. She doesn't believe what Jakub says. She felt the way his mouth wanted her, how his hand caressed her leg.

Atasha says, "Yes, Jakub. We understand."

The door to the boxcar opens abruptly. Jakub moves quickly behind the desk, clearing his throat. "You two can go back to your wagon now."

Mariana stands in front of the twins and looks down at them. Anna swallows hard. Mariana's voice is even. "Girls? Please, Jakub and I have some business to discuss."

Jakub quickly picks up the letter that he has written for the girls, crumples it into a ball, then throws it away.

ANNA AND Atasha lie silently next to each other. It is dark outside their wagon, and they now hear that the Great Feast has diminished into a group of men drinking and laughing around a fire. Atasha hasn't spoken one word to Anna since they left Jakub's boxcar.

Anna hears the tapping on the glass of the wagon, then speaks quickly, "Remember, Atasha, we promised Jakub we wouldn't say *anything to anyone*." Anna doesn't want Shanghai to know about the kiss that she shared with Jakub. Atasha doesn't respond.

Atasha pulls Shanghai to her and leaves quick kisses all over his face.

Shanghai laughs. "I missed you so much," Atasha whispers.

"We've only been apart for a few hours." Atasha keeps kissing him. Anna clears her throat.

Shanghai pulls away from Atasha, looking embarrassed. "Did you get the letter written to your father, Anna?"

"No," Anna snaps back.

"What happened?"

Both of the girls are silent, then Atasha says, "Mariana walked in and asked us to leave. We didn't get the letter written."

"Not at all?"

"Jakub threw away what we had done."

"Anna? Do you want me to write the letter?"

"No. It doesn't matter. Papa hates us. Nothing matters."

"I'm sure your father doesn't hate you. Come on," Shanghai tries to pull the girls up, "you should write to your father."

"Shanghai, I'm tired," Atasha whines. "Let's wait."

Anna listens as Shanghai tries to convince Atasha to write the letter, but all she can think about is that one kiss. Forbidden and sweet.

"Come on, Atasha." Shanghai tugs at Atasha's arm. "Don't you want to tell your father how you feel about your mother's death?"

Anna decides not to protest the letter because she is convinced that their father won't want them anyway. Jakub even said so. And she knows that Atasha couldn't possibly get her way to go to Bohemia. Jakub wants them now. Shanghai lights a lantern and finds his pencil in his pocket. "Dear Papa," Anna begins, but Atasha stops her.

"No, the letter you dictated to Jakub was horrible. You never say things right, Anna. You never say things the way they should be said." Anna feels a flash of anger but quickly sinks inside her own body.

"Dear Father," Shanghai writes as Atasha speaks, "Mother's brother found us in Keokuk, Iowa, and told us the news of Mother's death. We are disappointed that you decided not to tell us in a letter yourself. While we know that we are on the move, you do have the address to the headquarters in Fairbury, Nebraska. You know that you could write us there and they would get the letter to us."

Shanghai motions for Atasha to stop speaking as he catches up on the writing. "*. . . nenapadlo na'm sem napsat.*" Shanghai motions for Atasha to continue.

"We are . . . ," Atasha thinks for a moment and looks at Anna, whose head is bowed, "we are deeply saddened by Mama's death. Words cannot describe the sorrow we carry."

Liar, Anna thinks. *You have been carrying on with Shanghai as if Mother were still alive. Liar, liar, liar.*

"We are turning our thoughts toward winter. We spend only two and a half months more on this journey through America, and then the circus goes to its winter quarters. We are unsure of our fate. At this time, we are asking for our independence from you."

"I want to stay with Jakub," Anna says in English so that Shanghai cannot comprehend.

"After what happened today? You want to stay with him?"

"Atasha. You're not supposed to tell."

"He can't understand English, Anna." Atasha starts dictating to Shanghai once again. "Our friend Shanghai has told us of European circuses. They operate much the same way as this circus, and Shanghai assures us that we will make good money in the home country."

"This is my home country," Anna snaps.

Atasha ignores her sister. "We will be able to travel through all of Czechoslovakia and even see the village where Mother was born."

"I do not want my name on this letter," Anna says firmly in English.

"Well, what do you want to do, Anna?" Atasha asks angrily. Shanghai stops writing and looks back and forth between the twins.

Anna grits her teeth. "I want to stay with Jakub."

"And Mariana?"

"Yes." Anna looks down. She knows that Jakub doesn't love Mariana. She can see it in his eyes.

"Fine, then we'll ask Papa if we can stay with Jakub." Atasha motions for Anna to tell Shanghai what to write. "Go ahead, tell him."

Anna's face turns red; Shanghai quickly looks down at the paper in his hand. Anna cannot speak when her sister pushes her like this. She tries to feel the words on her tongue, *Papa, I want to stay with Jakub,* but her tongue gets twisted again.

Atasha continues, "We would like to go to Europe for the winter with our friend Shanghai. We would need to save money from our last month's paychecks and would not be able to send you any. Most of the performers here are going to Europe this winter, so we would be among friends. We, of course, would send you any available money we would make in the homeland, and we promise to return for the circus season next year. Shanghai believes that we could find work in a museum in Prague, a museum much like the ones Barnum had here in America."

"I don't want to work in a museum in Prague," Anna says meekly in English.

"Anna!" Atasha quickly takes a deep breath and softens her voice. "Don't you want to see where Mama grew up?"

"We will see that?"

"Yes, won't we, Shanghai?"

Anna glares at Shanghai, the intruder on her life. Shanghai's eyes widen. Atasha repeats the questions in Czech. "Oh, yes," Shanghai says quickly. "Jesenice is a day ride from Prague."

Anna sneers, "This is a decision between my sister and me."

Shanghai looks shocked. "Anna," Atasha says, "weren't you awake the other night when Shanghai was telling me about the village? He went there in the spring when the flowers were in bloom and the air smelled of lilacs and bees were everywhere collecting honey."

"I must have been asleep when Sh-Sh-Shanghai told you this story." Anna shakes with anger. "What else have I missed while I was sleeping?"

Anna stares into her sister's eyes, and Atasha turns them downward. "We'll wait and see what Papa says. If he says yes, then you'll agree to go to Prague with Shanghai?"

Anna wants to laugh at Atasha and her ignorance. Instead she pretends that she is experiencing a headache and says, "I need to lie down now."

Anna falls back on the hay, and Atasha is dragged with her. "Father, we ask for your response soon," Atasha finishes the letter as Anna closes her eyes. Anna knows that their father would never allow them to go to Prague with a stranger. He would never trust them to anyone but Jakub. "We need to know what you think of the situation so that we can make our plans for the winter months. Your daughters, Atasha and Anna."

"I don't want my name on the letter!" Anna protests.

"All right, fine then. 'Your daughter, Atasha.'"

Anna hears Shanghai scribbling on the page madly, and when the scribbling stops, he whispers, "Is she asleep?"

Atasha nudges Anna, but Anna doesn't open her eyes, doesn't move. She hopes in her heart of hearts that what happened last night was just a mistake. That Atasha won't let it happen again. Especially now that she knows what it feels like to be on the outside. She hears rustling, then feels fingers graze the skin between them. It is Shanghai's hands touching her flesh as he touches her sister.

"Atasha," Shanghai whispers, "it seems that I'm coming between you and your sister."

"No, no, no. Shanghai, it's going to work out. We'll make it work out."

"But she is so unhappy."

"She's unhappy because of Jakub, not because of you."

"Jakub?"

Anna almost holds her breath. Atasha can't tell Shanghai what happened. She promised that she wouldn't.

"I think she loves him," whispers Atasha.

Anna wants to tell Atasha to shut up, but she can't fight anymore.

"Jakub?!?!? Atasha, you cannot let her get close to Jakub. He uses women. And he's married to the *jezibaba*. Jakub would never allow us to be together if Anna were with him. He just wouldn't allow it."

Anna feels a flash of hope. Of course, Jakub wouldn't want his lover to be sleeping with another lover. And Jakub is the manager of the circus.

"It's okay," Atasha whispers. "Jakub refuses to get involved with her."

Anna can't listen anymore. She can't listen to Atasha's lies about her, to Shanghai's lies about Jakub. She wants to find Jakub, to tell him that she loves him and that they can do anything together. He doesn't love Mariana. She knows that.

Before she realizes it, Shanghai has his hand under Atasha's nightshirt. Atasha starts to moan, then gasp. Anna tries to shut herself out so that she doesn't have to listen, so that she doesn't have to know what they are doing. She feels an ache deep inside herself, something she's never felt before, an emptiness, a hollow space. An eeriness. Like when the minister put them underwater at their baptism and she couldn't hear the "Praise Jesus'" and the "Hallelujahs," and when they broke the surface of the water, she couldn't hear her mother weeping with joy, her father saying a prayer out loud, her sister singing "What a Friend We Have in Jesus."

It is like all of that, but it goes deeper, like a sliver, and it sits inside her as a vacuum. It is different from the sorrow she felt when she was separated from her mother, from the grief that has been sitting in her chest since she heard of her mother's death. And then she knows it for the first time. *This is what it feels like,* she thinks, *this is what it feels like to be lonely.*

Sunday-Night Respite

Des Moines, Iowa
July 15, 1900

akub taps his pen on the desk as Mariana wraps thread around the tip of her finger until it turns blood red. She snaps the thread. *Tap, tap, tap.* Jakub dips his pen into the well. He hasn't written more than ten words in his logbook over the past hour.

Mariana waits in silence. She moves to the hem of the dress, pulls out more thread, snaps it from the spool, wets the end in her mouth, and threads the needle.

Tap, tap, tap.

She waits for him to tell the truth. Her jaw aches from clenching it. She pulls the needle through the fabric quickly as she looks at him, but he is lost in thought. Lost in guilt. She feels a sudden prick to her finger and jumps. She watches blood bead to the surface. In the early years, Jakub would have rushed to her side. He would have begged to see the tiny wound and pulled it to his mouth. Now, she holds the wound out for him.

Tap, tap, tap.

She feels like she will explode if Jakub doesn't stop that annoying tapping with his pen. She pulls the blood to her lips.

Tap, tap.

She wants to rip the pen from his hand, throw it across the room, and say, *I know what you do, Jakub. I know how you cheat and lie and drink. You are no better than my father. No better!* And now he has done something with the twins. She knows he has. He has chosen a

206

Sideshow act. An anomaly. *How much do you want to hurt me?* she wants to scream. *How much do you want to break my heart?*

Instead, she waits.

"Uh, my dear," Jakub's voice trembles. It is a sign of his guilt. She knows it well. He puts down his pen and rubs his hands together.

She looks at him, expressionless. Inside, she wants him to say it. *I'm sorry.* If he would only show some remorse, some sense of what he's done to her. *I'm sorry.* She would take it to encompass all of these years of hurt. Those two words would wipe out all of the infidelities, all of the drunken nights, even the way he's forgotten about their baby. *I'm sorry.*

"I think the twins need a new dress. They are quickly becoming young women, and the dress they have now is too . . . it is too . . . " She watches indignantly as he twists his hands around in the air. His nervousness gives him away. "Well, they need something new."

Mariana lowers her eyes. She rubs the wound with her thumb. Tiny waves of pain stab into her finger. "Yes, Jakub," she says softly.

"Yes?" His voice booms. Like a true showman. "Very well then. They shall have a new dress."

Which one is it, Jakub? Anna or Atasha? Or is it both of them? That's what she wants to say. But she returns to her hem. Jakub slaps the logbook shut, tucks a cigar in his coat pocket, and leaves Mariana in the boxcar. Alone.

Mariana does not cry about Jakub's affairs anymore, but as the day wears on, she becomes more determined than ever to take this circus down. To make Jakub fail, to find a way home. She spins out all the same scenarios—fire, animal escape, injury—but there's always a problem with each plan, a loophole that she knows Jakub will talk his way out of. Mariana thinks and dreams and schemes, and before she knows it, night falls and the boxcar is filled with the orange glow of a campfire. The men's voices are low at first—the men are not quite drunk yet. Mariana lies on her bed with a cold cloth on her forehead. She closes her eyes as she listens to Jakub's sober voice, deep and soft. Her thoughts take her back to the old days. The days when she and Jakub were happy, when he was proud to call her his wife. On her first day with the cirkus, the troupers were all gathered in a semicircle when her carriage arrived on the grounds. Mariana quivered when Jakub offered his hand to help her step into her new life. He introduced her to the gathering with glee, "This is my wife. Mariana!" She scanned the troupers' faces, white and fearful. "Yes, Mariana is my wife, and she will be an equal voice in the business. She is young, but she can see the future. She knows more than any of us ever could. I suggest that you treat her with respect." She saw the doubt on their faces. Jakub leaned into her and said, "Go ahead, my dear, show them what you know." He gave her a small nudge. She stepped forward and looked several troupers up and down. The silence made everyone uneasy. She stopped in front of Milada's mother, who leaned into her husband and pulled his hand tighter around her waist.

Mariana, then fourteen years old, stood only chest high with the woman and looked up into her eyes. She said plainly, "You will have a daughter."

The woman looked blankly at her husband. Mariana put her hand on the woman's flat belly and said, "You are pregnant."

"No," the woman said quickly, a puzzled look on her face, "no, I'm not."

Mariana smiled, said nothing, and understood for the first time how silence was powerful. Jakub put his arm around Mariana. "Congratulations! My children, you will find out soon enough that Helena is, indeed, pregnant. If Mariana says it is so, it is so!" Everyone doubted Mariana that day, but soon enough Helena began to grow, her belly expanding with Milada.

"You amaze me," Jakub whispered to her one night as his head rested on her chest. She stroked his dark, thick hair as he said, "You, my dear, are the best thing that has ever happened to me."

Outside, Jakub slurs his words as he yells a mocking call-to-order to the men gathered around the now blazing fire. Mariana picks out each voice as they speak: the Lion Tamer, the Elephant Trainer, the Strong

Man, Ladislav. Vincent's voice rises above all the rest, his acerbic breath tainting the atmosphere. He complains of the twins' egg-juggling crate and how the blacksmith has not done an adequate job on the making of it. "It's not safe," he whines, "picking that thing up every day. Look at this! I sliced my hand on the corner edge of it last night." The men sarcastically give him pity, and Vincent starts cursing the "bastard blacksmith," but his complaints fall on deaf ears.

Mariana misses Shanghai's thin voice mixing in with all the other voices, his words rolling around his mouth like music. Even though he looks at her with fear and loathing these days, she finds comfort in his stories, in the way the words fall from his lips, how the vowels swallow his tongue. She thinks of his mouth now and the way his thin lips speak the language of home. She closes her eyes and wishes she would hear his faint tapping on her door. She imagines him stepping into the soft light that fills the boxcar and asking her, "Madam, is something wrong?" Just as he did those weeks ago when he paid her a visit, he would say, "I am concerned." And she would not scare him away this time. She would not challenge him. Instead, she would ask him to sit with her. To be close to her. Perhaps, this time, he would tend to the wound on her finger.

The flames dance outside her window, and she watches the shadows float above her head, on the wall, the ceiling, over her body. She longs to see Shanghai's face, to watch his dance—just this would make the hurt feel better. When she opens the door, a blast of hot air washes over her. Jakub's face glows from the blaze, and he swings his arms around with a bottle in his left hand. Anger once again rises in her heart. Jakub could go anywhere on these grounds to have his drunken night with the other men, but he chooses to set up camp *right here*. Right in front of her boxcar. He shoves it in her face—how he has become like her father, how he has deceived her with the twins. She wants to spit into the men's fire. She imagines her saliva like gasoline, blasting the fire into the air. The men would fall back, their eyebrows and facial hair singed by the flames. But no, she won't give Jakub the satisfaction of knowing how much he hurts her. Instead she makes her way to the edge of the compound where the elephants are chained to trees. She breathes in and out until she feels her body fade away. This gives her peace. This gives her power.

She closes her eyes, leans her head back, and tunes into nature's sounds: small animals scurrying in the brush, grass rustling in the slight breeze, even the stars make a sound in Mariana's ears. She turns her right ear to the trees when a sudden wind picks up, then falls into a whisper. She tunes into something unusual: a woman crying, gasping, no . . . something else . . . moaning. She follows the sounds that rise and fall in the air. She steps beyond the elephants and past the workmen's cars; she pauses at the trouper car of the women and hears Judita inside talking softly to Gizela. The moaning starts again, and Mariana follows it to the glass-sided wagon of the Siamese Twins. *Jakub, you bastard,* she thinks as she peers through the glass, through the darkness. Although she just saw him at the campfire, she is sure she will find him now with the twins. Both twins lie on the floor, but the stronger twin is arching her back; her face appears to be twisted in pain. The other twin lies with her eyes fixed on the ceiling. Sweat, or maybe tears, roll down her face.

It is Atasha that is in the height of pleasure. He is making love to Atasha; Mariana knows it now. She follows the curve in Atasha's arched back and sees the twin's fist curled tightly in a shock of hair moving between her leg and the one she shares with her sister. Just when Mariana feels that she will pound on the glass and confront her husband for the first time in all these years, it is Shanghai's face that suddenly appears from the space between Atasha's legs.

Mariana steps back in shock. Shanghai pulls himself up and sits on his knees. He unbuttons his shirt. Mariana quickly turns away. She covers her mouth with both hands.

No, Shanghai, not you too, she gasps, releasing all the air from her body. She feels her breath pass through her fingers, and she knows she is visible once again. She stumbles backward on the uneven ground.

The rocks beneath her feet grind together in a hollow rumble. Her ankle twists, and she can't recover. She feels gravel slam into her elbow, the ground slap her face. She moans softly as the stinging on her face subsides. Her elbow burns as she looks back toward the glass where Atasha's moan rises over her head, where Shanghai lay with his lover.

She almost wants to laugh at her own foolishness, but she can't stop crying. *Why?* she whispers. She takes a deep breath, but the air won't go in; it only comes out in little bursts. She pushes herself off the ground, holding her elbow as she stands. The glass is in front of her, and her eyes take her inside the boxcar. *No!* She turns her head away from the glass before she witnesses any more. Atasha moans in ecstasy. Mariana holds the sound rising in her own throat as she runs back to her boxcar, getting away from this spectacle as fast as she can. Her speed causes the men's fire to move as if a big wind has blown up from the west. By the time Jakub turns toward the gust, Mariana has disappeared.

It is steaming hot in her car, but she is chilled. She examines her bruised elbow in the lantern light as she tries to assimilate what she has just seen. She scratches at the peeled skin and thinks again of Shanghai's head appearing between Atasha's and Anna's legs. She feels a pain deep in her abdomen that rises like vomit. Her body begins to shake. She takes a throw off the bed and wraps herself in it.

How could I have missed this? All this time and I didn't see it? She watched Shanghai everywhere—in the Big Top, at the show, in the pie car—but never once did she watch him with the twins. Why should she? They are joined together! They are freaks! *Is he pleasing both of them or just the one?* Rage boils her blood. She tries to comprehend the act of sex that she has just witnessed between the Siamese Twins and Shanghai, how the one twin lay completely still as the other arched and twisted. And how Shanghai's face was buried between the twins' legs. Couldn't the other twin feel it? Mariana shakes the thought out of her mind.

How did I let this happen? Shanghai started as a toy, an object to keep her entertained, but then these strange feelings took over her heart and

211

now she is left with this. This ridiculous pain in her chest, her elbow, her face, her body. Now she feels something much more familiar rise in her chest as she thinks of Shanghai having sex with the twins. She feels anger, and the anger snuffs out the weakness in her heart for Shanghai. She sits up and wipes the tears from her face. Why does she allow this weakness to attack her over and over again? She didn't intend to fall in love with anyone ever! Jakub was simply a way out of her family, but then she found herself drawn in by his big talk and grand ideas. And she did fall in love with him. Time and again she suffers for that love. And Shanghai . . . How did I allow myself to fall under his spell? Allow myself to have feelings for someone like him who is not even the right size, someone as powerless as that?

She spits onto the floor with each thought: Shanghai the freak, *plah,* Jakub's cheating, plah, Jakub's spinelessness, *plah,* coming to America, plah, moving into the Sideshow Tent, *plah, plah,* both Shanghai and Jakub having sex with a two-headed woman . . .

Once again her stomach churns. She takes in a deep breath to fuel the anger in her belly, and the anger begins to take over her thoughts. Her brain spins like a multicolored wheel on a parade wagon: red and yellow, yellow and red, red and yellow. *Enough is enough!* she says to herself. *It is time to go home . . . and Jakub is coming with me.* Her eyes are fixed on the boxcar window where she sees the embers from the fire outside float up into the air and drift away.

I know what I must do, she whispers into the air. *I know what I must do.*

Anna Dreams a Letter

July 18, 1900
Red Oak, Iowa

nside the Sideshow Tent, Mariana watches from her curtained area as the twins stand on the main stage, juggling eggs in their synchronized rhythm. When Shanghai steps onto the platform to join his new lovers, Mariana feels the anger rise within her heart. She clenches her fists as Shanghai stands on top of the finely crafted egg crate, the same one that Vincent complained of cutting his hand on, and juggles to the delight of the audience. *Show me, Shanghai. Show me what I should have seen all along.*

Shanghai throws an egg over Atasha's head so that the twins are juggling three, but then Anna drops her egg. Atasha stops. Someone laughs. Shanghai jumps off the crate and pulls out another egg. He throws it to Atasha, who gracefully catches it and throws it into the air without hesitation. As Shanghai throws the third egg into Atasha's hand, Anna again fumbles and drops the first egg, then the second. More people laugh. Mariana sees how Anna's body droops compared to the strong stance of her sister. Anna's face looks worn and beaten down. Shanghai picks up another egg and throws it to Atasha, whose confidence has not been shaken, but Anna drops it once again. Instead of trying one more time, Shanghai takes his leave, and the audience politely applauds as the twins juggle two eggs.

It is evident that there is strife between the two sisters, and Mariana knows for sure now that Anna is not part of the tryst. *But is she involved with Jakub?* Mariana considers telling Jakub outright of what she knows, but he would find some way to keep it from his uncle Vladan, and everything would remain the same. No, she needs something much bigger to take down the Borsefsky Brothers Circus so that they can go home and leave this all behind. Inside her curtained area, she paces like a lion in its cage; she steps twice and turns, steps and turns, pondering her prey. The plan Mariana has in mind challenges everything she knows and believes, but Shanghai and Jakub have pushed her and she feels confident that it must play out this way.

The Sideshow Tent empties, and the performance begins in the Big Top. Mariana peers out from the curtains to watch Atasha and Anna talk quietly between each other. Atasha's face is full of anger. Anna looks down to the ground in shame. When Shanghai approaches, Anna is silenced and Atasha giggles and flirts. It seems that Anna practically disappears when the two lovers begin talking in low voices, her body shrinking into her sister's, her head lowered and defeated.

Jakub's voice booms from the back of the Sideshow Tent, "How did we do today, my children?" Mariana jerks back as if she were about to be caught watching the lovers, then carefully leans forward to see Atasha and Shanghai pull away from each other. Jakub takes no notice of the exchange between the two. Everyone in the tent gives him a general answer of approval, then Jakub turns to the one in the know, "Vincent?"

"Yessir. Things went well tonight. Atasha and Anna pulled in even more people during the evening show, but they had a few problems with their act."

"A few problems?" Jakub looks toward the twins. "Well, we all have our off nights, don't we, girls?" Anna raises her head, and, for a moment, her face pleads, but then she lowers her head again. Jakub smiles at her, then quickly looks back to Vincent. The interaction between Jakub and Anna was not what she expected. Mariana suddenly feels lost in her powers of perception. "And the rest," Jakub asks, "how did the rest do?"

"Mariana didn't fare well at all, sir." Mariana steps out of her curtained area and stares Vincent down. How dare he single her out in such a manner, how dare he break the unspoken rules? Jakub glances at Mariana, then quickly looks back to Vincent with disdain. Vincent nervously continues, "Well, sir, I'm sorry, but it's true. She had one, maybe two customers."

The Sideshow troupers become silent, and all that can be heard are the faint sounds of the band in the Big Top. Jakub grabs Vincent by the collar and drags him past Mariana and into her curtained-off area. "Listen here," Jakub's anger spills out from the curtains, "you do not talk like that in front of everyone else. This business is between myself and Mariana. Do you hear me? It is no business of the troupers, and not even you! Mariana is off-limits to your scrutiny. Do you understand?"

"Yessir," Vincent chokes out beneath Jakub's angry grip.

Vincent steps toward Mariana and says, "I'm sorry, miss," without looking into her eyes. Jakub clears his throat condescendingly. "Er . . . " Vincent glances toward her face, then quickly looks away. "I'm sorry, madam." Jakub nods at Mariana, and she nods back. She glares at every freak that is looking in her direction. Each one looks away as she stares them down, all except Shanghai. He looks right past her as if she didn't exist. Mariana smiles at him as a reflex, forgetting her anger, but he doesn't acknowledge her. It's as if she has become invisible again against her will. She looks down at her dark hands to see if she has disappeared and readjusts her serpent ring, which is slightly off center. She looks back to Shanghai, but he doesn't flinch, doesn't act as if Mariana were even present. He turns back to Atasha and whispers something.

It was his last chance, Mariana thinks, *his last chance to change my mind*. She didn't even realize how much she wanted that to happen, and now she feels disgust for herself, for her weakness. She was giving him more time, more time to prove himself to her, but he has failed. And she is ready.

MARIANA WAITS out the time in her boxcar. When the train begins to move at half-past midnight, she fights the weight of her eyelids by picking up her sewing. Her mother's voice echoes in her mind, telling her not to do what she is about to do. Mariana struggles to ignore that voice, telling herself that she will be protected and that the evil spirits won't surround her. She pleads her own case, as if talking to her mother, but her mother's voice is persistent. "No, Mariana," she says, "they are *bibaxt*. You will enter their bodies and never return."

I must do this, Mariana thinks. *They cannot hurt me any more than they already have.* Her mother's voice is silenced. The freaks have taken my baby; they have stripped me of my dignity and my power. There is nowhere to hide from their evil; I am surrounded by them.

After a long silence, she hears her mother's voice, soft and distant, "Do what you must do, my child, but be careful."

At one thirty, the train stops just outside of Omaha, and Mariana rests her head on her pillow. She lies in the bed and breathes in for ten seconds, then blows out for twenty. She churns the name in her mind. *Anna, Anna, Anna,* she whispers, *spirits protect me as I step out of my dreams.* Anna, Anna, *spirits protect me as I step out of my dreams.* Anna . . . Her voice trails off, and soon she is drifting through darkness.

She is wearing blue slippers, the ones she first wore when she came to the circus. Jakub bought them for her because she had no shoes. They were thin, so that, even though they hugged the skin on her feet, she felt as if she wore no shoes at all. Now, in this dream, her blue slippers glow like the brightest light of a firefly, illuminating her way.

In these slippers, her feet don't touch the ground, and she is drifting an inch above the high wire. She's somehow limited by its boundaries, and it takes her not through the Big Top, but above the circus compound. She is like a bird, looking down on the Menagerie Tent, the Sideshow Tent, the Big Top, all set up on a nameless piece of land in a nameless town; it is the circus she is tied to and nothing else.

She cannot find who she is looking for so she calls out, "Anna,

Anna," and her voice echoes as if she's in a cave. "Anna, Anna."

Bruno, the largest of the elephants, cries out, and Mariana is released from the high wire. A thick rope falls from the sky, so she wraps herself around it and drifts down to the ground. Bruno balances himself on a small box, his legs squeezed tightly beneath his massive body. It pains Mariana to watch him like this, but her attention is shifted by the persistence of his trunk pointing in the direction of the costume tent. Mariana nods to him, and he relaxes his trunk. He slowly turns himself around on the little stage, his large round feet squeezed together as he balances. Mariana yearns to take him out of his own recurring nightmare, but she has tried before, and the jungle is too far away for him to dream of anything else.

She steps into the costume tent to find Shanghai and Atasha intertwined on the dirt floor. She quickly turns away from the sight of this and focuses on the pile of costumes in the corner of the tent, where a small voice whimpers. She digs through boas and feathers, petticoats and colorful shirts, until she finds Anna at the bottom of the pile. Her body is curled up, her knees to her chest, her one arm wrapped around herself. Mariana pulls the last costume off Anna's head and shoulder, but Anna grabs it and holds on to it as if it is the only thing saving her.

Mariana restrains herself from asking Anna outright what it was that happened with Jakub. Instead, she whispers, mustering her most compassionate voice, "My dear, what is wrong?"

Anna looks up, her dull eyes circled with a ring of darkness. "It is Atasha, madam. She doesn't love me anymore."

Mariana forces out her sugar-coated voice: "Oh, my dear, it's not that she doesn't love you anymore. It's that she loves Shanghai in a different way. In a way that is suddenly more important to her than her love for you."

"But no love should be more important than that of sisters. Especially sisters connected as we are." Her sight is turned to the top of the costume tent. "And this, madam . . . It is . . . disgusting."

Mariana follows her gaze to find that Atasha and Shanghai are rising to the top, playfully dancing naked in midair as if showing off their love to Anna and Mariana. Mariana first sees Atasha's half-body dancing without her sister. If Mariana were in her physical body, she would vomit at the sight. She glances at Shanghai, then looks back toward Anna. And suddenly, she realizes what she just saw. *No. It cannot be!* She looks back at the dancing lovers and takes a closer look at Shanghai. Her eyes did not deceive her! Here, in Anna's mind—the only true witness to Atasha and Shanghai's love—she clearly sees that Shanghai has breasts. *A hermaphrodite?* Mariana thinks. Her eyes are fixed there, on Shanghai's chest, watching his small breasts bounce as he twirls in circles with Atasha. And when she finally comprehends what she is witnessing, she dares to look lower, expecting to see Shanghai's penis in contrast to his breasts. But no! There is no penis, only a triangle of hair, and, as he flips over, Mariana sees the folds of a woman between his legs. Mariana looks back at Anna in shock.

"It *is* wrong, isn't it, madam?" Anna says, looking down at the floor.

"My dear, you are dreaming. This . . . " Mariana feels confused. She usually visits the authentic mind at sleep, not the fantasy world of dreams. But these are the freaks; she doesn't know what to expect or where she might get lost.

"No, madam. This is real. I've seen Shanghai myself, when he lies with my sister. He is a girl." Anna starts to cry.

Mariana becomes weak. Her knees shake. She feels herself getting sucked into Anna's dream to the point that she will soon lose control. Just then, something pushes on her back like a gentle wave in the ocean. She looks around the tent. At the entrance she sees a slight movement, like the fluttering of a curtain in a summer breeze. She focuses on the motion and begins to make out the figure of the twins' dead mother. A protector. *No, Anna cannot have an ally.* Mariana's already too weak, shocked by the vision of Shanghai's femaleness. Mariana breathes in as much air as her lungs will hold and blows at the thin veil of a spirit. The figure rises and drifts out of the tent into the air. Mariana knows that their mother will be back, but she has bought herself a little time.

"Anna," Mariana whispers, "are you sure this is what you have seen?!" She looks again at Shanghai's small breasts, the triangle of hair between his legs, then she quickly turns away. Mariana must maintain control of her emotions.

Anna hides her face and sobs. "It *is* abnormal! Atasha tried to say it wasn't!"

"Shanghai is a woman." Mariana takes in the words and almost begins to cry herself. She must think quickly before the mother comes back. She looks again at the two women dancing above her, and she is sure that this is Anna's authentic mind now. This vision—it is too detailed, too real.

"Would you like my advice?" Mariana says quickly. Anna's gaze is fixed on the two women dancing above them. "Let me help you write a letter to your father."

"Our father? But Atasha wouldn't like that."

"Does Atasha really care about what you like or don't like right now?"

"She doesn't seem to."

"Your father and Jakub have an agreement. You are to be treated well, and there are to be no suitors unless your father approves first. Did your father approve *this*?" Mariana feels her anger rise, and she tries to calm herself.

"No. No one knows about it." Anna looks shamed.

Mariana's voice is even. "Would your father approve of this?"

"No!" Anna motions for Mariana to bring her ear closer so that a secret can be shared. Mariana leans down and Anna whispers, "They are both women. It's not possible, what they're doing. Don't you agree?"

Mariana looks toward the couple, then back to Anna. "Yes, it *is* unnatural." She tries to maintain control. She must deal with her emotions outside of Anna's sleeping mind.

"Father would be furious."

"And do you want this to stop?" Mariana's voice rises again. *Control*, she thinks to herself, *control*.

Anna begins to cry. "Yes. I can't stand they way they twist and turn, and pull on my body while they're at it. I want to vomit when they are together."

"Then write a letter to your father. Here, I will help you." Anna looks worried as she peers over Mariana's shoulder at her dancing sister. "Don't worry, she cannot hear you; she is too involved in herself and in Shanghai. Go on," Mariana tries to help her along. "'Dear Father . . .'"

"No!" Anna says strongly. "Atasha calls him 'Father.' I call him 'Papa.'" Her stutter is suddenly nonexistent.

"I'm sorry. 'Dear Papa . . .'"

Anna is reluctant. She tightly closes her lips and shakes her head no. Mariana says it again in a softer voice, "'Dear Papa . . .'"

"No! I cannot tell you anything. Atasha would not like it."

The mother's force tugs on Mariana again, trying to pull her away from Anna. Mariana resists at first, annoyed by the mother's persistence. But then she has a thought; she lets the mother pull her out of Anna's sight. Mariana feels herself getting weaker as they rise above the tent and out into the fields, and the twins' mother gains strength as they get farther from the circus grounds. Mariana knows she must make her move before the mother is too strong. The mother's image appears like a fog. Mariana reaches into the figure and pulls on it as if it were a sheet she was shaking out in the wind. She blows on the mother's spirit, and it once again leaves her there. She looks down and sees that her hands are now the mother's hands. She wears the woman's skin like a Sunday dress of the *gadje*.

She races back to the tent where Anna's dream continues to unfold. "Anna?" she calls out in the Mother's voice. "Anna?"

"Mama?" Anna whines as she looks around the tent, and then she sees the image of her mother standing in the entrance. "Mama!"

"Anna," Mariana drifts toward her and holds the girl's hand, "I see what is going on. I see you are not happy."

"Oh, Mama, it's been awful. See? Look how Atasha carries on with her. Mama, with a woman!"

"Oh, my dear, it breaks my heart." Mariana knows she has little time to wear the mother's skin, but she must have an answer. "Atasha with this woman and you with Jakub."

"You know about Jakub?"

Mariana tries to stay in control. "Yes, that you and Jakub have lain together."

"No, Mama, we haven't. We only kissed. Then Jakub said it must stop."

Jakub stopped it! In Mariana's moment of distraction, the mother's skin slips away from her. She quickly pulls it back before Anna notices. Her time is short. "You need to do it, Anna. You need to write a letter to your papa."

"But Mama, Atasha will see me write it. She will be there when I take it to Radovan to deliver. She will never let me send a letter to Papa."

"I will write it for you. I will get it to him for you. Just tell me. Tell me the letter."

Anna looks worried, her eyes dance around the mother's head, and then she looks into the mother's eyes as if it has all become clear to her. "'Dear Papa. I have some news for you.'" Anna stops suddenly, then looks at her mother. "Aren't you going to write this down?"

"I am taking it down it in my head. It will all work out, don't you worry. Go on."

"Dear Papa," Anna begins, and Mariana listens as the words pour from Anna's mouth and the mother's skin slowly peels away from Mariana's body until the dream is over.

221

MARIANA WAKES with a start. *She'chorne,* Mariana whispers in a gasp of air. *Homosexual.* She tries to catch her breath as she recalls the image of Shanghai's small breasts bouncing in midair. She begins to laugh at herself, thinking of the way she scrutinized that tuft of hair between his legs for any sign of his maleness. But there was none. She can't believe what she has seen. Could it really be true? But this was Anna's mind . . . this is what Anna knows. How could Anna possibly know of anything other than a man and a woman being together?

Mariana laughs in her disbelief, in her anger. Shanghai the storyteller has told his best story yet! She thinks now of the wide, curvy hips as she measured Shanghai for costumes. She had a moment of thinking how odd that was, but she knew that little people often had wider hips, so she dismissed it. *What else did I miss?* She thinks back on any of the signs, anything she could have caught. Milada! *Was Milada part of this conspiracy?!* Mariana churns this in her head and remembers seeing Milada that night long ago, outside of Prague, with her new lover. Yes, Mariana turned away before he was disrobed. And, yes, Milada *had* to know. Mariana has been deceived! She has been made a fool of not only by Shanghai but also by her only friend! How could Milada have lied to her?!

Last year when Shanghai joined the circus, Milada confided in Mariana of the love she felt for the dwarf. She often spoke of her regret for deceiving Zikmund by having an affair with her tiny lover. But never once did she confess that she was having an affair with a woman! That she was cheating on Zikmund with a homosexual! No, she never confided something as vile as that. But Mariana blames herself, too. She, the best fortune-teller in all of Europe, was blind to something as bold as this?!

She runs to her trunk and pulls out all of Milada's letters, looking for some indication, some sign that Milada knew. And what about Madam Zora?! She said it, that day that they took Shanghai from the brothel! Madam Zora said outright, "You know they may not be as understanding to your ways as I." That phrase has always stuck in Mariana's head, and now she knows why! She quickly tosses aside the letters and pulls out

Shanghai's diary. She scans the pages with her finger. "Here! Here!" she cries out in disbelief. She reads the passages that she should have seen. The passages that gave him away. Gave *HER* away! Mariana's voice rises as she reads each passage: " . . . the odd curves of my body; she will see beyond my stunted growth and find the truth!" Mariana slams the diary shut.

She laughs out loud at the ridiculousness of it all! And the laughter rolls around inside her like thunder, churning her rage with her hurt and her pain. Shanghai the Deceiver! She laughs again as she wipes the tears from her face. She swallows the vomit rising in her throat.

No! she says aloud. *You cannot have any more control!* She pulls herself together and focuses on the letter to the twins' father. This vileness, this deceit from Shanghai, will fuel her plan, she's sure of it. She reaches for the paper that she left by the bed and dips the pen into the ink, knowing that these words will come easily to her. She writes the letter in Czech, just as Anna spoke it to her. "Dear Papa. Something bad has happened, and I think you should know about it." Mariana scratches it out wildly, stumbling over the part about Shanghai's femaleness, but she gets it down. "Please help me, Papa. I don't know where else to turn. I cannot bear to have this go on any longer. Your loving daughter, Anna."

In Jakub's desk, Mariana finds the envelope that contains the weekly payment to the twins' father. She tears it open, slips the letter between two bills, and seals it into a new envelope. She tucks it in with Jakub's outgoing mail.

There is only one thing left to do. Mariana leans her head back and closes her eyes. The words spill from her lips in a fury; spit flies into the air like steam from the cauldron of an old witch's brew. The words bite and swirl, chew and spin. When she is finished, her hair is soaked with sweat, her body is exhausted, and the spell that she placed on Shanghai those months ago at sea has been released. He will feel it all now.

She feels satisfied, even justified, and her thoughts spin out all of the future possibilities of her final vengeance. And always, in the end, her mind returns to the homeland.

Purge

Plankinton, South Dakota
July 25, 1900

T he dream haunts her. Even one week later, Anna can't forget the Gypsy woman invading her dreams. Anna revealed her sister's secret to the woman, *but it was just a dream, she tells herself.*

Reality is plaguing her everyday life now. Here it is, the early morning hours, and there is Shanghai, once again curled next to Atasha's body. Anna glances over to see his head nestled next to Atasha's, his bare shoulder tucked under her arm. Anna does not want to see any more of his naked body than that, and she squeezes her eyes shut. Soon, he will kiss Atasha and leave this wagon before anyone knows he was ever here. It's the routine they have now, and it happens every morning—every night.

Every night as they make love, she lies still and tries to think of her mother, watching over her, protecting her. How vivid she came to her in that dream, her face soft, her thumb wiping away the tears, her warm hand cupping Anna's chin. But then her mother left—left her to face this dilemma alone. "Write a letter to your father," her mother said. But how can she do it without Atasha knowing? No, there must be another way to make this stop. She considers telling Jakub, but how does she do anything without her sister knowing, denying, shaming? And besides, she carries the shame of this just as much as Atasha because she is there with them every time they engage in such activities. What would Jakub think of her?

She fantasizes about blurting it out to everyone at the next Great

Feast. Telling them all how Shanghai is a woman and he/she sneaks into their wagon every night and makes love to Atasha, but Anna can't imagine the words escaping her lips. They are locked so deep inside her throat, and they are sinking into her chest, deeper and deeper. She cannot say it, cannot speak it, cannot even imagine what is going on right next to her night after night.

The words are buried so deeply that her body feels like lead, weighted to the ground and cemented to Atasha. Her head aches, not only from the discomfort of her body but also from the energy it takes to block all of this out of her mind. She imagines her mother smiling at her, talking softly to her, stroking her hair. She can almost hear her mother's voice as clearly as it was in the dream. *"Shhh, shhh.* Go to sleep now. Everything will be all right," her mother says as her fingertips brush through Anna's hair, pushing it back behind her ear. Anna closes her eyes. The circus grounds are quiet, and even the lions are still in these hours before daybreak. Anna focuses on her own breath and the way her own chest rises and falls. She is so aware of how different her body feels. She has sensation in her left arm and leg, she feels her own heartbeat, her own stomach, but the rest of her is dead. She cannot feel her connection to Atasha; she thankfully cannot feel any excitement when Shanghai makes love to her sister. There is a space between Anna and her sister now, a chasm, a dark tunnel. She tries to remember what it felt like to know her sister's thoughts and emotions. She tries to remember what it was like to hear her sister's heartbeat, gently drumming in her own ears. And as Anna falls into a deep sleep, she tries to dream herself whole again.

SHANGHAI WAKES to the feeling of blood between his legs, sticky and hot. As he pulls his trousers on, he looks at Atasha, peacefully asleep, her face relaxed into a dream. He knows the warmth of lying close to her breast, his arm wrapped around hers, her fingers caressing his forearm in those brief moments of waking. He yearns to return to sleep with her, but he has to stop the flow of blood. He leans over and gives her a kiss on the lips; she stirs, but keeps dreaming.

It is cool and misting outside, and steam rises from the ground. Before anyone is awake, Shanghai walks toward the costume tent where Mariana keeps a trunk full of rags for the female performers. He slows his pace as a memory floods his brain. Milada. He remembers how she took him by the hand and led him toward the trunk. She giggled, embarrassed, as she showed him the rags. He thanked her, and she told him to go into the woods to tie the rags between his legs. "Yes," he told her, "that will work." He remembers now that she was the one who taught him how to survive as a female traveling with the circus. She told him to take enough rags into the woods for the day and to bury the used ones. "Mariana stays up late and wakes early in the morning," she said, "so you must sneak in here and get the rags just before the break of day."

Yes, it was Milada. And now, without trying, he sees her clearly—standing on the trapeze bar, soaring toward him, and he yelled for her to be careful. She laughed and said, "Join me." Letting go of the ropes, she reached out her arms for him, then fell. He gasped, even cried out, but she caught the bar with her feet and swung away from him, laughing. And he laughed too. And they would sneak away—away from Zikmund, away from Jakub, away from Mariana—and make love in the Big Top, in the costume tent, in the woods at the edge of the grounds.

Suddenly, it's as if the blood coming from inside him has released every thought, and his body is completely remembering Milada. Every inch of her. Her hands—she liked to hold them up to his hands, their palms pressed together, her fingers spread out, his fingertips at the back of her knuckles. He remembers it all: the curves of her body, her disrobed body, and how he loved to look at her, walking toward him, the lamplight warm on her spine, illuminating her hair, her hips, her torso. And how she cried out as they made love, her yes soft in his ear. He remembers it all, and it fills his heart with longing, with sadness, with fear.

The blood trickles down his leg as he hurries into the nearby woods, and he can't stop the memories from coming. His chest tightens and his knees begin to shake. Before he can catch himself, he falls to the moist ground. He has no strength, no will, to push himself up; the smell of dirt fills his nostrils, and wet leaves stick to his face. His ribs rest uncomfortably on the root of a tree, but he can't seem to move his body. He soaks up the memories of Milada as quickly as the ground soaks up the light rain: walking across the Charles Bridge, seeing her first performance, whispers beneath the Big Top, a river of tears, hiding, sneaking, cheating. As day breaks, he clasps the rags in his hands and begins to cry. He can't stop himself, just as he can't stop the sharp pain that sits like sparking fire low beneath his belly. Just as he can't block the memory of seeing Milada for the last time at the train station, saying good-bye.

He curls up like a baby and shoves the rags between his legs. He is so lost in the memories that he doesn't realize how he drifts in and out of sleep. Present time slips away for he is suspended in the past with Milada. Hours later, he is awakened by the calliope, signaling the start of the circus parade. The rag between his legs is soaked with blood; his trousers are soaked with blood. He looks up through the canopy of trees and sees that the sun has finally come out, yet Shanghai feels nothing but darkness around himself. It is cold and damp in the shade. He shudders. Although he can't remember his dreams, he is sure that they were all about Milada because his heart has become so heavy with grief. He cries again as if the crying had never stopped before he drifted away in sleep.

He manages to pull himself off the ground and secures fresh rags between his legs. His trousers are ruined, but he puts them on so that he can get back to the circus. As he moves his body toward the clearing, he sees the empty grounds before him. There is no life around the Big Top or the Menagerie Tent. He hurriedly walks toward his sleeper car before anyone can see the stains on his trousers, but the flags on top of the Big Top snap in the wind and the stillness on the grounds causes him to panic. He looks toward the empty popcorn stands and the abandoned Bally-ho platform; the parade wagons are gone; there is no sound coming from the cookhouse tent; there are empty shackles on the ground where elephants are usually lined up. His thoughts spin out of control, and he wonders if Jakub and Mariana have discovered the truth. He takes deep breaths to calm himself as he pulls on new trousers and heads to the Sideshow Tent.

He tries not to allow the image of Jakub stealing the girls away, packing everyone up quickly, and leaving Shanghai behind. He fights the thought of Atasha saying that this wasn't the kind of man she wanted. His heart pounds in his chest. He can't stop the thoughts of Milada from coming—it's as if the *jezibaba* cast some new spell on him—and every word from Milada spins and twists its way into Atasha's mouth. As the circus parade comes back onto the grounds, he ducks behind the costume tent, relieved that he has not been left behind. But Milada keeps pulling him into the pain of his past, and he tries to convince himself that she has nothing to do with Atasha. She has nothing to do with the present. And while he is sure that Atasha knows the truth, he has not spoken the words to her. Suddenly he sees the words coming from Atasha's lips, "I don't know if I can do this anymore," the same words spoken by his ghost lover, and the pain from his back moves up through his spine and around his chest and into his spleen, and he feels an emptiness inside himself that no one can possibly fill.

"**IN A** land dark and dreary as a grave . . . Say it with me, Anna." Before they go onstage, Atasha tries to pull her sister out of her increasingly common bad mood, but Anna remains silent. "Grandfather

Knowitall had not been seen for many, many days . . . ," Atasha nudges the space that once had life but now feels numb, and Atasha can't decipher if there is anger or resentment or loathing coming from Anna, "for he had been under Jezibaba's spell . . . "

"Atasha, stop it!" Anna snaps, her voice loud enough for Gizela to turn her head.

"Okay, okay," Atasha tries to ease Anna back into silence.

While Vincent introduces Gizela, the twins remain quiet. Atasha doesn't care anymore—doesn't care about Anna's bad mood, her jealousy, her bottled-up emotions. Despite her sister's heaviness, Atasha feels light these days—giddy, happy, warm, independent.

She is so lost in herself that she doesn't see Jakub approach, doesn't feel his arm glide over the small of Anna's back. "Stand up straight, dear Anna," he says kindly, "or we will soon have to bill you as the hunchback twins!" Anna straightens her body, and Atasha feels pressure released from her own spine. Anna's bad posture is a burden she hasn't even been aware of. "Is everything okay, girls? Your show has been lacking enthusiasm of late." Jakub glances at Atasha, but focuses on Anna.

"Everything is wonderful, Jakub," Atasha says quickly. "We are very, very happy here. Isn't that right, Anna?" Anna looks up to meet Jakub's eyes, and Atasha sees her smile for the first time in a week—a shy, embarrassed smile that broadens when Jakub smiles back.

"Yes," Anna's voice is almost a whisper, "we are happy." Her smile disappears, and she looks down at the twisted handkerchief in her hand.

"Well," Jakub sounds unconvinced, "good. Then, let's see a good show out there today, shall we?"

"Yes, of course," Atasha says, pretending that they have given nothing but a good show of late.

"Yes." Anna's voice is small and without conviction.

Jakub takes Anna's hand, pats it, and says, "Good. I have faith in you girls." He winks at Anna, then walks away hurriedly.

Atasha is aware of the power Jakub has over her sister. "Let's have a good show today, Anna," Atasha says, "a show that Jakub can be proud of."

Anna snaps back, "And Shanghai, too?!"

Atasha says nothing at first, suddenly feeling shame for her love, shame for her happiness. She tries to understand the anger that Anna shows. Could her sister possibly know Shanghai's secret? Does she know about his small breasts? Does she know about the night that Atasha reached between his legs to touch his maleness, only to find her fingers tangled in hair? No. How could she know? She is only jealous that Atasha has found love and she hasn't. That the two-headed fair maiden's prince is a dwarf and not Jakub. *Anna is being selfish*, Atasha thinks.

"You could be happy for me." Atasha's words bite the air between them. As Vincent introduces the twins, Atasha turns her head to look into Anna's face. "I'm tired of this, Anna. You should be happy for me. Someone loves me. You should be happy."

Anna doesn't say anything at first, doesn't even act as if she heard her sister speak. But as they take their first step onto the stage, Anna says, "I'm someone who loves you."

The crowd applauds. Vincent brings out the crate, sets it behind Atasha, and shows off the conjoined twins, connected from shoulder to hip. The sisters. The freaks.

"**HOW IS** your back feeling today, Shanghai?" Jakub puts his hand firmly on Shanghai's shoulder. He is relieved that Jakub treats him as usual; Jakub doesn't know anything more today than he has ever known. "Make sure they have a good show today, *hmmm?*" Shanghai nods, takes a deep breath, and looks to the stage where the twins try to maintain juggling three eggs at once. The girls were so good just a month ago, but now Atasha hesitates before launching an egg into the air. He watches as Anna almost drops an egg. The twins' rhythm is off; their movements are slow. Everything seems off balance. He's noticed it before, but he didn't want to admit. He didn't want to believe that his love for Atasha was coming between the two sisters, that it was changing their relationship.

He forces himself to take one step up to the stage. The memory of Milada sits like a stone in his chest, like mud in his brain. It is a dull ache in his heart. His cramps have not improved, and he wants to lie down, close his eyes, and dream the pain away. His back aches in the dramatic curve at the base of his spine, and when he tries to stretch it out the pain only increases and shoots cramps into his femaleness.

Vincent urgently motions for Shanghai to come save the twins from their own stagnant performance. Shanghai digs deep within himself to find the enthusiasm to leap onto the stage and onto the crate. He towers only inches above Atasha, but he suddenly sees himself in the same game that he had with Milada: standing high off the ground with his lover, throwing his heart off the bridge. He closes his eyes and tries to focus. He holds up an egg, opens his eyes, then throws the egg to Atasha. Now Atasha juggles eggs, throwing one, two, three to Shanghai, Shanghai tossing them back; Atasha throws one, two, three to Anna, and Anna tosses them back. It is nothing spectacular. It is not the kind of act that Shanghai envisioned, but it is the best they can do now. Every time they perform, Shanghai tries to engage Anna. He throws an egg to her, but it takes her by surprise and sets her off rhythm. She drops one egg, then two, then three. Soon, the juggling continues between only Shanghai and Atasha while Anna's arm hangs limp at her side, her eyes cast downward.

Vincent runs up to the stage and asks for questions from the crowd. Shanghai doesn't look at Atasha as he exits. His thoughts are consumed with Milada's good-bye and how it started long before that day at the train station. For months, they had talked about going to America together. Zikmund was not coming along because Jakub could not use a Czech-speaking spieler in the American show. It was Shanghai's chance to be with Milada alone. They had planned and dreamed about the future, just the two of them.

He thinks of the night they lay peacefully together in the costume tent—weeks before the voyage to America. Shanghai looked at Milada, and Milada looked at their intertwined fingers when she told him, "I'm not going with you, Shanghai." He quickly sat up and looked down at her, her hair framing her head like a halo. "I can't . . . " she said, her hands shaking. "I can't go with you."

Shanghai was nearly speechless. "Why? Why not?"

"I can't . . . It's . . . it's complicated."

"What do you mean? Complicated how?" Shanghai was nearly begging.

"Complicated . . . " She thought for a moment, then the words spilled from her lips: "With Zikmund, with my father, with Mariana, with Jakub. With you . . . as you are." Sorrow came over him like a wave.

"Tell me, Milada." His tears fell onto her hair. "Tell me why. Just say it . . . "

She began to cry then, too. She cried so hard that she couldn't tell him. She could only shake her head and whisper, "It's complicated." He didn't know what questions to ask, what to say. His thoughts raced with the information, with the lack of information. He craved to hear a story, even a made-up one. A story about why this was complicated, how this came to be difficult. A romantic story of lovers who had everything, and everyone, against them. But Milada was not one to tell stories.

As he stands backstage, he swallows hard to choke down this memory. He looks around to get his bearings and sees that the *jezibaba* is peering out from behind the curtains. He looks her in the eyes, and she doesn't look away. He stares hard at her; a chill runs down his spine. The *jezibaba* smiles at him, a wicked smile that makes him shudder. She disappears behind the curtains, but they sway slowly back and forth as if telling him *She's still here, she's still watching, still lurking.*

The motion of the curtains stops, but he still feels the *jezibaba*'s presence. It hangs in the air like stale cigar smoke at the brothel. He can feel her eyes fixed on him, her black pupils burning into his brain. He understands now that there are so many ways he could lose Atasha. All these plans they've made for Prague. Will Atasha stay behind in the end because of the pain that he feels deep in his belly? Will she leave him because of those parts of him that are female? His knees shake as Atasha steps slowly down the stairs off the stage, pulling her sister along. He holds Atasha's hand to help her down from the bottom step. He wonders if she can feel him shaking. She looks at him, a smile on her face, but Milada used to smile too. Even when she was leaving him at the train station. Is Atasha trying to plot a way out? How easy would it be for her to use her sister as an excuse?

He feels the *jezibaba* behind him, he hears Milada's voice running wild through his thoughts, he sees Atasha smiling before him, he watches Anna look anywhere but at him, and all he wants to do right now is run. Run as fast and as far as he can before Atasha can leave him. He glances toward the *jezibaba*'s tent, then looks at Atasha and quickly says, "I cannot write a letter for you tonight."

"Why not?" Disappointment fills Atasha's voice.

Shanghai looks at Anna, who seems to have shut herself out of the conversation, her eyes following Jakub as he leaves the tent. Panic rises within Shanghai as he thinks, *What if Anna tells Jakub? How much does Anna know?* He needs to sort this out. He needs to see his relationship without Milada's memory lurking. "Jakub was asking about my back pain. I think it's best if I spend a few nights with the other men." He feels guilty for his lie to Atasha. But what if she is lying to him? "Just a few nights, okay?"

Shanghai wishes he could take Atasha away somewhere. Just her alone. He wishes they could run away, across the American countryside, into Mexico, or down to Brazil. He's heard stories of amazing circuses there. Atasha could learn the high wire. She could learn to love him as he is. They could be new people, without a past, without a memory.

Atasha squeezes his hand before she releases it. "Yes, of course. You're right. I know you're right." He leaves through the back of the tent, glancing at Atasha once more, seeing her smile before she is out of sight.

Milada's voice is clear in his head, and where he once had to conjure up the images of his former lover, they now saturate his brain without him even trying. He remembers how they met on a street in Prague and walked across the Charles Bridge. He went to see her perform. They made love that very night, and Shanghai instantly fell in love. Milada was always cautious. Cautious with her love for him, giving it only in small doses, then running off to be with Zikmund. "I'm used to him," she'd often say. "He's like an old comfortable shoe."

"Is it because I'm a woman?" Shanghai asked directly.

"No, Shanghai," Milada told him, holding his hand. "It's because he is a man." This made Shanghai furious, and he would walk away from Milada time and again. He would leave her for a few days, but then he would always come back. He would come back when she asked in her soft, sexy way, "Meet me in the Big Top?" and he would be there.

Now it makes him angry. Angry at her indecisiveness, at her ambiguity. Angry at her weakness for trying to make everyone happy. Everyone but him. And he feels angry at himself for his willingness to go along with her, to follow her whims. But there was something about her that made him feel different. In those moments when she called out to him, when she gave him a sideways glance, when she reached out for him from the trapeze . . . In those moments he felt larger than life. He felt wanted, loved, special.

"You go," she said. "Go to America with Jakub to work for the season. Then come back before winter sets in, and I will be here. Please, Shanghai, tell me you will come back."

"I don't understand . . . Why don't you just go to America with me and leave Zikmund behind?"

"I have to work things out for myself. Work things out with Zikmund.

I need you to come back in the fall, and then we can be together." She sat up and kissed his face, kissed his forehead, kissed the bridge of his nose. "Please, just do this for me, will you?" She whispered in his ear, "Don't ask me to explain."

He melted for her. "I will come back, Milada," he whispered, and she devoured the words as they came from his lips. The strength of her kisses wiped away any doubts he had, and he believed in her; he believed in each kiss; he trusted her completely. *What a fool!* he thinks now when he remembers how she came to the train station with Zikmund. She stood on the platform, her arm around his waist as the upcoming marriage was announced.

His heart aches at the memory. He goes into the woods to replace the rags between his legs before the evening show and soon finds himself running. Running over brush and rocks, running to release the anger held deep inside himself. He runs as hard and as long as he can, the rags falling loose from his waist and getting tangled between his legs and his pants. When he can't run anymore, he doubles over in pain, panting wildly. He closes his eyes and makes up a story, something to fill in the gaps of information that Milada wouldn't tell him. He imagines her father, his fist raised, demanding her to marry Zikmund. He imagines Jakub, agreeing with the father that it would be best for Milada. And Mariana, perhaps even putting a spell on Milada to push her toward Zikmund. Then he imagines Milada, making up lies, finding a way to get rid of *him*.

Shanghai goes to the beginning of the story and rehashes the conversation with Milada to find any hint of the lies she could have told. And he wonders, could Atasha be lying to him now? Could she be preparing to leave him, too? Just as Milada is not waiting for him in Prague, is Atasha not leaving her own country for his? Are these just things that women say when they don't know what to do with a man such as he? *No! No.* Shanghai tries to stop those thoughts from coming. *Atasha is not Milada.*

And then, like a show under the big tent, the pictures in his mind change quickly, and he recalls the day that Madam Zora made her grand appearance in the Big Top. He remembers how she had one of the whores tell Zikmund of the affair, and Shanghai ran to the Big Top to tell Milada that trouble was coming their way. And when he got to the Big Top, there was Madam Zora in the front row, watching it all with a smug look on her face. She destroyed his life with Milada. He remembers now the fight that he had with Zikmund in front of Milada, in front of her father, in front of a full-capacity tent. Yes, it was Madam Zora who started the trouble. After the spectacle of that, Jakub called Shanghai to his wagon.

As Shanghai sat there, his heart thumping wildly in his chest, he thought that Jakub knew he was a woman. But no, both Madam Zora and Milada held on to that secret. And now he doesn't know where there were lies or where there was truth. He doesn't know whose heart was full of evil or whose heart was full of love. And now, he wonders, what will stop Anna from telling Jakub the truth?

"I will not hold you accountable for what occurred today in the Big Top with Madam Zora." Jakub seemed to be choking down the laughter, but then he turned serious. "But we need to talk about your relationship with Milada. Shanghai, I do not have to tell you that Milada belongs to Zikmund. They are engaged. You need to step aside and let her be with her future husband." Shanghai protested, telling Jakub that Milada was in love with him and that Zikmund was in the way.

"Little one," Jakub was stern, "let it go. I have known Milada for many years, and I can tell you that she will only break your heart."

"No." Shanghai mocks himself now, for his own innocence. "No, I want to speak to Milada right now. Right here. We'll straighten this out."

Jakub laughed. "Shanghai, I am telling you, man to man, let it go." Jakub stood, but Shanghai didn't back down.

"We love each other, Jakub."

Jakub grinned. "Let it go, Shanghai."

Shanghai left the wagon and went to find Milada, but Radovan stopped him. "Where are you going?" That's when Shanghai saw them—Milada and Zikmund—kissing, out in the open for everyone to see. It was as if the whole scene was staged just for him.

"Milada!" Shanghai called out and she tried to pull away from the kiss, but Zikmund held his hand tight behind her head. Radovan nudged Shanghai away from the couple and toward the costume tent. "Why don't you go see Mariana? I hear she has a new outfit for you to try on."

Mariana, Radovan, Jakub, Zikmund, and Madam Zora. He's sure that they were all in it together. How they must have laughed at him that day at the train station when Milada and Zikmund announced that they would be married two weeks later.

Mariana. She was lurking just a while ago, behind the curtains, watching him. How are his thoughts getting so out of control? What has the *jezibaba* done to him?

He hears Milada whispering her last words to him, "This is the right thing to do." She held onto the window of the train car, and he leaned in to kiss her, his lips only grazing hers before she released her grip and returned to Zikmund's arm. *The right thing to do,* Shanghai thinks, *the right thing to do.* It was the right thing for Zikmund, for Jakub, for Radovan, for Mariana, but was it the right thing for Milada? Was it the right thing for Shanghai?

Now Shanghai falls to his knees and cries. And in the crying he tries to purge his love for Milada, the married woman, so that it doesn't take over his heart. He tries to make those feelings for her be just a tiny spot, a memory that sits next to the wound of seeing his mother for the last time. Milada and his mother, the women who left him—and Atasha, what will she be? Now all of these wounds seem to wrap themselves around the same pain, and he can't find his way out. He thinks of Milada, then his mother. And he tries to see if Atasha is any different. Milada at the train station; his mother a shadow in the doorway; Atasha holding his hand. Milada flying through the air; his mother brushing one hundred strokes through her hair; Atasha begging him to speak

237

words of legend and fable. Milada saying she couldn't go to America; his mother telling him a final story.

It was a story about a court fool—a court fool who was a dwarf. "The princess begged for the dwarf to perform for her and her alone," his mother said. "She was a beautiful young girl, with long legs and porcelain skin. The dwarf came in once a week to perform for her. He did forward flips and backward flips, somersaults, handstands. He danced and sang and made the princess laugh. At the end of his performance, the princess asked the dwarf to sit on her lap. He loved this attention. He loved how she combed his hair with her fingers, how she kissed his cheeks and nose. How she squeezed him so tight that it felt like she would never let go. The dwarf fell in love with her, and in that love he felt completely alive. But the princess thought of him as a doll, a toy that she could play with for a while and then cast aside. And when the dwarf heard that the princess had found a prince, his heart was broken." His mother pulled him onto her lap and held his head close to her chest. "You are special, Shanghai, but you will find people who will treat you like a doll. Don't become attached to those people, my little boy. You are special, but you need to find the person who will see that you are special in your heart."

It was his mother's good-bye story. It has always confused him as an adult, how his mother could tell that story and then leave him. Cast him aside like a doll. Just as Milada cast him aside. The story of his mother is so enmeshed with the story of Milada—and now combined with the suspicions or fabrications or truths about Atasha and her conjoined sister—that he feels like he is looking into a box of snakes, intertwined one around another, and he can't tell where one begins and one ends. He can't differentiate patterns from the head of one and the tail of another. If only he could reach his hand into these stories and pull them apart, separate them and let them exist without each other. He could put the reality over here, the fiction over here, the deceit over here, and perhaps he would be left with something to hold on to. He closes his eyes and tries not to think anymore. He is tired of filling in the gaps of all the stories of all the women who couldn't tell him anything. He's tired of feeling lost and abandoned. He's tired of the complications.

He sits up and wipes the tears from his face. He thinks of Atasha now. She is here, with him, and he still has a chance. He thinks of how she looks at him across the room, without shame, without fear. He thinks of the disappointment that shows on her face and sounds in her voice when they say good-bye. He thinks of how she makes him feel special. He wants to ask her to tell him the truth. He wants to know for sure that she isn't planning to leave him. And he realizes now that he wants to tell Atasha everything. He wants to tell her everything he can remember about Milada and the pain that sits in his chest. And in that telling, he can finally let go and begin a new story. A story without lies, without deceit. A story where he can begin to see himself as more than a freak, as more than a toy. A story where he tells her everything about himself.

He wants to speak the words to her: "I was born female, but I am a man, here in my heart." Only then will he know the truth that she holds in her heart.

ANNA FINDS herself daydreaming about Jakub more and more often. Even now, she can't take her eyes off of him as he stands on the other side of the cookhouse, giving direction to one of the workmen. He is like a juggler, too, keeping everything moving at once.

Sometimes she pictures herself in Mariana's place. She imagines being his wife, walking arm in arm with him. He walks proudly and says, "I'd like to introduce you to my wife, Anna," as he pats her hand. And when he helps her off the train car, he places his hand firmly beneath her elbow. She's seen how he whispers to Mariana behind the curtains, and sometimes she imagines herself behind those curtains, with him down on bended knee, professing his love for her.

She used to imagine how he would make love to her, and she wondered how that would feel, to have him inside her. But ever since Atasha and Shanghai began their indiscretion, she doesn't think about such things anymore. Now all the fantasies she has take place outside of the bedroom, outside of her new experience with sex. She concentrates only on the intimate words that would be exchanged between herself and Jakub.

Jakub leaves the cookhouse tent, and Anna looks down at her plate. She's barely eaten a thing, and Atasha has finished her food. Anna pushes the peas around on her plate, anticipating that Atasha will bark at her soon to hurry up and eat. But then Shanghai appears; his eyes are puffy and red.

"Atasha," he says desperately as he takes a seat next to her, "I need to talk to you."

Atasha twists toward him, and Anna feels pain in her ribs. She sighs, trying to release the pressure. Atasha's voice mimics the panic in Shanghai's, "What's wrong?"

"I need to know," he whispers, but Anna can still hear. "Are you planning to leave me?"

"What?" Anna is as shocked as Atasha at his question. But even more shocking to her is that Shanghai is nearly in tears. She's never seen a man cry before.

Shanghai holds Atasha's hand beneath the table, "Please, tell me the truth. Are you having second thoughts about being with me?"

"Shanghai, what's wrong with you?" Concern coats Atasha's voice.

"I was in the woods . . . I remember," he whispers as he looks around the tent. "I think the *jezibaba* lifted her spell, and now I can remember Milada. I remember it all. Everything that happened between us."

"Oh." Atasha squares herself to the table, and the pressure on Anna's ribs is released.

"I remember how we met and how hard our relationship was, what with Zikmund and Milada's father and Jakub and everyone being involved. And I remember how much it hurt. She told me, Atasha, that she was staying in Prague. I remember everything," Shanghai again looks around the tent to make sure no one is listening, that no one is watching. "And I need to know. Are you planning to stay in America alone, without me?"

Anna snaps, "What a ridiculous question to ask conjoined twins! We cannot be alone. Ever!" The words fly out of her mouth before she can stop them, as if someone else has taken over her thoughts. She immediately feels shame for herself.

"Shut up, Anna!" Atasha chastises, but Anna has already shut herself down. She puts her fork on the table and looks at her lap. She feels herself shrinking. She shuts out the frantic whispers between her sister and the dwarf. She isn't aware of time anymore. She simply blocks out words and sounds and emotions. When Atasha stands, she obligingly lifts her body and goes with them as they move the conversation to the steps of the Snake Charmer's wagon. It's automatic how her body follows her sister's will and she can't see anything in front of her or beside her, like she is moving through complete darkness in the middle of the night. When they sit on the stairs, her body sinks like a stone in a river. She goes underwater again, just like at her baptism, and she is alone. She hears fragments of the conversation between the lovers from time to time when she comes up for air. Atasha says, "Shanghai, I want to be with you. There is no place I would rather be. There is no one else I would rather be with."

Shanghai says, "Even with me, as I am?"

"Who are you, Shanghai? Tell me." Atasha kisses his palm.

"I cannot tell you," Shanghai cries.

"Yes, tell me, Shanghai. I know, so just tell me."

Shanghai whispers so softly into Atasha's ear that Anna can't make out a single word.

"Yes, Shanghai, yes. I will go to Prague with you at the end of the season." Atasha holds his hand, and Anna feels the darkness open up inside her now and fill her stomach and her chest as the words drift farther away. Shanghai speaks lovers' words and Atasha giggles as Anna keeps drifting, and now she can't even hear them anymore. This is how she's learned to cope with her life—with her sister's life. And as the lovers exchange discreet little kisses, her mind drifts into emptiness, and it is all black inside her brain as if she has disappeared into a land as dark and dreary as a grave.

Awake

Ansley, Nebraska
August 6, 1900

tasha sees their father first, standing at the back of the audience; his face is bright red, his brow furrowed. He holds up several pages and waves them above his head, then steps closer to the stage, pushing through the crowd. Atasha squints at the block printing on the paper clutched in his fist; the words are sloppy and childlike and look like they were written with a nondominant hand.

"Anna, look," Atasha says frantically.

"Papa," the word escapes Anna's lips on a breath, as if she has spoken it for the first time.

"What is that? A letter?" Atasha asks, but he is getting closer to the stage, and she knows that she will soon find out.

"Letter?" Anna says meekly. She starts to wobble, and Atasha tries to keep them balanced and upright.

"Anna, hold still." Anna's body rocks back and forth until her weight is too much for Atasha to handle. Anna falls, pulling them both to the floor. The thud of their bodies is followed by the thud of Vincent dropping their egg-juggling crate. He is suddenly above Atasha yelling "Get up! Get up now!" But Anna doesn't stir. Atasha hears a rush of footsteps on the stairs as the tent slowly fades to darkness, and Atasha knows that Anna has passed out because she herself now feels light-headed and dizzy. She cannot see Vincent, but she hears his voice drifting farther away, joined by their father, yelling "How dare you?"

243

His voice is like a far-away echo in a tunnel.

"Anna?" Atasha says in a whisper, but she feels herself fading, too, and soon the voices disappear in a point of light.

✦   ✦   ✦   ✦   ✦

WHEN ATASHA wakes, she and Anna are lying on the floor, bathed in a pocket of sunlight that streams through the small window of Jakub's boxcar. She still hears their father's voice off in the distance. She closes her eyes and opens them again, trying to focus on the sounds. "Anna?" she says, but again Anna doesn't answer.

"Your sister is still out," Mariana says. Atasha follows the voice to see the *jezibaba* sitting on the settee, watching over the girls.

The hair rises on the back of Atasha's neck. "What are you doing here?"

"I'm looking out for you. You and your sister passed out." Her voice is calm and matter-of-fact.

"Where's our father?"

"He is just outside, speaking with Jakub. He'll be with you soon. He very much wants to talk with you."

Atasha listens to their father's rant. "The Campbell Brothers want them, and for a good price. I want to take them right now, and you can't stop me! They are my daughters! Now get out of my way!" Jakub talks in a more subdued tone. Pleading. Negotiating.

"You told me that the men and women were separated, especially at night. And now this? You should have known that something as vile as this was going on here!" their father yells.

Atasha trembles at her father's anger. "What's all this about?" she demands of Mariana.

A smile slowly crosses Mariana's face. "You'll have to wait and see."

244

The *jezibaba*'s tone is cold and frightening. Atasha shakes herself violently, trying to wake her sister. She yells at Mariana, "Don't you have some smelling salts?"

"Radovan will bring some momentarily."

The voices again rise outside the boxcar. "Enough! Enough of your talking! This is inexcusable! I don't want to hear reasons. The Campbell Brothers want them, and I am taking them now!"

Jakub talks quickly: "As I recall, the Campbell Brothers are in Topeka right now. That's two days away. The season is nearly over. It seems like it would be much more financially prudent for you to let the twins finish their season here. I will give them $200 more a week; that will be $150 more for you. I will see to it that Shanghai will be near them only in the Sideshow Tent from here on out."

"This freak shouldn't be with them at all!" Their father's voice rises to a crescendo then lowers to an inaudible tone. Atasha flops around violently once again, like a dying fish, trying to rouse her sister. The *jezibaba* does nothing but sit and watch. Atasha stops shaking when Anna finally comes to with a moan, a whimper. Just as she does, Jakub and their father storm into the trailer, their faces looking down on Atasha.

"Are you well enough to stand?" Jakub asks tersely.

"Anna?" Atasha asks, but without giving Anna a chance to answer, Jakub and their father pull the twins to their feet. "Anna just woke!" Atasha yells. "Be careful!" Her father's grip tightens on her arm.

"Mariana, you can leave us now," Jakub shouts over the commotion.

"What?" Mariana sounds surprised.

"I said you can leave us now." Mariana doesn't move. "Mariana, please!" She frowns at Jakub but obeys him. She pauses briefly at the door and looks back at the twins.

Atasha fearlessly stares back at the *jezibaba* when she smiles wickedly at the twins. With her face turned toward Mariana, Atasha doesn't see her father's open hand coming her way; she only feels the sting as he slaps her left cheek. *"Je mě z tebe špatně,"* her father yells. *You disgust me*. Through the tears in Atasha's eyes, she sees that Mariana cringes at the slap, then leaves the car.

Atasha cries, her hand on her face where a red mark begins to appear. As their father raises his hand again, Jakub pulls him back. "Please, Mr. Shimerda, we're both upset, but this is not helping."

"You are not the father here!" he yells, his arms flying through the air. "I am their father!"

Radovan appears suddenly behind their father, grabbing him from behind and locking down his arms.

Jakub yells over the father's protests, "Radovan, take him outside while I have a word with the girls." Radovan is deceptively strong and manages to pull the father through the doorway as he curses Jakub and Atasha. The fear rises up in Atasha so that she cannot catch her breath; she tries to keep herself and her sister upright, but her knees are shaking. Anna begins to fall again, but Jakub catches her. "Atasha, come over to the settee," he barks as he puts his arm around Anna and eases her onto the couch.

"What's this all about?" Atasha demands, her voice shaking.

"That's what I would like to know." Jakub's angry words are directed at Atasha as he talks across Anna, putting his arm around her shoulder to keep her from falling into a dead faint. "We will talk in just a moment," he snaps. He pulls smelling salts out of his pocket and runs them under Anna's nose. She moans. "There, there," Jakub says to her, his voice soft like a caring father, "you're all right now." Atasha's heart quickens when Shanghai appears in the doorway of the boxcar.

"Ah! Shanghai," Jakub's voice is insincerely jovial. "Why don't you shut the door and join us?"

Shanghai approaches cautiously. "Sit, sit," Jakub says, motioning to Shanghai, who begins to sit on the chair across from the settee. "No, no, no," Jakub says, "on the floor, please."

"What?" Shanghai looks shocked.

"A chair is too good for you. On the floor, please." Shanghai obliges, all the while looking at Atasha, who feels the fear rise up from her feet.

"What's this all about?" Shanghai asks, leaning back on his hands, trying to muster a casual air.

"Are you all right?" Jakub whispers to Anna, and she shakes her head. He stands, "I do not appreciate a towner coming in here and telling me what is going on in my circus. Even if that towner is the parent of my performers."

"Just tell us what this is about," Shanghai demands, looking at Atasha.

Jakub moves in front of Atasha to block Shanghai's vision. "You are not talking right now!" he yells, pointing his finger at Shanghai. "You are listening, and you will listen with respect and patience!" Jakub begins to pace as he thinks, giving Shanghai the chance to look at Atasha inquisitively. She wants to tell him everything that she knows, but all she can do is shrug at him, unsure herself of what is taking place. Jakub becomes agitated and stands between the lovers again, his hands clenched behind his back. Atasha sees how he nervously twists his fingers, cracking the knuckles as he speaks. "It has come to my attention that you two have been involved in an affair." He turns to the twins. "Your father told me this. And how do you suppose he knows? *Hmmm*, Anna?" Atasha looks at Anna, who is gazing down at her lap, twisting the fabric of her dress between her fingers.

"Anna?" Atasha asks.

Jakub kneels down to Anna and holds her hand. "I only wish you would have come to me with this information. Despite anything that has happened, I am your guardian here. I should know what is going on." Anna nods her head and shamefully glances at Atasha, whose anger is rising above her own fear. Jakub turns his attention to Shanghai. "Now, do you have something you wish to tell me?"

"No." Shanghai does not meet Jakub's eyes.

"No? Well, that is very interesting. Perhaps Anna has lied in this letter to her father." Jakub pulls the paper from his pocket and unfolds it. "Have you lied in this letter, Anna?"

247

"You wrote a letter?" Atasha asks. She tries to comprehend when and how that could have happened.

"I, I . . . I only dreamed the letter."

"Well, here it is." Jakub waves three pages. "Let's see . . . Where is it?" he turns each page over, his eyes running side to side and up and down, trying to find the words. Atasha focuses on the handwriting, and it is, indeed, the childlike printing of her sister. "Ah! Here it is." Jakub's voice becomes dramatic and animated, punching the words like a showman. "'There's more, Papa, something so vile, I can barely write it down on this page. Shanghai, the dwarf that Atasha is involved with, is not a man. Shanghai is a woman, hiding her femaleness away from us by posing as a man. But I see her with Atasha, practically every night. She has small breasts. Oh, Papa, I'm so sorry I have to write this down, and may God forgive me for ever knowing these vile things, but they are true. And please understand that I am innocent in all of this.'"

Atasha wants to yell, *How dare you?* at her sister. *How dare you write to Father, telling him that I'm doing vile things, making it sound as if you and Jakub are innocent?* Instead, she feels Jakub's glare move back and forth between herself and Shanghai. She looks down at the floor of the boxcar, watching Jakub's agitated feet scuffle around. Then she can't stop herself. "Jakub. How could Anna write the letter? She can barely print, and she certainly can't write in Czech!"

"Enough, Atasha! Enough talking! It is clear that you two are sleeping together . . . I can see it in your faces!"

"But you kissed Anna!" Atasha whines.

Jakub glares at Atasha. He turns and walks away from her, pounding his fist on the wall. He suddenly whips around. "You cannot play this game, Atasha. You will lose, trust me." His voice softens slightly. "Shanghai, my old friend, do you wish to deny that you are involved with Atasha?"

Shanghai's voice is shaky, but defiant. "No, sir. I do not wish to deny it. I am in love with Atasha."

"Oh, I see. I see. And this business about being a woman? Is it true?"

Shanghai remains silent but never once looks away from Jakub.

Atasha is drawn even more to her lover now that the truth is revealed. She thinks of how he told her everything, just last week. How he came to her, desperate, and poured out his heart. "I am a woman, but I feel like a man," he told her. Atasha already knew this, before Shanghai told her. She knew that first night they were together, and it didn't matter. She was surprised at how it didn't matter. But Atasha didn't know that Anna knew the truth. And now, the betrayal she feels from her sister is almost more than she can bear. She tries to send a signal to her sister, to tell her how furious she is at this moment, but the bond between them feels paralyzed. She cannot feel anything from Anna; it is as if they have become two separate people.

"So, let me see here." Jakub rubs his chin. "How do we find out the truth of this situation? It seems to me that if you remove your shirt, that would be the best way. Tell me, Shanghai, would you like to remove your shirt here, for me? Or would you rather I call Mariana back and you can remove your shirt for her only?" Atasha's heart sinks.

Shanghai speaks in a monotone, "I would prefer, sir, not to remove my shirt at all."

"Uh huh. Well, you see, that is not an option at this point. Not unless you tell me the absolute truth."

"I have been telling you the truth."

"Well, then, if you are a man, you will have no problem taking off your shirt, right here. Will you?"

"I am very shy, sir. You know that."

"You don't seem to be so shy around Atasha, or Anna for that matter, since they are, after all, connected."

"I will not take off my shirt." Atasha admires Shanghai's bravery, but she can see how terrified he is just by looking in his eyes.

"Well, then, I have to assume that you are a woman, don't I?"

Shanghai's voice is cool. "You can assume what you wish."

Jakub stops for a moment, then his voice becomes controlled and edgy. "I will find out, Shanghai, one way or another, I will find out. In the meantime, you are to stay away from Anna and Atasha. And you," he looks back at the twins, "you will return to the bunk in the sleeper car. I'm sorry that it's uncomfortable for you, Anna, but I have no other choice now."

Anna nods, still looking down at her twisting fabric. "But Jakub . . . ," Atasha begins to beg. She can't believe this is happening. Jakub doesn't own them, Shanghai said so.

"No, Atasha! You cannot talk yourself out of this. Shanghai, you now have a curfew of nine p.m. You are to find Radovan immediately after the evening Big Top performance begins. He will ensure that you are locked in the Snake Charmer's wagon until morning. Girls, your curfew remains the same. You may go now."

"Do we get to see our father?" asks Anna, but that is the last thing that Atasha wants right now. She doesn't need their father's coldness. She would want to see him only to spit upon his feet.

Jakub kneels down and takes Anna's hand; his voice is soft. "Perhaps later. I need to know—do you both wish to remain here, or would you prefer to go to another circus?"

"We wish to remain here," Atasha says quickly.

Jakub glares at her briefly, then returns his attention back to Anna. He strokes her hand. "Anna?" Hope fills his voice.

"Yes, we wish to remain here."

That's when Atasha realizes what she must do. "We do want to see our father, Jakub," she announces quickly.

Jakub breathes a sigh of relief. "Very well, then. Let me have some time with your father first. I will try to convince him that you shall remain here, with our circus. Then I will tell him that you wish to see him." Jakub turns to Shanghai. "Get out of here, now. Go back to the sleeper car and gather your things." Atasha quickly looks at Shanghai before Jakub forces him out the door. She wants to yell to him, she wants to talk to him, to have some kind of interaction, but all she gets is a quick look as Jakub pushes him out into the dirt.

✦　　✦　　✦　　✦　　✦

ATASHA WAITS quietly for their father to join them in Jakub's boxcar. Every now and then, Anna sighs, but Atasha pays no attention to it. She cannot even look at her sister. The door swings open, and their father, dressed in his Sunday clothes, steps in. He towers over the girls; his face is tight, his eyes angry.

Atasha waits for him to break the silence. She waits to be spoken to, just like all the years when they were growing up. It's a habit she can't seem to break.

"This is . . . ," he begins, as spit flies from his mouth, "this is inconceivable!" He doesn't look at either twin as he talks.

"Did you get our l-l-letters, P-P-Papa?" Atasha is shocked that Anna speaks first. "The one about what we will do in the winter?"

"The ones the dwarf helped you write?" he chastises. Anna looks down in shame. "Well, you are certainly not going to Europe with that . . . that freak!" His arm flies over Atasha's head, but misses her by an inch. "Jakub will be taking care of you this winter in Fairbury. I will be in touch with him often to see that you are behaving. And he assures me that Shanghai, or whatever her name is, will be going back to Prague soon. Arrangements for her passage have already been made."

"Jakub is not any better, Father!" Atasha speaks quickly. "He and Anna have kissed! He has touched Anna. And he is a married man!"

Her father's face turns a deep red. His hand seems to move in slow motion as she watches it raise over her head, the back of his hand coming across her face, his knuckles burning on her skin. Anna jumps when contact is made. Atasha cups her hand over the stinging. "You are a disgrace! Now you're trying to drag your sister into it?! It is against God, what you have done! Do you understand?"

Atasha looks out the little window behind her father. She refuses to look down and she refuses to look at him. "Answer me!" he yells. He stands over the girls for a moment, then turns for the door.

"Papa!" Anna starts to cry. Atasha is sure that her sister wants to get up, but Atasha keeps them grounded.

Their father keeps his back to the girls. "Anna, you will stay with Jakub this winter. I cannot handle the two of you. That is obvious." Anna starts to cry. "Good-bye, girls." Their father doesn't once look back at them as he leaves.

Atasha waits to cry until her father is outside the boxcar. But unlike Anna, her tears are not for their father; her tears are for Shanghai.

✴   ✴   ✴   ✴   ✴

IT IS completely quiet inside the car where Anna and Atasha now sleep—as if everyone lies awake, looking into the same darkness that Anna has experienced for the past week. Not even Judita snores tonight. Gizela didn't say a word to either twin when they took over her bed. She obligingly took the top bunk.

Anna is crushed between the wall and Atasha, who seems immovable and takes up most of the bed. Anna cannot move her pillow so that she is comfortable. Her ribs ache. When she shifts position, her hip hurts. She tucks her arm behind her back, and her neck hurts. She asks her sister to move but gets no response.

After a long, painful silence, Atasha finally asks, "How did you write the letter, Anna? How did you write in Czech?"

Anna's heart quickens at the interaction with her sister as if she had been waiting for this her whole life. "I dreamed it, Atasha. I didn't write it."

Atasha sighs, angry and resigned. "Go to sleep, Anna." This dismissal becomes darkness and the darkness becomes silence and the silence becomes unbearable.

Anna tries to figure out how to make her sister understand. After seconds, minutes, hours, an eternity, Anna whispers, "It really was a dream." It feels as if everyone, and no one, is listening. "It was the *jezibaba*. She was in this dream, but then it was Mother. She helped me write the letter."

She describes her dream as best she can remember it, talking and talking and feeling that no one can hear her. She wonders if her lips are simply moving with no sound coming from her mouth. She clears her throat, then speaks in a louder voice and states again that it was just a dream. Gizela tells her to quiet down.

Jakub seems to be the only one who doesn't hold her responsible for all of this. Even their father is unhappy with both of them. He wouldn't even give her a hug before he left. She imagines one of his awkward, one-armed hugs. She imagines holding onto him, squeezing him with all her might, hoping that in that one moment, love would consume him. But she knows that he would break the hug before it seemed she could even feel it.

The train begins to move to a new destination, getting farther away from their father and from the farm. Every now and then, Anna cries for home. Her chest heaves, and she realizes that she cannot feel her sister, cannot hear her breathing. "Atasha?" she calls her name, but there's no response. She nudges the flesh between them but feels no movement. "Atasha," she says again quickly, but her sister is a dead weight at her side. She frantically shouts to the whole car, "Something's wrong! Something's wrong with Atasha! She's not moving! Help, please!"

Before anyone has time to respond, Atasha yells, "Anna! I'm fine! Go to sleep!"

Anna feels embarrassed and ashamed. She tries to release the tension of her body, focusing on her shoulders and arms, then her chest, torso, and legs. As she releases the hold on each muscle, she tries to forgive herself. Forgive herself for writing the letter in her dream, for making her father angry, for making Atasha angry. Jakub was the only one who treated her with kindness and forgiveness. He was so gentle with her when he took her hand in his, when he kneeled down in front of her and asked her to stay with him. How good that felt to be loved like that again. Happiness sneaks into her heart. She will spend the winter with Jakub. She imagines that he will have a house and that she and Atasha will live in it with him. But best of all, Shanghai will not be with them. He will be on his way back to Prague.

She feels safe now, and guilty satisfaction comes over her as she falls asleep with only her sister next to her. There will be no more nights spent with Shanghai.

* * * * *

SHANGHAI MINDLESSLY tugs at a piece of splintered wood below his hand as he sits in the locked Snake Charmer's wagon. Without a door open, the air is stagnant and suffocating. He has never been here without the twins. He will see Atasha now only from a distance. He won't be able to hold her, won't be able to feel her hand in his hair, nor will he be able to make her laugh or see her smile. Of all the anomalies accepted in this circus life, homosexuality is not one of them. It is a curse. A disease. A sickness.

A piece of wood from the planked floor comes off in his hand. He pushes it aside and picks at another splintered piece. He looks at his hands and tries to see any hint of the delicate fingers of a woman. But he has the hands of a man: his fingers are thick and strong, his palms are muscular, his nails are cut short. Even when he was a child, all he could see in himself were the features of a male being. It came from deep inside, and it was as clear to his mother as it was to himself.

She dressed him as a boy ever since he could remember. Before she left, she told him that he was to dress and behave as a boy long after she was gone. "You don't want to be like your mother. Do you understand?" He shook his head yes, but he didn't understand at all. He only understood that he felt like a boy, no matter what. He liked the boys' clothing that his mother made him wear, and, instead of dolls with button eyes, he asked his mother if he could play with wooden blocks. She often gleefully said, "You are my little boy, aren't you?" And she would tousle his hair. She taught him how to dress himself so that no one would see the truth after she was gone.

As he grew, he asked the women of the brothel to make baggy pants so that no one could see what he was missing. He wrapped his chest when his breasts developed. And then he understood his mother's plea. The more he looked and behaved as a boy, the less likely it was that Madam Zora would groom him for prostitution. But always, in his heart, he truly believed and felt that he was a boy. He still believes that he is male, even though his body denies that once a month.

He doesn't know what will happen to him now, and he doesn't really care. All he cares about is Atasha. He imagines her, lying peacefully in her bed, her lips gently creased into a smile. He closes his eyes and sees her. "Tell me a story," she whispers, and her eyes look into him, as if she can see right into his heart. As if she can see that part of him that is a man. The train begins moving, and he looks down at the splintered wood in his hand. He suddenly sees his only way out. He picks at the wood aggressively, trying to pull pieces out with both hands. He wouldn't need a very big hole to slip out of, and he has hours before the train stops. He pulls off two-inch strips at a time, digging his fingernails into the thick wood and tugging desperately, knowing that Atasha is waiting in the darkness for him.

Throughout his whole life he has loved only women. There was nothing he enjoyed more in his adolescence than the attention of the prostitutes. They would tease him and flirt with him, and he savored every minute of it. And when Madam Zora's attraction for him grew and she began to devour him with her eyes, he wanted nothing more than to share her bed. He played with her attraction like an experienced man. For a year, he toyed with her—stared at her, held back, flirted with her, became cool, kissed her—while he learned and mastered the game between men and women.

He held out until he couldn't stand it anymore, and when he and

Madam Zora made love that first time, she didn't seem at all surprised when she helped him strip. She was completely comfortable with his body. It was as if she were involved with the conspiracy from the beginning, and the secret was more exciting to her than anything she'd ever experienced in her life. She held on to the secret like a treasure, and it worked for her in so many ways because the advantages of Shanghai being male were present not only within the brothel. He also was able to conduct business for Madam Zora outside because the greater world saw him as male. He not only escaped the prostitution that his mother so feared for him but also lived his life in Prague as a free man.

Shanghai stands in the boxcar and stomps down on the splintered wood. He hears a crack, but the wood is still too thick. He stomps again and again and again. He looks around for anything that will help him free himself. But there is nothing in this boxcar except a bucket to urinate in. He sits on the floor once again and digs his aching fingernails into the wood. The wrap around his chest is burning hot, and he feels as if he will pass out from the heat in the wagon. He wants to rip off all his clothes and unwrap his chest, but he knows that is exactly what they want. They want him to reveal himself, and he will not fall into their trap.

In the darkness of the midnight hours, the train finally stops at their new location. He stomps on the splintered wood once again. One, two, three, four times. He bends down and pulls more of the dry, cracked wood away. His hands ache, but he won't give up. His heart races. He thinks only of Atasha and how surprised she will be when she sees him again.

Before he can get any farther, he hears keys in the lock of the door. He quickly covers the half-destroyed wood with hay and scatters to the other side of the wagon. When the door to the wagon opens, he sees the figure towering over him, a lion tamer's whip in the shadow's hand.

Shanghai's New Image

Ainsworth, Nebraska
August 7, 1900

he sound wakes her. Mariana shoots upright in bed, hearing it, like one of the animals is being tortured. A low, guttural scream—a whimper, a moan. It started in her dream. Her father was dragging her by the hair, and the sound was coming out of her own mouth, but when she woke, her mouth was closed and the scream continued. *It must be a camel,* she thinks. She runs to the door, wanting to stop the abuse on the animal. Only a camel could make that ungodly sound.

But she doesn't get any farther than the door. That's where Jakub meets her. "Everything is under control, my dear, no need to worry."

"But that noise . . . ," Mariana says desperately. She looks over his shoulder to see the workmen raising the Big Top.

"It's really not as bad as it sounds. Believe me, it is being overdramatized."

"Which of the camels is it?"

"Camel? No, no, dear, it is Shanghai. We are just teaching him, uh, her, a little lesson."

"Shanghai?!" Mariana can't imagine what they're doing to him to make him scream like that.

"Come, my dear, it's still dark out. Let's go to bed." Jakub takes off his shoes, lies in the bed, and motions for Mariana to join him. It is now quiet outside, and she suddenly finds herself craving to be close to Jakub. He puts his arm around her waist and lets out a relaxed moan.

"Go to sleep, my dear," he whispers in her ear. He smells like cigars, and she takes a deep breath to inhale his scent. The chirping of crickets outside comforts her, and she relaxes into the bed, into Jakub's arms. In her dream, she is with Jakub, and they are back in Bohemia. They are home again, and everything feels right as they walk through the streets of Prague.

But then the screaming starts again. She pulls the blanket over her ears and tries instead to focus on Jakub's snoring. She tosses and turns, and now when she slips closer into a dream, it gravitates toward evil. Her uncle is in every vision, smiling at her, telling her to relax. He tugs her away from the family, pulls her to the edge of the caravan, pushes her head into his lap, his grip firm on her hair. Mariana forces herself back to waking, only to slip away into the same nightmare over and over. The screams outside the tent burn in her ears and mix with her dreams. She wakes and dreams, wakes and dreams, and each waking makes her anxiety rise and surge until she can't contain it any longer. She can't stand the screaming.

She shakes Jakub until he wakes. "Did you rape him?" Mariana whispers, trying to control her voice so that it doesn't quiver.

"What?" Jakub whispers back.

Her throat aches. "I said, did you rape him?"

"Shanghai? No, no, dear God, what do you think I am?"

Mariana gulps hard. The scream stops for a moment, and the silence almost becomes worse than the screaming. Mariana knows the loneliness in that silence. Her shoulders tighten; her head feels as heavy as a bag of sand. She does not want the responsibility for something as vicious as this. "Did someone else rape him?"

"Rape her? Mariana, Shanghai is female. No! Now, stop this talk right now."

"What did you do then that would cause her to make such noise?"

"I told you, she is overdramatizing. Simply overdramatizing."

"What did you do?"

Jakub focuses his eyes on Mariana's, as if he were trying to see into her soul. "You've never had an interest in the anomalies before, so why are you starting now?" He begins to tease. "Did you develop a fondness for Shanghai on that ride over from the home country?"

Mariana feels the anger rush into her face. "Jakub! Whatever is being done to Shanghai must stop right now!"

Jakub becomes furious. "You want to know what's going on?" He jumps out of bed and pulls on his pants, yelling at Mariana. "Get up! Get some clothes on, and I will take you to Shanghai." He lights a lantern as she gets dressed, and they go out into the pitch-black night. He leads her to the animal cages, past the lions, the tigers, and the camels. As they approach the kennels, the poodles yelp wildly. Jakub leads Mariana to the end of the kennels, stacked up neatly on the ground, where one poodle cage sits alone. He casts his light on the kennel, and Mariana sees Shanghai, curled up with his feet cramped on the top of the kennel wall, his arms folded over the shirt lying across his chest. His wide eyes are filled with loathing, with anger. She recognizes the look on his face from her own childhood. She recognizes the shivering, not from cold, but from rage and fear. She's felt the terror, the shame, the helplessness. Mariana clutches Jakub's sleeve but keeps her eyes on Shanghai. "Get her out of there." Her tone is controlled, but she feels herself slipping toward rage.

"No." Jakub's eyes are fixed on Shanghai.

Mariana bends down to release the catch on the cage only to find that there is a padlock. Jakub pulls Mariana up. "What are you doing? We are teaching her a lesson."

"A lesson? Jakub, open your eyes! She has been violated, and I want her out of there now!"

"No, she has not been touched." Mariana hears the deceit in Jakub's protest. "I told Vincent to teach her that there are consequences for lying. He has locked her in the cage, which she deserves. You must agree that she needs to pay for her deceit."

"You let Vincent handle this?" She grips Jakub's arm, her fingernails digging into his skin. "Get her out of that cage right now!" Her rage burns into Jakub's eyes.

He backs away from her in fear; he suddenly sounds helpless. "Vincent has the key."

Mariana feels herself losing control. When this all began, she thought that Jakub would have to wire Vladan—that he would have to admit that things were going terribly wrong in the circus. She didn't think he would ever have it in his heart to do this, to violate Shanghai, the man turned woman, to lock him up. It makes her want to spit in Jakub's face. To slap him. To make him suffer in some similar fashion. She is near panic. "Get the key from him right now." Jakub takes the light and darts away without saying a word. In the darkness, Mariana crouches next to the cage. Shanghai labors in breathing; his voice bursts short, uncontrolled sounds with each breath. It stops only when he swallows, and then the grunting continues. It's not a cry, it's not a moan—it's the sound of fear. The sound of fury. Mariana forces out the words, "What did they do to you? Did they hurt you?"

"Vincent . . . ," Shanghai spits out, "he violated me." He starts to scream out that awful sound again and shakes the entire cage violently. When he stops, he clutches the bars of the cage. His voice is hoarse, but he talks loudly to Mariana. "All three of them—Jakub, Radovan, and Vincent—they tore off my shirt and my pants, and then they whipped me. They beat me until I passed out, then they dumped a bucket of water on me to wake me up. Then Jakub and Radovan left me here with him . . . Vincent . . . He, he stuck his fingers inside me, and he . . . " Shanghai cries in a way that is uncomfortably familiar to Mariana. It is a cry of anger and disgust, of terror and degradation. Mariana wipes a tear that sits as a drip from her chin. "I know, Shanghai," she tries to quiet him from telling any more, "I know." She reaches her fingers through the cage and touches his bare shoulder. He is startled and pulls away from her. Her body tenses, and she pulls her hand out of the cage. She stands, then crosses her arms over her chest to embrace herself, to keep herself from the cold. She tries to detach herself from this moment as she peers into darkness, waiting for Jakub to return.

✦　✦　✦　✦　✦

AS MARIANA sews the lace on the trim of a new dress, her head aches. She's had only a few hours of sleep since Shanghai was released, and that sleep was labored. Her heart fills with sorrow and regret for what happened to Shanghai. As much as she tries to fight it, she knows that she is responsible. She thought in her heart that Jakub would call Vladan. That Jakub would admit defeat. She didn't realize how he had changed since arriving in America.

Jakub shows no regret for what has happened. She felt disgust for him this morning as he spoke with joy, "Just imagine, we now have a female dwarf who throws fire! It's spectacular! Absolutely spectacular. The Bailey Brothers will be swimming in jealousy." She didn't realize that the man she was married to was now so heartless, so absent to the suffering of others. She wasn't aware of how blind she could be to matters involving her own heart.

And now, there will be no letter to Uncle Vladan to tell him that everything is falling apart. If anything, the receipts for the Sideshow will increase with Shanghai's new act as a woman. Vladan will beg Jakub to stay. Mariana can see the same vision as Jakub: people crowded around the stage to watch a dwarf woman throw fire around her head. They will gather despite the fact that Shanghai's act will have to be toned down, *ladylike*—that was the term Jakub used, *ladylike*. "I want you to make her into a beautiful woman, Mariana," that's what Jakub said. "Make her someone who attracts men's attention, despite her stature. Help her out with her hair, and definitely make her a suitable dress."

When Mariana left early this morning, she told Jakub that she couldn't wait to get started on Shanghai's dress, but the truth was that she couldn't bear to be around Jakub any longer. His good mood was shocking to her. As she sits in the costume tent, Mariana turns her attention back to the seam of satin and lace. "Shanghai?" she calls out, and Shanghai lifts himself off a mattress of fabric slowly, painfully. "Why don't you try this on and let me know how it feels." She notices bruises on Shanghai's arms and legs, finger-mark bruises, and Mariana diverts her eyes from their awful blue color. The screams she heard last night echo in her ears.

"Are you feeling all right today?" she asks, noticing that Shanghai's movements seem strained.

Shanghai doesn't respond, and he snaps the dress from her. His anger surprises her. Behind the dressing wall, she hears him moan as the fabric rustles in his hands. "Do you want me to put a salve on your back?" Mariana dreads the thought of doing such a thing, imagining how awful the whip marks must look, but she can't stand this level of suffering. Shanghai doesn't answer. When he comes out from behind the dressing wall, his face is locked in a grimace; he appears to be in excruciating pain. Mariana takes a deep breath, then stands back to study the dress. She is shocked at how awkward it looks as Shanghai stands before her. The dress hangs to the ground; the length is perfect. The ruffles in the bodice are exactly right. The seams all line up exactly where they should. The arm length fits right. The neckline is appropriately high, and there are no gaps between Shanghai's neck and the fabric. It makes his small breasts round and lifted; it shows off his wide hips. But still, it looks like Shanghai's head has been put onto someone else's body. "How does it feel?"

Shanghai glares at Mariana the same way he's done for the past year. She steps back and looks at the overall appearance again. It's perfect, but it looks awkward. "Does it feel all right?" she asks again, and when Shanghai doesn't respond, Mariana becomes angry, the silence stinging as much as any harsh words could. Does she deserve this treatment after getting him released from his prison last night? Does she deserve to be treated as the enemy? Any regret she felt minutes ago has melted away.

"Take the ponytail out of your hair," she says.

Shanghai complies, and his hair falls to his shoulders. She thinks that maybe a ribbon, or a bow, would help. But even the vision of that seems ridiculous.

"Am I expected to throw fire in this thing?" Shanghai's words are biting and sarcastic.

"Yes." Mariana doesn't appreciate Shanghai's tone. "What's wrong with it?"

"It is ridiculous."

Selfish, Mariana thinks. *Ungrateful and selfish.* "It is your dress. You will wear it. And you will figure out how to make it work with throwing fire." Mariana hears Jakub's voice coming from her own lips, and it makes her cringe.

"Why can't I just wear pants? I'll catch myself on fire wearing this."

"The canvas is being repainted right now, as we speak. Jakub has you appearing as a woman."

"Give me my other clothes back until showtime then." Shanghai's demanding tone makes Mariana seethe. It is the same tone he uses to call her *jezibaba* under his breath. She can feel his loathing, and it makes her turn inward. She thinks back to the stinging words Shanghai spoke to her on the ship, in the cabin, on those two nights that they were alone. Those nights when she let her heart melt for Shanghai, let her thoughts turn from her husband and into something abnormal—into feelings for a dwarf. And not only a dwarf but a dwarf who turned out to be a woman!

None of this matters now, though, as Shanghai stands before her, pulling the lacy collar away from his neck. "No, Jakub has taken your other clothes away. You are to dress as a woman at all times now, onstage and off."

Shanghai glares again at Mariana, then turns to leave; his dress twists between his legs, and the front gets caught under his feet. He nearly falls, but he catches himself and straightens the dress out.

"Lift it as you walk," Mariana says like a teacher.

He pulls the dress up enough to expose the tight black shoes with tiny heels under the skirts. Mariana thinks she hears Shanghai say, "I was right to never trust you," as he steps out into the burning sunlight.

263

✶   ✶   ✶   ✶   ✶

JAKUB CALLS Mariana out from her little fortune-telling tent. "I need you to come see Shanghai with me," he says as they make their way to the Bally-ho platform. "We need to see how the new costume works out." He puts his hand on her back and talks to her about how wonderful business will be for them. "Our circus will do very well with Shanghai appearing as a woman." *Our circus,* Mariana thinks, and the dread of seeing Shanghai is quickly replaced with hope. Jakub hasn't called it our circus since the day they left Prague. In that moment she feels content, important, an equal partner. Jakub has once again pulled her into the decision making. *Yes, this is the way it should be,* she thinks.

"Ladies and gentlemen, boys and girls," Vincent's voice is lyrical and smooth as he continues his introduction of Shanghai to the crowd. Mariana stands next to Jakub at the back of the audience, like discerning parents waiting for their child to perform. "Shanghai, the female fire-eating dwarf!" Vincent yells out. Shanghai steps onto the stage. The crowd gasps. Jakub starts cursing, his face turning bright red. He stomps out his cigar under his foot and storms off. In that moment, Mariana realizes Shanghai's brilliance. After reading all of those pages in his diary, she should have known that he would be up to something. She should have known that he was about to create a new story. Mariana is pleasantly stunned as she watches Shanghai spin his batons around his newly shaved head. He is nearly bald; only a fine stubble covers his smooth white cranium. His dress wisps around him, and he throws fire up, catches it, twirls it. From neck to toe, he looks like a dwarf woman, but his head, his face, is that of a man. The vision is so freakishly strange that the crowd can't focus on the fire that is being thrown. "Is that a man in a dress?" they mumble. "What kind of Sideshow is this anyway?" Men pull their wives and children away from the spectacle.

Mariana delights in how this is going to work to her benefit. Now that people are walking away from the Sideshow altogether, the receipts will be a disaster. Jakub will finally be forced to explain this to his uncle. Yes, he has managed to keep all of this chaos from Vladan, but now there is no hiding and Jakub will be sent back to the homeland, with his wife by his side.

Jakub yells something at Vincent, who, in turn, tries desperately to gain back the attention of the crowd: "That's right, folks, her hair was burned off by a baton just last week. It's a dangerous sport." But it is too late. Only a few people come back to watch. The rest are already petting the camels and feeding the elephants, waiting to take their seats in the big tent. And Shanghai, standing firmly in place with his new dress, throws batons around his head, a vengeful smile on his face.

★　　★　　★　　★　　★

BACKSTAGE AT the Sideshow Tent, Anna hears the anger in Jakub's voice as he warns the sisters, "If you don't perform well, you will be sent to the Campbell Brothers." Anna tries to smile at Jakub, to assure herself that his fury is not directed at her, but he doesn't look her way at all. "I will be watching your performance. Do not test me on this, Atasha." He leaves the twins without further explanation. Anna has never seen him so angry. She looks at Atasha, whose face is like stone. Anna tries to tap into Atasha's thoughts, but she feels nothing between them. The skin that connects her to her sister is numb, and she has no sensation in the leg they share. It feels like Atasha has claimed it as her own.

Atasha leads them onstage, walking forward as if Anna is not even attached. Anna tries to keep up but feels like she is about to take them backward down the stairs. Her own will has been overpowered by Atasha. She nearly gives up, resigns herself to failing, but then she sees Jakub's face off to the side of the stage. She sees his edginess in the deep-set lines on his forehead. She desperately wants to please him. She knows that she will have to compensate for Atasha somehow, but she doesn't know how to be the leader. She doesn't know how to be the one who comes through in the end.

Anna notices how thin the crowd is, with only a handful of people, all men, in attendance. No women, no children. "Atasha, what's going on?" she whispers, but Atasha doesn't answer. Vincent introduces the twins and sets their elaborate crate down a few feet behind Atasha. He pulls out two eggs from the crate and hands them to the twins. Anna waits for Atasha to begin their routine, and the crowd anxiously readjusts. There's a cough, a whisper—Jakub is staring the twins down. Anna nervously throws the egg up, and it lands on the other side of Atasha, its yolk bleeding onto the stage. Jakub storms up the steps and glares at Atasha. "You were in this together, weren't you?" he says.

"No," Anna says, thinking that he means the two of them.

Jakub ignores Anna and turns to the male audience. "The Borsefsky Brothers Circus Siamese Twins will only be taking questions today." He glares at Atasha once again before leaving the stage. Anna keeps her eyes on him until he takes his place in the crowd, his hat tucked beneath his arm.

The men in attendance call out the usual inquiries. "Do you share each other's feelings?"

"No." Atasha's sarcasm fills the space between the twins and the audience. "It barely feels like I even have a sister." Anna quivers at Atasha's anger.

"Does the other head talk?" one man yells.

"No!" Atasha snaps. "The other head doesn't talk. Doesn't think. I don't even think it feels."

Anna struggles to maintain her composure. She looks toward Jakub, who is signaling for her to speak. "I . . . " She forces the words out, her speech clumsy. "I d-d-do talk."

The men gasp. They look at each other uncomfortably until someone else calls out, "If one of you becomes ill, does the other become ill?"

Atasha says nothing, but Anna knows that Atasha is staring at her, waiting for her to respond. "We d-d-don't fall ill often, b-b-but yes, we get sick t-t-together."

"What happens when one of you falls in love?" a small but loud and determined voice calls from the back of the tent. Anna focuses on the little person in a dress with a gleaming white head.

★　★　★　★　★

SHANGHAI TUGS at the collar of his dress as sweat rolls beneath the lace trim. "What happens when one of you falls in love?" he yells out defiantly. He doesn't care about consequences or what Jakub might do to him, and he refuses to let anyone take away the love he and Atasha share. When he first saw her tonight, she looked defeated and worn. Now, as she looks at him, a smile fills her face. Jakub pushes his way through the crowd, his fists clenched at his sides. Shanghai looks up at Jakub's towering figure, but Shanghai doesn't move, doesn't even flinch. "Atasha is going back to Prague with me," he says sternly.

Jakub jerks Shanghai off the ground and starts for the exit of the tent. Shanghai kicks and grabs, scratches and struggles. "Let me go! You can't do this! You can't!" The dress snaps between each one of his kicks.

"I *can* do this, Shanghai. You have taken this far enough!" Jakub's voice booms. As Shanghai throws his arms wildly through the air, he manages to claw skin from Jakub's face. Jakub throws Shanghai to the ground, and the force knocks the wind out of him. As Jakub sits on top of him, holding his arms down into the dirt, Jakub yells, "Don't test me, Shanghai. You thought last night was bad? You haven't seen anything!"

Shanghai struggles, but his entire body is locked in place from Jakub's weight. "Do you think I'm afraid of you? I know you, Jakub. I know that you're all talk."

"You knew me man to man, little one. You are a woman! Now, you will be treated as such. Do you want to walk out of here with dignity, or do you want to make a spectacle of yourself?"

Shanghai spits in Jakub's face, and before Shanghai knows it, Jakub's fist flies. Shanghai feels the burn around his left eye.

"Hey mister!" an onlooker yells. "You can't treat a lady like that!" A few men attempt to pull Jakub off of Shanghai, but Jakub fights back, his arms flailing, his knees firmly planted as they straddle Shanghai.

"This is my business!" Jakub shouts. "Leave me alone!" The men manage to toss Jakub to the ground. "Hey, Rube!" he cries out, the signal to other troupers that he needs help.

As the men try to subdue Jakub and wrestle him to the ground, Shanghai wipes away the blood trickling from his nose. He sees Jakub lying on the ground, helpless, his arms and legs contained, and the rage that Shanghai has kept pushed down in his chest explodes outward. He runs to Jakub, who is now defenseless, and begins kicking, and with each kick he remembers one moment from the night before. *Hold him down,* Jakub ordered Vincent.

Shanghai kicks Jakub's hip and legs as he feels, once again, the memory of the pain of the whip cracking against his back, pain seared into his flesh.

Shanghai kicks Jakub's stomach, trying to get around his flailing hands. *Take care of him, Vincent.* Jakub threw the whip in Shanghai's face.

The men push Shanghai back and he tries to catch his breath, but he thinks of Vincent, ripping off his pants, forcing his fingers into his vagina. *How does it feel?* Vincent asked as he licked Shanghai's neck.

Shanghai pushes his way back toward Jakub, sees him yelling at the men, saying, "Do you know who I am?" And Shanghai hates him. Hates him more than anything in the world. He kicks Jakub's ribs, his stomach, his arms . . . Shanghai kicks and kicks and kicks, trying, just trying, to deplete the anger in his own heart.

✦   ✦   ✦   ✦   ✦

ANNA IS stunned as she watches the commotion at the back of the tent. Atasha yells out Shanghai's name so loudly that it rings in Anna's ear.

Mariana slides up next to Anna. She is strangely and uncomfortably close, and that closeness makes Anna feel uneasy. She and Atasha haven't trusted the Gypsy from the beginning. Anna glances at the *jezibaba* then back toward the commotion, then back at Atasha, who is still yelling out for Shanghai. Dizziness spins in her brain.

As she tries to maintain her balance, she feels ice-cold fingers squeeze her collarbone. Anna's heart jumps as she sees the *jezibaba* standing next to her. She jerks herself away from Mariana's grip, and the force of that movement throws Atasha off balance. The *jezibaba's* icicle fingers graze the back of Anna's neck as she tries to readjust their middle leg to regain balance. But Atasha is trying to move that leg, too, and they become even less composed. As they fall to the ground, Anna hears a crack, then Atasha moans. It's a low, soft moan that quickly turns to silence. The commotion offstage is so loud that Anna can't get anyone's attention. She watches Mariana's skirt as it moves away from them; she watches Vincent's feet run past them. And Anna can't feel Atasha at all. She doesn't know the pain Atasha felt as her skull cracked on the crate of eggs that Vincent placed on the stage. Anna doesn't even know that Atasha is unconscious, her head bleeding from a cut made by the sharp corner of the box. She only hears the now muffled sound of voices. She watches the sun peek in through the tiny bit of air that circles the pole at the top of the tent, its openness split apart by white rope.

The sun is directly above them, burning on Anna's face. She closes her eyes, but the brightness still fills her vision. She feels something warm in her hair, like warm water soaking in through the thick layers and settling on her scalp. It reminds her of home, her mother pulling the girls back over the sink and pouring warm water over their heads, gently massaging their scalps with raw eggs. It fills her chest with sadness. Her vision begins to fade; she opens her eyes to blackness, only blackness. She hears Atasha gasp and the yelling voices are farther and farther away, and then Anna closes her eyes and her leg and arm tingle. She tries to move, but she can't move, she can't see, she can't think. And then, just before she tries to shake herself awake, shake her sister awake, she slips away—slips away to the countryside, to the farm, to her mother. And then there is just nothing.

✷   ✷   ✷   ✷   ✷

ANNA TRIES to will her eyes open. She gets a glimpse of dark cherrywood before the weight of her lids forces her eyes shut again. Jakub's voice is across the room, soft and deep, along with another man's voice, one she doesn't recognize. She hears water dripping into a basin, someone wringing a cloth. Her eyelids are too heavy to force open. She tries to form Jakub's name with her lips but has no control over her mouth.

"I don't know. I can't tell you the extent of this," the unknown man says. "I don't know how much connection they have, but it must be profound from the looks of them. Keep the cold compress on the one's head. The cut is superficial, but the swelling indicates damage to her skull. I just don't know. I've seen worse than this. She may come out of it."

The man leaves, and Jakub curses him. "He calls himself a doctor?!" Mariana quiets him, pleads with him to wire the girls' father. Anna tries to speak her sister's name, but again her mouth won't form a word. She manages to moan and feels Jakub's hand grazing her forehead, stroking her hair.

"Anna," he whispers. She can feel his breath on her cheek. "Anna, wake up." She forces her eyes open enough to see his face briefly, his eyes inches from hers. She feels weak. Her eyes close again against her will. "It's okay. Rest now. The doctor said you'll be fine. Sleep now and we'll talk tomorrow."

She moans again, trying to tell him not to leave. She wants to feel the warmth of his hand, to smell the sweetness of his breath.

SHANGHAI SITS impatiently in the cookhouse with Radovan when Jakub enters, his face ablaze with rage. "I hope you know that this is all your fault, Shanghai," Jakub spits out as Radovan holds him back.

Shanghai ignores his impetuousness. "How is she?"

"How is *she?!* THEY, Shanghai. THEY. There are two of them. They are connected." Shanghai waits for the answer to his question. Jakub stares him down.

Shanghai stares back at him, fearless. His only desire is to talk to Atasha, to make sure that she is all right. The only image he holds is of Radovan bent over them, calling out for help. Shanghai saw only the bottom of Atasha's feet. "Can I see them?" Shanghai asks.

Jakub glares at him and tries to control his anger. "How dare you. How dare you ask that after all that has happened. No! You may not see them." He stands, and Radovan steps between Jakub and Shanghai, prepared to hold someone back.

Radovan asks, "Jakub, what do we do about the father, and Vladan? Do you want me to send telegrams?"

"No. No, there is no need to overreact. Everything will be fine. They will rest for the next few days in my boxcar with Mariana watching over them. We will go on as scheduled." Jakub rubs the stubble on his face as he thinks. He squints his eyes at Shanghai. "The Sideshow will be lacking without the twins and with Shanghai as she is." This is part

271

of Shanghai's new existence—to be talked about as if he weren't in the room.

"We could put her back in men's clothing and have the audience think she's a man."

"No!" Jakub yells. A smile fills his face as he looks directly into Shanghai's eyes, his voice becoming sly. "We will sell her in the blow-off. With that shaved head, we'll display her as a juggling hermaphrodite."

"I'm not a hermaphrodite," Shanghai yells. Radovan puts his hand over Shanghai's mouth and restrains his arms.

Jakub continues, "Dress her as a man. Have her juggle as a man. Then, at the end of her act, she removes her top only."

Shanghai feels his stomach twist; he tries to think of a way out—out of this situation, out of the circus, out of America. There are no more shows today, and tomorrow Atasha will be better. He has time to think this through. Time to ponder his escape with Atasha.

"Radovan, take her back to the Snake Charmer's wagon. I don't want to see her face." Jakub takes Radovan aside for a moment of whispering, and that's when Shanghai sees it. He quickly pulls the knife off the cookhouse table and tucks it into his sleeve, cupping the blade in his hand.

MARIANA PUTS the basin next to Atasha and brushes through her bloody, clumped hair with a wet cloth. Mariana tries to stay composed, but then she touches the blue crescent-shaped bruise that dips out from the girl's hairline and her hand begins to shake. She runs her fingers over Atasha's soft white skin, but the girl doesn't move, doesn't twitch. Anna moans. Mariana holds the matted, sticky mess of Atasha's hair in her left hand and gently pulls the twisted, dried pieces apart. She rubs the hair with the cloth, softening the blood, tugging on the strands, thinning out the clumps. Blood reddens her hand. She wrings the cloth into the basin, and the water turns to crimson. She soaks the cloth and works more aggressively; blood drips onto the pillow. Mariana quivers and chokes down the tears. She tries to rub the stain out of the white pillow, but the stain turns into a smear. She returns her focus to Atasha's hair, rubbing, brushing, cleaning. She tries to tell herself everything will be okay.

She throws the bloody water out into the darkness. The circus grounds are quiet. Crickets fill in the eerie silence. She turns back toward the twins, who lie on her bed. They are washed-out-pale. Anna moans again; Atasha remains silent, motionless. Mariana can't hold it anymore. She begins to cry as she pours fresh water into the basin. She wants Atasha to return to normal—to look as if she had never hit her head, as if the blood had never soaked into her hair. Mariana works over Atasha's hair again and again—brushing through it, wringing out the cloth, scrubbing gently—stopping only when she notices that blood has seeped into the lines of her hand. She dips her hand into the reddened, tepid water, but the stain will not leave her. She desperately calls out Atasha's name, but the girl doesn't move. It seems that she is lost so deeply in sleep that she may never become restless again.

Now Mariana can't seem to stop the tears. She places her stained hand on the girl's head and softly whispers regret into Atasha's ear.

SHANGHAI WAITS in the wagon, the blade clutched close to his chest, hoping with all his heart that Vincent won't pay him another visit. His jaw is clenched as tightly as his fist around the knife. *I won't let it happen again,* he vows. *Never again.*

The train starts to move and Shanghai relaxes his grip. He works quickly. He knows he has only the time of travel to make his escape.

Now that he knows he is safe, his mind is solely on Atasha. He begins chipping away at the splintered wood. He uses the blade to pierce, twist, pry, and crack. He strips down to his bloomers. Wood flies around his head in splinters, chips, and chunks. The train rattles, quivers, slows, and quickens seemingly to each of his movements.

He breaks through one tiny spot of the floor; the train jerks. It is a hole big enough for three of his fingers, but it gives him hope, and momentum. He works feverishly, knowing that he does it all for Atasha. Knowing that he must see her, must hold her in his arms once again.

The wood creaks and squeaks, as if it is crying with him. Sweat drips from his face, splinters pierce his hands, his fingernails begin to bleed. His arms and shoulders ache. None of this stops him. Wood particles stick to his bloomers. He kicks and stomps. It seems impossible, but he keeps working with the knife, his feet, his fingers. Wood gives way. The hole now seems just big enough, just painfully big enough. He waits for the train to stop moving, then puts his dress around the sharpest edges of the hole and forces his body through a space slightly bigger than his mother's womb.

Falling

hanghai scans the campgrounds for any sign of movement. The workmen are putting up the cookhouse tent, but they are not paying attention to him. He takes a deep breath and knocks on Mariana's door.

"Please, madam," he says quickly before she even has the door halfway open.

"Shanghai?" she whispers, looking out over his head and around the corner. She pulls him into the boxcar quickly. "How did you get here?"

"Please, let me see Atasha." Shanghai is prepared to plead, beg at her feet, even kiss the serpent ring that twists all the way up her finger.

"If Jakub finds you . . . You are at great risk. You know that, don't you?"

"Please, madam, please." He feels the heat from her hand as he holds it tightly.

"Your hands?" She examines each of his red, aching fingers. "What happened? And your dress ..." She releases her hand from his and picks up the bottom of his dress where there is a large tear in the fabric. Anger swells in her voice. "Did Vincent pay you another visit?"

"No, no, madam. There is no time to explain. Please, let me see Atasha."

She quickly nudges him toward the twins' bed. At that moment, all Shanghai sees is Atasha. There is no Anna; there is no Mariana. Atasha's skin is stone white. If he didn't know she was sick, he would think she was a fair maiden from a fairy tale, lost in a deep slumber, waiting for her prince to kiss her to life again.

He holds her cold hand and kisses it, then he places a kiss on her cheek. He strokes her hair and pulls his hand back quickly when he feels the massive bump caked with blood. That's when the reality sinks into him. That's when he knows that Atasha is seriously ill. He rests his hand on top of her wound and feels heat rise from her head.

★ ✶ ✶ ✶ ✶

ANNA WAKES with a headache after the night ride on the train. She hears Shanghai pleading with Mariana at the door of the boxcar. "Please, madam."

"Atasha?" Anna whispers with a faint breath, but her sister doesn't respond. Anna shuts her eyes when she hears footsteps approach the bed. "She has not been awake once since the fall," Mariana says softly.

Shanghai calls out Atasha's name but gets no response. Shanghai cries quietly.

Anna thinks she hears their mother's voice, soft and low, saying, "I'm so sorry. I didn't know they were hurt."

Anna forces the word from her mouth, like a baby learning to speak, "Mama."

Shanghai says, "What about Anna?"

"She opens her eyes now and then, but she can barely keep them open."

Anna catches her breath when Shanghai touches her hand. "Anna?" He rubs her forehead just as Jakub did. Her anger swells. "Anna, please wake up." Shanghai cries, resting his forehead on her shoulder. Her heart melts in pity and she opens her eyes. For the second time, she sees Shanghai in a dress, and it brings back the whole terrible scene of yesterday's fight. His face is bruised and swollen beneath the left eye.

He talks quickly, "Atasha . . . Can you feel anything, anything at all, from her?"

Anna closes her eyes and rolls her head away from Shanghai. She knows he doesn't care about her, only Atasha. She doesn't want him touching her, talking to her, crying on her shoulder.

"Anna, talk to me. I'm sorry I didn't tell you. I've lived this way my whole life. Please understand."

"Shanghai," Mariana whispers, "I think you should go. Before they find out that you were here. I have stopped them so far, but they will not be kind to you, you know that."

Anna focuses on the lifeless mass of her sister. She is a weight at Anna's side. She is a darkness, a pain, a bottomless well. Anna hears an echo, a ping, one little bit of life that swells through the darkness. It is Atasha's faint heartbeat.

Shanghai cries again on Atasha's side of the bed. She can hear him trying to get the words out. He gulps to swallow his tears.

"Shanghai," Mariana's whispers, "you need to go."

Anna hears Shanghai sobbing, but his cries are farther away and then they are gone.

"Anna," Mariana says quietly, touching her shoulder, "how are you doing?"

Anna shivers. "I'm cold," she says. "Atasha's heart ..."

She feels Mariana's cool hand on her forehead. "You've got a fever. I'll get a cold cloth for your head. Just rest now."

The next time Anna wakes, she hears the music playing in the Big Top. Her heart is frantically pounding in her chest. Sweat causes her clothing to stick to every part of her skin. She tries to form a sentence, but her tongue feels thick. She's too exhausted to get all of the words out.

"Everything is fine," Mariana says, her voice as caring as a mother's. She strokes Anna's hair. "Sleep now. Just sleep."

IT IS dark in the boxcar. Anna opens her eyes and sees Jakub talking to Mariana. She can only breathe in small amounts of air before she has to take another breath. *What's happening?* she wants to say, but she can't get her lips to move. *Is Atasha okay? Where's my papa? And mama?* Did you send for Mama? Her eyes close again, but she can hear the couple talking.

"We cannot move them again tonight. It's too much for them."

"We have to move," Jakub says. "We cannot shut down the show unless we tell Vladan."

"You have to tell Vladan. Send a telegram tonight when you go into town for the doctor. We cannot move them again."

"He'll send me back to Bohemia, Mariana. He'll send us all back."

"Jakub, you have to get a doctor tonight. *Please.* They . . . they are young girls. *Please, Jakub.* I cannot help them anymore."

★　　★　　★　　★　　★

ANNA IS at the farm, the soft, cool grass between her toes, the sound of birds and wind in the trees, the smell of fresh country air, the sun warm on her face and back; her mother is holding the twins' hands so that the three of them form a circle. *"Ring around the rosie,"* their mother sings, and Atasha and Anna join in, *"pocket full of posies, ashes, ashes, we all fall down."* When they fall, Anna hears the crack of Atasha's head, but they stand again. "I did this!" Anna yells. "I did this!"

She feels a cold cloth on her head.

"I'm sorry," a man says. "There's nothing I can do now."

"Surely there must be something."

"The one is nearly gone. The infection is spreading quickly. The other will be gone by morning."

Gone by morning, gone by morning. The words spin in Anna's head, but she doesn't understand them. She tries to comprehend, but the words change. *I did this. I did this.* What does it mean? Her head is pounding. She can't stop shivering. She opens her eyes, and a dark woman sits next to her. *Who are you?* She pushes the woman's hand away. "Mama?" she yells out. The dark woman says something to her. "Atasha?" But there is no answer. Her eyes close against her will.

✦   ✦   ✦   ✦   ✦

MARIANA SITS under a tree in a small tent. She and Jakub argued about moving the twins here, but Mariana couldn't have them die in her bed. Even worse, she didn't think that the twins should die in a small space where their spirits might not have the chance to escape. The wind shakes the tent that they wait in. She had the workmen lay the twins on the ground, thinking that the girls might like the prairie grass of home beneath them.

After the doctor and Jakub left, Mariana began the task of washing the girls' bodies. It was difficult for her to undress them and to see the connected tissue between them. But this is the Romani way—to prepare the body before death. She kept a white sheet over their bodies as she worked. Washing one arm, one chest, one stomach. Now she washes their feet, starting with the middle one, the one they share. She washes them slowly, meticulously, prayerfully.

How did it come to this? she wonders. When she was young, all she wanted was to get away from her uncle, from her father. All she wanted was to have a baby, someone to love, someone to love her back. She never wanted this. She never wanted to be the one responsible for so much heartache.

She holds the girls' foot in her lap and rubs the cloth between their toes, gently massaging each toenail. In her younger years, she knew that her heart was full of love and compassion; she felt it so strongly that she had to build a wall around herself for protection. *A wall of words.*

279

Just like Shanghai. And the wall seemed to build higher and thicker as she got older. As she lost her baby. As she watched her husband turn into her father.

She swipes the cloth down the arch of the foot, rubbing it around their heel, their ankle. Their foot feels just like anyone else's foot. It feels like her own.

All this suffering, all of it was because she couldn't see past the twins' deviation. She couldn't see that they were human. She couldn't see that they could be capable of feeling pain. *I am no better than my father, no better than my uncle.* She puts the girls' shared foot gently on the ground and starts washing Anna's foot, the left foot.

She wishes that she would have held on tighter to the twins before they fell—maybe she could have stopped them from falling. Or if she would have checked on them after they fell. She tries to remember that moment; Jakub was screaming and Shanghai was kicking and her grip on Anna's shoulder loosened. Or did they slip from her grasp? She glanced behind her, and she's sure that Anna's eyes were open. She remembers thinking that they were fine; that they simply fell. She became so consumed in the drama between Jakub and Shanghai that she didn't think to look closer at them. She could have looked closer, just turned her head and let her eyes rest on them for one moment longer. Or better still, she could have left it all alone. She could have found a different way to get back home. *What have I become?* she wonders. She has destroyed Shanghai's life, Anna's life, Atasha's life. She left the twins after they fell, and before that, she stood by as Shanghai was violated, listening to his awful screams late in the night. And she wrote the letter to the twins' father, and she revealed Shanghai's secret.

I did it, she whispers as she mindlessly rubs their toes.

I did it. She holds their foot in her hand.

I did it.

She swallows down her tears and tries to focus on the twins. She whispers her final prayer. She struggles to redress them, pushing her hands beneath Atasha's back; she tries to roll them. Atasha gasps for air; a horrible, raspy, suffering sound comes from her mouth. It is too much; Mariana cries. She strokes the girl's hair and whispers, "I'm sorry. I'm so sorry."

"Mariana," Jakub sticks his head into the tent. Mariana quickly makes sure that the sheet is properly covering the girls' bodies. "A word?"

"No," Mariana says, wiping the tears from her face. "We cannot leave them alone now."

"Mariana!" Jakub demands.

Mariana returns her attention to the twins and meets Jakub's tone. "Bring Shanghai here, Jakub."

"Mariana!"

"Jakub!" She stops whispering. "He needs to say good-bye. It is important that her spirit is released without ties to earth. Her spirit will return if she is not satisfied. Get Shanghai now."

"Mariana, you are in the world of the whites. Your Romani customs are not necessary here."

Mariana closes her eyes and begins to say a spell for the girls' spirits. Not only does she know that Jakub will think this is a curse on him, but she also needs to ask for forgiveness. Forgiveness for all of the suffering she has brought to these two young women. The words fly quickly from her mouth like sparks from a stone.

"All right, all right," Jakub says, "I will go get Shanghai."

She stops speaking and looks at Atasha. "Shanghai will be here soon," she whispers. She looks at Anna, whose eyelids flutter as if in a dream. "Anna . . . Anna I tried to get Jakub to send notice sooner to your father. So that he could be here. I tried." Mariana worries that the twins' father will not gain forgiveness before they die. That he will be plagued throughout his life by muló.

"Mariana?" Jakub nudges Shanghai toward the twins.

"Leave us for a moment, Jakub."

"I will not. Shanghai should not be here alone with them."

"I am here! Leave us!" Mariana knows exactly the tone to use to gain Jakub's fear.

"I will be right outside, Shanghai," he warns.

"Help me get them dressed," Mariana whispers to Shanghai.

"Madam?" Shanghai is shocked.

"Their dress. Behind you."

Shanghai looks ashamed, but Mariana quickly gets him involved in the task. They pull the dress gently over each twin's head. Shanghai puts his arms beneath Atasha and lifts her as far as he can, pushing the dress beneath her body. Mariana pushes her arms beneath Anna's body and tugs at the dress, pulling it down as far as she can. Shanghai slides his arms beneath Atasha's back and pulls the dress down farther. Mariana does the same on Anna's side. They keep going until they have the dress completely down to the twins' legs.

Anna's chest heaves. Atasha's breath is shallow.

"You should say good-bye," Mariana says quietly and leaves Shanghai alone with the twins.

✦   ✦   ✦   ✦   ✦

RING AROUND *the rosie, pocket full of posies* . . . Anna's mother is laughing, happier than Anna has seen her in many years. The girls twirl around in a circle with her, laughter echoing off the wind.

The wind calls back, "Atasha? Atasha?" It's a faint, distant voice. Familiar to Anna. Who is it? Her mother tugs at her arm, and Atasha pushes Anna around in the circle.

Anna hears chattering. It is Shanghai. She can't make out what he's saying. Ashes, ashes, we all fall down! Anna, Atasha, and their mother drop. There is a crack, and she and her mother stand again. Atasha does not stand up. Anna has the shared leg but only one arm. She and her mother dance again and fall again, but this time only Anna stands up.

MARIANA SEES the death on Shanghai's face when he leaves the tent. "And Anna?" she asks, but Shanghai just shakes his head.

"Come, Shanghai," Jakub says quietly. As he walks away with Shanghai, Mariana grabs Jakub's arm. "You should come say good-bye to Anna now."

"Mariana, I ..."

"Jakub, you need to say good-bye." Mariana knows Jakub must ask forgiveness. She cannot risk having Anna's spirit follow them all over Bohemia.

"I don't need to do anything."

"Jakub, you have wronged her. I know that you kissed her. You need to ask for forgiveness."

"Forgiveness for what?!"

Mariana stares Jakub down.

"Mariana, you are crossing a line."

"Jakub! It is your last chance to do the right thing with her."

"All right, all right. Stay out here and watch him." Jakub goes into the tent. Mariana knows that this is the first step for them to right their lives. She knows it is the beginning of their journey back to the homeland.

RING AROUND *the rosie.* Anna is standing alone, rocking back and forth, humming the tune, her body oddly misshapen. She reaches out with her one arm toward the voice. That voice.

"Anna, please forgive me for not taking care of you like I should."

Anna wants to stay here. She wants to talk to Jakub. But her lips won't

283

move. Her eyelids are too heavy.

Ring around the rosie . . . Her mother's voice sings out to her.

Anna wants to stay.

Ring around the rosie . . .

But she can't help but finish the song. Just one more time.

Ring around the rosie . . . her mother's voice calls.

Pocket full of posies. She is on the farm. The sun is fading beyond the Nebraska horizon. It is huge and orange, and it drops like a balloon. *Ashes, ashes.* And everything turns to black, and Anna falls down, down, down until there is nothing.

Shanghai's Sorrow

Cozad, Nebraska
August 10, 1900

he band starts the procession, playing a mournful song, heavy on the trumpet with a drum that thumps . . . thumps . . . thumps. Jakub takes Mariana's arm in his as the workmen lift the wooden box onto their shoulders. It is the largest, oddest box that Mariana has ever seen.

"Jakub," Mariana says softly, "Shanghai." She looks toward the women's sleeping car, where Shanghai's face appears in the small window, his forehead white against the glass.

"No. He doesn't deserve to be here."

"Their father didn't come. What's the harm?"

"Mariana, this is a funeral. We shouldn't argue."

"So let him come, and I won't argue."

Jakub sighs, then grunts, then says something under his breath as he walks toward the train car where Radovan stands guard. Jakub and Radovan argue for a moment, then Radovan quickly runs to the front of the line to stop the procession.

After a few moments—with the band quiet and the troopers patiently standing in line—Jakub finally leads Shanghai to Mariana. It still strikes her, how awkward he looks wearing a dress. Shanghai doesn't lift his eyes to her when he speaks his "Thank you." His voice is hoarse. He clears his throat and says "Thank you" again.

Mariana takes Jakub's arm, and Shanghai falls in line behind them. The twins are taken out over a hill and laid to rest under the shade of a cottonwood at the edge of the open prairie.

Jakub throws in the first shovel of dirt, then steps away. Radovan follows with another shovelful and hands the shovel to the Strong Man. Everyone throws a shovelful of dirt on the grave: the band members, Gizela, the high-wire performers, Ladislav, the Lion Tamer, Judita. Mariana digs her fingers into the dirt and throws a handful onto the wooden box, quietly speaking a prayer, quietly asking for forgiveness. The troupers look at her expressionlessly, fearful as usual. Mariana quickly steps aside when the Strong Man picks Jarmil up and holds him like a child, allowing the legless man to also throw dirt on the grave.

Shanghai is last. Mariana is surprised at how he grieves like a man. He doesn't show his tears; he holds the sorrow in his eyes, wearing it on his face. Shanghai pushes the shovel into the dirt, raises the small mound, and holds it over the hole. He opens his mouth and Mariana expects eloquence to fall from his lips, but he says nothing, as if the words stick to the roof of his mouth. He tips the shovel and dirt slowly falls like sand in an hourglass. When the last bit of dirt falls down into the grave, Shanghai drops the shovel, turns, and walks away.

The procession follows Shanghai back to the circus grounds; the trumpet wails, the trombone moans, and the drum pounds out a rhythm slower than a heartbeat.

Business as Usual

Hastings, Nebraska
August 11, 1900

ust after the train arrives in Hastings, Mariana hears a gentle knock on her door. When she opens it, Jakub holds up a plate of food. "I've brought you some breakfast." She is surprised by this, not only because Jakub should be working but also because he hasn't made such a gesture since before their baby died.

"Breakfast? Yes, yes, come in." Mariana's heart has felt so heavy in the past days that she hasn't wanted to eat, hasn't even thought about eating.

"I had the cook make up a plate of fruit, and some porridge. Just as you like it." He clumsily sets the food on a small table; the bowl of porridge rattles against the plate. Jakub takes a handkerchief from his pocket and wipes his brow. Mariana's concern rises with his anxiety.

She has been waiting for this visit since Vladan arrived after the funeral yesterday. He left abruptly after his conversation with Jakub. She knows that Jakub was chastised for his failures: the twins' deaths, bringing Shanghai into the circus, the dwindling receipts in the Sideshow. But she feels the burden of her own failure. She blames herself for the twins' deaths, and now she almost feels that she deserves whatever Vladan has planned for her.

Jakub sits next to her on the settee. "You took very good care of the twins after they fell, my dear."

"I only did what was right." Mariana looks down at her fingers, thoughtfully rubbing each one the same way she massaged the fingers

287

on the twins' hands.

Sweat again collects on Jakub's brow. "Tea?" Mariana lifts her cup and Jakub fills it; his hands are shaking.

Mariana uncomfortably waits through the silence a few moments, then says, "Vladan's visit was short yesterday."

"Yes. Yes. He said, 'Now that the funeral is over, it is business as usual. I have two acts on the way to replace the twins.'" Jakub imitates his uncle, lowering his voice, raising the index finger of each hand to mock Vladan's way of showing "two." Laughter sneaks out of Mariana's chest. It feels good to laugh, after spending so much time the past few days crying. Jakub laughs with her and tugs at his collar, then straightens his vest, still imitating Vladan's mannerisms. It is in these little moments with Jakub that she feels her heart open to him. She suddenly feels shy with her husband's attention.

Jakub looks around the boxcar and quickly becomes serious, "Mariana? My dear, . . . " He swallows hard. "You are going to New York early next week."

"Next week?" Mariana sits upright. She thought that Vladan would banish her to cleaning out dog cages or helping in the cookhouse. But now she imagines herself stepping off the ship in Amsterdam, watching the hills of her homeland pass through the window of the train to Prague, walking through the familiar streets, putting flowers on their baby's grave, holding Jakub's hand, gaining back their old following, and making a new life in the old country. Jedu domů, she thinks. I am going home. For the first time since the twins fell, she feels light.

Jakub clears his throat. "Yes, next week. I have arranged for a carriage to take you to New York."

New York to take a ship bound for Amsterdam. She will be so far away from here by next week that this will soon be like a bad dream, and she will feel right again. And at the end of the season, Jakub will join her, and it will be like when they traveled together in the old days.

"Mariana," he takes her hand in his and strokes it, lovingly, tenderly, "I'm sorry. I'm so sorry, but we just can't use you here. You're not pulling in enough business." When he begins to cry, Mariana is shocked. She hasn't seen him cry . . . not since they buried their baby in Český ráj. This second business failure is too much for him. She sees that now. She cups his face with both of her hands and lifts his eyes to hers. He hasn't shaved yet, and the stubble she feels beneath her palms reminds her of those days when they were first married, when she woke up next to him every morning. She strokes the hair on his face. He brings his hands under her elbows, then runs his fingers over her forearms, grasping her wrists. He is shaking; his hands tremble from her touch. Now she can't resist; she pulls his face closer and kisses him. She almost forgot what it feels like to have her lips on his, what it is like to have someone kiss her back, to welcome her lips with a tongue, to have his hand tangled in her hair, pulling her closer as if he could never possibly let go. She starts to cry with him and says, "It's all right, Jakub." She strokes his sideburns. "Everything will be fine. I will stay in Prague until you come home. It will work out, you'll see."

"Prague?" Jakub pulls her hands away from his face, and for once she finds his fear endearing.

"Is there somewhere else you want me to wait for you? Do you want me to go to Český ráj?" She again holds his hands in hers. His fingers are trembling, and as she caresses his wrist, she feels his rapid pulse. She has memories of the night that they made their baby: how much passion they had, how she made him tremble then, too.

"Český ráj? No, no, Mariana." He wipes the tears from his face and stands abruptly. "I have to go. The parade will start soon."

"Yes, of course." Mariana grabs his hand and looks him in the eyes. She wants to tell him that she is happy now and there is nothing to fear from her. She wants to say, *I love you, Jakub. I have always loved you.*

Jakub looks down at his hand and pulls it away from her, then rushes to the door. "And Mariana?" He doesn't turn to face her.

"Yes?"

"Vladan does not want you to perform this week." His voice has an odd tone, and Mariana sees that his knees are shaking. For a moment, a feeling of suspicion sneaks into her heart. He talks quickly before she has a chance to say anything else. "The Strong Man has learned to throw knives, and Judita has agreed to be his target. So our Sideshow is complete! That should give you time to pack for your journey."

"Yes," she says simply, and, like a magician, he is gone. It almost seemed like Jakub was holding something back from her. *Is Jakub perhaps staying?* No, Vladan is so angry at them that he has no choice but to send the both of them home. And they are married, husband and wife. She thinks over Jakub's words, searching for a lie. *Cynic,* she calls herself and realizes that Jakub would never leave her. Not after all they've been through. She knows deep in her heart that he loves her—she knows it in the way he held her hand, the way he kissed her. She now realizes that they are going to have to learn to be a couple again; they will have to learn to trust one another without all of these silly games.

No, she is not the least bit upset that Vladan has stopped her show. It gives her time to pack, to straighten out her things, to leave everything in the costume tent orderly. She opens the trunk at the end of her bed. She takes scraps of fabric—silk, cotton, wool—and folds each piece, stacking one on top of the other on her bed. She takes that square of blanket that belonged to her baby, kisses it, and sets it aside. As she takes her clothing out and refolds it, she finds the stack of letters addressed to Shanghai.

Milada. She should contact Milada and tell her that she is coming home. How she misses her old friend; she has already forgiven her for lying about Shanghai. She hopes in her heart that Milada will forgive her for coming between her and Shanghai. Mariana unties the letters and opens one of the first envelopes that arrived at the beginning of the season. "My dearest Shanghai," it began. "I can't stop thinking about that day in the train station. Believe me when I say that I hoped to tell you the news myself, but I couldn't break away. My heart broke at the sorrow on your face. I know that sorrow, Shanghai, because it was the same sorrow I held within myself."

The calliope wails outside. It's true that both Milada and Shanghai had a sadness about them in those last days together. But Shanghai, he carries that underlying sadness with him everywhere. It's planted beneath the surface of his skin like a seed. Even when he is happiest, Mariana sees his sadness. As if he's lost something, something as precious as a baby.

She continues reading Milada's letter. "I had no control in this, Shanghai. You must believe me. My father arranged the wedding with Zikmund. He had been trying to plan it before you even came into my life. I kept resisting, trying to delay it. I thought that if I agreed to stay in Prague with Zikmund, I could stop it. But you know my father, Shanghai."

Milada never seemed to take control of her life, Mariana thinks.

"I don't know if this letter will find its way to you, but I need you to know this one thing: I love you even more than you can realize. I think about ways to bring us back together every day, every night. Please, please think of this, too."

The circus grounds fill with people, and the sounds swell outside. Mariana picks up Shanghai's diary and rubs the cover with the palm of her hand. The sound of the calliope comes to a halt, and she knows that the show at the Bally-ho will start soon. She gently puts the diary and the letters back into the trunk, tucking them under her finely made *diklos*.

She wants to see Shanghai. She wants to watch him throw fire on the platform. She will miss him. Already, she misses the mystery of him. She misses the desire to seek him out night after night. Long ago, the Romani queen told her that she would be blind to reality if her heart truly wanted something. That she could never truly see her own future. That she would manipulate the truth to believe what she wanted. Now, Mariana realizes that Shanghai wasn't the master of deceit, but that she saw what she wanted to see. She saw a man with a secret that she couldn't discover on her own.

✹　✹　✹　✹　✹

SHANGHAI CHANGES into the old clothes that Radovan gave him. Radovan told him that he was to dress "in the old way for the blow-off." It feels good to be in his old pants, his old shirt, his old shoes, but he knows what is to come, and it makes him sick to his stomach.

His body feels like it has been filled with wet sand, and he labors to crawl into his bed, the bed that, briefly, belonged to Atasha. He turns over and lies on his stomach. This is where he wants to stay forever, his face pressed into the pillow that was once hers, his body melted into the bed so that he can sleep the rest of his life away.

He sees a long, thin hair stuck in the frame of the bed. He wraps his finger under it; he can tell by the chestnut color and the slight twist in the middle that it belongs to either Atasha or Anna. He plucks it from the frame and suspends it in front of his face. He feels happy in that brief moment as he twirls it, watching it dance in the air, spinning and spinning until it slips from his grasp and drifts to the floor.

His false sense of security is suddenly broken by Radovan's voice outside the car. "She's not going to Prague, Jakub! It's too late! Vladan has sold her to the Brawly Circus."

Shanghai's heart sinks. The Brawly Circus is a low-rate circus out east. He has heard stories of their deceit. Grifters and thieves roam the grounds, stealing from the audience. The women are treated like slaves, like animals. Shanghai scrambles on top of Judita's bed and looks out the window. He can see only the top of each man's head.

"A carriage will be here Tuesday to pick her up, Jakub. You cannot change things now."

Shanghai fights the tears that he's been holding back since Atasha's funeral. He didn't think anything could possibly get worse than this, but now he is going to the Brawly Circus. Tuesday. He didn't think that he would ever care about anything that happened to him now, but this . . . He starts talking to Atasha, asking for her to help him, to watch over him, to get him out of this mess. Atasha, his mother, some higher being, anyone. *Help me,* he thinks. *Help me.*

"It is unbearable," Jakub says, "to act as if everything is normal."

"You have to do it, Jakub. Just until Tuesday. Business as usual."

Tuesday. He's got to think of some way out. Some way to get back to Prague on his own. He could just start walking, tonight after the sun goes down. Or he could travel tonight with the train and start walking early tomorrow morning. But Jakub would find him. He would find him because Shanghai would not have paid for his freedom. Or worse, the Brawly Circus, who has already paid for him, would come and find him. They would punish him worse than Vincent punished him that night at the poodle cages. It would be easy for them to find him. They would simply ask around, wondering if anyone had seen the dwarf. And people would say, *Yes, just this morning, I gave him bread.* How can he possibly disappear into a crowd? How can he make his escape?

Suddenly, Vincent's flat white palm is pressed against the window. "It's showtime!" Vincent's booming voice causes the glass to vibrate.

"Showtime," Shanghai whispers. His larger problem is now consumed by his immediate situation. He tries to separate his mind from his body as he walks to the Sideshow Tent. It feels strange, to feel his breasts bounce without the support of the wrap he's accustomed to wearing. He walks through the backyard and passes the spot where he used to step out to the Bally-ho stage. His throat aches. He ducks into another part of the Sideshow Tent, a curtained-off area, dark and lit only by dim lanterns. He hears the crowd of men mumble and cough as they wait for Gizela to appear. She doesn't seem to mind stripping down to her bloomers, turning herself around as the men laugh at her nude appearance. She is covered head to toe by the same coarse hair that covers her face.

Shanghai feels anger flash through his body. If only he could feel nothing. If only he could separate himself like Atasha could separate from Anna. *If only. If only. If only.*

Vincent says, "Gentlemen, you are about to witness something so spectacular that you will not even want to tell your wives about it."

He motions to Shanghai and whispers, "Don't stand directly in the light. We can't let them see that bruise on your face." Shanghai steps onto the stage, just left of center, and throws juggling batons over his head. The men start to boo, and Shanghai fights the urge to throw the batons out into the audience, knocking out one or two or three men. Vincent gives Shanghai a nudge and Shanghai glares at Vincent.

He shoves a baton into Vincent's abdomen with such force that Vincent doubles over. Breathless, he says, "Just do it, little woman, or you'll be sorry." Vincent rips the other baton from Shanghai's grip.

Shanghai scans the faces in the audience of men; he looks each and every one square in the eye as he unbuttons his shirt. But the men's eyes are already diverted to Shanghai's body. To the curves below the fabric of this man's shirt. And suddenly, at the back of the crowd, he sees Mariana's face. She looks horrified as Shanghai pulls the shirt off of his shoulders and lets it fall down to the ground. He chokes down the emotion pushing up through his throat.

He looks away from the men's staring faces. He wants to scream, *I'm not abnormal!* But he bites his tongue so hard that blood fills his mouth. He swallows it back. He stands exposed for several minutes so that the men can completely take in his appearance. His shaved head, his men's clothes, his chiseled jaw.

His nipples rise as a chill runs through his veins.

MARIANA RUNS outside the small tent and closes her eyes against the bright, burning rays. The air is so stifling that she can't seem to catch her breath. It's too much to make Shanghai suffer like this. She can't believe how low Jakub has stooped. She angrily pushes through the crowd thickening around the entrance of the big tent. Heat rises from the ground and sticks to her skin like molasses. The English language clucks around her head, cackling out words that she suddenly can't understand. The band in the big tent begins to play, and Mariana pushes harder against the crowd, knowing that the show will start soon. The crowd is stagnant for a moment, not moving forward. Mariana is paralyzed. Then the people move forcefully, pushing her toward the entrance of the tent, but she fights her way to the other side of the entering crowd. She takes a deep breath when she finally makes it to the performers' side of the tent. Jakub stands just inside the performers' entrance, and Mariana feels her anger break through the heaviness in the air.

"You have to stop, Jakub." Mariana grabs his arm.

Jakub looks terrified and tries to pry her fingers from his arm. "Stop?" His breathing becomes shallow. "I don't know what ..."

"With Shanghai. You have to stop this now."

Jakub returns his eyes to the clipboard shaking in his hand and clears his throat. "Mariana, I'm busy now. Can we discuss this later?"

"No. You've punished him enough. Promise me, Jakub. Promise me that this will stop."

"She did this to herself, Mariana. I don't want to hear any more about it." He pulls her aside to make way for a line of white horses that dance sideways into the ring.

"Are you going to let him go at the end of the season?"

"Yes, yes, Mariana," Jakub seems annoyed. "Her passage back to Prague has been booked. She can live any way she wants to after that." He sniffs and mumbles, "Any way she wants to."

"Promise me, Jakub," she pleads. He doesn't respond, but she doesn't give up. "Jakub! Promise me!" She grabs his chin and makes him look at her, face-to-face. His jaw tightens in her hand, and tears seem to pool in his eyes.

"I promise. She is going back to Prague." Mariana lets go of his chin. It's obvious that something is wrong, and she knows she should push him harder, but his face shows tenderness and all she can do is believe him. She wants to trust him, as his wife. Yes, Shanghai is going back to Prague. Jakub looks away quickly, and his voice cracks, "Now, unless you want to go out there with the elephants, I suggest you move."

Mariana looks behind her and sees the Elephant Trainer lining up Bruno and the other elephants. Jakub yells at the Elephant Trainer, "Let's move!" He hits the trainer on the back of the leg with the same whip the man uses on the elephants. Mariana quickly moves out of their way as they walk past her in a perfect row, the ground vibrating beneath their feet. Once in the ring, they rise into the air so they are standing on hind legs, turning around to the audience's applause. Their trunks are high above their heads, and their mouths seem to form a smile. They are always performing, knowing the consequences if they don't. And now they turn and turn, the sorrow held deep inside them, as they perform a well-orchestrated dance.

AFTER THE evening show, Shanghai walks back to the train, his hands in his pocket, watching his feet kick up dirt with each step. He feels nothing but heaviness, like gravity is pulling on him harder than metal to a magnet. For a moment, he thinks about giving in to the gravity. He could throw himself off the platform in the Big Top. The platform where Milada stood so many nights, above his head, yelling out an "I love you" as she took flight and the words flew from one side of the tent to the other. The same platform where he stood and looked down on Atasha and Anna when they found him in the Big Top. The platform where he could jump and let the earth suck his body into oblivion.

"Shanghai," Jakub yells from his boxcar, "a word?" Mariana sits on the settee. Shanghai feels shame rise in his heart for what she saw earlier. When he sees the pity on Mariana's face, he wants her to look away, but she doesn't. Jakub begins to speak, and Shanghai looks down to the floor. "I have made arrangements for your journey back to the homeland," Jakub says.

Shanghai feels a flash of anger. He knows that Jakub is telling a lie. He knows he is being sent to the Brawly Circus. He feels like tackling Jakub right here, right now, spilling out all of the rage, the sorrow, the disgust he feels.

"You will leave here in eight weeks. It will take you a week to get to port. There is no point in trying to get a job with another circus here—Vladan put the word out that you are not only difficult but dangerous as well. I suggest you start to think about your future. Perhaps you should contact Madam Zora."

Shanghai looks up and tries to discern what Jakub is up to. *Eight weeks from now?*

"But I overheard you and Radovan today," Shanghai spits the words out. He is tired of Jakub's lies. "I know that I am leaving next week. I know that I am going to the Brawl . . . "

Before Shanghai can get any more words out, Jakub speaks quickly and loudly over him. "No! Shanghai, you are not going next week. Mariana is leaving next week."

Shanghai looks to Mariana. She smiles at Shanghai and nods. "You, madam?" Shanghai is confused by her apparent joy.

"Yes. I will leave for New York on Tuesday."

He looks at Jakub, whose eyes are filled with fear, and he suddenly understands the scope of Jakub's deceit. He looks back at Mariana, the fortune-teller, and wonders why she can't see it. But then he remembers something that Milada once told him: Mariana can never accurately see her own future.

Jakub's voice trembles as his eyes plead with Shanghai. "Mariana is going to New York on Tuesday. That's what I was telling Radovan." Jakub swallows, then his voice rises to a higher tone, "She . . . she will be leaving us next week." Jakub doesn't look at Mariana at all, but she looks at him like Atasha used to look at Shanghai. Jakub wipes the sweat from his face.

Shanghai looks at Mariana once again and considers blurting out everything that he heard; it would be so satisfying, to get back at Jakub for all he has done. He looks toward Jakub, whose face has produced another layer of sweat. Suddenly, Shanghai sees how to best use this situation, how to ensure that Jakub won't bamboozle him as he has bamboozled his own wife. Shanghai considers his words carefully, then speaks loudly and forcefully, "I will give you back two weeks' pay in exchange for my ticket for the voyage back to Europe."

Jakub looks surprised. "It's all taken care of, Shanghai. The voyage is already booked."

"But I want to be the holder of that ticket."

Jakub looks at him suspiciously. "There's no need to worry, Shanghai. Your ticket is much safer locked away than being kept with you."

"You can hold my remaining pay until the very day I leave here. All I ask in return is that you let me be the holder of that ticket."

Jakub squints his eyes at Shanghai. "Why? Why are you asking this?"

Shanghai thinks quickly. "If there is anything I have learned from you, Jakub, it is to be savvy in business. You have something I want, and I am willing to negotiate for it. It's as simple as that." Jakub smiles and puffs out his chest. "Besides, I know that you paid a good price to Madam Zora for me. Two weeks' salary will easily cover that price, and you won't lose a thing. Or, I could tell you what Radovan said earlier . . . "

"No, no, no!"

"What?" Mariana leans forward. "What did Radovan say?"

Jakub quickly takes his keys from his pocket and jiggles them in front of Shanghai. "I will get you your ticket, Shanghai."

Shanghai glances at Mariana. "He was talking about my future in the Sideshow, madam."

Jakub hands the ticket over to Shanghai, but before he releases his grip on it, he says, "Just to clarify . . . I am holding back two weeks' salary in exchange for this ticket."

"Make that one week's salary," Shanghai tightens his fingers on the ticket until Jakub lets go. He opens the envelope and checks the printing on the ticket. The date of departure is October 13; the destination is Amsterdam. "And Jakub," Shanghai says, looking at Mariana, "I want to go back to the Bally-ho platform."

Jakub laughs. "I cannot do that, Shanghai. Uncle Vladan wants you in the blow-off, and that is where you will stay."

"Madam . . . " Shanghai talks slowly as he approaches Mariana.

"All right, all right." Jakub steps between Shanghai and Mariana. "With the two of you nagging me, I can hardly think. Fine, you will go back to the Bally-ho." He slaps the ticket in Shanghai's hand. Shanghai turns toward the door, averting his eyes from Mariana's gaze.

"But!" Jakub raises his index finger. "You will stay here for the eight weeks, no? I cannot afford to lose another act in the Sideshow right now."

Shanghai can tell by this voice that it is his uncle Vladan that Jakub fears.

Jakub lowers his voice. "It would be easy to find a dwarf traveling without a circus, Shanghai."

Shanghai looks down at his ticket and sees the date once again. October 13. Where else would he go before then anyway?

Shanghai reaches his hand out to Jakub, clutching the ticket to Amsterdam in the other hand.

Jakub grips Shanghai's small hand and shakes it. The deal is sealed.

Red-Winged Blackbirds

Syracuse, Kansas
August 14, 1900

ariana steps onto the carriage and takes one last look at the circus grounds. The Sideshow Banner flaps in the wind, and the parade wagons are all lined up, ready to draw the town to the show. Shanghai stands by the train, watching her, that sadness creeping into the lines on his face. She can tell that he hasn't found Milada's letters yet.

As she sees him now, he seems to be forgiving her. His face has softened, and he seems to look right at her. She waves good-bye, and he waves back, hesitantly, thoughtfully. She feels a burden lifted from her shoulders. She holds her smaller bag to her chest. She packed Shanghai's diary close to the top, so that she could read it on the train. She has kept it for herself so that she could read his stories, so that she could remember his voice.

She looks out over the prairie and thinks about how Jakub visited her this morning. He cried once again. He didn't even have to tell her that he would be joining her soon. She simply reassured him about their new life in the old country; she told him that she was sure they could gain back their old following.

He spoke to her then in a low, soft voice, crying as he told her how much he would miss her. And he took her hand, kissing it and saying her name over and over again. "Oh, Mariana." A kiss. "Mariana, my dear." Another kiss. "Mariana."

It feels like they are in love all over again. Mariana wants to believe, in her heart, that they will reconcile their marriage when he joins her back in the homeland.

AS THE wagons are lined up for the circus parade, Shanghai watches Mariana step onto a carriage that will take her to Kansas City where she will get on a train to New York. Jakub helps her up and kisses her hand as he releases it. Shanghai sees the joy on her face and suddenly understands that she is not a witch at all. *She's just one of us,* he thinks, *being fooled like the rest of us.* Mariana thinks she is going home, but Jakub has sold her out. He has sold out his own wife.

Her carriage passes Shanghai. She stares out at him, and for the first time, he notices her different-colored eyes: *green and brown,* he thinks, *and full of life.* He smiles at her, a sad, almost pitying smile. She cocks her head, in disbelief, and smiles back, innocently, unknowingly. She hangs out the window of the wagon and waves. He waves back, suddenly feeling the urge to run after her. To tell her what Jakub has planned. But it's too late; the wagon is too far away.

As he watches Mariana's square being painted over on the Sideshow Banner, he feels guilt for Mariana's eventual suffering. Mariana's face is halfway gone on the canvas; her skirt is turning from bright purple to mud gray to white. She is no longer the best fortune-teller in all of Europe. She is no longer Jakub's wife, the grand dame of the circus. She has been stripped of all that she knows, of all the power that she holds.

He goes back to the sleeper car. His heart still weighs him down, every day, every night. He lies on his bed, the twins' old bed, hoping to erase that vision of Mariana from his mind. He feels tired, but he can't close his eyes. He could have stopped this. He could have warned her. But then what would happen to him? He rolls to his side and slips his hand between the pillow and the sheet. He pulls out a stack of envelopes, neatly tied together with a ribbon. He sees that the top letter is addressed to him. He quickly unwraps the bundle and opens the first letter. "My dearest Shanghai." His eyes quickly dart up to the date on the letter: 1900 May 2. "I was wrong. There is no other way to say it. I have married Zikmund, but it is you that I am in love with and I don't care who finds out. I was wrong to be so afraid of it."

Shanghai's heart beats harder than it has since Atasha died. He flips the page over and reads frantically, picking up words here and there, trying to comprehend. He opens the next letter and the next letter and the next. Each one is from Milada, all expressing her love for him. They are all begging him to return to her in the old country. "I will leave Zikmund by the end of summer. I have a plan, Shanghai, and I will get away from him." He reads quickly, skimming over some sentences, looking for the words he has craved to hear from her since the beginning. His eyes pause on those sentences until he absorbs the information. The final letter tells him what he has always wanted to hear. "I have left Zikmund. Please return to me, Shanghai. I long to have you by my side. I cannot tell you where I am right now for fear that this letter will be intercepted and they will tell Zikmund where I am. If you write back, I will tell, Shanghai. I will tell you where I am."

Shanghai's hands begin to shake. He pulls the final letter to his face and draws it to his lips. He can almost breathe in Milada's soft scent. He feels alive for the first time in weeks, but then he realizes that this is another cruel joke that someone has played on him. He cannot possibly reach Milada before his voyage home. In seven weeks, he leaves here and travels to New York to get onto a ship bound for home. It's not enough time, he thinks, to get a letter to her now, and to get a response in return. The *jezibaba*, Shanghai thinks. *She did this to me.*

What can he do now? Jakub wants him to write to Madam Zora and tell her that he will return to the brothel, but he has decided that he will never reconcile with her—he will never return to that life. He will find some other way to live, without Madam Zora. And now, not only has he lost Atasha but he has lost Milada, once again.

Angry, he runs to the window and looks out to the road leading into the countryside. The *jezibaba*'s carriage is a tiny dot in the distance. He spits out the words, "You deserve what you are about to get, Mariana." The calliope wagon begins its chorus as the parade takes off down the dirt road that leads to town. The blasting sound of the organ frightens a flock of red-winged blackbirds. They lift up in the air, their wings flapping madly like the beating inside his chest, and they fly to the east, then dart upward and shadow the sun like a cloud. The birds spin downward, streaking the horizon with red as if their wings were setting the sky on fire, and then they land in exactly the same place they began.

Shanghai laughs to himself, wiping the tears from his face. *It's all an illusion.* Every part of his life seems to disappear, spinning itself into fire, and he ends up in the same exact place. Suddenly, the images flash through his mind like a flame. Milada's shadow flying across the tent wall, his mother's figure in the doorway saying "Now don't cry," and Atasha's body white and drained of blood.

Pain shoots into his kneecaps as he labors to crawl into his bed. He looks through the letters that surround him. He has devoured most of them, and they are scattered like empty candy wrappers. He looks for any that he hasn't read, hoping that something will give him a clue. Something will tell him where he can find Milada. Then he sees the one letter, sticking out from beneath his pillow; it is written by someone else's hand.

He scans the back page of the letter. It is signed by Mariana. Shanghai reads it cautiously. "I know I have wronged you in the past. I am regretful of this and want to give you something to make up for it. Jakub didn't want you to have these letters, but I have kept them for you." Shanghai fights the urge to rip this page into tiny pieces and throw it out into the wind. He chews the inside of his lip as he continues reading. "I do have a way to contact Milada. I know you don't believe me, but I can prove it to you. After you get to Prague, take the train to Český Krumlov. You will find her in Staré mesto. Ask the woman who sells fresh-baked Šumava. She can tell you where to find Milada. She wants you to know that she loves you, Shanghai, and she cannot wait to see you again. She will be counting down the days."

Shanghai crumples up the page in anger, looking for somewhere to throw it as far away as he can. But the letter won't leave his hand. He flattens it out again, pushing the wrinkles out across his thigh. He cries as he reads it over and over, slowly, methodically. Hope fills his heart, but then he is pulled down by the possible reality that this could all be another trick. But what would the *jezibaba* have to gain now? He notices a black cloth sticking out from under his pillow. Mariana has left him clothes. Two trousers, three shirts, and under his bed, he finds a pair of his old shoes.

Vincent pounds on the window, and Shanghai looks just in time to see the birds rise up again through the small square of glass, but this time they fly away. "It's showtime!" Vincent yells. Shanghai quickly gathers up all of the letters and shoves them under his pillow, between two of the little suits.

"Shanghai, my dear woman." Jakub comes from the doorway of the sleeper car. He is holding the dress that Shanghai wore the day that Atasha fell. He sits on the bed next to Shanghai and touches the hair behind Shanghai's ear. Shanghai quickly pulls away. "Your hair is growing back, so it is time for you to present yourself accordingly." He throws the dress in Shanghai's lap and stands up.

"But Jakub, it's hard to throw fire in this dress." For the past week, Shanghai has been appearing as a man on the Bally-ho platform. His life has almost felt right again.

Jakub doesn't turn to look at Shanghai; his voice is cool and even. "Mariana is not here to protect you anymore, little one. I suggest you wear the dress, or you will go back to the blow-off. And I will need that suit back."

Shanghai quickly throws the dress on top of the pant leg sticking out from under his pillow. "Yes, Jakub," he forces out through his teeth. He pulls on the dress and realizes that anything could happen now that Mariana is gone. She was the one who let him see Atasha; she begged for Jakub to let him be there when she died. She was the one who made Jakub allow him to attend the funeral. She was the one who helped him get out of the blow-off. He picks up the letter from Mariana and reads it again. "...take the train to Český Krumlov. You will find her in Staré mesto. Ask the woman who sells fresh-baked Šumava ..."

Vincent pounds again on the glass of the car, more insistently than before. "Let's go, you little freak!"

Shanghai quickly buttons up his dress. He puts his hands on his breasts and pulls them closer to his ribs. *Less than eight weeks,* he thinks. *Ninety-one more performances.*

As Shanghai stands backstage, Vincent taunts the crowd with the "wedding" that will take place between Ladislav and Judita. It reminds Shanghai of Atasha's story about her first night onstage. She yelled over to Judita in Czech that the audience was making fun of the pair, that the audience thought they were married. Atasha laughed about how innocent she was that night. She didn't understand the show value of a tall, thin man being married to a woman of Judita's heft. How funny Atasha would think the fake wedding was between the two when, every night, Judita throws the bouquet into the waiting audience. Yes, Atasha would laugh about this now.

But Atasha is gone, and Milada waits for him in Český Krumlov. He must get through the next seven weeks, complying with whatever Jakub asks of him, with his ticket secure, with his letters from Milada safely tucked away.

Home

New York, New York
October 13, 1900

hanghai stands on the pier with a large group of immigrants. He intentionally edged his way into the middle of the gathering, fearing that someone might be following him, that someone may snatch him up at any time and carry him away into a life of prostitution. *How easy would it be?* He imagines Jakub contacting a madam in New York City, telling her to have her man look for a dwarf on the pier waiting for this ship.

Shanghai left the Borsefsky Brothers Circus dressed as a woman. It was the final thing that Jakub could force him to do. But Mariana left him with these clothes, and now he is dressed as a man. He wears the pants, the white shirt buttoned up to the neck, the old comfortable shoes. His hair is almost back to normal: he is nearly able to tuck it behind his ear, to push it out of his eyes.

As the immigrants walk up the platform toward the mouth of the ship, Shanghai holds his position at the center of the group. He glances around—watching, waiting, ready to dart between legs if someone tries to grab him—just in case Jakub gave them a description of a male dwarf as well. Just in case Jakub tries to do to him what he did to Mariana.

He settles into his bunk below deck. When the ship's horn wails as it leaves port, he begins to relax. He opens his suitcase and takes out Milada's letters. He reads each one again, consuming every sentence, every word, every syllable, every character. At the end of each letter he kisses Milada's signature. He runs his finger over the ink, feeling each tiny curve. As his fingertip vibrates over the curls in her writing, he feels anticipation, then fear, excitement, then sadness, trepidation, then hope. His emotions rise and fall like the waves beneath the ship.

He comes across Milada's first letter and wonders if he will ever feel happy, if the longing will ever go away. Sometimes he talks to Atasha in his head, and sometimes he feels like she can hear him. He tells her everything about his miserable final days in the circus, about the letters from Milada, and even about Mariana's lamentable future.

The thought of it haunts him. He often thinks about Mariana's happiness when she stepped onto that carriage. He thinks of how she reacted when she got off the train and never made it to the port. How angry she must have been when they took her to the circus. But there were rumors going around the Borsefsky Brothers circus grounds before Shanghai left. Judita overheard Jakub tell Radovan that there was a fire. The Brawly Circus went down in flames. It started in the Big Top, then quickly spread to the Sideshow Tent. A performer died; the animals escaped harm, their cages suspiciously moved far from the blaze. Mariana had disappeared; it was feared that she, too, had died in the fire. But Jakub said he knew better.

Yes, Shanghai thinks, *if the rumors are true, Mariana is certainly capable of this* . . . He looks over Mariana's letter, searching for any untruths, any manipulations, any evilness. He keeps wondering if she had anything to gain by sending him to Český Krumlov. But he's been over this letter a thousand times, and he cannot see anything that she would have possibly gained. Perhaps Mariana really could talk to Milada after all. It is his only hope now.

Shanghai picks up Milada's letters and holds them to his chest as he closes his eyes. And in his head, he tells a story. It is the story of a court jester who is a dwarf. How he fell in love with a beautiful princess and how—after many journeys together and many journeys apart—how he thinks she may have fallen in love with him, too.

Acknowledgments

THIS NOVEL could not have been written without the incredible support of friends, coworkers, and family. Thanks to my five siblings for giving me the experience of a circuslike atmosphere in my childhood development. Thanks to my grandmother Fern Frazee for the gifts of storytelling and imagination.

Thanks especially to Helena Cervinková Case, who gave me the history, stories, and language of her homeland, the Czech Republic. To Zuzanna Bracknell for additional help with the Czech language. To Marian for helping me put the pieces together. To Terri Scanlon for entertaining me on the trips to Baraboo, Wisconsin, and for sifting through all the information at the Circus World Museum.

Thanks also to Erin Foley, archivist at the Circus World Museum, for sharing her wealth of knowledge and for being generous with her time.

I'm deeply grateful to the faculty at Hamline University—especially Mary Rockcastle, Sheila O'Connor, Deborah Keenan, Scott Edelstein, and Judith Katz—who encouraged, taught, and mentored me.

And finally, thanks to Julie Neraas, Leni deMik, and the late Jane Rice, who all believed in me from the beginning.